Shattered Destiny

James Fisher Series
Book 3

G J Stevens

Copyright © GJ Stevens 2012-2023

The moral right of GJ Stevens to be identified as the author of this work has been asserted by him in accordance with the Copyright, Designs, and Patents Act 1998.

British Library Cataloguing-in-Publication Data
A catalogue record for this book is available from the British Library

ISBN: 9798876402257

Other Books by GJ Stevens

James Fisher Series

Fate's Ambition
Their Right to Vengeance

Post-apocalyptic Thrillers

IN THE END
BEFORE THE END
AFTER THE END
BEGINNING OF THE END (Novella)

SURVIVOR
Your Guide to Surviving the Apocalypse

Agent Carrie Harris Series

OPERATION DAWN WOLF
LESSON LEARNED
THE GEMINI ASSIGNMENT
CAPITAL ACTION (Novella)

Agent Carrie Harris – Undead Thrillers

STOPPING POWER – SEASON ONE

1

James

15th October

Rain drummed against the corrugated metal, each beat echoing around the vast warehouse. Fisher stood motionless in the centre of the windowless expanse, his eyes wide despite the brilliant glare pouring from above, transfixed on the razor-straight edges of his suit reflected in the tall rectangle of glass at arm's reach.

The glass, one side of a transparent box, was a little taller than him and sat on a polished stainless steel plinth seeming to float just proud of the grey, featureless floor.

He blinked, refocusing on a muscular naked body lain across the cold steel inside. Facing away, white cuffs bound the man's hands. Despite not being able to see his face, he was a fine specimen, toned muscles obvious and skin pale, but coarse scars ran up his legs, jig-sawing his torso to the back of a smooth, shaven head.

The body stirred.

Fisher's calm gaze switched through the thick pane on the other side, catching the smooth fleshy curves of a woman in her prime, standing with her stomach flat, her sides punctuated by tight obliques. He followed up and over pert breasts, her stiff nipples seeming to point in his direction. He willed his view to move up her body, desperate to glimpse her face.

Instead, he found a metal hatch opening inside the glass cage. Watching the slick motion, he blinked before he returned to her skin, watching her hands busy on a series of controls in front of her.

A glint of light drew him back to the roof of the one-man prison. Fisher's gaze flitted to her right hand resting on a thin metal control. The body in the cage twitched against the restraints. The tremor subsided, then rocked with a second jolt.

Fisher winced at the sight of the two missing feet, but he couldn't force himself to look away and he watched in horror as a mechanical arm, gleaming in the brightness, uncurled downward like a snake.

Catching movement on the other side of the glass, the woman edged her way around the chamber and his gaze fell to a neat triangle of auburn hair between her legs. Then, looking up, he sucked in a breath when he saw Harris gliding towards him.

Their eyes locked and her smile washed away his fear.

Taking in her sweet scent, she nestled her head in the crook of his neck and, pulling his arm around her, she settled his open palm on her warm, silk buttock.

"It won't be long," she lamented in her soft husk.

Together they watched the extending metal arm, its end punctuated with a sharp pick.

As she stroked his hair with the tenderness he'd craved, the silvered forearm drew back like a scorpion's stinger.

With her delicate kiss at his ear, he stared at the man's bloodshot eyes and a face he recognised so well.

"I love you," she whispered, and the arm sprung down and punctured Fisher's bald head.

2

With the bright light penetrating through his dark lenses, Fisher drew a sharp breath as he woke to a constant rush of hot wind. Butting his hand against his face, he squinted at an endless haze of blue sky and a die-straight road, marvelling at dusty tarmac sandwiched by a vast carpet of straw-dry brush.

"Are you going to get that?" Harris said, the gravel in her voice dripping with nectar.

Fisher turned to his right, his neck sleep stiff as he watched her strawberry hair dance in the turbulent air. Glancing down, he followed her thin white blouse, flashing peeks at the white of her bra as it flapped in the wind. His gaze soon drifted to her smooth flowing legs, bared to the tight jean of her shorts, then followed up her slender hands resting loose at the leather wheel.

Their eyes met. Hers moved down, expectant at his lap where he found a cheap phone he remembered buying before they'd flown, its irritating chirp springing into focus and the screen flashing with Susie's string of digits.

"They were beautiful words," his friend's sombre voice said in his ear. "He would have said the same about you."

"There would have been a lot more swearing, but thank you," Fisher replied, and listened to her gentle laugh from the other side of the world.

"You know where I am if you need me," she said.

He nodded, a pointless gesture, before closing his eyes. "And you can call me if you want to talk."

"Thank you," she said, and the line went dead.

His gaze settled back on the road and an approaching tall green sign.

Cunnamulla, five. Mt Isa, over a thousand.

Harris's voice cut through the rushing wind as he blinked away the thoughts.

"The same dream?"

Fisher nodded without looking away.

He hadn't seen Andrew's desperate face since catching

a plane to Brisbane after the funeral. It was in the comfortable seats when he'd first lived the new nightmare.

She'd known as he'd woken. He'd been quick to tell her all, describing the visions, except for an unknown stranger taking her starring role.

During the long flight, they'd resolved to find Luana and each of the terrible places, test chambers or whatever nightmare name they used, and to shut them down, release the captives, and figure out who was behind it all.

They'd agreed to move under the radar of their employer. Although they didn't outright suspect their involvement, they knew powerful people played an integral role. Despite how desperate they were to halt the suffering, gathering evidence was the only way they could hope to end the torture once and for all.

Keen to discard the literal meaning of the recurring dream, Fisher had decided it was his mind's reaction to not going in guns blazing, and he counted himself lucky not to be imprisoned in a glass box beside the other freaks.

Although he couldn't impress with accelerated healing, his ability to influence the minds of others made him a clear target for those people, and despite the terror incited by the visions and his attempt to step over the obvious, it was Harris's part that bothered him the most.

He longed for their futures to be together and she gave off signs, however subtle, that she wanted the same, making any betrayal unthinkable, even though he knew she was more than capable.

"How far?" he said, turning back to the road. A folded map, curled at the edges, landed on his lap. "Old school," he said, turning the paper over in his hands.

"Don't start that again," Harris said, laughter coming easily.

He turned to the dimples in her cheeks, but watched as her expression sank when she saw something in the rearview mirror.

"Shit."

Turning his head between the seats, his gaze fell on a helicopter wrapped in stark orange and green camouflage flying low to the road with a cloud of dust at its back.

"For us?" he said, turning to the resignation on her expression.

"I take it you didn't tell them about our field trip, either?" she asked.

Fisher shook his head with the pounding of the blades building.

She slowed the car, bumping the wheels from the tarmac while the roof closed over their heads. Clamps secured against the metalwork just as the chopper shot over, showering sand across the paintwork.

Fisher stared as the chopper swung through ninety degrees then halted, the wheels touching down on the tarmac.

They watched as the side door of what looked like a smaller version of the Merlin opened, and a man in a sharply-pressed uniform emerged, holding an attaché case.

Harris let go of a deep sigh as his face emerged.

"Ryan Kelly," she said to Fisher's surprise. "What can we do for you on such a fine morning?"

The uniformed sergeant glanced at his thick black watch as he stood at the driver's door.

"It's afternoon. Twelve zero one," he said, the accent Australian. "It's my turn to be the post boy, Miss Trinity, and not for you this time." Stepping around to the other side of the car, he pulled open the case. "For you, sir," he said, presenting it at Fisher's window.

Inside, a plain white cardboard box nestled in a foam surround. Recognising the box, Fisher turned to Harris, who shrugged and looked across the horizon.

As the handset announced *'Identity Verified',* he thanked the sergeant.

"How'd you find us?" Harris said, looking towards the chopper with its rotors still turning.

"The orders came through this morning. We were told to follow the road."

Fisher's new iComm vibrated.

"See ya round," the Australian said.

Harris raised her hand and Fisher thanked him again with a wave of his palm.

"Are you going to answer it?" she said as the chopper lifted.

He drew a deep breath and slid the green icon.

***

Jane Doe

Present

The itch was incessant. A constant irritation on the thin boundary between her skin and just under.

Lethargy kept her eyes closed, the drugs muddying her thoughts as her nails scratched at the hand which was no longer there.

Her eyes opened with a jolt to the heart-shaped face of a stranger sweeping aside short blonde hair from her face.

The stranger smiled, and she felt her body glow. She took a deep breath and relaxed back into the mattress, watching the girl sitting at the foot of her bed, her slender form wrapped in a light blue tunic.

The girl squinted as she leaned forward and spoke, her voice gilded with sugar.

"Good morning. I'm Amy. Do you know where you are?"

Contemplating the question, she tried to move past the floral syrup of the voice. She knew she was in hospital, but which, she wasn't sure.

"It's okay," Amy said, squinting as she smiled. "Let's try something easier. Can you tell me your name?"

Her name, that was difficult too. She knew who she

was, but it wasn't clear which name she'd been using when she'd arrived at wherever *here* was. Concentrating, her gaze lingered on Amy's youthful face. She liked the name. It brought back memories of her first experience.

Reaching to scratch at the itch, her gaze fell to the covers.

"Don't worry. It's not uncommon to experience temporary amnesia after going through a traumatic experience."

Trauma. Ha, she thought to herself and kept looking at the white spread of the bed, pulling her left arm from under the sheets.

She knew something was wrong before she was free of the material, before she saw the space meeting the bandaged stump at her wrist.

The fog cleared in an instant and her eyes locked with Amy's.

"Where's that bastard? I'm going to fucking kill him."

3

James

"You didn't have to come," Fisher said as he strolled along the Brisbane street, its length dotted with residential buildings, each different from its neighbour. Across the wide road, he looked at a fenced-in garden at the foot of a black and white apartment looming over the street, tall palms splaying out their fronds, wild behind their wooden boundary. His gaze landed on a pair of semi-detached houses that wouldn't have been out of place on the street he'd grown up on.

"Something cut my plans short," she replied, as she pulled on her grey jacket.

He turned to the road and looked along the high curb lined on either side with drab, paint-faded cars. Just two brightly-painted vans were in amongst them.

Tugging at the base of his own suit jacket, he stretched out a suitcase crease.

"Remind me what Clark told you," Harris said.

He swapped his gaze from the bright red of the Australia Post van to the gleaming white of the Telstra.

"It's an Interpol arrest warrant. Johannas Häll. The local office had a tip-off. He's in an apartment just down there," he said, nudging his head forward.

"Why's he wanted?"

"Multiple homicide. He set fire to an office block in Bergen," Fisher replied, not taking his gaze from along the road.

"Terrorism?" Harris said, but he didn't look over.

"No. It was his office building. He'd worked for the company man and boy. Almost twenty years," Fisher said.

"Did he say why they're sending *you* in?"

"My unique abilities. They think I can keep the death toll down," Fisher replied, and for the first time he glanced over his shoulder at her thoughtful expression sweeping the street. "He said I should be careful. The guy's paranoid, probably armed, and may not be alone."

Harris laughed. Fisher wasn't altogether sure it was an appropriate reaction.

"Did you say I was with you?" she said, the corner of her mouth upturned.

Fisher shook his head.

"Do they know you're not armed?"

He nodded, and she made a strange noise with her mouth as she squinted across the line of parked cars.

"What have you seen?" he asked, his eyebrows raised as he followed her gaze.

"Nothing. Just pretend I'm not here."

"You've seen something." Fisher turned to her as she twisted her thumb and forefingers around her lips, then mimed throwing something over her shoulder. At the sight of the indents in her cheeks, he smiled, picking out his phone as Clark answered his call. "I'm here."

"You've got ten minutes before the local police arrive. Have him ready."

As Clark's voice cut off, he looked up at the target's building; a three-storey sandstone block, its height jutted with bright orange balconies and a tall, garish purple fence marking the perimeter. In the otherwise deserted street, a postman in a bright-orange jacket sorted through the bloated saddlebags of his red company-issue motorbike.

Fisher turned to Harris and smiled before checking each way and then crossing the road. The postman looked over and gave an almost imperceptible shudder as Fisher approached.

"You've got a parcel for one three five."

With a shallow nod, the postman followed him back across the road, then pressed the door number on the apartment's videophone before pushing his mouth up to the chromed microphone slot.

"Postie," he announced, his tone resonating with Aussie enthusiasm.

The latch on the gate clicked and Fisher turned to the

civil servant.

"You've already delivered it."

The postman shuddered, turning with a shrug.

Fisher pushed at the wide wooden door and stepped into the communal hall, the latch clicking closed as they got halfway up the carpeted steps, where his search followed a line of silvered numbers across the top floor landing before flitting to the right and finding the second door ajar.

Glancing back, he found her lips in a playful smirk.

***

Luana

Present

She felt no pain. The drip in her arm ensured that.

Her thoughts were clear, her mind sharper than it had felt for months. A pleasant side effect of the drip, at least for her.

She saw no alarm on the young girl's face. The badge on her tunic told her she was used to all sorts of reactions.

"Do you think I'm mad?" Luana said, edging herself up the bed.

Amy went to stand, but relaxed when Luana's head shook.

"You need company in these first few hours. I'm here to help you understand what's happened. To assist with the transition."

"Transition to what?" Luana replied.

Amy's gaze fell to the stump. "To your new way of life. I'm here to help you cope."

Luana's expression relaxed. "Do you think I'm not coping?"

Amy's head swayed from side to side. "I think you're

doing really well."

She felt a smile building on her face. "Anyway, I don't need to cope," Luana replied, the edges of her mouth drifting downward. "I know what happened. Can you pass me my clothes?" she said, as she glanced at the closed door to her right.

Amy leaned forward, her voice like silk. "You're twelve hours out of surgery. You need rest." Amy's head lifted, edging forward in her seat as Luana tried to pull herself toward the side of the bed. "Without the Morphine you'd be writhing in agony. The doctors will be here in a few hours and they'll give you the full medical picture, along with details of your ongoing care."

"Did they scan my head?" Luana said, cutting off the nurse.

Amy looked back with a noncommittal shake. "I doubt it."

"Can you check?" she said, leaning forward.

The nurse stood and picked up the chart hanging unseen on the end of the bed. After flicking through the pages, she shook her head again.

Luana closed her eyes, relaxing into the plump pillows. Neither said anything for a long time.

Without opening her eyes, Luana broke the silence.

"I'm sorry, Amy. You seem very nice. Another time and I could talk to you for hours. Maybe at a bar with a drink in both of our hands, but right this minute, I need James Fisher to explain why the fuck he didn't give me back my hand."

Amy leaned forward and placed her palm on the white of the bedcovers with the volume of her smile turned up full.

"A drink would be nice, but not while you're on medication," she said, raising her eyebrows. "Just lay back and rest. There'll be plenty of time to get hold of your friend."

Luana's eyes burst wide.

"My friend? You've got the wrong end of the stick. James fucking Fisher is not my friend. James fucking Fisher is a cunt that used all the fucking elixir on his fucking fuck-buddy." She lifted her stump into the air. "He didn't save even a drop for me."

Amy's smile didn't waver and Luana winced as she dropped her arm back onto the covers.

"You're a brilliant listener," Luana said, her tone softening as Amy stood and walked around the bed, their gazes locked.

She stopped by the monitor at Luana's side, with its clear plastic drip snaking into the back of her arm.

"Can you get my clothes please, Amy?"

"I will, but first…" she said, reaching for the white plastic thumbwheel, "you need a little sleep. I'll speak to the doctors about adjusting your medicine and see if we can get rid of those hallucinations."

Before Luana could protest, her gaze fell on Amy's delicate fingers on the plastic.

4

James

Only lingering on her unusual behaviour for a moment, he pushed at the heavy door with his knuckle and peered into the dark hallway. As it gave to the left, a heavy sweet aroma of burning pipe tobacco pinged at a forgotten place from a time long ago.

For a second he tried to follow the wisp of his past, but as the door prematurely thumped against something soft, he was back in the moment.

Glancing behind, he found her smirk hadn't changed, then stepping around the door into the heady darkness, he looked again. Intrigued at her growing lopsided smile, he followed her stare at the floor behind the door, his lids opening wide at the shadow of a figure slumped against a wall and a trail of darkness dripping from a neat hole in the centre of its forehead.

The fluctuating rhythm of fingers on a keyboard caught in his ear and he looked down the shadowy hallway. Habit turned his head to the left and he took a step back, a sharp breath catching as he watched her dab her finger at the trail of dark treacle dripping down the motionless forehead.

Drawing back, he watched her touch her finger to her mouth.

His alarm turned to a smirk as her expression changed to shock, her lips batting against the sleeve of her white blouse; all at once he realised Harris had thought this was a training exercise. She'd thought it was fake blood.

His amusement gave way as instinct turned him from the dead man. The background rhythm had ceased, replaced for a moment with two thuds he recognised.

Fisher's feet fixed on the spot as a debate raged in his head, but the choice was short-lived as a man in a bright-blue tracksuit appeared at the darkened end of the corridor, striding towards them, his hands out in front working a cloth across the butt of a silenced handgun. A sliver of a grey plastic case was tucked under his left arm.

The guy looked up and stopped, then let the object under his arm fall, his hands blurring as he fumbled to aim.

Fisher, still passive, watched as a white vase he'd barely noticed at his back flew past his shoulder, thumping against the guy's face with a crack of breaking bone. It sent him reeling against the wall to the sound of ceramic shattering. Shoved at his shoulder, Fisher stumbled into a dark bathroom just off the hallway as he caught a flash of Harris rushing toward the danger.

Stunned into inaction, with his gaze rushing around the damp room, he strained to the sound of footsteps running down the hall and crushing porcelain chips before breath pushed from full lungs.

Harris's call from between gritted teeth pulled him from his daze and he peered out to an empty hallway.

Driven on by a newfound impulse, he ran from the small room. As he rounded the corner, he found her with her arms gripped high around the guy's torso, his arms trapped to his side in a tackle that would have been illegal on the pitch, her momentum charging them down the corridor and forcing his legs to flail backwards.

As a single entity, they burst through a thin door, but she didn't let go, her slight torso pushing back his bulk. Spotting the gun still in the guy's hand, it felt like ice stabbed him in the heart.

Together the two bodies smashed square into a stud wall, the plaster buckling against their press.

Fisher ran after, his gaze darting side-to-side, searching for something to use as a weapon. Pulling up, he burst into the room and looked again, his breath catching in his throat when he found his target slumped at a dark wooden table with a clean entry wound in the back of his head and blood pooling over the varnished oak. To his side, tobacco smouldered as the treacle-like liquid flowed over spilt embers.

Snapping himself from the stare, he searched for

something substantial as the tussling cries grew louder. A yelp of pain shot from the melee and Fisher glanced over. With a face full of anger, muscles tight in his neck, the guy was forcing her back and straining to point the gun towards her stomach.

A half-full bottle of whiskey caught Fisher's eye as he turned. Without thought, he swept it off the floor and, in one movement, swung it over his shoulder before flinging it towards the grapple. Glass smashed against plaster and the tang of liquor filled the air; the missed shot failed to force the guy's reaction, but the same wasn't true for her.

With shards of glass raining down, she shot a look in Fisher's direction. The distraction gave her combatant an edge, and the gun came around to her middle.

***

Luana

Before

Sun streamed through the round skylight two stories above her head. Waking to the portal was one of her first memories, back when the mould hadn't greyed the glass. In the summer, it would wake her early. In the winter, it would wake her late. Today was the first time she could remember wishing she could turn over.

Rising out of the bed, she swayed to the side, then collapsed onto the billowing duvet, groaning with the pain rising in her head. Her first hangover hurt, but in a satisfying way, the pain a reminder of the excitement she'd felt last night. A reminder of her first time alone with someone of her own age.

Pulling back the cover, she stood, eyes closed against the bright morning. She leaned against the mattress, her feet meandering toward the long frameless mirror near the foot of her bed as its edges hung just proud of the wall. None of her furniture, not her stainless steel dresser nor the tall sheet metal wardrobe, or transparent boxes stuffed full of under-used toys, fitted tight against the roundness of the continuous wall.

She summoned herself tall and let her eyes peek back open, sweeping them down the length of her body, her hand pushing long brunette hair behind her ears.

She looked rough, at least by her standards, her face sleep-creased down one side. Eyes, red as Miss Piggy, stared back, telling her to smile.

Looking down, she decided once the fallout from last night had subsided, she would have to ask Zio for new nightwear. It had been a few months since the fabric had covered up the curls between her legs. She would ask for colour for the sheer white walls. Maybe light pink, and to get rid of the toys.

Judging from her new friend's reaction, she was too old for Barbie and Ken. They'd giggled together as she'd listened to the more interesting things to do without the need for imagination. Her expression turned thoughtful as she traced around the campus in her mind, ideas soon revealing themselves and a plan forming for a second trip out for the night.

With a rush of air at the outer door, she pulled in a deep breath, blinking her eyes bright and wide.

5

James

With Fisher's panic near overwhelming, he turned from the tussle and scoured the desk, his hands touching at a tiled mantlepiece, grabbing at small ornaments before discarding them to the floor as he realised their worth. When a shot rang out, his whole body clenched, desperation gripping his stomach.

Preparing for the worst, he turned. Expecting to see Harris falling backwards, his spirit buoyed as she stood upright. The smoking weapon held, locked in both the attacker's shaking hands, pointed only a hair's breadth from her delicate flesh.

Determination took control and Fisher's panic washed away. He had a second chance and wouldn't let this guy destroy her.

Without conscious thought, he took a step toward the battle. Drawing a deep breath, he pushed his hands out and screamed, "Stop."

The sounds of battle halted as if time froze. The assailant paused, staring at Harris.

Fisher's mouth gaped wide, but Harris didn't wait to question and with a flick of her wrist she had control of the gun, then swung it down and pulled the trigger.

Fisher winced as the second shot tore through the guy's crotch. She stepped back, giving him room to grab at the bloody mess that had been his balls.

Stepping aside, Fisher didn't know whether to hug her or grab himself in sympathy. Instead, he watched as the guy fell to the floor and curled in a foetal position, whimpering. She didn't pause or gloat; she just moved to the window, racking at the net curtains and waving.

Together they left the sparse room, heading through the hallway now lit from above, as figures in shorts and T-shirts burst past. Handing the gun's components to the last guy in the procession, they stepped over shards of broken vase and the two halves of the laptop the assassin had held under his arm.

"I'm sorry," she said, not turning back, her hand outstretched for a cab.

Before he could answer, Clark was on the iComm.

"It didn't go well," Fisher said.

"I heard. Are you okay?" Clark asked, his voice subdued.

"I'm fine, but I was lucky." Fisher hadn't finished his sentence before Harris grabbed the phone from his ear.

"What the fuck's going on?" The venom in her voice chilled the calm. "Don't sound surprised," she continued. "Yeah, someone fucked up. We could have lost him."

Fisher had never seen her so emotional, her voice spitting at the handset, her free hand clenched in a fist.

After seconds of silence hung in the air, she relaxed.

"I'm on rest," she replied, then paused again. "Okay. We'll get the next flight." She passed the phone back, whispering as she leaned in. "He said sorry. It was a test."

Fisher's mouth hung agape.

"The warrant was real," she added. "They didn't know about the other guy. They didn't know he was someone's target. There wasn't meant to be a problem."

"I guessed that much," Fisher replied.

"We need to head back to the UK. They want you," she paused and turned towards him. "Training."

Fisher nodded.

"And," she paused again, looking away. "They've reassigned me. There's been lots of chatter in the community."

Fisher furrowed his brow as he tried to meet her gaze.

"Something's imminent," she added, turning around.

"What does that mean?" he said, a mix of excitement and panic rising in his tone.

"It's probably nothing. It happens two or three times a year and nothing comes of it," she replied.

His shoulders slumped. "What about the place by the lake?" he asked.

"This could be serious. We agreed the day job comes first," she said.

"So we're six months from our next chance," Fisher said, his eyes wide.

She stared back, her expression unreadable.

"But you'll be in a better position," she replied.

"We will be," he said, and she nodded before turning away. "But…" was all he could get out before she cut him off to look him in the eye, her brow raised as she held up her hand.

"Make a choice. You're in or out. If you want to run, then I'll give you a head start. Just pray they don't send me after you."

Fisher couldn't help the shiver that ran down his back.

***

Luana

Before

The hairs on her body stood to attention as she turned to him glaring from the doorway.

He wore a slim white polo, the buttons, as always, closed up to the chin, the sharp tang of aftershave rolling in behind him. Despite his height, he imposed on the room with a straight stature and cold blue eyes that cut through her bull.

"You look like shit," he blurted out, his American accent elongating the words.

"Thanks," she replied with a smile as big as her face.

"Tell me who you were with?"

"Just my new friend," she said as her smile held.

"It's not time for boys yet," he replied with a raised

brow.

"I know," she said, her smile widening further.

"Or girls," he said. "Get some clothes on. We're going for a walk."

"What about school?"

He shook his head. "You're eighteen and not a child anymore. You proved that last night."

While he spoke, she pulled her nightdress over her head, leaving her perfect curves naked with her gaze locked to his as she watched for that reaction. The one she'd grown to love.

"No more school," he said. "It's time for work."

"I'll miss school," she replied, her brow furrowing as she flung the nightdress onto the bed. "There's so much more to learn."

"And learn you will. Now get some fucking clothes on."

Turning to the cold metal dresser, she pulled out a pair of knickers from the top drawer, then short socks frilled around the edges from the next level down. Tight jeans came from the third and a vest top from the last before she dropped the pile of white clothes to the floor. With no other choice of colour, she turned and dressed whilst watching him in the mirror.

Expressionless, his gaze fixed on her behind.

Pulling the top over her bare breasts, she turned around and smiled, his gaze moving to her face.

"What about my exams?" she said, reaching to scratch at the round skin-coloured plaster on her left forearm.

"We'll start after labs," he replied, ignoring the question as she followed him to the door.

"What sort of work?" she asked as it sealed behind her.

"You'll see."

6

James

Fisher woke with a start, panting as the pick dove into his skull. Wide-eyed, he settled his breath, watching the privacy screen lower to his right with Harris appearing through the gap as her bed climbed upright.

"Morning. I think," she said, wiping her eyes with the back of her hand.

He forced a smile and leaned back in his seat as it rose.

"We have people you can see," she said, searching around the cabin.

"They'd throw away the key," he replied and watched her cheeks dimple. "What time are we due back?" he added, blinking the sleep from his eyes.

"It's another three hours to Delhi, then it's eight to Heathrow. Are you in a hurry?" she said with a raise of her brow.

"No." He was silent for a long time as he glanced around at the other passengers rousing, their beds transforming back into luxury seats. "Do you know how long your next assignment is?"

"It could be a day, or a month. Longer perhaps."

A light perfume caught his attention and a cabin attendant with shapely legs and flowing brunette hair appeared at his side, holding a silvered steel jug with light steam whipping from the spout.

"Coffee, sir?"

Fisher accepted, pulling down his tray where she placed a steaming porcelain mug and smiled, then moved to the next row. He was about to speak when he noticed Harris was out of view, replaced with the rustle of thin plastic.

"What's up?" Harris said, startling him as she appeared back at the gap.

"Um…" he stuttered, watching her brows raise, her eyes full and energetic.

"Take a deep breath," she said with a sympathetic smile.

Fisher did as he was told.

"Did you see what happened in Bris…" he stopped mid word as the seatbelt symbol lit above their heads and a bong sounded across the cabin. Out of the corner of his eye, he watched an overweight passenger speaking with a male attendant, her face contorted with concern, then his gaze caught the brown liquid in his mug as it leaned to the left.

A deep male voice came over the speakers as he was about to speak.

"Hello, this is First Officer Silsbury again. I hope you have had a pleasant sleep as we travelled on the first leg of our journey. The keen-eyed amongst you would have noticed we have made an unscheduled turn. That's because we're diverting to Mumbai."

Fisher swapped looks with Harris, then turned as a murmur built in the cabin.

"On behalf of British Airways, I would like to apologise, but this is due to an incident at Delhi airport which is out of our control. A British Airways representative will be in the baggage claim hall to take care of your onward travel arrangements."

Harris fidgeted in her seat. "Call Clark," she said, and he pulled out his iComm, sliding the call icon.

After a moment, he removed the phone from his ear.

"That's a pain in the ass," he said, putting it back to the side of his head while turning to Harris's scowl.

"I don't like being told where to go."

Fisher's brow raised as he listened to the beeps before the call ended and he looked at the phone, then showed it to Harris.

Twisting her neck for a better angle, her eyes narrowed. "*Busy?*"

Luana

Present

She stared for what felt like forever. Her eyes were open, but the images only drifted, barely registering. Instead, she lay watching her cute nurse sitting at the foot of her bed with a tattered old paperback open in her lap.

She took comfort in her urge. She wasn't broken. It was just a missing hand, and she looked around the room as if for the first time.

It was a stark magnolia space dotted with dark furniture, a disorderly surreal mass of green and orange framed to her left, and a lone, tall wooden door to her right. In front stood a mirror the width of the room, with a light curtain set at the side. Peering at her reflection, she took heart at her punishing good looks and chestnut hair with a cute streak of blonde she loved so much, even though it had taken them so long to engineer.

Making a mental note to top up her tan, she looked at the side of her bed. There were no flowers or balloons or get-well cards, but she'd have been shocked to find any.

"Where do you live?" she said, much to Amy's surprise, her eyelids creasing as she placed the book open on her lap.

"The nurse's flats. How are you feeling?"

They sat in silence as Luana ignored the question. Instead, she watched Amy's fixed expression of empathy as Luana's eyes wandered down Amy's tight-fitting tunic wrapping her full breasts.

"I'm leaving today, no matter what you say."

Amy's head tilted to the side. "You'll need ongoing care."

Luana smiled.

"Two weeks minimum. Ignoring the pain, your biggest risk is infection," Amy continued.

"It's only a short-term concern," Luana said, and watched Amy's expression change as an ingrained alarm rang.

"Don't worry, I'm not going to kill myself." Amy's expression relaxed. "But I do have a proposition for you."

"Okay," Amy replied, her smile broadening.

"Why don't you come with me? Take some time off?" she said, concentrating on Amy's reaction, but all she saw was a rise of her brow that almost made her change her mind. "I can pay you. How about ten thousand pounds? That's not bad for a couple of weeks' work."

Amy relaxed back into her chair, her face revealing nothing new.

"I'm not kidding," Luana added. "If you can get my things, I can show you."

Amy sat forward and picked up her book. Then, turning down the corner of the page, she placed it on a side cabinet and pushed her palms together.

"You only had the gown you arrived in," Amy said, pausing.

Luana's palm flattened below her neck and she took a slow breath.

"Do you want to talk about that?"

"No," Luana snapped. "Best not."

Amy turned away as her gaze wandered to the door.

Luana swallowed, knowing it was a hopeless endeavour as Amy stood, moving to the end of her bed.

"And we only have your name down as Luana."

Luana shook her head. "It must be a misprint. Call me Lara."

Amy bunched her cheeks as she smiled and pulled out a pen to update the chart at the end of the bed, then stepped towards the door.

"So how about it?" Luana said, surprising herself, her brow raised with hope. Giving second chances was rare, but the warmth inside her built as she saw Amy's hesitation, her gaze moving between the woman in the bed and the heavy wooden door.

Luana's heart rate climbed as Amy took a step towards her, then halted as the nurse stopped and smiled. She knew the answer before she heard the sorrowful words.

"It's a flattering offer, Lara, but I have responsibilities here. I'll get the doctors and we'll have a chat about your ongoing care."

Luana sighed and lifted her right arm before she remembered. Swapping the movement to her left, she beckoned Amy over. "Can you sort out my pillows before you go?" Her tone was flat.

Amy's perpetual smile grew with her patient's first request for care and she stepped to the side of the bed, her hands either side of Luana's head to grab at the pillows. As she leaned in, Luana pulled herself forward, her head close to the tightness of her tunic.

"One last chance," Luana whispered under her breath as she looked at the woman's clear complexion, breathing in her delicate perfume.

"Huh," was her only reply, and Luana's left hand shot around and grabbed at Amy's soft neck. Her thumb pushed hard against the small cavity in her throat, her grip pulling Amy's mouth into the crook of her shoulder, making the perfect seal around her airway and stifling her gathering scream.

Amy flailed to break free of Luana's single-handed hold, but it wasn't long before they both felt her fight ending.

With a deep sigh, Luana turned her head to the lifeless ear. "We could have been fucking amazing."

She kept her grip a long while after the fight was over; long after she knew all function had stopped. Then with another heavy sigh, she let the lifeless body slump onto the hard floor, then pulled herself out of bed with her hand already around her back, pulling at the gown's drawstring.

7

James

"He must be on another call," Fisher replied, but Harris shook her head.

"The call should re-route, but it sounds like it didn't get that far," she said as she stared at the outstretched phone. "I've never heard of SkyNet being busy before." Slumping in her seat, she disappeared out of sight, only to reappear at the gap a moment later. "Try again."

After tapping at the phone's screen, he listened to the same tone.

"Check the news feeds," she said, nodding over. "You'd have lost the signal just after take off, but you might find something useful."

Fisher looked back, his expression blank, and she beckoned him closer. Then under her instruction, he double pressed the home button and found a news icon. A simple text list appeared, entries punctuated by arrows on the left filling the screen.

With the phone between them, they read together.

9 hours ago – SECRET - INTERNAL – UK – SRC: SS (Verified)
> SS / SIS / MET Leave cancelled as second suspect device difuss… MORE

9 hours ago – FLASH – USA – SRC: CCN *(Not Verified)*
> Pipe bomb explodes in LA mall. 20 killed, 36 injured. 2 suspects… MORE

9 hours ago – SECRET - INTERNAL – PAKISTAN – SRC: SIS (Verified)
> Reports of a gun battle in outskirts of town of Hyderabad… MORE

9 hours ago – FLASH – CANADA – SRC: CBC *(Not Verified)*

No injuries after explosion outside barracks in Montreal. No warn… MORE

9 hours ago – FLASH – UK – SRC: BBC (Verified)

Suspect device found in a fast-food restaurant. Police calling for wit… MORE

Fisher clicked the link for the top story and a pop-up window appeared.

No Connection.

Harris took the phone and tapped at the screen.

"The chatter was right," she said, looking over the list again. "There's lots going on, but nothing linked to Delhi. The closest is a gun battle in Pakistan, but that's on the other side of the country. Not even in India."

Fisher sat back in his seat. "A lot can happen in nine hours."

"That's an understatement," Harris replied, her eyes wide. "We should start getting updates as we descend in a few hours. Try the call again."

Fisher turned off the screen as its speaker squawked with the busy tone.

"We should speak with the captain," she said, tilting her head to the side.

"Will he speak to you?" Fisher replied.

"No, but he might with you," she said, raising the corner of her mouth, already pressing the call button.

After five minutes, the red-lipped cabin director was back, her line-thin eyebrows raised as she beamed her uniform smile, leaning close and speaking in a near whisper.

"I'm really sorry, sir. I told him who you are, but they've had strict instructions from air traffic control. They're not leaving the cockpit or allowing anyone in." She smiled and turned away as a plump lady bellowed for coffee across the cabin.

Harris leaned forward to the divider and shook her head. "I don't like this at all. It feels like something big."

"I'll try Clark again." A few seconds later, Fisher shook his head.

"Then our hands are tied until we descend," she replied before sinking out of view.

Fisher sat in silence, watching the staff busy around the cabin, but after ten minutes, he leaned between the partition to find Harris staring right ahead, her eyes glazed as she shook her head. It was the first time he'd seen her so frustrated, her usual calm absent.

She was so used to taking control, or analysing a situation for what to do next. It was easy to understand how she must feel stuck in the air, cut off from the outside world.

With nothing else to do, Fisher's mind wandered back to their first meeting near Heathrow Airport, then not long after they drove to North Wales, before following Susie's kidnapper's trail to Barbados, where they led the women destined to be slaves to safety.

She'd kept him strong after his best friend's murder, then watched him from a distance whilst he worked alone to find Farid's boss.

She'd risked her career and her life, taking severe heat for her choices. If he mentioned it, he knew she would say he'd paid her back, first saving her from the psychopath trafficker who'd had a penchant for pain. Then saving her life in Chile and making the connection to what they'd found in the concrete prison. The people they'd found with their own abilities.

When she'd come around on HMS Dragon, she vowed to save them all from their terrible fate. He'd never seen her so despondent before as he leaned forward to the divider.

"So what's involved in training?" he said, almost in a whisper.

Breaking her stare, her expression hardened and she

turned toward him. He smiled, despite the discomfort of her glare.

"You said you'd tell me about it when we had time," he added and forced his smile wider. "I think we've got a couple of hours."

Her eyes narrowed and she sat up in her seat.

"Most of the first month is class work," she said, her words quiet. "With PT in the mornings. You'll learn military theory and strategy. They'll open your eyes to the brutal world we live in. The other candidates will be from all backgrounds. Regular soldiers, sailors, special forces, graduates, intelligence officers, civil service," her eyebrows raised. "And sometimes people off the street."

Fisher nodded, holding the smile.

"They'll assess you all the time to gauge what you already know. Month two and classes continue. You'll be out on the range and learning basic fieldwork, along with PT for six hours a day. Month three and the suitability tests start.

"They'll subject you to trials of endurance, mental and physical. You'll train alongside special forces squadrons and your class will shrink away. You'll be training sixteen hours a day.

"Month four and every bone and muscle in your body will ache, then they'll step up a gear. You'll be acting out your newfound skills, living on five hours of sleep. Your class will be a shadow of its former size."

Fisher's smile eased.

"Month five, *you'll* want to quit," she said, pointing at him. "If you don't, then you're not human. Next will be the military escape and evasion course." She shuddered. "Then tactical questioning. Month six, if you've not given up or aren't in hospital, dead or disabled, then you go through total immersion."

Harris leaned forward, a smile building on her face.

"I shouldn't tell you this, but," she said, leaning closer, "The survivors think they've passed. They'll have a passing out ceremony. But," she added, before looking around the cabin, "That's the last test. They'll deploy you to hell. They'll throw everything at you, but it's not just about survival. If you make it to month seven, then you'll get your pass or fail."

Fisher realised his mouth was hanging open as Harris sat back in her seat, her expression blank.

"But you'll be fine," she said, monotone.

"How many people go through training?" Fisher replied, struggling with the words.

"Each year?" She bunched a cheek in thought. "About five hundred."

"Oh," he said, letting out a held breath and looking away, then his head snapped towards her. "How many pass?"

A smile rose on her lips.

"About twenty percent."

Fisher matched her smile as he sat back in his seat.

"Of those that survive," she added unseen.

His eyes widened, and he moved back to the gap. "How many survive?" he said, barely breathing.

"About ten," she paused, then spoke again. "But remember, not all the rest are dead."

***

Luana

Present

She knew she was on a train with her eyes closed and head leaning against a hard window, but her mind was in the past, the images, thoughts and feelings as crisp as the time they'd formed. She saw the white round room just missing the boxes once full of toys, now full of CDs and DVDs and the curve of a composite bow leaning against her flat screen by the piles of worn discs, stacked haphazard on top of each other.

Under the plump white duvet, she rubbed the hard calluses on the fore and index fingers of her right hand, the product of training for a month non-stop.

She felt eager to stretch her muscles as she stared at the bow. She was getting quite good and hoped to put her skills to test in competition soon. She'd assumed that was the point. At least then she'd get to leave the compound and meet people.

Since that night months ago, Zio had been her only human contact, apart from Gretta in the lab, but she was a mean old bitch that only spoke to tell her to roll up her sleeves, or to get her to lie down still as a corpse so she wouldn't fuzz the image.

Looking up at the skylight, she knew Zio would arrive soon. Yesterday, as he led her back, he said they'd do something new, something special to celebrate her coming of age.

Hearing the outer door, she pulled off the covers.

8

James

The tone in his head wrenched him from a restless sleep. Wiping his hand across his brow, he watched Harris appear at the gap.

"Looks like we got a connection," he said, pulling out his iComm just as he heard the first officer over the speakers confirming they'd started their descent.

Coming around from her seat, Harris knelt in the aisle beside him as they scrolled through the chaotic headlines. The avalanche of information kept coming as they struggled to process the sheer number of reports of explosions and inevitable deaths confirmed across the globe.

"Ring him," she snapped whilst the list continued, as if without end.

"Is she with you?" Clark said.

"Yes," Fisher replied in a near whisper. "What's going on?"

"It's a coordinated attack. Soft targets in the most part, but the scale is like nothing we've seen before. Twenty devices in the UK, ten of which have failed to detonate, but the death toll is nearing a hundred already. This is bigger than seven seven. The US is worse, hundreds more dead."

"Hold on a minute," Fisher said, then whispered the gist of the conversation in Harris's ear.

"Why the diversion?" she said, as Fisher pointed the bottom of his iComm to her mouth.

"It's everyone," Clark replied. "Not just you."

Fisher's eyes went wide as Clark continued. "There's been a threat of a mass nine eleven style attack and, with what's been happening, it's being treated as credible. The UN has grounded all commercial air traffic. It's chaos out there. Planes are landing all over the place. Delhi's full. Mumbai is your nearest overspill. There's already been a midair collision near JFK and countless near misses. There's a barrage of other threats. We're concentrating our own efforts on the UK at the moment, leaving the other sections to their own countries. Someone wanted us to sit up and listen. We're waiting to hear what they say."

"What are our orders?" Fisher replied as he stared wide-eyed and breathless at Harris.

"Find a hotel and sit tight. The situation is fluid, and we're not expecting the flight ban to lift for at least forty-eight hours. Let me know when you're down and I'll get more details."

Harris stared at Fisher as he replayed the conversation. Then, without comment, she walked back around to her chair.

A few seconds later, he heard her quiet voice. "I'd get some sleep if you can. It looks like it's going to be a busy few months."

She'd already closed her eyes by the time Fisher looked through the gap. As he sat back, his mind raced over all that Clark had said, but in that moment, his brow raised at the thought it might all be another training exercise.

With a shake of his head, he dismissed the thought, not willing to repeat Harris's mistake.

Smiling, he remembered the bloody finger heading to her lips and his eyes drifted closed, snatching a moment's sleep before he saw the first of the warehouse's bright metal siding.

The first officer's voice pulled him from his nightmare. They'd arrived at Mumbai but were stacking; a spiralled, three-dimensional queue, letting other aircraft with less fuel land first.

Taking a sip from his water bottle and wetting a cotton napkin, he leaned forward, freshening his face and lids. Through the gap in the partition he saw into the darkening sky and stared in wonder at the spider's web of orange streetlights, the bright city glowing as the aircraft banked, before rolling back to darkness.

Lurching in his seat, he saw lights flashing across his narrow view. Then he looked at Harris with her eyes closed, feeling himself calm as he took in her beauty. After a moment, he shook his head and took a deep breath, watching the blinking beacons off in the distance.

With his eyes closed, the aircraft rocked left then right, and a scream from over his shoulder filled the cabin, replaced with the hum of chatter as each passenger turned to the source, a plump, brunette, fifty-something woman, her face buried in her hands as her body shook.

Fisher jerked a look back to the window but saw nothing other than lights layered across the horizon.

After a moment of counselling by the attendant who'd served his coffee, the woman calmed, slowing her gesticulations toward the window. As the attendant walked away in her hugging pencil skirt, the seatbelt light came on and the heavy woman screamed again.

Unclipping his metal clasp, Fisher stood. Approaching, her hands were clamped tight to the arm rests, her knuckles white as long manicured nails buried deep into the leather. He crouched at her side, her gaze darting his way as he touched her shivering arm.

"It's going to be okay," Fisher said in a soft voice.

Settling back into his seat, he glanced to see her already asleep and as the attendant passed by, she brushed a warm palm on his forearm, her mouth and eyes forming a silent thank you.

Without warning, the plane lurched to the right, sending everything that wasn't strapped down into the air. The flight attendant flew, along with the cabin's flotsam, towards the front of the plane, her rag-doll limbs flailing into seat backs as she went.

The aircraft then swung in the opposite direction, its nose pointing towards the ground. With debris raining down and then up again as the pilot fought to correct their direction, the attendant thumped against the floor.

Luana

Before

"What is it?" she said, regretful as the words left her mouth. Cowering, she looked up, surprised to see the lines on his face tightening to a smile. When it turned to a laugh, she smiled, relaxing as he shook her by the shoulder. They both knew she recognised the Beretta, the same 92F model John McClane had brandished so many times on the small screen.

Looking back down, she felt the warm metal, the grip solid in her hands. It was lighter than the bow and easier to wield. Her rough index finger tightened as she moved to the trigger.

"It's loaded," his warm voice warned from somewhere behind and she flinched her finger behind the guard. "Give it a go."

Looking down the whitewashed walls, she eyed the dark silhouettes that replaced yesterday's straw circles.

9

James

As if frozen in time, the cabin was calm until, with a jolt, screams erupted the length of the metal tube when the aircraft twitched from side to side with the pilot's fight for the hundreds of lives.

A ragged voice boomed over the speakers, the words fuelling the screams as he announced that something had hit their left wing and they'd be making an emergency landing. Before going silent, he left them with hurried orders to brace.

Forcing himself to calm, Fisher peered down the aisle where he found a growing crimson pool darkening the carpet along with the attendant's head and limbs bent at awkward angles. Certain she was the first of the fatalities, he drew a sharp breath when her chest rose and fell.

His glare soon confirmed the pain washing over her face, just as the cabin dived left before correcting right and the aircraft dropped through a bubble of pressure. Her face glimmered with renewed agony as it lifted just enough to crash against the metal of a seat upright.

Knowing he couldn't sit alongside the other passengers and watch her die, he loosened his grip on the armrest's leather and pulled open his seat belt. Uneasy on his feet, he slipped the belt from his suit trousers, grabbing at his seat back as his feet lifted and dropped back to a chorus of gasps.

Edging his way along the aisle, he gripped hard, buffeted side by side as they shaved altitude in bursts. Dropping to his knees, her pool of blood stretched the width of the aisle. Despairing at her blank expression, he longed for any sign of brain function. Even pain would give him hope.

A violent lurch slid him down the aisle, sending his head into the metal of a seat. He turned and clawed back into the sticky pool, looping his belt to the nearest metal seat mount and wrapping the ends around his fist.

Gripping tight, he leaned down to her face, taking heart

in her rasping breath. With the little he knew, he guessed the acute angle of her neck caused her labour. Desperate for advice, he scanned around the cabin but saw only faces fixed ahead in terror, their heads buffeting this way and that, hands gripped to first class opulence.

Looking down, racked with indecision, he couldn't help fear that despite making it this far, he wouldn't be able to help the wretched woman. His first aid skills were almost non-existent and her injuries were more severe than any practiced Samaritan could hope to manage.

The angle of her neck looked the worse, with blood oozing from a large gash above her ear. The multitude of other grazes and cuts looked painful, but wouldn't kill her. More important were her limbs at random angles, bending in places where they shouldn't.

It was then he heard the command. Shooting a look back, he saw Harris belted in his aisle seat, leaning forward and staring over, her mouth moving in a one word command. "Airway."

Flourished with new confidence, he used his free right hand to turn her head, heeding Harris's shouts.

"Slowly."

The patient repaid his actions with deep breaths and a pink hue returning to her face as his focus changed to the new gush of blood from the deep wound near her ear. A thick napkin appeared at his eye level. Looking up, he saw a middle-aged man, his face grey with fear.

Fisher nodded and pushed the material to the wound and then, being careful not to smother her, he lay her on her side, his mass stopping the bounce of her limbs with each arbitrary swing of the cabin.

Before he could relax, rubber screeched and rapturous applause filled the cabin. Harris soon arrived by his side with a warm pat on his back before she knelt by the stricken hostess. He stood, his clothes stiff with blood, and the applause grew to a deafening volume.

Together they held their vigil as the passengers were

anything but calm, rushing the aisles to evacuate down the inflatable slide. Within minutes, ambulance crews took over the care and Harris led him into the humid night.

Once down the steps, he spotted jagged metal and a spaghetti of wires rolling out where the rest of the wing had been.

Taking a deep breath, Fisher peered up to a sea of blinking lights mingling with the stars.

***

Luana

Before

Her eyes widened, her gaze darting around the room, her lungs pulling at the air as though she'd just risen from under water. She knew she was in the same sterile place she always woke, but being alone surprised her.

Rolling to her back, her face lit up with a smile, her shoulders relaxed into the soft mattress as the dream drifted from memory. A thought caught her off guard.

He'd arrive soon, and he'd know what she'd dreamed of when he looked her in the eyes.

She looked up, then jumped from the bed, the bright light her only clock. Today she'd dress before he opened the door.

Without lingering, she pulled on her exercise whites that had supplemented the meagre range of clothes she'd had for years.

At first she'd enjoyed the running, especially the new range of clothes and savouring the warmth of finishing. But now he pushed her so hard each morning it was only a matter of time before she puked, despite her fear of that bitch's wrath.

As the outer seal hissed, she drew a deep breath.

10

James

With a blanket wrapped around Fisher's shoulders, not sticking around for praise or favour, together they hung their heads and blended back into the crowd. Programmable passports stamped, they walked past the queue for the besieged British Airways rep and into the sweaty chaos of the baggage hall, soon passing straight into the arrival's washroom.

To strained looks, Fisher scrubbed at his bare arms until, with a flash of strawberry blonde, a pair of hanger-straight tan trousers and a crisp white t-shirt landed at his feet. Gritting his teeth, he pulled off his cardboard-stiff clothes, wincing as what felt like most of his body hair went with them.

Clean, at first look at least, he found her through the bustle as she leaned with her ear to the black plastic of a payphone and a second bulging carrier at her feet.

A smile bubbled up past the thought of the blood scraped from his skin, the bag a reminder of a rare insight she'd let loose as they'd set off for the airport heading to Australia.

When she'd refused to pick up his clothes from his flat and carried no luggage herself, she told of her thoughts about bags left to linger on a commercial flight, her distrust of the baggage process and the gaping opportunity it gave for interference. Instead, with money no object, she sourced everything at her destination, discarding again as she jumped on the next plane.

Hanging up the phone when she spotted him heading over, and with her expression sullen, red hinting around her eyes, she barely acknowledged his presence as she made eye contact.

Out in the sticky night with cloud blanketing the stars, water stood proud under foot. To the blare of horns almost as loud as her silence, Fisher clung to the door handle as the creaking cab twisted and slipped across the packed roads.

Peeling his hand from the mock leather, they arrived under a glass canopy; the rain running a river across their path leading to the comfort of an air-conditioned foyer.

As Harris checked in with short answers and hurried writing, the colourful receptionist's corner mouth smile hinted at an unusual transaction that had bagged one of the last hotel rooms in the city.

Fisher didn't doubt it for a minute.

With his skin still tight with the hostess's blood, he turned to find Harris glancing over her shoulder as she walked back under the scores of slow fans towards the glass entrance.

"I'll meet you up there."

She missed the protest of his raised eyebrow, having already turned back towards the revolving doors.

***

Luana

Before

She opened her eyes to the darkness, wide awake as if someone had thrown a switch. She searched the room for comfort and the tiny red LED on the TV proved it was her own.

Closing her eyes, she found tiredness a long way off. With her lids unable to stay closed, she stared through the grime at the sprinkling of stars. Although the darkness was alien, she felt no unease.

She was an amazing sleeper. Lights out and she was gone, never waking until the sun. Unable to slumber, she couldn't help thinking something was wrong. Nothing had changed, apart from the training, but she'd been doing that for months.

She turned from her back as his face reflected from the skylight.

He was her only contact, and she was human. It was natural to think of him that way.

Rolling to her left and the opposite shoulder, the bed felt like stone. She didn't want it to be him. Why not someone extraordinary like John McClane?

Zio was her father and mother and brother and sister, and had been since her real kin long abandoned her. When she wasn't alone, she was alone with him. Alone to train. Alone to watch a movie. Alone to eat and alone for laying back for the examinations.

He hadn't abandoned her.

Rolling onto her back, she told herself she was bound to have feelings for him, and if they were so wrong, then why was she allowed to keep them? She knew she'd never see that girl from her brief trip outside again.

Surprised by the warmth of her hand between her legs, she pressed, picturing the short hair curled around a face, and that vixen's smile she'd stored away so well.

Her fingers rolled in circles, her back arching as she varied the pressure, only pausing at a noise outside her door. Her hand moved again as the silence continued, her shoulders relaxing into the bed as she closed her eyes, only to freeze as Zio's face smiled back.

She pulled her arms over the covers and turned to her side, tears rolling down her face.

11

James

Refreshed and scrubbed clean with a towel wrapped around his waist, Fisher found Harris sitting on the left twin bed in the lamplit room, her renewed smile glowing a welcome.

"So what now?" he said, looking down through the full-height windows toward a dark sandy beach a few roads over.

"We do as the man says," she replied.

He heard the smile in her voice. "And?" he said, turning to the crease of her grin.

"We figure out how the hell we're going to get home," she said, pulling an iPad from its fresh white box, which she threw into the waste bin. "Ganners is pretty close, but the journey would be a bitch. We'd have to go right through Terry land to get to Butlins." Her eyes seemed to glow with excitement as she spoke, her demeanour so much brighter than when he'd left her in the foyer.

Fisher stared without speaking and she looked up through the pause, smiling at his confused brow.

"I forget how green you are." Her tone was stoney as she shook her head. "No disrespect, of course," she added, the edges softening.

"None taken," Fisher replied as he turned back to the blackened sea view.

"Afghanistan. And it's still full of Terry Taliban. Butlins is what the guys call Camp Bastian, the British HQ in Helmand. I picked up a bit of bullshit talk over the years out there."

Fisher opened his palms and smiled as he turned to take in her inevitable look. "So the choice is between a few days at the beach, or a war zone?"

Harris shot him a scowl.

"Did you listen to Clark, or those TV reports at the airport? This is bread and butter stuff. It's what we... I, trained for," she said, pausing for a moment before resuming a smile. "Anyway, if it's sand you want…"

Fisher chuckled as he grabbed his phone before speed dialling Clark on speaker. "It was worth a try," he said, tightening the towel with his free hand.

"They've scored a direct hit," Clark's tinny voice came back. "It's chaos out there. There are no commercial flights airborne. At least three planes crashed and there are hundreds of aircraft unaccounted for. You two were lucky."

Nodding, Fisher drew a deep breath before moving to sit beside Harris.

"We're predicting seventy-two hours before they lift the flight ban. The airlines are racing against the clock to find the five thousand aircraft that landed at their closest airport. Then they've got to get fuel, ground and air crews all to the right place. Airlines are going to the wall as we speak and the cost to the world's economies could be over half a trillion dollars."

"Okay," Harris said, not hiding the resignation in her voice. "So we're not going anywhere for the time being. What should we do in the meantime?"

"You won't like it," Clark replied.

"Why doesn't that surprise me?" she said, placing the tablet on the bed.

"We're in third phase."

"Already?" she replied as her expression sunk.

Fisher's confusion pulled his brow low.

"With phase one already over, Five are taking the lead on phase two. We're sharing three with Six, at least for now. New reports and intel are inundating all agencies, plus we're reviewing everything from the last few years to see if we've missed anything. That includes police files. We've already found leads for at least two of the devices, so I'm afraid it's old-fashioned trawling. I'm going to fire over a case for you to review. Once you're done, I'll send you another. They've given me my own pile."

"Sure," Harris sighed. Her face lit up with a question. "What happened to SkyNet?" she said, looking out into the darkness.

Fisher followed her gaze to the pitch-black sky void of blinking beacons.

"Sheer traffic, I'm told. I think we had every offshore asset calling at the same time."

The handset beeped and Fisher saw a second call, then Susie's face filled the screen as Clark signed off. Switching from the speaker, he pushed the phone to his ear and stood.

"You're not involved, are you?" she said, desperation peaking in her tone.

"I'm fine," he said, and heard her release her held breath. "Are you okay?"

"Yeah, I'm fine," she paused. "I guess."

"Get some sleep."

"I've been trying."

"Call me if you need to chat, but now's not a great time," Fisher said as he closed the call, then he turned from the window to Harris. "Dinner?" She shook her head. "What's wrong?"

"We're stuck in Mumbai, thousands of miles from the action. I don't know. What do you think?" she replied, tilting her head to the side.

"Maybe you're hungry. Anyway, this could be fun?" Fisher said, flashing his eyebrows.

The hint of a smile rose in the corner of her mouth as she looked him up and down.

"I suggest you put some clothes on."

After dressing in his tan airport clothes, he checked his iComm.

"Email from Clark. Shall I?"

Harris nodded and leaned back with her elbows on the bed as Fisher relaxed into a wicker chair in the corner of the room. He opened the file's attachment.

"It's from Thames Valley Police. Files relating to a string of fires at the University of Reading in 2006 and 2007," he said, looking up with a raised brow. "That's three years ago."

"I can't fault your maths," she replied and Fisher sighed before looking back at the screen.

"May 2006. Miller Building. No cause or accelerant found."

"Is that it?" Harris said, her brow low.

"The notes from the fire investigation classed it as a chemical fire, but the accelerant was never identified." He looked up again. "How's this interesting?"

"Keep going."

"It's probably a student prank gone wrong," Fisher said, bunching up the corner of his mouth.

"Work it through," Harris replied, not hiding her irritation. "What did they do in the Miller Building?"

He stood as he read, pouring two glasses of water from a frosted bottle in the minibar.

"Admin. Teacher training. Geography and Environmental Sciences."

"Not chemistry or explosives, then?" she asked with a raise of her brow.

"Nothing that exciting. The seat of the fire was in the Environmental Sciences storage facility."

"Any injuries?"

"A guy in security," Fisher said, reading down the page. "He died, and the damage was extensive." He paused as he read on and Harris coughed and raised her eyebrows.

"Fire Two," Fisher started reading again. "Same building, but in November the same year. No cause or accelerant found, but again, they classed it as a chemical fire. Maybe the police think the geography department was developing untraceable chemical weapons?"

"Take it seriously," Harris said, picking up the iPad, then after tapping at the screen, she took over narrating the file. "The second fire was in a lab in the early afternoon. Students were carrying out low-risk experiments. The survivors, all students, described the air catching fire. Three floors of the building were gutted. One fatality and a case of serious burns."

"Gas?" Fisher asked, looking over.

She shook her head. "They ruled it out."

"Why?" he replied, waiting as she read on.

"The flame was invisible," she said.

"What the fuck burns with an invisible flame?" he replied, frowning.

Harris tapped on the tablet while Fisher typed a phrase into the iComm's search engine. He clicked the top result and a grainy video of a racetrack filled the screen. In the pit lane was a seventies single seater race car, its colours washed out. He watched as the driver jumped from the low seat and pranced around the pit lane, his arms flailing as if he was shaking off a swarm of spiders the camera couldn't quite pick out. It took way too long before the pit crew realised he was engulfed in an invisible flame. Dousing him with powder extinguishers, the fire fighters jumped back as unseen flames licked out.

"Ethanol," Harris said, interrupting his wide-eyed glare.

"You should see this. It's the stuff of nightmares," he said, pointing the iComm her way.

"And Hydrogen," she added, watching at a distance.

"Ethanol. Isn't that alcohol?" he replied. Harris nodded as Fisher's mouth broadened into a smile. "I think they made this too easy for us."

***

Luana

Before

The darkness had become a pattern. She'd wake to the stars bright through the skylight, her thoughts circling around *that* time, dreading the minutes till the first signs of the sun.

The day started like any other, with a blistering run

around the campus. The heat of the shower did its usual job, rousing her until she lay back against the couch's soft leather where she'd teeter near to sleep, despite the pokes, jabs and photographs, before breakfast perked her back up. They'd spent an hour on the range, four hundred rounds at forty metres, half in the red heart zone and half square in the brain.

He pushed her out to fifty. Her results made him smile and, surrounded by the air thick with propellant, he made the promise of a moving target. She watched in wonder as they skipped the door to the gym where they would spar in hand to hand. Instead, they walked, bringing back vague memories before they were outside and standing at a lone white car.

Wide-eyed, she sat straight-backed in the passenger seat, a grin filling his face, matched only by hers as she saw the red and white gates pull open. She watched the alien world fly by. Her grin turned to an open gape as she took in the blur of unfamiliar faces and buildings and cars and buses as they shot past. The buildings disappeared, after how long she wasn't sure, the ache in her jaw and stretched muscles in her face giving her only an idea.

Still deep in wonder, she watched the rolling green hills and bright yellow fields, the lazy cows cutting the grass and fluffed sheep flocking like grounded birds. She hadn't seen another car or person for an age before they slowed and took a turn, the tyres crunching on the gravel, stopping in front of a slatted fence that kept a fascinated heifer at bay. It wasn't until he raised his eyebrows that she knew she could pull the handle.

Still surprised it wasn't locked, she rose, closed her eyes and took in the deepest of breaths.

The air was cleaner than she ever thought possible. The silence quieter still. She'd never realised before, but at home there was always a constant hum of process from the huge tangle of metal a mile away in the centre of the campus.

She looked across the vista and stumbled back, the metal of the car saving her from falling. The lack of walls and fence struck her eye, her heart pounding; she loved the wide open space but she felt so vulnerable.

The silence broke as Zio pulled a small pack from the boot before turning down a gravel track. Then, with a glance, he motioned for her to follow. Standing by the door for security, she moved only as he held his hand out.

With his fingers interlocked with hers as they walked, her heart calmed with the warmth. She loved the man, her father, in the most important ways, keeping her secure and teaching her the way.

Catching sight of a rabbit, she pointed in the distance. He looked over but couldn't see until it moved, soon spotting another bounding ahead. She stopped them dead, her hand at his chest, and they stood still. Her gaze fell to a four-legged creature with great antlers rising from its head.

He complemented her eyesight as he squinted. They moved again, and the deer shot away, her gaze roving across the green horizon as the sun beat on her skin and the wind wafted fresh across her face.

They walked until her legs ached, the gravel track left long behind and a huge void in her belly. He smiled with a blanket in hand and pulled a wrapped picnic parcel from his pack.

Sitting on the soft down of grass underlay, she marvelled at the thick, rough cut sandwiches. He'd made them himself and they were nothing like the die-straight thin bread from the canteen.

As they ate, he pulled out a green glass bottle and a plastic beaker. She knew wine, of course. She'd seen and tasted it last time she'd been free of the place and lapped it up from the plastic glass, despite his protests to slow.

Like last time, her head swooned, and she felt that tug as her eyes drifted across the horizon. Before she knew it, they were kissing. It was good, but the fireworks stayed in their cardboard packaging; nothing like she'd felt that night out over the fence.

It was pleasant enough to carry on, and they ended up undressing. To be one with the wilderness, he said.

She stood and twirled her arms out like a helicopter, then turned back and marvelled at the difference, his body so dissimilar to hers.

She had vague memories of her brother naked, back when they were very young, but his was different. It was huge and angry as it pointed towards her, getting closer as he walked.

At first she took her own steps closer, intrigued by this new thing, then stopped and he held her hands, pulling her into a kiss. He guided her to the ground, too busy to aim for the blanket and it was inside her, her face full of surprise as the pain died, her body stiff with shock.

It was over quickly, his face contorting as he gasped, rolling back onto the blanket, his thing shrivelling in the wind. She lay still, each breath hard fought, silent tears streaming down her cheeks.

She flinched as his face filled her vision.

"I lied. It was training." Seeing her tears, he shrugged. "Get used to it. It's your best weapon yet."

He dressed and turned, walking back down the track. She hurried her clothes on, gagging as she pulled her knickers up, then ran to catch him on the horizon.

It wasn't his fault, was his only comment as he drove. "You have no idea what you do to people," he said as the gates closed.

The next morning, they didn't leave her room. Arriving, he told her to get back in bed before stripping off his bottom half and pulling a sheath over what protruded.

Afterwards he lay at her side, his breath heavy with the seconds of effort.

"I'll get that cleaned," he said, staring at the skylight.

They dressed and went to the range.

After that, the sex was the least of her worries.

12

James

"Case closed," Fisher said, not hiding the triumph in his voice as he perched forward in the hotel room chair. "They were making vodka."

Harris sighed as Fisher picked up his phone and unlocked the screen.

"The cops aren't incompetent. There would have been plenty of physical evidence," she said, shaking her head.

Relaxing back into the chair, he raised his brow. "Do they always get it right?" he asked after a moment.

"More often than you think," she replied, and he stared out into the night.

"So if it's not an illegal still, then what else have we got to go on?" he said, turning from the window.

"There're loads more details at the back of the report, plus there was another fire in a different building."

"Go on," Fisher said, trying his best to remain interested.

"Thanks," she replied, not hiding the sarcasm. "It was in an accommodation block. The ignition source wasn't in question this time, but the chip pan fire wasn't what caused the building's structure to warp and collapse. They found a secondary seat of the fire in the bedroom next door."

"Another chemical fire?" Fisher said, looking around the room.

"Yes, but they figured it out too late. Or didn't have enough time. The fire took most of the evidence with it."

"But it's still the same. A chemical fire with an unknown cause?" he replied, catching her eye.

"In a nutshell," she said, nodding.

Fisher shook his head and Harris couldn't help but smile.

"This is what we have to do. After the immediate threat is over, we go through phase one and hunt for the perpetrators. In phase two, we seek the players pulling the strings."

"So what's phase three?" Fisher asked, looking her in the eye.

"After nine eleven, we had all the field teams, analysts, even the cleaners sifting through cases like this for months. In the end, we found three people with links to the attack and stopped a whole new tragedy from hitting the news. The process works."

"So what do we do now?" he asked.

"We work the information and sift the angles the cops dismissed for whatever reason. When we send our conclusion," she said, raising her brow, "they'll pass over the next case and we'll accept it with gratitude."

"These fires happened a long time ago, and it's not like they made headline news…" He paused, searching for the right phrase. "I'm not sure why we're interested."

"The fires were unusual enough and the fact that they occurred in such a short timeframe makes them interesting. Universities are great places to breed terrorists. Students are vulnerable, at least when they start. It's their first step into adulthood. All you need is one dodgy member of the academia and they can inspire almost anything."

"In the geography department?" Fisher said, raising a brow.

"I admit it's unlikely," she said, her finger sliding down the screen. "There should be a summary from the investigators somewhere. Bingo. Three fires… blah, blah, blah… two common links… blah, blah, blah. They looked at those expelled, or that might hold a grudge. They looked at rival universities and anyone with personal issues, but no one fell out as a suspect. The research profile for the university is bland. No GM. No vivisection. There was extensive CCTV, and they accounted for everyone."

"Does it say who occupied the bedroom?" Fisher asked, and Harris scrolled down the page.

"A twenty-five-year-old Philosophy PhD student called

Francine Madeleine Bissette. She came back squeaky clean."

"So it's someone from outside of the University?" Fisher replied, glancing at the phone on the side of the bed.

Harris shrugged, leaning back.

"You want a beer?" Fisher asked, but before she answered, he'd moved over to the phone and had reception on the line.

Her expected protest didn't come; instead, she went back to staring at the screen.

"So where would you start?" she said, looking over when he'd sat back down.

Raising a brow, he pressed his lips together in thought.

"Three things interest me," he said after a moment.

Harris nodded for him to elaborate.

"What caused the fire?" he said, holding out his hand and lifting his thumb into the air. "How does Bissette come into this, or was it just a coincidence it was her room?" he added, lifting his forefinger.

"We don't know what started the fire," Harris said, looking at the screen.

Fisher lowered his hand.

"We must know what was in storage?"

Harris ran a finger along the smooth glass and he smiled as he watched her concentrating.

"Ice," she said, and Fisher let his smile drop a moment before she looked up.

"Ice?" he repeated, shifting in the chair.

"Industrial floor to ceiling freezers containing ice core samples. Outside of the freezers were a lot of rocks, packed up in steel boxes sitting on metal shelves," she replied.

"Could a freezer have blown up and ignited a gas pipeline?" he said, despite knowing he was reaching.

"There weren't any gas pipes in the vicinity," she replied as she span the iPad around in her hands. On the screen were two dark images. In the first, a black soup rose up the wall with a chalk mark on the charred paintwork showing thirty-two centimetres off the ground. A computer-generated red circle ringed the mess with an arrow and a caption in white. *Freezer remains.*

The second image showed scorched metal shelves piled with blackened boxes, all leaning to one side.

"It was so hot the shelves melted."

"Destroying the evidence as it burnt," Fisher said with a sideways smile as his eyes lit up. "Like a copper still."

"It burnt for four hours," she said, continuing to read down the screen. "Suppressant foam eventually brought it under control." She paused again as she read. "The scene was under investigation for an entire week before it landed in the *too hard* basket."

"Did they analyse the molten gloop left behind?" Fisher asked, letting his smile relax.

"It doesn't say. It would be useful, I agree. At least we could rule out your illicit operation."

Fisher rubbed the light stubble on his chin. "Is there any more detail on the contents of the freezers? What sort of ice was it?"

"Core samples from Antarctica," she said after reading the screen.

Fisher shrugged.

"Explosive rocks?" he said, raising his brow and she stared at him as if she were a million miles away. "Can rocks explode?"

"I've seen that before," she said, her voice vague. "But it's not that," she added, shaking her head. "The building would have come down." With that, her gaze snapped back into focus.

He thought better of asking.

Even though he didn't speak, she felt the need to comment. "It was a long time ago, and I'm assured it couldn't happen again."

Fisher raised his brow and shook his head when it was clear she wasn't talking to him.

"Perhaps there was residual gas inside the rocks," he eventually said. "I'd have thought they'd protect against that."

Harris nodded as if she hadn't paid attention to what he'd said. "Give me a minute," she added, jumping from the bed. "Can I?" she said, reaching for the iComm in Fisher's hand.

Fisher let her take it and she disappeared into the bathroom, before reappearing a moment later with what looked like a satisfied smile.

"I just had to check something. And it's all good. Anyway. I think someone was storing something down there they shouldn't have, but to find out, we'd need to know who regularly accessed the room and then hope they kept any records so we could interview everyone."

Fisher relaxed back into the seat. "What about the security guard? Why was he down there?" he said, his voice quiet as she went back to reading.

"He had no set routine," she said, pausing as she read. "There was no reason for him to be there rather than somewhere else. They can't place him at the time the fire alarm went off. They think he was investigating the cause of an alarm, even though it was against policy. It adds weight to the Fire Service's theory. They say the door was opened when the fire was in progress. The cause of death was a broken back after the back draft threw him across the room."

Fisher turned to the windows as sheets of water ran down the glass.

"An electrical fault with a freezer?" he said, looking back before he caught himself staring.

"You still need something to ignite," she replied.

"How old were those freezers?" he asked, touching his chin.

"I'll email Clark," Harris said, already tapping at the screen, but froze with a knock at the door, before her hand shot out towards Fisher as he stood from the chair.

Luana

Present

"I need help," Luana said, her tone flat as she spoke into the handset with her back against the gloss-red metal frame. Watching as people came and went in the distance, she waited for a reply, savouring Amy's perfume as it rose from the tunic and trousers hugging her body.

She'd expected the pause.

She'd expected the shuffling and the slam of the door.

She expected the rhetorical question from the American.

"You're alive?"

She'd expected the surprise in his elongating tone.

She hadn't expected what came next.

"Why the hell are you calling me on this number? Are you crazy?"

"Zio, it's me," she said, her voice cracking. "I really need help."

"Don't use that name. They think you're dead. I can't help," he said, spitting the reply before her coins clattered against metal as the line cut off.

Staring at the hospital, she drew a deep breath and dialled the long number from memory again. "Tell them they're wrong."

"They think you've paid for your mistakes," he said in a whisper.

"Tell them I'm sorry. It was out of my hands," she said with a glance at her stump. "We can still do this."

She listened to his racing breath.

"You cost them so much," he replied after a pause.

"They're not short of money," she said without thought.

"It's not about the money. The samples were very rare," he replied, spitting out the words.

"But *he's* still out there," she pleaded.

"And that's why I'm able to answer the phone. You paid the debt with your life and that's how it needs to stay."

"But I can help get him," Luana replied, her voice tailing off as she stared out beyond the glass.

"You can't. You're dead," he snapped, giving her no time to interrupt. "The decision's been made. The other team is in play. Stay a stiff, if I were you. It's better for all of us."

"But I don't know anything else. It's all I am. It's all you made me."

"All you were," he replied, and she detected a slight softening.

The line went dead and black plastic showered across the ground as she smashed the handset against the brushed metal.

13

James

"It's room service," Fisher whispered, leaning towards her. "You heard me order it?"

"Stay there," Harris said, pulling an empty glass from the top of the dresser before moving to the door as the knock drummed again.

"Room service," said an Asian-accented voice from the corridor.

Avoiding the spy hole, she stood beside the door, holding the glass behind her back. She jerked the door open to a man in a gold-edged uniform holding a silver tray with four beer bottles, his eyes wide and a practiced smile broadening as she beckoned him in.

"Wasn't that a bit over the top?" Fisher said as the footsteps disappeared. "Who could know we're here?"

She turned to meet his gaze. "They'll know alright and you'd do well not to think otherwise."

Fisher pulled himself up out of the seat and twisted the cap off two frosty bottles, passing one over as she sat back on the bed.

After a long pull, she raised the bottle towards him. "You said three things."

"Oh, yes," he replied after taking a swig. "The second fire."

"The second fire," she repeated, pulling the remaining contents of the bottle. "Same building, but six months later with same MO but in a lab a few floors up. Only a handful of experienced PhD students using it."

"Any ideas what the experiments were?" Fisher asked.

Her gaze lingered on the page before she spoke. "There's plenty of detail, but you'll need a geology degree to understand what the hell they were doing. It says the experiments were ruled out as the cause."

Fisher nodded as he upended the damp bottle.

"The room was a copy of the scene before. Scorched earth. Nothing but metal, ceramic and rocks left. The guy who died, Gerald Soley, was reviewing projects for his mid-term dissertation. His notes were lost in the fire. The guy with third-degree burns, Spencer Robbs, was sitting next to him and experimenting with light refraction through quartz. His statement said Gerald was cleaning up an old rock. He was washing it and chipping away dirt when the air seemed to explode."

"Can we assume the guy who died was ground zero?" Fisher said as he twisted the cap off a fresh bottle and passed it to Harris.

"Assume what you like."

"Is there any more on fire three?" he asked as he pulled the cap off his own bottle before motioning it towards her. "Cheers."

Harris nodded as their bottles clinked.

"Another building and three months had passed. It was a relatively small fire which started in a kitchen and led to an explosion in a bedroom next..."

"Does Bissette link to the other two fires?" Fisher interrupted.

"Apart from the location?" Harris scanned the screen for a long moment before shaking her head. "There's nothing obvious."

Fisher grunted. "Is that about all we can get from the file?"

"I think so," she replied, still reading.

"What do we do next?"

"We investigate," she replied, looking up with her brow pinched.

"But we're in Mumbai?"

Harris relaxed her expression and forced a smile. "There's plenty we can do from here. Where would you start?" she said, laying the iPad beside her.

"Aren't you the expert?" Fisher said, tilting his head to the side and Harris mirrored his expression.

"You're the officer in training. We may as well make use of the time."

Fisher nodded and turned to the window where the rain had slowed to form spots on the glass. "Are we doing this right now?"

"What do you mean?" she said, a smile creeping on her face.

"After what we've been through?" he replied, looking over.

"What else is there to do?" she said, seeming to stifle the smile.

Fisher leaned forward. "I mean, there's a global terror situation and we're looking at fires that happened over three years ago. If we're doing something, then it must be more…" he said, choosing his words. "Immediate."

Sitting forward on the bed, Harris's expression dropped. "I understand. I do," she said, speaking slowly. "Sometimes *I* struggle with taking orders, but I'm sure when we're back we'll be in the thick of it. In the meantime, you have to understand, we do the James Bond shit and *then* we put in the hours at the desk." It was her turn to pause as she stared over. "You need to ask yourself if you can handle that."

Fisher turned to the vast window and stared out at the black Arabian Sea distorted by sheets of water coursing down the glass again.

"It stopped with the girl," he replied. "I think she's important. Maybe she was storing something in her flat and somehow got rid of it before the investigators could find it."

Harris had relaxed back on to the bed as he turned.

"Her own personal vendetta against the geography department?" she said, raising an eyebrow whilst picking at the label of the empty bottle.

"It's not as good as my hooch theory, I admit."

"We discount nothing yet," she replied, still picking at the paper.

"We should find out what she has to say," Fisher said and Harris nodded, before placing the bottle on the floor and picking up the iPad.

"Let's see what happened to her," she replied, her fingers animated on the screen.

Sitting next to Harris, Fisher leaned over and watched the screen, enjoying the subtle aroma of fading perfume. She tapped in twelve numbers with a full stop between each group of three, and pastel pink hues of a Scottish florist's website appeared on the screen.

Fisher's eyebrows bunched as she filled in a username and password, before relaxing as the screen went white and he recognised the grey letters of FALCON, the Security Service intelligence database, sliding into view.

With the images settled, a search box appeared in the middle of the page. Francine Madeleine Bissette's name and age, taken from the witness statement, jumped into the box with a flurry from her fingers. Within a blink, he was reading a stark chronological listing.

She was born in Brittany, France, before attending two schools with similar addresses, both listed on the screen. Her parents were named, as were her two siblings, each highlighted as a link.

Scrolling down the text, she'd passed through the Port of Dover three times, and it displayed her enrolment details for the university and her entry on the Electoral Register in Reading. Next was the police file. The police interviewed her twice before she moved to Ealing, North London.

"She's straight," Harris said.

Fisher looked sideways.

"Her file's clean," she reiterated, looking back down.

He watched her fingers tap at a contact tab he'd noticed for the first time.

"We have contact information?" Fisher said, leaning down over her shoulder.

Harris turned towards him. "You'll be surprised by the information people give away for free."

He watched her gaze move to the digital clock underneath the deep-bodied TV.

"It's still early. Give her a call."

"What do I say?" he replied, pulling back.

"Just ask her what she remembers about the fire. Play it by ear."

Tapping the number into the iComm, he hung up as the call timed out.

"No answer. What if the fires didn't stop? What if they just happened elsewhere?"

She nodded. "Are you hungry?"

"Room service?" he asked, but she was already shaking her head as his last syllable dropped.

"Never eat room service," she replied, her brow bunched as she gave him her cold teacher glare. "Always find your own food and pick somewhere random. Never pre-book. Do anything to limit the time for players to prepare."

A smile raised in the corner of Fisher's mouth. "Players?"

"The other side. The bad guys. I'm serious," she said, although her glare was already melting. "Never eat room service," she said again as her eyes brightened. "Unless it's meant for someone else," she added, flashing her brow.

"I understand," he said, his body language saying the opposite. "But there's no way anyone could know we're here. We're supposed to be in Delhi."

The glare returned.

"Don't assume," she said, typing in another memorised IP address and Fisher watched as a pop up appeared asking if she wanted to obliterate all the machine's stored information. Hitting okay, she caught his eye. "Never relax."

Fisher threw his hands in the air.

"Come on," he said. "What are you expecting?"

"When I'm with you," she said, her expression deadpan. "Anything."

Luana

Before

"We found him," he said, buckling up his thick leather belt. Luana didn't reply as she turned away, pulling clothes from the drawers and dressing with her back to him. "He had the necklace."

Halfway through pulling a white fleece over her head, she turned with her brow raised. Watching his hands move to his trouser pocket, she turned away whilst peering out of the corner of her eye. As a thin silver chain emerged wrapped around his thick fingers, her head snapped back, her eyes wide as her breath felt thick in her throat.

The glistening heart pendant hung as she'd remembered.

Drawing a deep breath, she pushed out her hands, the last ten minutes erased. Closing her eyes, she cupped the necklace to her cheek and wept. Tears rolled down her face, the silver heart turning in her fingers as she leafed through vague memories. Her short, haggard nails dug at the tiny catch and she closed her eyes as it opened.

"Be strong," she heard him say, and felt a touch against her cheek.

Dabbing her eyes with the offered handkerchief, she looked at a younger version of herself at the top of the triangle with her brother and sister, their faces almost a match. Her mother looked back from the left and she remembered the time they'd picked out the photo together, handing it to Zio, who'd cut it down with a knife. She remembered the golden paper they'd wrapped it with before he tucked her to sleep, then the look on her face as she presented it, the smile no one could recreate.

Standing tall, she held it out. "Can you?" she said, her voice barely heard.

Stepping towards her, he undid the clasp before clipping it around her neck as she leaned over.

"What now?" she said, her palm spread below her neck.

"It's time for target practice."

Closing her eyes, she nodded.

14

James

Fisher watched from under the sagging canopy, the street filling with life moments after the clouds had dried, as he attacked his meal with a fork whilst those around him scooped rice with clawed fingers.

Glancing at Harris, her stare fixed into the distance, she picked disinterested at a full bowl.

To his left, the lamplit street was full with carefree tourists soaking up an energetic atmosphere of traders in their multi-coloured sweat-stained shirts playing up to the crowd. The right was cluttered with natives, their faces turned down with everyday matters of passing the night.

Men in yellowing shirts sat on flattened cardboard boxes playing cards, their table an upturned wooden crate next to a queue of haggard beggars standing frail, their hands pushed out in hope of passing benevolence.

"We're being watched," Harris said, her tone conversational and her posture unmoving as she pushed the full bowl to the side.

"Huh?" Fisher replied, mopping up the last of his food.

"It could be the DIA or CIB," she added with her usual confidence.

"No. I'm still lost," he said, shaking his head as he scanned the faces dotted at wooden street stalls, all of which looked out of place.

"Indian intelligence. Pass me your phone and I'll check in."

As she hung up, Fisher spotted a dark-skinned man who'd leaned on the side of a wooden stall laden with oranges and alien green fruits. He tweaked the side of his thick, unkempt moustache and answered a phone Fisher didn't hear ring. Nodding as he listened, then unseen by the stall owner, he picked an orange and disappeared into the throng.

"He's gone," Fisher said, looking over.

"Nope. I'm still eyes on," she replied with a false smile.

"Then there were two of them," Fisher said, explaining what he'd seen.

"Drink up," she said, standing and dropping a red rupee note to the table while turning her wrist. Fisher looked behind, frowning as he found the view was a match to his. Twisting back to question her, she was nowhere to be seen.

Standing, he caught sight of her rolling red-blonde hair and jogged up to her shoulder while watching the crowd out of the corner of his eye.

She set her mouth in a veneered smile whilst every one of her neurones absorbed in her task. Her head swung from side to side, eyes acting their flowing glance from one colourful curiosity to the next, her hand up and pointing to bright spices whilst she made no mention.

"What are we looking for?" Fisher said, glancing ahead as casually as he dared.

"Somewhere with a back door," she replied, as she moved her hand to the small of his back to guide him to the edge of a throng of tourists at a small souvenir shop, its table laid at the entrance piled with colourful, decorated tins, their gold adornment glinting in the streetlight. Picking a box swirled with pink and purple plastic jewels, he turned it in his hand, wafting it in front of her.

"A great centrepiece for your cottage?" he said.

For a split second, her smile melted into a frown, then his heart picked up speed as she drew herself up to his face. Fisher closed his eyes, leaning forward until he heard her whisper. "Stop mucking around and take note of who you see behind. But don't be too obvious."

His heart sank as he took in the warmth of her face, her delicate breath prickling the hairs on his neck. His eyes began to close as he revelled in her satisfying touch, until out of the corner of his vision he spotted an Asian man in loose black trousers and a once white shirt paying them too much attention.

Glancing up, the man turned side-on, examining a

golden multi-armed idol he held in his hand as his moustached face fixed in a scowl. Fisher snapped his eyes wide as he felt Harris move away before he pulled her in close.

"I've seen him," he whispered, his gaze falling on another. Wearing the same uniform shirt and blank expression, he stared at a bemused carpet seller speaking at a frantic pace. Each time Fisher flicked his gaze, it settled on another suspect, whose appearance was only a minor variation of the last.

He pulled from the embrace. "They've sent an army," he declared and Harris glanced with an exaggerated laugh as she playfully slapped him on the chest.

"Stay sharp," she snapped before sliding back into the flow of human traffic, leaving him wondering if he was right or not.

Side by side, excusing their way through, the flow narrowed and faltered, the shouts of traders rising in volume, the heat growing stronger as waves of spice crashed across them. Zigzagging through the crowd, they sidestepped split piled sacks revealing every colour and hue whilst struggling forward, their gazes fixed toward a towering skyscraper filling their vision, its modern straight edges set against the tinned roof stalls and shanty wooden shops whose contrast would be no greater than if born from different centuries.

Just as Fisher was about to relent and look behind, he spotted a narrow shop filled with rolled carpets stacked by colour and pattern, lined up against both walls and leading through to the dark street on the other side.

Not turning, he hugged her arm, then as if unhurried, he pulled her to the side and towards the narrow shop. Without discussion or conference, they were soon out the other side to find a near mirror image of what they'd left behind. Out from cover, Harris took charge with their fingers intertwined as she guided him swiftly along a few steps, dodging the thick crowd on either side.

Pulling him down the first alley, they left the glow of the streetlights behind. Instead of people, they stepped around a sickly sweet slick of strewn rotting fruit and small bodies lain against the warm crease of bricks. Without warning, the air rang with a polyphonic tone. Fisher's nerves jumped and he looked at Harris.

Her sharp expression told him everything he needed to know as his hand jammed into his vibrating pocket and fumbled Susie's call to silent.

"Sorry," he mouthed, wide-eyed, but she was already leading them further down the alley and away from the noises of bodies stirring, making quick changes of direction around corners this way and that in the maze of offshoot alleys, guided only by the moonlight and distant skyscrapers. Soon the rot of fruit underfoot receded, giving way to dark, long-rotted squalor. Their pace slowed as caution increased and after a few changes of direction, the path opened out between two brick buildings, the concrete floor swept clean.

"I think we lost them," she said, speaking for the first time since the main street. As she spoke, a pained groan punctuated the air, followed by a squeak of protest.

Fisher scowled as they looked at each other, peering ahead as they walked between the two smart buildings, then along a passage adjoining the wide alley.

Fisher barked a command and four feral heads, browned with rags covering their bodies, darted from the darkness before shooting across their path. At first, not sure whether he should take chase, he looked between the buildings and saw a mound of pitiful brown flesh, the colour composed of Indian skin and Mumbai grime, punctuated with dripping scarlet. As Fisher rushed over, two bright blue eyes, circled with crystal white, opened and the boy winced back.

Holding his hands up, Fisher stepped away.

"Are you okay?" he said, his words overstated and clumsy. The boy's eyebrows raised, looking back with a mixture of emotions shadowing his face.

Fisher reached out. "I won't hurt you. Can you stand?"

The boy laid still, contorted and awkward, his eyes growing wide and darting to Fisher's side. Fisher turned to

Harris, squinting into the darkness. She gave a sharp native shout and his chubby face winced as he dragged himself up.

"Take it easy," Fisher said, holding out a steadying hand until, much to his surprise, Harris ushered him backwards with a sharp edge to her tone.

"Watch these street rats. They're thieving little shits. They'll pick your pockets clean if you get too close."

Fisher regarded her with surprise. "You would too if you were starving," he replied, pushing a yellow and green rupee note out towards the child's wide eyes, but Harris pushed his hand down.

"He'll buy drugs or get robbed. Let's go. We have our own problems."

She turned and as Fisher reluctantly followed, he looked over his shoulder, the child staring back until he dropped the note on the floor as they rounded the corner.

***

Luana

Present

As if a hoard of threadworms wriggled beneath her skin, she moved her hand to satisfy before pulling back when she remembered her predicament.

Distraction had become her best friend and the train rushing through the station served her well, but she couldn't hide from the two new growing sensations, the beginnings of what she'd been dreading since pulling the pipes that had snaked from her arm. No matter how she'd hated being closed in, laid up, a source of pity, she'd been thankful for the endless supply of morphine to dull the pain and keep her on track.

However, back on her own terms and the master of her destiny once more, being reliant on no one but herself, the pain was a low price to pay.

There wasn't much left in the floral purse, just useless plastic and a few coins. A world away from the endless support she was used to. Not daunted, she'd trained to be out in the cold and took comfort in her quiet insurance set aside in case someone betrayed her again.

She tried to brush aside a loose hair from her face, then repeated to more effect with her remaining hand. She knew her goal and felt the intoxicating lack of fear. They'd take her back, or pay.

Seconds after the call, she'd come to terms with her new status as a mere tool, procured and trained as a small girl away from the wider influence circling above her lifetime mentor.

She rarely had regrets, but if that motherfucker in Chile hadn't recognised her, she would be somewhere else altogether. Then, of course, there was James Fisher. They should have locked him up with the others. His old life over, along with his dead companion.

Death was her next thought. Death to all involved.

She sniggered at the drama running through her mind, but soon recognised she'd fallen to that place once again.

She needed something for the pain and a leveller and she looked at each of those standing on the platform, their daily mundanity rolling around their minds. If they heard her thoughts, they'd run a mile and she knew if she couldn't get something to slow her, things would get a little dark.

Dropping her smile, she cycled the scenarios, and an idea floated above the rest.

It wasn't a time for vanity. Hand first, then revenge, with maybe a little fun in between. Perhaps she could deliver Fisher, and maybe she would still get whatever reward she was due. She corrected her earlier self with a sly smile.

Darker. Things were already a little further down the track.

The grin grew as she noticed the train arrive and the door slide open.

15

James

In silence they stood side by side and as the plush lift car rose, Fisher watched the changing illumination around the silver-ringed controls.

"Are you sulking?" she said, speaking for the first time since they'd left the boy. Her tone had softened and their eyes met in the shine of the mirrored doors.

"That was cold," he said as their reflection disappeared, replaced by their floor's plush wooden trimmed lobby.

"But the right thing to do," she said, rolling her head to the side as they walked. "If you want to help those feral animals, then give money to charity. *Your* money. Give them shelter, not hand…" She halted and leaned into their door, holding Fisher back with her arm outstretched behind her.

After what seemed like furious seconds of examination, she motioned down the corridor with a swing of her head, then walking in the opposite direction of the lift, they passed the line of doors in silence until they reached a stairwell which Harris seemed to be familiar with.

"My markers are missing," she said as Fisher followed her down seven flights of stairs.

"Huh?" came his breathy reply.

"I hope there's nothing in there you needed."

"Just my toothbrush," Fisher said, stepping through the double doors on the ground floor before jogging to keep up with Harris as she led them through the restaurant, ignoring the questioning looks as they tramped along the kitchen and past the huddle of smokers in whites by the staff entrance.

"What's going on?" he said, touching her arm as the humid air hit them.

"I placed threads of hair around the door frame. They're all gone," she said, asserting them through the still thronging orange-lit streets.

"Where are we going?" he asked.

"I need to get hold of my contact again. He won't thank me at this time of night," she said, showing the first sign of strain in her voice as she guided them along a wide and busy road lined each side by sprawling buildings spilling out light.

Fisher looked up at the first concrete and glass structure, its entrance haloed in blue and punctuated with bright-red lettering.

"Let me," he said, veering left through the revolving doors.

Five minutes and a handshake later, a handsome young couple from Minnesota were packing their bags for the short trip to their new hotel. With the new key in hand, he walked beside Harris for ten minutes before shaking hands again, this time a short Canadian in a shirt and tie who seemed grateful for the exchange. Only a few moments later, Fisher rolled the lock into place and Harris jammed a rubber wedge under the door.

"Scan the room," she said to a blank-faced Fisher, inspecting their surroundings. "On the iComm. There's an icon that looks like a ladybird."

"Huh?" Fisher replied as he thumbed his phone. "A ladybird?"

"A bug scanner."

"Very droll," he said, rolling his eyes. "The techs have a sense of humour."

"No, they don't," she said, her expression cold. "It's a ladybird, so you can find it quickly."

Fisher double-pressed the home button and as he pushed the icon, a concentric circle radiated from the base of the phone, disappearing off the edge of the screen, only to be replaced by another, repeating the sequence.

"Now what?" he said, looking up.

"Walk around the room."

He moved around the king-sized bed, its silk covers pulled tight, over to the dark wooden dresser, then the wide flat screen TV, past the tall wardrobe and into the bright bathroom, the small screen giving no reaction.

"It's clean," Harris said, peering over his shoulder.

Following her commands, he selected an icon formed of a row of three zeds, each shrinking in size to the right. "You've just scanned for transmissions from a device, not the device itself. New kit can beat the scan by intermittently turning off, so we have to search deeper."

"How?" Fisher said, turning back to Harris as she laid her jacket on the bed, its arms outstretched on the silk.

"We use the iComm's sensors in a different mode, but they're not as sensitive, so you have to get in close. Run the end of the handset over the jacket."

He moved to the bed, her perfume rising as he ran the end of the phone over the grey cloth, then stood tall. Harris shook her head, then clamped her hand onto his wrist, pushing it back to the thin jacket.

"Slow down. You need to cover every nook," she said, her gentle touch guiding his hand along the flattened arm and across every square of the material. He paid no attention to the glass display, concentrating instead on the warmth of her touch. Reaching the end of the opposite arm, he took a deep breath as she let go.

Feeling the electricity from her touch on his shoulder, Fisher held his ground.

"I need you to do me," she breathed.

Standing in silence, his mouth hung open.

"Come on," she said when he didn't respond. "You need to scan me."

"Oh," Fisher said, his eyes widening as she spread her arms out to the side as if poised for jumping jacks. Still, he didn't move.

"What are you waiting for?"

Blinking his attention back into the room, Fisher took a tentative step towards her, then stopped with his arm outstretched.

"I don't bite," she snapped, as if in a hurry. "Run it over every inch of my body. Or wait for the next time it turns on whilst you stare. You choose."

With a slow step, he slid the phone over to her left hand, then with care, he moved the iComm from the edge of her finger, past her thin wrist before easing it up her slender arm. He watched her muscles building through the vague thinness of fitted cotton as he moved up to her armpit and the strap of her bra. She lifted her head as he ran the iComm across her neck and down to her other hand, then he paused.

She looked up, resting her hand on the back of his palm, guiding it across her sternum and tracing from her armpit and around her left breast. Catching the edge of the phone on her blouse, it sagged open, and he caught a fleeting show of lace against goose-bumped skin. He looked away for a moment before she guided across her chest.

"Do you think you can do the rest?" she said, her voice breaking his concentration.

His mouth was too dry to speak, so he nodded and moved the phone with a side-to-side motion as he tracked down her body, slowing across her navel before reaching the fly of her tight jean shorts. Bending his knees, she opened her legs as he pulled the phone over the material as he felt the heat of her crotch, then tracked down her silken legs one by one before she turned and he found his face level with her behind.

After a pause, he snapped himself out of the stare and rushed the search up each leg, his breathing heavy as he scanned the metal edge over each globe, slowing as he travelled up her back and stood to reach across her bra strap and the backs of her arms.

As she felt the phone reach her last untouched spot, she turned, stepped back, then pulled the thin band from the back of her hair and bent forward, sending her strawberry blonde locks flowing down like a waterfall.

Fisher ran the phone over her fresh smelling hair before she flicked her head back up, each strand landing clean and straight to curtain her face.

"Now your turn," she said, looking up.

Fisher gulped.

Luana

Present

With her mind clearer than it had been since she'd woken in the hospital, she remembered the funeral for a dead friend, tempering her excitement as she didn't know if the date had already passed. She pictured the pair she sought paying their respects, and just as she did, a small bell rang twice unseen and the sharp clinical smell renewed with a new breath.

Applying a little extra pressure at the sole of her foot, she peered down to a pair of mascara-smeared eyes squinting back. Cropped black hair shook with a nod in a silent promise she wouldn't make a sound even if she hadn't crushed her windpipe.

Luana leaned her head around shelves piled high with crisp boxes and brown, white-capped bottles, stifling all surprise at the yellow fluorescence of a young blond police officer walking toward the counter wearing a bright smile.

"Is Mary in?" he asked, his deep voice betraying affection for the woman under Luana's shoe. "Are you new?" he added with a tilt of his head. "I'm Simon, her fiancé."

Luana congratulated herself with a rising smile at the warmth of his offered hand. Shooting a look back at the floor out of his view, she eased her foot away, leaving a tread print across the woman's neck as she stepped around the tall shelving. Her smile evaporated as the officer's gaze moved down to her bandaged wrist.

"She's just popped out. I'm covering. I expect she'll be back in half an hour," Luana said, knowing her smile radiated.

"Oh," he said, glancing at the door. "She didn't say anything when I spoke to her a moment ago."

"It was an emergency. She rushed off after a call."

Pushing up to the counter, she blocked his view should he decide to shift to his left, then grasped the cold steel of a long pair of scissors on the desk below whilst pinpointing precious veins rising over his stab vest.

"I'll call her," he said, his cheeks rising. "It was nice to meet you," he added, as he turned and reached into his pocket.

The bell chimed twice, and knowing she didn't have long left, she resigned herself to just the pain killers as the discarded mobile rang, stopping only as the screen cracked under her shoe with the insides filling with thick scarlet.

The bell chimed again as she left large gaps on the shelves, a half-naked pharmacist and metallic tang hanging in the air.

16

James

Harris's narrowing gaze ran along the length of his body as she swallowed.

At arm's reach, Fisher held himself still, poised and afraid of breathing as he ached for her first touch to explode them into an unstoppable fury. But when she turned and stepped away, Fisher's eyes grew wide as she rushed to the door.

"I need to make a call," she said, low and breathy.

Fisher pulled in a deep breath as the door slammed against its jamb.

"Holy shit," he said, panting for the cool air still full of her perfume, his body rocking with waves of relief and disappointment deep in his chest. After gathering his thoughts and realising he held the only phone, he smiled and stripped to his Calvin Kleins before running the iComm over his skin, dressing seconds before the door swung back open.

Running the bolt across the door to the corridor, Harris turned and leaned against the wall with a curated smile.

"Are you clean?" she said, her voice more controlled as she looked him in the eye.

Fisher forced a smile, unsure he could trust his expression.

"It looks that way," he replied, relieved at the interruption when the iComm rang in his hand, Clark's voice coming over the speaker.

"I've got you a flight in thirty hours. It's one of the first out of the country." Fisher looked at Harris and her rising smile. "If you miss it, there's a few thousand pissed off people to take your place."

"We'll be there," Harris called out.

"And I got the information you wanted," Clark added. "The university's systems are oddly efficient, if not too secure. Their asset records show the freezers were fifteen years old, and I found a maintenance ticket, which was never closed off." The pair stared at each other as they listened. "The day before the fire, maintenance raised a job for a new coolant pump."

"Aha," Fisher replied, his eyes wide as he nodded.

"If the freezer failed, wouldn't you just get a rather wet floor?" Harris asked.

"I'll leave that with you. The tickets will be in the usual place," Clark said before hanging up.

"What time is it in the UK?" Fisher asked, searching the room for a clock.

"Six PM," she replied, turning her wrist to the face of her thin golden watch he'd not noticed before.

With a nod, he tapped at the iComm and listened as it rang twice before a woman's unmistakable French accent rose from the speaker.

"Hello?"

"Hello," Fisher replied, his voice formal. "Is that Francine Bissette?"

"Yes," came the unsure reply.

"I'm calling from the Home Office."

"Okay," she said, her volume retreating.

"Considering the recent terrorist attacks, we're reviewing certain unresolved investigations," Fisher said.

"The fires," she replied without pause.

"You were expecting the call?"

"I wondered how long it would be, but I don't know how I can help," the woman replied.

"Did you have any connection to the Geography and Environmental Sciences Department?" Fisher asked.

"No," she said, then laughed. "I had a boyfriend for a short time who was studying geochemistry. Is that what you mean?"

Fisher glanced at Harris as she nodded.

"Can you tell me his name?" he said, peering at the phone.

"Robin Gasper," came the accented reply. "He was

forever bringing me beautiful rocks," she said as her voice hardened. "They were his only romantic gestures. After the fire, I made a change."

Harris moved toward the mini bar.

"Thank you. We'll be in touch if we need anything else," Fisher said, hanging up the call. "We have a link," he added when he found Harris flicking the caps from two beer bottles.

"At least they've got a better mini bar here," she said, handing a bottle over.

"But we still have no idea how at least two of the fires started."

Bottle in hand, and after pulling the twin bed apart with the other, Harris took long pulls as she sat up against the pillows.

Staring at the opposite wall, Fisher took her silence as a hint. He tipped up his bottle with long pauses in between while he double pressed the iComm's home button and thumbed through the rows of unconcealed icons. His gaze caught on the scanner, evoking in his tired mind the hotel where two goons had tried to abduct him for Farid. It wasn't long before his thoughts turned to the colonial Caribbean palace as he held the iComm out in his search for Susie. The green dot pulsing on the twin bed disappeared as a call came in.

"Are you okay, Susie?" Fisher said, taking a deep breath.

"I just wanted to talk," her quiet voice replied. Not sensing any fear or hurry, Fisher relaxed. "What are you doing?"

"Talking to you," he said, smiling.

Susie laughed, and he could tell she was tired. "You know what I mean."

Fisher laughed. "I'm just about to sleep. You?"

"The chance would be a fine thing."

He was about to ask her to elaborate when she cut him off. "Oh. I just remembered. Someone was looking for you at the wake."

"Who?" Fisher said, taking more interest.

"I didn't catch her name, but she was wearing a nurse's uniform. She was very nice," Susie replied.

"I don't know any nurses," Fisher said, glancing at Harris.

"She knew you."

"Okay. Thanks. Anyway, I better be getting to bed," he said.

"When are you coming home?" Susie replied as Fisher watched Harris slip down the bed, her head resting against a plump white pillow and eyes closed as her chest rose and fell.

"Soon," he said and hung up, his eyelids feeling heavy as he let them close.

A moment later and he was back in the corridor of the Australian flat with the assassin grappling with Harris. Then he said it. He issued the command.

The guy had done as he'd told, compelled to stop the assault even though he must have known it meant losing the battle.

The moment played over in Fisher's mind, each time he couldn't help but wonder if there was more to come next time.

***

Luana

Before

A single shot started a chain of memories she'd never forget. Not that she'd even tried.

Battered wooden furniture littered the range. Soft cover, she soon found out.

At the distant end, the rule running the length of the

wall showing a hundred metres, was an open door she hadn't noticed.

Zio didn't speak as he led her through the main door, handing her ear defenders as she stepped in. He pulled a key from his back pocket and, as before, unlocked the metal cabinet, but this time held out his palm for her to wait.

Stepping onto the range, he found a long chain laid across the floor, its new grey links sweeping along the dust of the concrete before snaking up through the handles of a tall wardrobe. She stared at the dark oak cabinet, its edges battered with age. It quivered, or so she thought.

As Zio bent at the waist and reached for the chain, she realised what was happening and stepped backwards, flexing her hands. When the chain fell from around the dark metal handles, the doors burst open and she saw him. With a quick glance, their eyes locked for a split second but she saw no recognition.

He was quick to figure out the challenge. It was some sort of bargain. Get to the end and live, or something like that.

She waited, not because she wanted to give him a chance. She waited because she wanted to give him hope.

After he took ten quick paces, she couldn't hold herself any longer, and she flung open the metal cabinet. The gun sat where she expected it, with rounds already crammed into the metal.

With the magazine pushed home and the safety in kill mode, she turned but couldn't see him. Pointing the barrel out, she smiled and looked at each piece of furniture for a tell. Hearing a whimper, she spotted the top of his head bobbing behind a thick antique cabinet.

If he was trained, then it was badly.

Taking only seconds to aim, she fired into the cabinet. Not wanting it to be too easy, she watched him leap up without a glance.

He was faster than she'd expected. A death bargain will do that, and a fear rose that he might get to the door.

Throwing the thought away, she relaxed her shoulders.

She knew the theory and told herself she had this.

Aiming for where he would be, not where he was, her first shot missed. With a glance over to Zio, he nodded with encouragement and she pushed her arms further out, lining up the sight just ahead of the man bobbing and weaving but with a predictable flow.

Glancing at the long ruler, she knew it was time to end it.

He fell to the ground behind a pine dresser. Blood sprayed in a flower of success and she stepped onto the dusty concrete, the walk seeming to take forever.

Hearing a murmur, she found him alive, but a second shot to the chest was all it took to stop that.

Zio clapped and grinned wide. She'd seen the grin before and didn't like what happened after. With twelve rounds left, and still wearing the smile, he held his hand out for the weapon.

She paused, but only for the briefest of moments.

"How does that feel?" he said as he took the safetied weapon.

Luana shrugged just as he spoke again. "I have someone else I want you to meet."

17

James

Conditioned air breezed across his face, his right hand swiping at the pick as he woke. With his breathing rushed, he searched the day-lit room to find he was alone, the covers of her bed tight and dressed. Sitting upright, he drew deep breaths as the terror faded.

Without warning, the door swung open. Still dazed, he glanced to Harris as she bounded in wearing a skinny black trouser suit over a white blouse buttoned high to her neck. He'd not seen the outfit before, but he got the message. Today was for business, nothing else.

Her energetic smile beamed at his sleep-tired face. His levels were in the opposite state as he wallowed in a daze. Despite his reaction, her smile broadened as she threw a brown paper bag onto his lap.

"Rise and shine, sleepyhead," she called. "We've got a busy day."

"I thought we could lie by that beautiful pool and mull over our case with a Master P or two." His smile rose at the thought but fell again when he pulled out pressed black trousers and a shirt.

"We're going hunting," she replied, and he didn't miss the glint in her eye as he followed her hand to a Glock 17 pulled from under her jacket. The brass of the first round gleamed as she checked the magazine.

Hauling the clothes into the bathroom, he raised his dry voice. "And mine?" He heard the smile as she replied.

"*You* don't want to be caught with a stolen military firearm."

There was no point in replying.

"Very handsome," Harris quipped, her eyebrows raised as he left the bathroom with a black jacket held in one hand over his shoulder. "Show me the iComm and we can start this little game."

Fisher grabbed the thick black phone from the bedside table and the screen glowed with the start of a message.

Can't sleep. You awake?

With a sigh, the words disappeared as he double pressed the home button, the hidden screens darting in from the left and, guided by Harris, he pressed a Bluetooth icon with a notepad in its corner.

"It's a log of all the Bluetooth handshakes. Are you familiar with the system?" She looked up at Fisher's nod. "I forgot you're an IT geek."

"And you're a gun geek. Enough said."

She smiled and looked at the phone.

"If these guys are sloppy, their phones would transmit away. This is a log of the phones the iComm has seen."

Fisher raised his brow. "So we can see what devices were handshaking when we knew someone was watching. If their phone is called Mr Big, or KGB, then we're laughing, right?"

"I said sloppy, not stupid. We mark the phones we're interested in and then if the iComm gets a second handshake we know they're with us again. The chances of randomly coming in to contact with the same people from last night are not worth thinking about."

Fisher nodded. "Okay. That's pretty cool."

Harris showed him how to scroll down the list of phone names and times, then selected twenty handsets around at the end of their meal.

Much to Fisher's disappointment, there were none with any giveaway names.

Luana

Before

"I have to pee," she said in the darkness as a red bus bright with a wash of rain rushed past, spraying the windows of their compact car.

"It's not been an hour since you last went," Zio said without looking back, instead facing towards the newspaper spread across the steering wheel but with his gaze fixed on the entrance of a stone and dark glass building, whose height disappeared out of view. "Learn to hold it."

Groaning, Luana shifted in her seat and turned towards the building's entrance as a white van sprayed the window with water, smudging the night view into a multicoloured light show. As the water settled, her gaze caught on a man and woman holding hands and she ran through the checklist in her head whilst squeezing her pelvic floor.

The right age. Third quarter.

The right height. Around six feet.

Right build. Slight.

His skin was a little tanned. That was another tick. He wore thick, black-rimmed glasses, but that wasn't on the list. She wasn't sure if it was an oversight.

The man turned to the woman draped on his arm and laughed. Luana was closer to her age than his. Her golden sequinned dress was just visible through a woollen coat glistening with water. She thought perhaps they'd left a cab somewhere local, otherwise she'd be soaked through.

Watching them walk in through the entrance, Luana turned to her right with her brow raised.

"Glasses," he said without moving his head.

Luana turned back and glanced down at her new blue jeans as she squeezed her legs together, still enjoying the new colour.

Zio coughed into a balled fist and she blew out a deep breath, her gaze tracking back to the pathway where she found another tall man, his hair gleaming silver under a wide black umbrella held by the thick outstretched arm of another walking at his side. Both wore tuxedos with black coats over their shoulders. One man dripped with water whilst the other remained dry under the umbrella. To the older man's side, but two steps in front, another walked. A second towering bodyguard. Obvious to anyone, and he was the first in through the hotel's revolving doors.

"That's him," she said, then startled by the engine, she squealed in fear she might lose control of her bladder when the car set off along the wet road.

Concentrating on the image in her mind, the shine of his grey hair, the roughness of his skin, his flat, serious expression, she thought of all the bad things he'd probably done until she agreed he was the kind of man she could kill.

18

James

"Remind me why we're back here?" Fisher said, sitting in a wicker chair opposite Harris as she sipped from a tall glass of orange juice, its surface beaded with condensation.

"If they followed us here last night from the restaurant, there's a good chance that's who we're looking for," she replied, placing the glass on the table.

Fisher looked around, watching the busy comings and goings of the hotel reception whilst listening to the hum of partial conversations. He looked along the row of slow turning ceiling fans, each blade in line with its neighbour strung from the reception to the lift lobby.

"Would you do the same if you were them?" he said without turning away from the mesmerising action.

"No," she replied in an instant. He looked over. "I'd have finished the job on the first attempt."

Fisher's smile slipped, and he turned away as déjà vu washed over him, not doubting the truth in what she'd said.

"Do you think they're trying to kill us?" he asked, his voice quieter as he watched smart suits walk with purpose through the reception beside tourists dragging kids behind, others coupled and holding hands, their faces warm with holiday smiles.

"Assume the worst," she replied without a pause.

"I do."

Fisher's gaze headed to the dining room and its bustle of occupants just visible through a pair of open double doors where, after glimpsing the buffet, he wished he hadn't just grabbed a pastry as they passed through their own hotel, scoffing it as he hurried behind Harris.

"How long do you think it will take?" he said, hoping to take his mind off the subject.

"They're already here."

His head twitched towards the receptionist, their gazes

locking for what seemed like an age. He was young, fair skinned with pristine manicured eyebrows, but he was missing a smile and turned away to beam at a guest as he tapped at a keyboard out of sight.

"Cool it," Harris said in a low voice.

"The receptionist?"

"Yes. Stop looking," she replied, and he turned back.

"What are we waiting for?" he asked, poised to stand.

"I want to give them time for backup to arrive," she said under her breath.

"What?" Fisher replied, almost forgetting to check his volume.

"I want the best they've got."

Fisher drew a deep breath, then with a sip of his coffee, he turned to Harris as an unrecognised tone rang in his head.

"Leave it in your pocket and drink up," she said, after reading his body language.

Fisher guessed the tone meant a phone they'd been in range of last night was here again.

His lips pulled at the edge of the cup before he looked at his watch and slumped back into the chair. His gaze fixed on a spot in the foyer as he sought shapes in his peripheral vision. All he could make out were the blank ovals of faces.

"What are you doing?" she said as she leaned across the low wicker table between them.

"Maybe I'll recognise them."

"You look constipated. Just relax and drink up. I've got this." Harris stood, watching him drain the cup and wipe foamed milk from his lip. "Very slick," she said, before setting off towards the entrance.

Luana

Before

A voice called from far away. The words were so soft it took her a moment to realise it was a man's voice, but she couldn't quite place who spoke. Reaching out in the darkness, she felt restricted, unsure if it was a dream.

Feeling a waft of cold air around her, she realised her bottom half was exposed and her eyes snapped open to the light, as her legs were pulled apart by some unseen force.

There he was, looking down, eyebrows raised.

"Good morning," he said, and she pulled in a sharp breath with his hard thrust.

19

James

Passing into a wall of heat, together they stepped from the hotel with a casual rhythm, a pace welcomed by Fisher, despite his concern Harris was making it too easy for those who followed.

Faces soon streamed past, with vibrant colours rushing at their sides and moustaches hanging bushy on faces as a continual assault attacked his nostrils, leaving him to wonder how these people could exist in such oppressive heat.

Disordered lines of battered Premier Padmini taxis clambered for every square of blacktop, but the tone in his head drew him away and he glanced to Harris as an answer to her unspoken question.

"You'll keep hearing it as long as they're near," she replied.

"So what's the plan?" Fisher asked, edging closer. "Are we just going to tire them out?" he added, dodging a cyclist whose loose orange smock threatened to catch in the bike's chain.

"Just follow my lead," she said with a smile. "There are two reasons for surveillance. Either to gather information, or to trap. If they're just keeping tabs on us, perhaps trying to figure out our agenda, they won't take too many risks. All we need to do is let them know we've identified them and they'll disappear. Or try to, at least."

"And if it's more sinister?" Fisher said, his eyes wide as he stared back at the surging footpath.

"Then it's a good job I went shopping this morning," she said, raising her thin brow. "Either way, we'll find out soon enough. I've informed our hosts and they know better than to follow me, which means I'm very interested in who these people are."

"How do we ID them in all this?" Fisher said, motioning with his head to the crowd.

"We draw them into being spotted. If you see the individuals three or four times, they're not just a coincidental face in the crowd," she said, her smile widening. "And because they're following us…"

"We can make them go wherever we want," Fisher replied.

"Exactly," she said, her face lit with approval.

"But we don't have eyes in the back of our heads?"

Harris nodded. "With two of us, we'd split up and force them to choose one or to divide their effort. But…" she said, looking over as she tilted her head.

"Not until after training," he replied and, still smiling, she nodded.

"You'll learn from the traditional rule book to do everything by the rule of three, but afterwards they'll train you in ways the players are unlikely to use."

Fisher nodded, raising his brow as he stepped around a stack of wooden crates filled with peaches.

"I'd say these guys are pretty lazy from what I've seen. They'll have a three-man team. One will follow with a gap of three people behind us," she said, side-stepping a stack of oranges leaning toward the middle of the path. "With this crowd, they'll be pretty close behind. He's called the Eyeball, and it's his job to keep sight of the mark."

"The mark?" Fisher asked, battling against an urge to glance back.

"You and me, or one of us. Maybe. If we were travelling in a vehicle, the same would apply. He'd leave three cars between us."

Nodding, Fisher concentrated on the back of people's heads as they moved through the crowd.

"Behind the Eyeball, another three people between them, is the Backup. Their job is to keep visual contact with the Eyeball. He doesn't need to see us. If for some reason the Eyeball's compromised, taken out or just can't continue without risking exposure, the Backup would take over."

"And the third?" Fisher asked.

"They'll be on hand, ready to advise, or cover the Backup. They should be out of sight, but if that's not possible, they'll at least be out of the ten to two."

"Come on," Fisher said, drawing out the words.

"Sorry," she replied, shaking her head. "I keep forgetting just how much you've got to learn," she said, with no hint of a smile. "Almost all of your perception is in the field of vision between ten o'clock and two o'clock," she said, pausing for his nod of understanding. "Anything in that angle risks being noticed, or at the very least, adding to the library of faces you would recognise if you saw them again. If I had to guess," she continued. "The Trail, the third member, will be on the other side of the road," she added, pointing across the colourful sea of traffic. "Anyway, enough of that. Let's make their lives a little more difficult." She swung her arm high and veered into the path of a yellow-topped Padmini, its brakes screeching to a halt just in time.

Fisher's butt barely touched the discoloured seat cloth before Harris shouted something native to the white-bearded driver and the car lurched into traffic, with the rainbow beads swinging across the cracked rear-view mirror.

After ten minutes of weaving to a cacophony of horn blasts, they pulled up to the front of the R City Mall, a wide tall building of white stone and glass.

Harris already had the fare bartered before the brakes complained to a stop, and together they followed the throng of westerners and natives surging into the antiseptic sheen of the whitewashed mall.

Welcoming the wave of air-conditioned chill, Fisher regarded the anonymous building where all signs of the country of origin were gone, replaced with brands at home in any town in Britain.

As the tone rang, he nodded over.

"That was quick," Harris said, diverting them into the nearest shop where they walked across a wooden floor in a forest of mannequins dressed in western splendour. Fisher watched her scan left and right as if giving curious glances to this outfit and that before they were back in the polished atrium.

Soon into another shop with a similar offering, they were out again within a minute before skipping the next shop, as Fisher tried to force himself to remember each stranger's face when the tone confirmed they were still being watched.

The next shop took up double the size of the last and Harris broke with the routine as she spotted an escalator inside the department store.

Fisher followed, sauntering across the floor before stepping aside at the last moment to let the mechanical stairs lead them higher. Climbing, their attention soon fixed on three couples and two men following.

"If they're any good, we won't see the guy in the black trousers and grey shirt again," Harris said as they arrived at the peak.

Fisher drew a deep breath when he couldn't recall anyone with that description.

"Don't worry," Harris said as they crossed the polished floor, gazing at the colourful window displays. "It's all about experience. Check the hands. Look for clenched fists, or a pressel switch sticking out from a sleeve. Or hands touching mouths, or at their ears. Most agencies don't have our up-to-date kit."

Still trying to look over the sea of faces with causal glances, Fisher thought most were holiday shoppers, not natives, each relaxed and ambling with early stage tans, their smiles and slow pace highlighting their insignificance. Stepping through more premises, Harris halted in one, seeming to take a genuine liking to a thin white bikini Fisher would love to see her in.

As Harris turned away, Fisher picked it from the hanger.

"Let's get it," he said, and she grinned, but her smiled dropped as she looked over his shoulder.

"We're working," she said and walked past him toward the exit.

With a quick in and out of a perfume shop, they strode towards the central escalator heading toward the ground floor, but nearing the precipice of the rolling stairs, Harris stopped, blocking the way.

As a group of people hoping to use the moving stairs soon formed, she stepped to the side and fumbled in her pockets. Looking up moments later, her eyes wide and mouth hanging open, she looked the perfection of panic.

The tone in his head reminded him it was an act, and he had a part to play. Turning around, he nodded his apology to those stepping past as he tried his best to note each of them as they moved by. Within a moment Harris sighed with relief and held out a hotel room key, beaming, then stepped further to the side to let the queue shuffle by.

Fisher's heart rate peaked as a man in black trousers and grey shirt crossed in front of them and stepped onto the metal stairs.

"Amateurs," Harris said under her breath, before leading him to the escalator heading in the opposite direction. With a slow walk through the centre of the mall on the upper floor, dodging prams and pushchairs, they were soon outside with another Padmini's brakes screeching as she flung out her hand.

***

Luana

Before

Her instructions were simple. Wait at the bar and don't put people off.

"Sit and smoulder," were Zio's words. "And don't drink too much," he added as she'd left the car.

When they'd first spoken about the project, she raised

lots of questions, but he'd insisted she was more than proficient. "A natural," he'd said as he looked her up and down with a slow shake of his head.

Regardless, she'd put in the hours, leafing through her collection and spending hours studying Cruel Intentions, Wild Things, and Diane Kruger blistering the screen. Now here she was, following the orders to the letter.

Perched on the edge of a leather-topped stool in a dim lounge with a large glass of white warming on the bar top, her gaze glided along the mirror image behind.

She'd seen off two guys in suits so far and, after the first, the barman changed the way he looked at her.

Another girl sat further along. She was attractive, if not a little underdressed. The barman wore a false smile as he asked her to leave.

Listening to the piano's tones floating through the air, she sipped at the wine, its tang already tingling her brain.

With a sudden wave of panic, she realised her attention had slipped, her mind having wandered.

Out of the corner of her eye, she saw the bodyguard who'd held the umbrella. Sitting three stools away, his eyes drooping with fatigue, she thought perhaps he was off duty. Concentrating on the row of drinks behind the bar, not his surroundings, he still noticed her.

20

James

"One down and two to go," Fisher replied.

"If they're using the old book," Harris said, before uttering something guttural and intense to the driver as the car bounced forward into the flow.

Another ten minutes, and through a journey of extremes, they passed tall buildings of glass climbing to the sky, then imperial stone whose complexity Fisher couldn't begin to describe, and dilapidated structures that looked like the city officials had forgotten to take down.

Parked in a nook between two fresh white air-conditioned coaches, Harris furnished the driver with Rupees and waited as he scribbled on a square of paper before handing it over with a yellow-toothed smile. Fisher double took at the thought of Harris claiming expenses.

The thread fell away as they crossed through a break in a tall hedge-line. Stepping into an oasis with a fountain flowering in the centre of a courtyard, the surrounding gravel paths thronged with tourists as they headed toward a stone building imposed with a white dome, it's design as if the architect had started with a castle then, when three quarters finished, he'd changed his mind, continuing the build but as a religious temple.

By her will and pace, Harris pulled Fisher towards the entrance, weaving through the loose line of shorts and skirts sauntering with guidebooks.

Just as they were about to cross the threshold, she stopped and fumbled in her pocket before continuing.

Their pace picked up through the reception, where Fisher peered up into a wide hall rising to a high-domed ceiling with two floors striped around the edge. Evenly spaced pillars of ornate stone supported the first floor, the next level edged in wood to the waist with dark oaken columns rising, all sitting on a mottled marble floor with not one tile the same colour as its neighbour.

In the centre stood an island of wood surrounded with a moat foaming with green ferns in place of water. At intervals on each floor were glass cabinets Fisher had barely enough time to register, let alone investigate their contents as their footsteps echoed at pace up the marbled steps. On the first floor, they stopped, with light flooding through a tall arched window at the front of the building. Together they crept closer to the edge, Harris pushing her hand across his stomach to hold him from going too close as they watched a stream of white, black and brown faces channelling through the courtyard and heading to the entrance.

"We're never going to spot them. There must be fifty people out there," Fisher said, still staring.

"Just watch," she whispered, her hand moving to his arm. "Concentrate on the middle of the pack. One of them will bend down."

"Huh?" Fisher mouthed, glancing over.

"They'll be desperate to check out the piece of paper I dropped."

True to her words, an Asian man almost identical in his blandness, dropped to a crouch and, ignoring those flowing around him, was soon back to his feet and examining the taxi receipt.

***

Luana

Before

Her gaze locked onto a bead of sweat as it soaked into the pillow's cotton cover, its filling plumped to a mound by her hands either side as her body still bucked, riding his throws. As her pleasure subsided to a glow, she felt disappointment that his fight for breath was over.

He'd let out a deep moan as she felt the explosion in the latex sheath. His breath was gone before she'd covered his face, his muscles relaxing as the blood emptied from the flesh inside her.

She smiled, recounting the ease with which she'd convinced the bodyguard to meet his charge and then to be taken for his own.

Her smile grew as she recalled the twitch of his muscular jaw as his charge dismissed him. Then a second of delay as he thought over his choices, only for common sense to prevail.

Maybe Zio was right. It was her best asset, and who knew it could be so much fun when she took charge.

A wave of nausea washed over her and she felt a chill with the excitement and adrenaline already fading. Her body grew heavy as she pulled herself up, rushing to the ensuite. With no time to spare, she threw up in the bowl.

A few seconds later she stood, wiping her mouth on the towel only for her gaze to fall on the mirror, where she admired her naked form with tears welling in her eyes. Her smile fell when a low groan came from the bedroom.

She watched his wide-open eyes as he died, her hand covering his mouth and nose with her gift to him; her image burned into his brain for eternity.

21

James

"Now we wait," Harris said, turning to the main hall, her gaze running across the fine walls, then between the tall cabinets and mingling faces. Fisher stepped forward and leaned up to the edge of the wooden balustrade, whilst taking care not to expose himself as he peered down at the crowd of heads spreading out amongst the exhibits.

He'd seen two of the guys twice now; they'd stood out as if they wore fluorescent vests. Switching between the opposite ends of the hall, he watched their concentration as they scanned each face in the crowd. Moving back to the other end, his survey stopped halfway on a pair of eyes peering at him.

Holding his breath, Fisher stepped back in the hope it had just been the casual glance of someone unconnected.

Turning around, he followed Harris, disappearing up a second marble flight of stairs and as they arrived on the top floor, he looked at the round of the wall and the out-of-place camera, its LED blinking in their direction.

"Let's find where those cameras are controlled from. I can put in a quiet word," Fisher said as he glanced over the almost deserted level.

"Do you speak Hindi now?" Harris whispered as she turned with a familiar smile and headed back to the stairwell. Fisher didn't answer.

"I think I spotted another player," he said after a moment.

She nodded and swept her head from side-to-side in search of cover before she hurried Fisher with a pull of her palm into the furthest alcove, tucking themselves beside a tall cabinet. Trying to calm his rising panic, Fisher glanced inside the tall display case at a polished suit of armour standing tall, which blocked most of the view to the other end of the domed hall.

On either side of the alcove were more glass-fronted cabinets. Inside each were medieval weapons, maces, flails and all manner of curved blades, hanging or laying at angles with light glinting from the softened spotlights above. In the back of the dark wood-lined alcove stood a tall wooden door with a thick, tarnished, round metal handle. Above, he spotted the luminous green of an emergency exit, its diagonal crossed with thick black tape, a second strip hanging loose by one end.

Tucked in and staring at the glass, not the weapons inside, whilst trying to act naturally, Fisher used the polished surface, concentrating on the reflected view on either side of the tall medieval robot-like figure guarding their way.

"Let's hope they don't look too hard," Fisher said, flicking his head from side to side as he caught movement at the edge of his vision. Keeping his expression as relaxed as he could, he watched a white couple with suspicion as they pushed a stroller around the glass cabinets.

"Relax," Harris said, but not able to reply, Fisher listened to the echo of distant whispered conversations, the occasional squeak of the stroller's wheel and the high pitch of the toddler as it marvelled at bright jewellery and ancient implements of torture.

"Did you know knights started their training when they were seven?" Fisher said out of the blue.

"Fascinating," Harris replied, raising her eyebrows half-heartedly.

"I've more."

"Rain check and keep your voice down."

Fisher looked over with a smile, but instead of seeing the grin repeated, he found her reaching under her jacket and he followed her gaze to the white guy he'd locked eyes with on the floor below.

Luana

Before

"We'll have to get you an alarm clock," Zio said, his voice cutting into her sleep.

Sitting up in bed, Luana shielded her eyes from the light. She couldn't hear him moving and didn't want to look. She didn't want to see him naked, his body ready for the morning ritual. Instead, she concentrated on her own breath, then on his as it came into focus. A wave of nausea rose, and she jumped from the bed, her eyes wide as she just made it to the white porcelain before her stomach erupted.

Without looking, she sensed his shadow at the door. The light flicked on and she turned. He was fully clothed and grabbed a glass from the sink, filling it with water.

"You've not been yourself," he said, his voice dry.

"You've noticed?" she said, not hiding her surprise.

"I notice a lot."

"What do you think it is?" Luana said, her voice quivering.

"I have an idea. Don't bother dressing. We'll go straight to the lab."

Through watery eyes, she found the glass.

Gretta was her usual self. Stark questions spat from her harsh, lined face as Luana lay back in the reclined leather examination chair.

"Are your breasts tender?" she said.

A strange question, Luana thought, but they were sensitive from his rough handling each morning.

"Any strange tastes, sights, or sounds?"

Luana didn't reply.

"We know you're tired and you've missed your bleed."

Luana thought back. Perhaps it was a week late. Zio spoke from the doorway, reporting her nausea and incessant need to pee.

"Can you cure me?" Luana asked, trying to keep her

voice level.

"Oh yes," Gretta replied with authority as she turned to a stainless steel tray and picked a syringe from the array of silvered tools before squirting clear liquid into the air. "You'll be fixed when you wake," she said, plunging the needle into Luana's arm.

Used to not being consulted, she let herself relax and watched Gretta's delighted nod to someone out of view as her eyelids grew heavy.

22

James

"Carolyn," came the rising English voice. Its owner, a middle-aged man dressed in brown cords and a white polo shirt, his leathered face beaming with a smile, walked towards them with arms open for an embrace. "Of all the places."

Expecting to see her trademark calm, when Fisher turned to Harris, he found her wide-eyed and blinking hard as she relaxed her hand from under her jacket before stepping up to meet the man.

"Uncle Tom," she said, leaning forward to accept the hug, but holding back in hope he wouldn't press against her holster.

"What a small world," he said, loud and bold. Her widening eyes told of her desperation for him to lower his volume. Taking his hand, she drew him into the recess.

"What are you doing here?" she eventually said, somehow keeping her voice neutral before nodding for Fisher to remain vigilant. With relief, he found the second-floor hall still clear.

"We're on holiday. Did you get caught up with this God-awful terrorist thing? We're supposed to be in Thailand by now. And who, may I ask, is your friend?" he said, not giving her time to answer.

As Fisher turned around, he found Tom offering his hand out.

"No, don't," Harris snapped, before Fisher could do something he hadn't considered. He shook the offered hand, nonetheless. "He's a friend from work," she added as Tom turned to her. "We're out here for a trade show and taking in the sights between meetings."

Letting go of Tom's hand, Fisher stepped out of the metal man's shadow when he saw the grey shirt who'd followed them across the city to his right, his beady eyes peering to every nook and alcove, all discretion abandoned.

Stepping back, he looked across the glass with the armour inside and his gaze landed on a bearded face in a grey turban doing much the same as the other man.

"Um," Fisher said, catching himself from saying her real name. The sound caught her attention.

"Is Aunt May with you?" she said to Tom.

"Of course. She's on the ground floor looking at some wonderful paintings, I think. She'll be astounded. Let's go find her."

"I tell you what," Harris said, doing her best to hide the urgency of her voice. "I can't right now. We've got a meeting in a few minutes. Why don't I surprise her at dinner while you're still in the country?"

"That sounds like a lovely idea," he said, his face glowing with the thought. "We're staying at The Emerald. Room 564. I've got my mobile, so just call me when you're out of your meeting and we'll set something up," he said with a wink. "Mum's the word."

Fisher watched the undiminished excitement as the older man turned, leaving him with a nod before heading into the main hall. Glancing away, Fisher couldn't find the men he'd spotted only seconds before.

"That was too close," Harris said as she drew a deep breath.

"A coincidence?" he replied.

"I bloody hope so," Harris said. "I'll call him later to say something came up."

"We're not out of the woods yet," Fisher said as the men appeared from different alcoves. "There's two on this level," he added, nodding along the side of the steel man. "And they'll be here any second."

Turning, he found Harris facing away and peering around the edge of the door. "I don't think it's alarmed," she said, gripping the handle as sunlight shone through the crack.

Fisher followed into the wash of heat, blinded by the bright day as he eased the door closed behind him only to find they were standing with the dome towering at their backs and on a rusted, cross-hatched metal walkway raised just off the roof's brown-stained stonework.

Paint flaked from a handrail leaning at an acute angle on either side of the metal as it followed the roof's undulations, until it ended at the top rung of a ladder tracing over the edge through one of many gaps in the low perimeter wall.

Following Harris, Fisher's confidence in the steelwork ebbed each time his gaze fell on crucial joints rusted to a mere residue of paint with spaces as wide as his thumb in the cross braces and hand holds. The constant shower of brown dust from under each step didn't help.

Averting his eyes, he chose ignorance and a light touch as he concentrated on Harris's flowing hair glinting in the sun. His soft steps matched hers, despite the metal's constant complaint as their path lowered with the walkway's profile.

"Down," she said, twisting around.

He ducked, thankful he'd reached the dip in the stone.

Twisting around, his gaze crowned the stonework where it hovered only for a moment before he ducked when he caught sight of a grey turban at the door. With heat radiating from the stone below, he gritted his teeth against the beaming sun as sweat rolled into his eyes, despite pushing them closed.

Only with a vibration in his pocket did he open them again, his heart rate spiking at the low sound with Harris reaching for her gun.

***

Luana

Present

She'd found the funeral easily enough. With her newfound

bulge of money, she pumped the phone for an hour before a name she recognised came back from the drab voice. A name he'd mentioned so many times.

But she was too late; aside from the gravediggers patting down the earth, the deserted cemetery left her pondering her next move. Spotting an official between the horizontal stones, and with the deft application of her own well-practiced skills, she headed to the wake.

Ignoring questioning looks from the full room, she found a pretty blonde woman with brunette roots whose eyes lit up when she mentioned his name. If it wasn't for the news he'd left for Heathrow only moments before, she would have spent more time getting to know her. Instead, she stored away her face together with that special little feeling and a name.

With no more information to be had by social grace alone, the friend tight lipped, the same wouldn't be true if she could get her alone.

"Heathrow Airport, please," she said to the taxi driver.

"Which terminal?" the Asian man replied, pulling the car away from the curb.

"Where does Qantas fly from?"

23

James

Blind to their foe, their heads below the stone lip, Harris's hand readied at her jacket whilst Fisher wished for his own weapon.

Waiting for what seemed like an age, he tried to stop himself from peering off the building's edge. The fragile metal was the only thing keeping him from falling between the gap in the perimeter wall and down three storeys to the concrete courtyard. Instead, he concentrated on the only comfort, knowing the rattling walkway would give them miles of notice before any action.

Unless, Fisher thought, the man knew to bound the disjointed metal and pad along the hot stone to mask any approach.

A dull call came from inside the building and Fisher's gaze darted to hers, her hand relaxing as the door's slam echoed. Taking a deep breath, he flapped the leaves of his jacket to cool boiling flesh, but an ear-splitting shriek from the metal beneath their feet sent them lurching to the left.

Fisher's hand darted for the handrail, but it gave way in his grip with deep orange snow showering to the stone as they toppled. Before he could fall, Harris grabbed his wrist and held him back from the long fall. With their eyes locked and their motion paused, they waited in the hope the metal had found its new resting place.

Unable to hold back any longer, Fisher's hand moved to her right whilst the other clung behind her as they stared at each other wide-eyed.

With the structure seeming to hold firm, Harris was the first to move and Fisher drew him towards her as she climbed the steps, her grip on his hand never wavering. Back at the main walkway, they climbed over the metal barrier and onto the stone with the heat from the fiery surface soon radiating through their soles. Stepping with a renewed vigour, but not heading for the door and the air-conditioned shade, Harris moved towards the edge of the roof, crouching by the thick waist-high wall.

"Perfect," Harris whispered as Fisher joined at her side, both of them peering over the edge at the bird's eye view of the bustling courtyard. Turning away from the flow at the museum's entrance, Fisher's gaze followed her slender finger pointing to the grey shirt and black trousers walking away with a hand mopping a sodden brow.

Fisher shuffled for comfort, still crouching as he stared, but unable to look away from the turbaned man as he walked to the edge of the courtyard, where a plume of smoke rose through the partial camouflage of a tall bush.

"Four," Harris said, keeping her vigil on the courtyard. Fisher followed her gaze, watching the two men joining the meeting as they lit cigarettes. "It's no fun when they make it so easy."

Fisher raised a brow, unsure if she was serious or not. He watched as the group stared at the building's entrance.

The turban soon took something from his pocket and pushed it to his ear, turning his head and glancing up, but too preoccupied with the conversation to spot them. With the phone pushed away, his lips moved before he rushed off, soon disappearing around the green border.

Once he'd gone, the others stubbed out their cigarettes on a low wall and left in different directions, soon blending into the crowd.

Fisher turned to find Harris rushing across the walkway without care for its fragile condition. With more diligence, he followed, mindful of where he placed his feet.

"Now it's our turn," she said as Fisher joined her at the door, her fingers testing the edge as he noticed no handle on their side. "Shit," she said, peering past him. "We need to be quick," she added, glancing over the edge of the building.

Squeezing past him, leaving Fisher to cringe at the metal's complaint, she called over her shoulder. "Come on."

He tried his best to follow with light steps, but each

press against the metal felt like it would be his last. Still, he carried on down into the dip, stepping over the section which had failed before climbing to the highest point where he glanced around, then squeezed his eyes closed. After plucking up the courage to look again, he found Harris climbing down the metal rungs where the walkway stopped and the ladder hung.

With a deep breath, and not willing to be left behind, he took bold paces, holding the handrail tight as he arrived at the ledge she'd disappeared down.

Peering over, his throat gave an involuntary reflex, gulping air when he saw the sparse hoops of metal circling the browning steel. Unsure how they'd stop him falling the three storeys to the ground, he tried not to linger on the danger as he watched her hair from above as it floated from side to side with her feet speeding down the rungs.

Feeling every vibration from her descent, he lowered himself, gripping the delicate metal as it swayed, sending paint flaking down as the steel rattled on its mounts. Soon down the first storey, he heard feet crush the gravel and, out of the corner of his eye, she rushed off to his right.

Another storey down. With his next step, the metal moved, grinding against the stonework as the distance between the ladder and the wall grew. Instinct turned his attention to the ground, but with the metal hoops stopping him from jumping back, he scrambled lower as the steel pulled away from the building at an ever-increasing angle.

Missing a step, he stumbled to keep a hold, but as he passed the last of the hoops, he took what he hoped was his chance and jumped to the side as he tried to remember the best way to land.

Pain shot up his left leg as he hit the ground.

Luana

Before

The dream was obvious. The symbology clear. Instead of her bed, she lay in a basket of twigs, her cotton duvet replaced with a white lace blanket. The walls were pastel pink.

She woke in her room, her mouth in a wide smile that wouldn't shift.

Hearing the outer seal breach, she shuffled to sit up. She was tender, like she had been after his passion, but with what felt like a thick towel between her legs.

Zio stood in the doorway, making no move to undress, his eyes narrowing as if shocked at her wide smile. He held his down-turned palm out as she sat up.

"Stay in bed. I'm going away for a couple of days."

She remained seated.

"I'm pregnant," she blurted out, the excitement rushing to her voice.

He blinked and turned away, speaking a moment before the door sealed shut.

"Not anymore."

24

James

"How's the leg?" Harris said. Not replying, he watched her sip from the china bowl of foamed coffee as she stared across the traffic-clogged road.

"It's fine, but I still can't believe you left me behind," he said, rubbing the slight swelling around his ankle. He wasn't upset. Even in the short time he'd known her, he knew nothing got in the way of her work. She'd given him a backward glance at least, and made sure he'd got up off the ground.

He'd followed, just about able to keep her in view, despite his discomfort. They'd sat in the coffee shop for the last twenty minutes, watching the man in the turban as he drank alone.

Arriving, she confirmed he'd made three calls during the journey, changing direction after each. Whoever was on the other end of the call wanted to be sure the caller hadn't been followed.

Feeling pain tug at his ankle, he moved his hand away when the gloss of a dark Mercedes pulled up outside the coffee shop and blocked their view. The bulk of its door on the other side slammed closed, the blackened glass obscuring any detail, and it was only as it pulled away that they saw a sculpted brunette sitting with her back to them at the turban's table.

"Is that who I think it is?" Fisher said, the first to speak. "Luana?"

Luana

Present

Sitting on the anonymous toilet seat, Luana pulled in a breath, hoping her composure would return as she cradled the stump. Looking away as the crimson blotted out more of the crisp white bandage, she threw her head back against the tiled wall. Despite her swimming vision, she repeated the blow again, then stood, knowing she'd let the pain get out of control as the craving crowded out her concentration.

Easing the bag off her shoulder, she gritted her teeth as the rucksack fell, its weight cracking against the bridge of her foot.

Staring at the black sports bag with the pulse of pain across the two limbs, her gaze circled the neon strips winding between the fabric joins. She wasn't meant to need it for a long time. She'd placed the bag to retrieve in the years to come, not in the time it would take to conceive a new life and give birth. Or not.

As a new wave of nausea rushed up from her gut, she told herself it was from the pain and not a side effect of the tablets. They would come later.

Gritting her teeth, she pulled her back straight and drew out the thin sports bottle from under her coat, the pills rattling as she drew a smile. With two eased down her neck, she stared through the brown plastic.

All she had to do was push down the rest and the pain would stop forever.

Returning the bottle to her coat pocket, she cracked her head against the wall once more, her punishment for such weak thoughts.

With a swig from the sports bottle, she dropped it to the floor and sat back down to wait. After all, she had plenty of time to get through.

25

James

"What the hell's she doing here?" Fisher whispered, glaring at Harris.

"Just wait," she replied, holding up a finger, her eyes narrowing as she peered across the road. "Check out the guy at the next table? The one in the grey suit with the collarless shirt. Round cheeks and pointed features."

Fisher refocused, spotting the guy she was talking about. "He looks like a goblin?" he said.

"Yes, he does," Harris replied, her words dripping with venom. Despite the description, he wore a crisp white shirt and was clean shaven as he made no efforts to hide his attention which focused on the brunette out of the corner of his eye.

With a metallic clatter at Fisher's side, he looked away from the coffee shop and found a man in an off-white Kurta Pyjama pulling himself from his motorbike laying on the ground, surrounded by a spreading pile of oranges as an argument in the native language ignited.

With a murmur at his side, Fisher turned back to the table where the woman faced along the street. He couldn't help but laugh when her wrinkled face turned in their vague direction.

"Sometimes you just see what you want to," he said, chuckling to himself as he turned to Harris, who wasn't smiling.

"That's Connor fucking Tucson. I bet you my gun he's the one who had us followed."

Luana

Before

The contents hadn't taken long to collect, most of which she'd acquired in the normal course of business. The hardest part had been storing the spoils before she could get them to the safety of the locker.

Unsure if they searched her room, her stuff rifled as they put away her laundry, she'd found quiet spots around the campus. Little places no one ever went.

She'd had to wait for the last item, the most difficult to find, and she couldn't hide it anywhere where they might discover it. It had taken six months for the right target, and when it happened, she almost shook as she punched in the safe's code. It took doing things she didn't want to remember to get the four digits from his lips.

With her fingers still dripping with his blood, she found the package behind the thick, steel door amongst rafts of paperwork she had no use for. Then, dressed, and all tucked away, she let them discover her. With the contingency plan in place, she watched Zio's car race away as she set off on the elongated route to the emergency extraction point, which just happened to be at Heathrow Airport.

With her head empty of pain and feeling, she pulled open the neon zip, moving the bundle of sterling and dollars, seeking the precision-milled metal. The old revolver felt solid in her hand, so different from the composite handguns she'd carried whilst on the payroll.

Those were more accurate and reliable, but this one was hers. The first thing she'd ever owned.

26

James

The building sat isolated and alone. A brick two storey, although three in places. The roof lay flat, jutting like the peak of a cap, its motive the same as the headgear it took its inspiration from.

The lack of grandeur surprised Fisher, with only the eagled crest an indicator of its purpose. Thick glass doors, their diagonals banded with steel, swept open on their approach, pouring out chilled air.

Fisher followed a step behind as Harris led them inside and past a long queue of people in faded clothes sweat-stained from past effort, their hopes and dreams of a new life bundled under their arms in cardboard folders whose array of colours ranged as much as their clothes. As the queue snaked left, a Marine in uniform dress stood guard, his jaw compulsory square and giant frame blocking the gap in a long wall of smoked blast-proof glass.

"Do you have an appointment?" the deep American voice said and even Harris's smile didn't move the mound of muscle.

"Can you let Brandon Sword know I'm patiently waiting?" Harris replied as she stepped to the side of the arch. The tall Marine pushed out his thick arm, pulling a handset from a waist high plinth.

Fisher leaned to the side, looking past the Marine to a plain walled passage which turned out of sight to the left.

"Whom shall I say is waiting?" he said as he pulled the phone from his ear.

"Tell him it's his long-lost mother," she said, off handed, her back at an angle to the smoked wall. The Marine spoke down the phone before replacing the handset and turned with an unchanged expression as he stepped to the side.

"Someone will collect you shortly," he said, his thick

hand motioning for her to step through.

"I'll wait here. It will save a lot of paperwork," she said, glancing at the question in Fisher's frown.

"What?" she said.

"Long-lost mother?" he asked, tilting his head to the side.

She beamed back with a mischievous smile. "I've known Brandon a long time and I've got him out of the shit more than once. He says I'm like his mother. It's funny because he's always wanted more," she said, laughing to herself.

Fisher turned away, his gaze taking in the spacious hall as he scanned the long line of natives that stopped at the main door where one by one they were called forward to present their case to what looked like bank tellers behind bulletproof glass, sliding across their documents as they prayed in silence.

"Have you spoken to Susie?" she said, stepping into his view.

Fisher nodded, turning back to the queue.

"Is she okay?" Harris pressed, touching his arm.

He looked over, nodding. "What's it called when you save someone's life and they won't leave you alone afterwards?"

Harris smiled. "Sweet," she said, "and annoying. A consequence of attachment, I'm afraid."

"She's nervous because I'm not right by her side," he said, shaking his head. "She needs to get on with her life. There's nothing for her to be afraid of anymore."

"Except living," Harris replied, the smile gone from her voice. Fisher turned to see her eyebrows fall. "She'll learn to get back to herself. She just needs a distraction."

They turned, hearing the squeak of the Marine's boots, and Fisher watched as her face lit up when she spotted a figure at the end of the corridor.

Fisher had expected some John Wayne type; tall, with weathered skin and sharp chiselled features cut against a tight crew cut. Instead, he spotted a chubby man standing shorter than himself with the hair on his head long since vanished. His focus landed on grey curls across his chin and a wire-thin pair of glasses pushed up his nose.

Half expecting her expression to fade at the sight of the washed-out green tattoos running up his arm to a crinkled short-sleeve shirt bulging at his waist, he found her expression lighter than he knew possible as they held their arms open. Stepping through the transparent border, the edges misted with red smoke and a loud tone forced all eyes to the embrace.

Fisher watched the Marine go for his gun, but Brandon's expression and his outstretched palm calmed him as they held their clutch.

"You wouldn't like what you found, son," Brandon said, his words elongated by a thick accent. The Marine squeaked back into place with his stare turning on Fisher, who looked anywhere but the uncomfortable show of affection. Still in the embrace, her face nuzzled into the crook of his tattooed neck, Fisher stepped through unseen, except by the Marine, who didn't relax even though the archway lit with a pale green.

The two chatted as they headed down the corridor, neither checking Fisher followed.

He listened to their excited conversation as he tagged along, catching code-locked doors as they were about to close. They spoke of a library of friends, or colleagues, he couldn't quite tell, talking as if they'd spent a lifetime together. Walking close, like lovers, he thought, he caught Franklin's name a few times until they stopped at a lift, both turning and looking at him with surprise after catching his reflection in the shine of the metal doors.

"Where are my manners?" Harris blurted, her eyes wide. "Phineas, this is Brandon Sword. Brandon, this is Phineas."

Fisher deflated as she gave the code name he hated.

Brandon pushed out a thick hand. Fisher leaned forward and met with his own, but stood out of range, worried he would reach out to pat him on the back. Their palms locked

117

in firm grips. Brandon shook as if they were best friends, or Fisher had done him some great service. Still prickling from the awful codename she'd inflicted on him in Argentina, a thought occurred as he released his hands.

They knew each other very well and for a long time, they were in the same game; he'd let her carry her weapon without checking, they'd talked about Franklin and he was sure he'd maybe heard Clark's name mentioned too, but still she'd used his codename. He was very interested in hearing how Brandon referred to *her*.

"Nice to meet you," Brandon said and then turned back to Harris. "So what brings you to Mumbai? Is there anything I need to know about?" he said, still smiling even as he peered over the round glasses.

Harris beamed, leaning in with a dimpled laugh. "We're just minding our own business. It's an unscheduled stop, what with everything that's going on. What about you? Kicked out of Delhi?"

"How did you know I was in Mumbai?" Brandon asked, raising his brow.

Her expression dropped with the reminder of why they were here. "Never mind that. I want to know why your prick of a deputy had me followed."

Brandon's expression faltered, his hand going to her forearm as he shook his head.

"Shit. I'm real sorry. He's keen, but got no hands-on experience." He moved his hand to rub his chin. "I don't know why he'd do that." He shook his head towards Fisher the same, then turned back to Harris. "Look, it's about time you two got along. Why don't you bond over a meal? We're here with the ambassador, in answer to your question, and she's having a private dinner tonight before hosting a trade event tomorrow."

Harris didn't reply straight away, but a quick glance at Fisher made him feel like a child stopping his mother from going out.

"Bring him along. He's more than welcome," Brandon

said, laughing before they turned to the door at the end of the corridor as it flew open.

"Tucson," Harris said, her tone flat as in bounced the man from the cafe, his eyes wide with surprise.

"Shit, Trinity, what the fuck are you doing here?"

***

Luana

Present

She felt the presence before her eyes opened with a deep breath. Her codeine woozy head had passed, and she'd melted into her favourite phase. Chilled, but still with some focus.

She'd sat for hours paying no attention to the discomfort of the plastic seat and she'd seen the old lady mooching around the arrivals lounge before she'd claim the next seat, despite it being one of many that were empty. The airport was barren, deserted of people with real lives, but with a baggy thick-knit cardigan and oversized bag under her crossed hands, the woman appeared to want the company of the sweet-looking girl who'd been in the place as long as her.

"My husband was coming from Belgium," the old lady said, her voice shaking.

Luana tried her best, turning to look at her with a well-practiced smile.

"He needs to get home soon, or he'll run out of medicine." The wrinkled woman watched as Luana's stare didn't move. "I've brought them all the way from Reading. Have you come far?"

Luana smiled, but didn't glance over when the old lady ran her hand over her puffed grey hair. "Do you think they'll let them fly soon?"

Luana's smile dropped as she glanced back. "Not in

time for your old fella," she replied, her voice calm. "I'm afraid he's worm food."

The woman's lined eyelids widened, her mouth pinching as she picked herself up before limping to the furthest bench.

Luana closed her eyes and concentrated on her breath.

27

James

The Mumbai bolthole, as Brandon had called it, was a white stone mansion invisible from the road. The tall chimneys, long pillars and arched entrance only hinting halfway through the ten-minute walk that wound along the Royal Palm-lined private road.

Two Marine guards flanked the dark double-door entrance and ushered them in with open palms while the doors parted. The grand dining room was no let down either. Panelled in dark wood, chandeliers twinkled in the soft light with the Star and Stripes pinned die straight against the wall at the head of the long table.

In his rented black tuxedo, Fisher sat with the ambassador to his left, obeying his briefing and keeping his mouth shut.

He had no problem with that. He struggled to do anything but snatch glimpses of Harris opposite in her long, ankle-length dress whose tight fit kept stealing his breath.

The ambassador was a tall, older woman with elegant short grey hair, and she'd welcomed them with a bright smile that seemed used to its job. To her left was Sword, opposite Tucson. Placing Harris and Tucson next to each other was optimistic, but at least the ambassador's presence would hold back her temper.

For most of the meal, her excellency did the talking, keeping clear of conversation about their guest's day jobs. Connor only spoke a few times, seeming to have orders much the same as Fisher's, or so his subdued tone indicated. When he spoke, Fisher got the impression he was from the same state as Brandon, their voices almost identical, but he didn't come across as the asshole Harris had described many times since his first sighting.

Harris kept her attention on Brandon. Every so often they would share a smile, or a raised brow, and he couldn't help imagining their feet intertwined under the table.

The one-sided conversation ended after a couple of hours and, as waiters served coffee on a polished silver tray, the ambassador took her leave, a week of entertaining local dignitaries having taken its toll. With the drawn out opening of a new orphanage for street children on the agenda for tomorrow, she left the four alone.

With crystal glasses topped off with brandy and the door barely back in its hole, Harris took a swig and stood. Moving around to Fisher's side of the table, she narrowed her eyes and took a seat.

"Why the fuck did you have me followed?"

Leaning back, Fisher watched Connor's eyes widen with his gaze flitting between Harris and Brandon.

"I. Uh…" was all he could manage before Brandon leaned across the table.

"I think you should apologise," he said before turning to Harris with a wide smile.

"I… I'm sorry. It was a mistake. I thought I could test our team," Connor said, raising his glass up to his mouth.

"Bullshit," Harris spat. "Next time, I won't leave anyone standing. Do you understand?"

Connor nodded and gulped back the contents of his glass.

***

Luana

Present

"Your information was wrong," Zio said, his words replacing her surprise that he'd taken the call. "They're in Mumbai, but not for much longer."

Not knowing what to say, she stared at the closed doors

and the empty arrivals board. Just as the line went dead, the screens filled with yellow lettered entries; new flights with arrival times replaced the unending list of cancellations.

After taking a moment to work out which plane they were on, and with an extra dose of codeine, she relaxed into the plastic seat and gave in to sleep.

In a haze the hours came and went, then waking, she took the brief journey to the fourth terminal where she stood expectant in front of the arrivals board, which confirmed nothing had changed. Only after staring for what seemed liked hours did her elation spike when the first line's status changed to *landed*. Realising they were waiting for their bags on the other side of the doors, she pictured them standing in creased clothes, their faces weary from the flight and not altogether sure of the time.

Peeking over the glossy magazine, she leaned against the wall in the furthest corner of the wide arrival's hall. The first of the passengers were as she'd imagined; families and couples lugging bags with children at their side as they met with friends and lovers waiting beyond the barrier. She paid the most attention to those that walked through without stopping.

A crowd soon built, and she glanced at each face. With an excellent memory, she felt confident she'd recognise the companion and nothing short of brain injury would erase the image of James fucking Fisher. As the flow thinned, she tensed with reasons for their delay flourishing in her head, each of which she soon discarded.

After a few minutes since the last had come through, she held firm for another half an hour before she made the call.

"*Your* information was wrong. They weren't on the flight," she spat as the call connected and the digits raced down her credit.

"I'm not your mother," his sleep weary voice came back.

"They weren't on the flight. You were plain wrong,"

she replied.

"Maybe this is the reason you fucked up? Have you forgotten everything you learned?" Silence filled the line before he spoke again. "Where are you?"

"Terminal Four."

Zio sighed. "There were two flights out of Mumbai. They flew British Airways, and it landed half an hour ago at Terminal Five. The other side of the airport."

Smashing the handset onto the hook, she turned, her foot connecting with a plastic chair, sending it skidding across the tiled floor. Before the echo died, the thin crowd of faces turned towards her, and two figures dressed in black and wearing body armour walked toward her.

28

James

With brandy still reaching their veins, their reclined first-class seats soon sent them into an uneventful journey. A stiff BA suit met them on the tarmac, ushering them to a waiting car and driver. With the buildings not entered, their credentials not checked, the 7 Series BMW soon breezed past the two Warrior-tracked vehicles flanking the main terminal entrance.

As Harris caught up on sleep, Fisher scrolled through the messages filling his phone.

Susie, *who else*, James thought, had heard a noise in the night, chasing him for a reply after only ten minutes of silence. With none forthcoming, she spoke of her upset, worried about how she would cope if he abandoned her.

With a deep sigh, he sent a brief reply, letting her know he was back in the country.

Within an hour, they were through the steel and concrete barrier, walking through the packed car park in Vauxhall, elbowing their way through the crowded corridors. With a quick call, a conference room emptied, and Clark's ragged features projected on the wall. Behind him, the dark operations centre buzzed with activity.

"You look like shit," Harris said, and Clark's right eyebrow twitched. "When did you last sleep?"

"I caught a couple hours…" he said, then looked at his watch. "Sometime yesterday."

"Go rest," she replied, turning to Fisher. "We can take more on."

His head shook. "Direct orders. One case at a time."

"Where is he?" Harris said. Clark glanced somewhere behind the camera.

"In a meeting," he said, with more words hovering in his mouth before he spoke. "Please, just do what he said."

Harris turned to Fisher, her voice stuck in her throat, before she turned back to the projection and nodded.

"Can you do me one thing?" she said, but didn't wait for a reply. "I need a quick round up on Connor Tucson?"

"The Company man?" Clark replied, his eyebrow raised.

"Please," she said, nodding.

"Do I want to know?"

Harris scowled. "He's selling me a dumb story. Even by his standards."

"Shall I add in the station chief?"

"Don't bother. Sword's fine. Did the old man say where he wants us?"

"Sit tight. This place is fit to bursting," he replied.

"Get him to call me, please?" Harris said, and as the screen went blank, Fisher watched her eyes roll in the reflection. Staring at the blank wall, she lowered her brow as her breathing slowed. Tendons tightened in her forearms as she clenched her fists. Fisher kept quiet. It didn't look like Harris was in the mood for talking; instead, he pulled the iPad from inside his jacket and scrolled down the screen.

"What's with you and Connor?" Fisher said, hoping to break the tension. She turned to him, scowling.

"Remember, they're part of the game," she said. "Don't believe a word they say."

Fisher nodded. "Even Brandon?" he said, but spoke again when she didn't reply. "I've been thinking. What if there are more fires like ours which no one has connected?"

The silence continued for what felt like an age, then after a few moments, her fists unclenched. Without speaking, she raised an eyebrow, her expression softening as she pulled a keyboard from where it sat in the centre of the desk. Her fingers tapped on the keys.

"Let's take a look," she finally said.

Fisher turned his head to the side. "You have a database for that?"

"Of course. We have a lot of data on many things," she replied, not looking over as the projected screen came to life. "It's called the internet."

Fisher mirrored her smile and turned to the screen as she tapped *University Fires 2008* into the search engine. Five and a half million results came back, and she scrolled down the screen.

"Try deaths instead of fires," he said, and Harris tapped again.

"We'll ignore those which are alcohol or suicide related," Harris said as she scanned the information.

"That leaves us with Dr Willie Somerfield, Fine Arts Lecturer from Edinburgh University, and Professor Norman Wafford," Fisher said, reading aloud in a slow voice. "Department of Earth Sciences, Cambridge University." He looked up at Harris with a beaming smile as she clicked a link and took in the projected information.

"It says he died of asphyxiation, not fire."

"But I bet there's a link to Reading," Fisher replied.

Harris typed again and found his obituary.

"He lectured there until 2007, then moved to Cambridge to take up a professorship."

"The other guy?"

Harris drummed at the keyboard and they both read on. "Nothing jumps out."

"So Wafford links to the right place, but no fire," Fisher said, nodding.

Harris opened another window and logged into FALCON, then within seconds she scrolled through the police and coroner's report from his death. "Confirmed asphyxiation."

"Does that mean he couldn't breathe?" Fisher asked.

Harris nodded as she read. "He was found in the morning, assumed to have been working late."

"Was it a lab? Could it have been hermetically sealed?"

Harris shook her head, bunching her brow. "It was a standard office, by all accounts," she replied, shaking her head.

Fisher turned back to the projection and a mosaic of photos of a wood-panelled office, the professor slumped over his desk. "The air conditioning was turned off and there were floor vents," she added as she continued to read.

"They must have found some medical condition? A postmortem would have been mandatory," Fisher replied, squinting at the photo.

Her nod changed to a shake. "He was a weekend runner and surprisingly fit for a sixty-year-old."

"Foul play?"

"Nothing," she said.

"What *did* they say?" he replied, lifting his chin.

"It was an open verdict. They couldn't find anything, even after a second postmortem. The coroner put it down to a condition undetectable on examination."

"Do you believe it?" Fisher asked as he turned back to her. Harris raised her eyebrows. "Who found him?"

She scrolled back up the screen. "A colleague and friend. Dr Steinfield."

They sat in silence, each staring at the words but not reading.

Fisher tensed as his phone vibrated. It was Susie.

"Just checking you're okay?" she said.

"I'm fine," Fisher replied in a hushed voice.

"I knew you'd be the first back. Don't worry about me. I bet you're busy."

"Thanks, Suse. Are you okay?"

"Yes," she replied, and he heard the smile in her voice before he hung up, catching Harris's eyes pinched with concentration.

"I found something," she said as he pushed away his phone, looking up to find a newspaper's front page projected on the screen.

Fourteen die in a week of furious fires, the headline read above a story about the professor's death.

Luana

Present

She peered along the lamplit street, its length shadowed by towering Victorian houses. Along the roadside, a rainbow of super minis parked at right angles to the pavement. Bowing her head for the high mounted camera, she was through the second door with a flick of her wrist.

Dust floated in the stale air, sparking against the orange glow as it streamed through the room's only window. Her gaze followed the light, bouncing around the room from one dust- covered surface to another before settling on a wooden framed cork board, its surface pinned with glossy photos abound with reoccurring faces. She recognised two of the smiling expressions. The corner of her lips lifted as she reached for the short brunette hair. Three more were in the picture, one only just buried.

She turned, following the specks of dust to a wooden tabletop strewn with paper. She picked up the birth certificate and couldn't help but chuckle. Underneath she saw that photograph, the one that had started it all. The girl in Alana's hands was meant to be her. Stood next to her mother, at least for a few years, were the parents of James Fisher, or so he had thought. She smiled again. It was all so complex and well thought out. She'd wished she'd been a part of its design, the tangled web it had taken him over twenty-five years to pick at.

Pausing when voices came from the front door, her hand moved for her gun until she realised the flaw. Instead, she went for a small paring knife from her pocket with her other, then pushed it back home as the voices disappeared.

Sweeping through photographs in the pile, she couldn't find what she sought and moved to the bedroom. The room where he'd slept for so long, oblivious to his part in the great plot. Rifling through drawers, she wasn't hopeful. No one kept address books anymore, but when her gaze fell on the cracked screen of a black iPhone, she nodded.

129

"That'll do," she said to herself.

29

James

The paper was the Cambridge News, but before Fisher could read the detail, the image changed to Franklin's tree bark rough face with his eyes pronounced by deep black bags.

"Harris. Fisher," he said with a dry edge to the usual gravel in his voice.

"Sir," Harris replied. "I want in. You must have some leads by now."

Squinting, Franklin rubbed an eye with his thumb and forefinger.

"You are in. You should have a case to deal with," he said, scowling off screen.

"We have, but it's not leading us where we need to be anytime soon," she replied.

Franklin continued to scowl and stared at Harris for a long while. "Stick with it. We'll get you here as soon as we can." As his head left the shot, the video cut off, leaving Harris staring at the blank wall.

"Are you okay?" Fisher asked, regretting the words as she met her narrowed eyes.

"I'm pissed off," she snapped before turning away.

"Do you think they're keeping you away because of me?" he asked, his voice quiet. She looked over and nodded. "I'm sorry you have to babysit."

"No. *I'm* sorry. I shouldn't have snapped. It's just…" she said, then stopped with a knock at the door. "Come in."

The door opened and a thin wiry man entered, followed by five others in suits.

"We have this room," he said, glancing at his watch. Harris nodded, casting her head down then logging out of the computer. Fisher followed her out as the room filled. In her One Series she probed her new iComm with the bright fluorescent light pouring in from the underground car park.

"We can't do this here," Fisher said, breaking the

silence.

"You're right," Harris said, and pressed the button to start the engine before gunning the accelerator.

"Where are we going?" Fisher asked, pinned back in his seat as they raced towards the closed gates.

"Let's get to the bottom of these fires, then we can move on to the next case," she said as the barrier slipped to either side.

***

Luana

Present

Leaning back in the leather seat, she breathed with slow, steady purpose. The sweetness of the coating soon fell away as the round tablets disappeared down her throat. In the last few days, she'd become well practiced and knew to take the tablets twenty minutes before she changed her bandages, saving herself the need to bite down to stop the tears welling.

With the bandage changed, she closed her eyes, only opening briefly to guide her hand to the switch and let the window drop open a crack to ease the sharp smell.

With a buzz from her phone, her eyes shot open, and she stared through the sea of cars just as the first streetlight turned orange. Edging upright, her gaze fixed on the gilded main doors as they opened and she watched, waiting for each of the faces to arrive in focus whilst reminding herself who she was looking for wasn't part of the audience.

30

James

Beside Harris, Fisher sat in a wooden-panelled corridor, his feet resting on the black and white checker tiles with memories of school days drifting through his mind. He'd never taken this seat at his school, but had watched so many others with dread pulling down their expressions as they waited for a call from the headmaster.

He wondered about Harris's teenage years. She was a sports star, he knew that much, but what was she like out of the gym? A flurry of laughter from passing students pulled him back into the corridor, their dress sense teetering on the edge of fashion.

The door to their left opened unseen and a man shuffled out, his back arched and weight resting heavy on a pale wooden stick with his frame barely filling a rough tweed three-piece suit. As he hobbled away in the opposite direction, another man, younger by at least a decade, stepped over the threshold. He wore a white shirt cropped at the sleeves with a burgundy bow tie holding the collar together. Brown corduroy trousers, patched at the knees, completed the stereotype.

"Sorry to keep you waiting," he said, his voice dry and unhurried, with a sag of skin flapping under his chin as he spoke. Following him into the long thin office after invitation, the pair perched themselves on chairs in front of the wide desk, cluttered with dark wooden display cases trapping motionless insects pinned to creamy white boards.

"Thank you for agreeing to see us at such short notice, Professor Chapman," Harris said as she settled.

His eyes wrinkled and he replied with a warm smile. "I'm always happy to help the police where I can."

"Thank you. I'll get straight to the point. The original police report showed you were the first to find Professor Wafford. Is that correct?"

The professor twisted a wiry eyebrow.

"Yes. He was a friend of mine. It was awful."

"I'm sorry to drag it all up, but it may have some bearing on a case we're working on," she said, and Fisher watched her warm him with her smile.

"It's okay. Ask away. I imagine you're trying to figure out the cause of death," he replied.

She nodded and turned to look at Fisher as he spoke.

"What was he working on?"

The professor drew a deep breath. "He lectured geology and was putting together an expedition."

"To where?" Fisher asked.

"Somewhere cold. That's all I know. You should have seen the amount it was costing for the thermals alone," the professor replied with a raised brow.

"Did you see anything unusual when you found him?" Fisher added.

"Other than he was dead?" he replied, not smiling despite the flippant comment. "No," the professor said after neither of them smiled.

Harris shuffled forward in her seat. "Can we see his office?"

Chapman shook his head. "I'm afraid it's locked."

"Who has the keys?" Fisher asked.

"It's used by Doctor Finch now, but he's quite difficult to get hold of."

"Is he in today?" Fisher asked.

The professor laughed, the wrinkles in his face tightening.

"I'm sensing that you two don't get on," Fisher said.

"It's not that. He's a different…" Chapman paused. "He does things differently. He's more focused on tying up commercial deals rather than educating."

Fisher glanced to Harris, watching as she nodded, then he turned back to the old man. "You seem a little distracted. Nervous, perhaps?"

The professor's hand moved from his brow and he shook his head. "I didn't kill him, if that's what you're getting at."

"No one's suggesting that. In fact, no one is suggesting anything," Fisher said with a shake of his head, then stood, reaching out towards the man as Harris remained seated. "It was nice to meet you."

The professor shivered as their palms touched and Fisher spoke in an even tone. "You're not in any trouble. We can't, and won't, cause you any harm. We're only interested in solving the mystery. No one outside this room will ever know what you tell us."

The professor nodded.

"Now tell us how you found him. From the beginning," Fisher said as he sat back down and watched as the professor leaned to his side and dragged open the lowest desk drawer. Pulling out a heavy crystal tumbler, he placed it on the table, then reached again and grabbed a stumpy half full bottle of Aberfeldy Whiskey. After offering with an open palm, the pair declined with a shake of their heads and its sharp smoky aroma caught in their nostrils as he poured the dark straw-coloured liquor.

Swirling the tumbler, he spoke in a low voice.

"I was in early to finish work on a paper," the professor said with a glance at the door. "I pass his office on my way in. I saw his light on. He would sometimes be an early riser like me. You find you need less sleep as you get older." He took another sip. "I opened the door," he paused, cupping the glass in both hands. "And there he was, face down on the desk, next to a bottle of the good stuff and the most magnificent example of geology I've ever seen," he said, glancing at the stout bottle on his desk before taking a long drag from the glass. "I dropped my briefcase and rushed around the desk. He was blue and cold to the touch. I'll never forget that feeling. I don't know why I touched him when it was obvious he'd been gone for hours."

"What else?" Fisher said, leaning forward.

The old man looked over before turning to Harris and taking a deep breath.

"When I opened the door," he paused, draining the glass. "I felt a presence."

"A presence," Fisher repeated, on the edge of his seat.

"It's difficult to describe, other than to say it felt like someone had thrown a blanket over me. It took my breath away."

"Then what happened?" Fisher said.

"Nothing," the professor shrugged. "The feeling subsided."

Fisher nodded and stood. "Thank you, Professor Chapman. You've been a great help. One last thing. Could we get details of what he was working on that night?"

The professor nodded.

"I'll get it brought up from storage and have it sent on."

***

Luana

Present

The first out of the door was the girl with the blonde hair, brunette roots and beaming smile, stepping from the darkness into the orange-bathed car park. With a pale, thin cardigan wrapped around her shoulders, Luana could still make out the tightness of her middle, the fullness of her breasts and the radiance of her cheeks as she watched her laugh with a woman who was wider in body and draped in a smock.

They walked side by side, stopping for a kiss on both cheeks before parting company two rows away. If spotted, it was cause to change the plan, perhaps an escalation of the timescale. Just in case, she pushed her new phone to the side and fingered the cold metal.

With the flash of a black Mini's hazard lights, the girl pulled open the door and Luana made a mental note, her face lighting up as she pressed the power button on the smartphone.

"It's me," she said. "It's time for you to pay back that favour," she added, before reciting the registration and hanging up.

31

James

As the barrier lifted, Fisher pushed the case file down the side of the seat.

"They found broken glass in the bin," Fisher said. "And a glass of whiskey on the table."

"What's the significance?" Harris replied, not looking from the windscreen.

Fisher shrugged. "But it wasn't Wafford's ghost," he replied and her mouth turned up in a smile as she parked the car. Then the pair walked with purpose up to the police headquarters.

***

Luana

Present

"Make it look like an accident, but if you fucking harm her, I'll pay you a late-night visit you won't wake up from," Luana said into the phone.

Listening to the stunted reply, a deep repetitive knock came from the back of the car until the thump replaced with a clash of metal vibrating through the chassis.

Luana sighed.

"I'll call with the location. Be ready."

Without haste or hurry, she hung up, then with considered steps, walked to the back of the car, raising her brow as the boot eased open.

"Shut the fuck up," she said, just before she drove her fist into the darkness.

32

James

Harris scanned the case file, its pages spread across the desk as they sat opposite a man in a white short-sleeve shirt and navy blue tie who traced his index finger along a thin jet black moustache. A stack of similar files waited in front of him.

"Were you involved in these cases?" Harris asked, and Detective Inspector Wilks sat up straight as he shook his head.

"Only to review them twelve months ago," he said, sending stale cigarette breath across the table.

"What did your gut say?" she asked, her voice soft as the officer lifted his chin and glanced between them.

"The Prof was holding back," he said as his gaze settled on Harris.

"You were right," she replied, nodding. Raising his brow, he leaned forward. "But it was inconsequential," she added, and he sat back.

"Are these all the similar cases?" Fisher said, and the officer nodded, sliding the stack towards them.

"Where are the investigators?" Harris asked.

"Retired," Wilks said with a shake of his head. "One of them passed away just last month."

"Cause of death?" Harris replied, looking up from the file.

"Heart attack. He'd just turned sixty," he replied. "Old age, for the likes of us."

She nodded and turned her attention back to the pages. "Give us half an hour. Please."

Realising she'd dismissed him, he left them alone in the simple square room while Fisher took a folder from the pile.

"Only two investigators for all of these?" he said, flipping through the papers inside the dogeared cardboard. "Could it mean they suspected a link?"

"Perhaps, but more likely they didn't have enough people to involve anyone else," she replied, not looking up.

"DC Knox and DS Watkins," Fisher said, reading the file header, not able to stop himself from wondering which one was dead.

The summary described the death of four students. A house fire on the outskirts of Cambridge, with no evidence of criminality found by either the police or the coroner. Pushing the file to the side, he waited until Harris finished with hers.

"It's the same MO, but in a sheltered housing block. A fierce fire," she read aloud. "Killing a retired firefighter. Despite a lack of evidence, they concluded his oxygen cylinder leaked."

Fisher didn't reply. Instead, they both pulled another file, and he read of the six lives lost in a fierce blaze within a set of commercial units. With the entire block decimated, the fire service couldn't determine if it started in the plumber's offices or that of a recycling venture. They ruled both arson and a gas explosion out despite matching their characteristics, as none of the survivors reported smelling the fishy additive Mercaptan. The crew commander's statement ended the file, but raised more questions than he gave answers.

Recognising the name, Fisher flicked to the back of the previous file, soon confirming it was the same guy in charge, with the final report ending almost word for word.

As Harris pulled the next file, he did the same and read about a school, but even with his lack of experience, everything told him it was arson, despite the cops failing to find a culprit. Catching Harris looking up, he summarised what he'd read, whilst she simply said hers wasn't connected.

With a knock at the door, the detective inspector returned and made himself comfortable.

"Is this it?" Harris asked, her tone short.

The detective nodded, his gaze swapping between them. "After my review, I called Knox and asked him the same thing. He'd tried to find others with the same MO, but there were no matches in this force area. When the fires stopped, he took on a different case load."

"Did he tell you anything I won't read in these pages?"

Harris replied, leaning closer.

Wilks shook his head.

"Nothing?" Harris asked, tilting hers to the side.

"No," he replied, still shaking his head.

"Doesn't that strike you as odd?" Fisher said.

Still looking at Wilks, she nodded.

The inspector shrugged. "I asked, but you've got to remember he's retired. Who wants to be reminded of the cases they didn't solve?"

"What's his number?" Fisher asked, and the detective pulled a folded square of paper from this shirt pocket and slid it across the desk.

Staring out of the car window, Fisher watched the barrier raise and lower to let out a marked police car followed by a delivery van as he listened to the phone ringing through the speakers.

"I told Wilks I'm busy today," a rough, aged voice replaced the tone as the car crept forward.

"Mr Knox. This is..." she said, but didn't get far.

"I know who you are, and I'm still busy."

"It's important," Harris replied, pulling out of the junction and speeding up to a fire-red Porsche queuing at a roundabout.

"I'm not in your world anymore," he said.

"You've never been in my world. I'll visit if you prefer," Harris added.

Silence filled the void until the guy spoke.

"Listen. The same crew commander visited each of the fires. He's out of Cambridge station and knew more than he was letting on." The line went dead.

"What was that all about?" Fisher said, glancing over as they slowed for a roundabout.

"The inspector's right," she said with a glance. "It's like that for some when they leave the job. We'll talk to the firefighter. If he can't help, then we'll pay Knox a visit, whether he likes it or not."

Luana

Present

With her arm hung in a sling and a mannequin's hand protruding from the bandage, Luana sat on a wooden bench outside the florist with her back to the bright arrangements. Her gaze fixed into the distance as she watched the parked Ford Focus out of the corner of her eye. Switching her glance along the quiet town road, she found no sign of what she wanted.

It was the slow turn of the Ford's front wheels that made her force another look. The driver had clocked the black Mini ambling along the road before her. The man in the Ford stared straight ahead. Despite doing everything by the book, the Focus hit the Mini in the side, squealing its tyres over the curb and forcing Luana to lift her legs as it came to rest by the bench.

The roar of the engine filled the air as the Ford shot back; the driver wrenching the wheel and jumping left, scraping its crumpled metal along the Mini's rear quarter before speeding off into the distance.

Locking her wide eyes with that of the Mini's driver, they shared their open-mouthed shock at what had happened. Even though one of them was a trained actor, it was the other that gave a stellar performance.

Relaxing to let her shock subside, Luana stood, pushing a middle-aged woman to the side of a gathering crowd. She had to be the one to console her first.

33

James

"It's Professor Chapman, from Cambridge University," he said over the speaker.

"Hello," Harris replied as she pulled the car into the lay-by beside a quiet country road.

"It's missing," he said.

"What's missing?" Harris replied.

"What Wafford was working on. It was booked in, but we can't find it now. I've had one of my team looking for an hour. It's not anywhere in the basement."

"Where else could it be?" Fisher said, looking over at Harris.

"The system is based on trust," the professor said, his voice high. "Most of the materials have little monetary value, so I don't know why someone would take it."

"Could you speak to Wafford's replacement and find out if he has it?" Harris asked.

"I'll talk to Doctor Finch, but he was not Professor Wafford's replacement. After Professor Wafford died, Professor Peters replaced him," he added before his voice lowered. "He would have taken over Norman's projects if he hadn't died in a tragic car accident."

"You didn't mention that," Harris said, mirroring Fisher's raised brow.

"I didn't think it was important. He liked a drink, I'm afraid."

Luana

Present

"Where's your kettle?" Luana said, leading the blonde through an unfamiliar hallway and into an alien sitting room sparse with retro art deco furniture.

"There really is no need," the woman said, with Luana positioning herself to give the woman no choice but to sit.

"Sweet tea for shock. Don't they say?" Luana replied.

"I should get you a drink," the woman said, looking up, but without further word Luana disappeared into the next room, coming back with two steaming cups pinched together in her hand a moment later.

After shuffling herself back into the deep chair, the blonde pursed her lips on the edge of the mug, her gaze never leaving Luana's. "I'm so grateful, but I don't even know your name?"

"It's Lara," Luana said, sipping from her cup as she took the seat opposite.

"I'm Susie, and it's been an absolute pleasure to meet you. It feels like I've met you before," Susie said.

"I know what you mean," Luana replied, her smile rising high in the corner of her mouth. "But I'd remember if we had."

Susie's smile broadened. "I still can't believe that guy drove off."

"That's people, I'm afraid. There are some real bastards in this world, believe me," Luana said, holding eye contact.

"I know firsthand," Susie replied, looking away.

"I'm sure the police will sort him out, especially with all the details I gave them when I reported it."

"Thank you for taking control and making sure I was okay. It looks like someone should look after you," Susie said, nodding to her guest's wrapped arm.

Susie smiled wider as Luana leaned forward. "Do you live alone?"

She shook her head. "My flatmate's at work and she won't be back for a few hours. What about you? Please don't think I'm trying to get rid of you, but aren't I keeping you from something?" Susie said, hugging the mug between her hands and resting it on her drawn-up knees.

"No. I'm my own boss. I spend my days in the sun with a cocktail, or scouring the streets finding new friends," Luana said, watching Susie's eyes widen. "Do you have a boyfriend?"

"No boyfriend," she said, raising her brow.

Luana felt her tingle amplify, knowing if it wasn't for her missing hand she'd move beside the woman and touch her goose-pimpled thigh. But she knew she'd have to take her time. She could be patient when needed.

Instead, she watched Susie lean forward and place her empty mug on a black, stubby-legged wooden table next to her chair.

Pushing herself up to the edge of the leather, Luana's anger flared at the vibration in her pocket, until she realised only one person had her number. "I've got to go."

Susie's smile dropped. "Call me."

"I'll do one better. I'll come back," Luana said, before standing and heading out of the front door.

34

James

"It's getting complicated," Harris said, sitting back in the driver's seat. "We have an exploding fridge which kills a security guard. An invisible fireball incinerating a PhD student. A building destroyed. Then Cambridge. A hall full of students, and of course, the professor. Could they be connected?"

Knowing she didn't need a reply, Fisher stared out of the windscreen as she spoke again.

"Not to forget the retired fire fighter and the business address. But both of those feel more random. Then there's the death of Wafford's replacement."

"Murder?" Fisher asked, staring over to a large combine harvester as it reeled large swathes of yellow straw into its giant rotating mouth.

"For what purpose?" she said, turning to face him.

"The next big money-making breakthrough in geology?" Fisher said, shrugging.

"I imagine all the big questions are answered by now," she replied.

"Maybe they found a way to predict volcanic eruptions, or earthquakes or something?" Fisher said.

Harris nodded. "Is that geology?" she said.

"I guess," Fisher replied, shrugging again.

"But the old fire fighter. The business units. A plumbers, for goodness' sake? They don't fit."

"No," Fisher agreed, turning away as she pulled out the iPad, his gaze instead falling on split rubbish sacks overflowing with decaying food and plastic spilling across the gravel.

"Sure Plumbing, or Cambridge Recycling," Harris said, reading from the screen.

Fisher turned, his eyebrows raised. "Huh?"

"The two companies in the units. Cambridge Recycling

is a house clearance firm," she said, her brow raising as Fisher followed suit.

"Could it be something else causing the fires?" Fisher said.

"Like something stored in the freezer?" Harris said, biting her top lip. "Or maybe someone is looking for it and covering their tracks. The freezer catches fire, killing the security guard, but the object survives. The PhD student gets hold of it and has it with him when he died."

"Robin Gasper gives it to Bissette," Fisher added.

"She leaves it for lost in the rubble. Somehow, it gets to Wafford and to Cambridge."

"Then a student, who takes it back home and kills their flatmates," Fisher said.

"A fire fighter picks it up from the ashes and gives to an ex-colleague or family member," Harris said, tapping her finger on the screen.

"The sheltered housing," Fisher chipped in with a nod.

"They clear the house and the destruction follows."

"Someone is killing whoever has it? But why?" Fisher said, twisting in his seat. "And still they never get hold of whatever it is."

"Maybe that's not the point," Harris said, staring out of the windscreen.

"What the hell is this thing?" Fisher replied.

"There's only one person alive that might know," Harris said, turning back.

"Bissette," Fisher said, nodding.

Luana

Present

Scribbling the words spoken down the phone, she took a cab back to the sleepy high street. With no interruptions at the chemist this time, she almost broke down when she saw the strip of the deep red pills. A few moments on the level would be a holiday from herself, which was worth so much more than a break from the pain.

The timing was perfect if she wanted to enjoy her new-found friend, although she'd have to wait for now. It was enough to know they were safe in her pocket, as she still needed her edge to complete the most important mission of her life.

The sight of her ride still in the car park snapped her into focus, sending a breath of relief filling her lungs.

She wasn't worried about the metal; it was the contents of the boot that would complicate things. Another reason for holding off on those magic tablets. When she was back to herself, or how she used to be, she knew the guilt might overcome her.

With the streetlights bright as the sky glowed somewhere between night and day, two hours on the road went by the window before she pulled over to let the blue-lit fire engine pass.

35

James

"It's a rock," Fisher said as he cleared the call.

"Of course," Harris said, raising her brow.

"She said her boyfriend always gave her stuff like that. When the department ran out of space for their samples, they'd let students take the surplus. She remembers one particular rock because it was like no other she'd seen. A mixture of two beautiful stones sparkling with life. Her words, and she sounded almost dreamy when she talked about it."

"Where is it now?" Harris said, her brow still raised in hope.

"Destroyed in the fire."

Harris nodded. "But it wasn't."

Fisher mirrored her motion. "There's something about it that keeps it in circulation."

"Wafford could have rescued it from a skip when they were clearing the rubble."

The pair sat in silence, looking out of opposite windows.

"How can a rock cause a fire?" Fisher said, gazing at plumes of dust rising from behind the harvester.

"Radiation perhaps. I'm not sure. We could have the areas tested. There may still be residue," she said, starting the engine. "But it would take time," she added, just as the rear tyres spat gravel as she swung the car through a U-turn.

Luana

Present

Her heart beat against the walls of her chest, despite the supposed depressing effects of the painkillers.

Her gaze followed the silver BMW with the two on board and, winding down the window, she listened as the siren disappeared. Conflicted between playing the long or short game, she stroked the cold metal stowed beside the seat.

As the blue tint of their xenon headlights snapped on, she'd decided and turned the engine over.

36

James

With the sun falling low through the plate-glass window to their left, the crew manager, promoted to station manager in the intervening time, sat opposite the pair. With his frontline now, more often than not, a large wooden desk, his long, noble features and the bulk of his wide shoulders imposed on the room.

"Thank you for seeing us," Harris said, her voice slow and simmering with respect.

His lips moved with the start of an uneasy smile. "No problem. I'm on call. I'd be here anyway," he said, after seeming to consider his words.

"I'll get to the point," she said, leaning forward. "Can you remember a series of fires about six years ago?" The firefighter's brow raised with a question before she'd finished. "They shared certain unusual signatures, and the causes were never found."

"A house full of students," Fisher said, taking over. "And a row of business units on a trading estate, then a sheltered housing block."

The man lifted his chin as if in thought, but kept silent.

"A retired firefighter was amongst the victims," Harris said, breaking the quiet, watching as the man leaned back.

"I remember," he said, but didn't elaborate as he stiffened in his seat.

"We're investigating a potential link with something we're working on," she said, but offered nothing else. "We've read your reports and wanted to ask if it was unusual to leave them without conclusions."

The man's Adam's apple rose, then fell as his eyes narrowed. "What are you investigating?" he said, rearranging himself in his chair.

"I can't say anything other than it's a serious matter," Harris replied, and he nodded, glancing between the two of them before looking at the darkening skies through the window.

"I was under a lot of pressure at home," he finally said, glancing at the pair again. "I didn't get around to it," he added, raising his chin.

"To be clear," Harris said, still leaning forward. "We're not here to damage your career. Whatever you say remains confidential," she added, bunching her cheeks with a smile that didn't reach her eyes.

"So, why *are* you here?"

"We need your insight. We think you were close to figuring it out, but you didn't put it in writing," Fisher said. "We want to know your thoughts."

The fireman's gaze landed on Fisher again and he drew a deep breath through his nose, then looked down at the keyboard as if counting under his breath. The pair let the silence continue unchallenged, watching the confidence drain from his posture, his shoulders slumping before he nodded.

"Off the record?" he said, his voice low. The pair nodded, and he stood, climbing to over six feet tall as he walked from behind the desk to close the door.

"When I first qualified," he said, arriving back at his seat and not raising his voice. "I worked for an American petro-chem as a member of their emergency response team. They trained me on a vast range of chemical fires, the likes of which your average firefighter wouldn't come across in a thirty-year career.

"I've seen fires rage underwater and chemicals that seem to spawn beasts from the deep as they burn."

Fisher looked over at Harris, but found her intent on his words.

"Over the five years, I carried out over a hundred fire investigations across their sites. I saw some nasty stuff. After that I went into the public sector and, because of my background, I would get called in by colleagues for anything unusual."

"Like the first fire?" Harris said, sitting back.

He nodded. "The student house. Hearing what my colleague had to say, I told them to use foam as I rushed to the scene. It still raged as I arrived, and despite the fire being relatively tame, the heat was beyond anything I'd seen since those early days. After the two hours it took to get under control, I talked over my theories with the investigation branch, but they couldn't find any evidence of accelerant or fuel consistent with its chemical presentation."

Fisher's head swayed back and forth as the station commander spoke from across the table.

"I was late on the scene at the second fire because I came with the third pump. Again, I deployed foam, with more success this time, but the damage was already done. I arrived at the same conclusion."

"Why didn't you send this up the chain of command?" Fisher asked.

"I did. In fact, I made a lot of noise at the time." The commander looked around the room as if checking for someone he hadn't seen before. "I was practically shouting from the rooftops after the third fire. In the end, they gave me the chance to put in a formal report."

"But you never submitted a completed version," Harris said, her gaze fixed on his.

The fireman nodded. "I submitted a draft," he said, catching Fisher's look. "It's normal for the brass to review them before publishing."

Fisher nodded and looked over at Harris.

"Off the record, they advised me that with no evidence borne out by the fire investigation team, it would be a death knell in my career. I was due to take my Watch Manager B interview within six months." He looked back down at the desk.

"We're not here to judge," Harris said. "What *was* your first conclusion?" she added, her voice warming as she edged forward in her seat.

Sucking in his bottom lip, the fireman looked back and forth between them.

"Sir, it will be confidential and…" she said, her voice calm. "…And I shouldn't say this, but you'll be saving lives."

Twitching his head to the side, his eyes widened as he leaned back.

"It was hydrogen gas," he said, raising his chin, but as he did, a two-tone alarm lit up the station and he picked himself up from his seat. "Please excuse me for a moment," he said, closing the door behind him.

***

Luana

Present

At the edge of the car park, Luana sat away from the warm orange glow spreading from the streetlights. Parked out of sight by the trimmed lawn, she stared at the silver car as it pulled in beside the entrance, then leaned forward as he pulled suitcases from the boot. They both laughed as if sharing a joke, or so their body language told.

Luana's gaze passed over the blister pack of scarlet pills, and she raised a smile. "Not yet," she said out loud.

With an accuracy that improved each time, she tapped her thumb across the phone's screen and soon scrolled down a list of key staff along with their names and positions within the hotel, each one keen to promote themselves to future employers.

A quick phone call to the reception desk and she knew they were short staffed. With help expected in the next hour, she moved her car to the staff car park around the corner, then it wasn't long before she was following the car of a young woman with angled, eastern European features who rose to the same height and had a close enough body shape.

37

James

"It's highly combustible in an oxygen atmosphere," the station manager said, his eagerness easy to make out despite the background roar of a six-cylinder turbocharged seven point two litre engine emerging from the shuttered appliance bay below. He paused as the wail of a two-tone added to the deep rumble. "It burns with a colourless flame and ferocious heat. It's the same gas in the Hindenburg and the space shuttle's main engines. In the right mixture, a spark, heat or just sunlight would be enough to ignite it."

Still hanging on his words, Fisher interrupted. "And it reacts with water."

Much to Fisher's surprise, the station manager shook his head and raised an eyebrow. "Not particularly. One of the textbook extinguishants is a water spray as it cools the ignited gas."

Fisher's eyes narrowed. "But these fires got worse when they were fought with water."

The station manager nodded. "That was one of two issues with my evaluation. The source of the hydrogen and the fire's reaction to water. I believed that because hydrogen is lighter than air, the lightest of all gases in fact, it collected in ceiling cavities and the powerful water jets displaced those cavities, pushing more fuel into the fire."

Each of them was silent, Fisher imagining the fires as he tried to process the new information. "We're investigating three more fires," he blurted out, shooting a look at Harris to check for an objection, even though it was too late. When he found none, he turned back to the fireman who'd raised his brow.

"The first was in a rarely used confined space so the gas could have collected over a period. A spark from a faulty piece of electrical equipment could have been the ignition source." Fisher turned to Harris as he spoke. "The chip pan fire at

Bissette's flat would have been more than enough to start the blaze, and the lab would have been full of Bunsen burners," Fisher said, then looked across the desk. "Is hydrogen poisonous?"

The fireman shook his head as his thick eyebrows raised further. "But it displaces other molecules in the air, like oxygen, so with the right conditions, you could asphyxiate in an unsealed room."

Fisher swapped a glance with Harris, closing his mouth when he realised it was hanging open. "So where could the hydrogen come from?" he said as he turned back to the fireman.

The station manager held his hands up. "I'm afraid that's where my expertise ends. If it's not in a bottle or a pipeline, I can't help."

The alarm startled Fisher for a second time.

"Guv," came a call as the door sprung open. The station manager turned to the pair as he stood.

"I've got to go. They've called for the second pump. Mary downstairs will show you out." Striding around the desk, he went to move through the door, but turned back.

"There was something else," he said. "There was another shout that sounded similar, but we were called back just as we arrived. The in-house crew dealt with it themselves, but now I think of it, the initial report was so close to the others. As we turned the appliances around, we saw smoke billowing up from deep in the compound."

"Where?" Fisher blurted out as he stood.

"Stamp Pharmaceuticals," the fireman said as he stepped into the corridor and disappeared.

Taking the passenger seat, Fisher stared at the fire station from the car park opposite as sirens sounded off in the background.

"This rock was storing hydrogen," Fisher announced.

"Is that even possible?" Harris replied. Neither of them answered the question. "Either way, it's not terrorism," she said, pulling out her iComm. "We'll have to drop it."

"Straight away?" Fisher asked, turning in his seat. "Just as it's getting interesting."

Harris looked over. "Clark?" she said as the tired voice replaced the ringing tone.

"Yeah."

"Send the next one over. The fires aren't connected."

"Okay. File your report and I'll ping you another," he replied, just as Harris set her gaze on Fisher.

"We'll keep looking into the fires as well. We want to tie up the loose ends."

"There's no need. I'll pass everything back to TVP," Clark replied.

"How's everything panning out?" she asked before he could hang up. With his slow pull of breath, Fisher visualised Clark rubbing his eyes.

"It's not good. We're still missing two aircraft. Which means we're having to go through all their records and flight data to help the airlines find them. I gotta go."

***

Luana

Present

The long-sleeved blouse was just as she needed. Despite being tight over her chest, the fit was good enough. All she had to do was ease out the creases with her palm. The black skirt was a little longer than she'd wanted, but hitched up, it would have the effect she aimed for.

Checking for any out of place bodily fluids before smiling with satisfaction, she winced as she pushed the mannequin's hand against her stump.

38

James

Fisher read from his iComm as the traffic raced past the parked car's window.

"Laurence Chalmers. The alarms triggered when he bought up large quantities of hydrogen peroxide from an American seller on eBay. They also found him buying hydrochloric acid," he said as Harris drove. "Apparently, they're two of three ingredients used to make a rudimentary bomb."

"It's called AP," Harris said as she pushed the start-stop button to shut off the engine. "All he needed was acetone."

"Nail varnish remover?" Fisher replied, looking over.

Harris smiled, raising her eyebrows as she nodded. Fisher read on.

"They placed him on a watch list and passed it onto the security services, but nothing ever came of it."

"I guess we can clear this one up with a visit," Harris said, turning the dial to switch on the lights.

Before long, the pair sat on an aged brown sofa, its arms worn to beige as light poured from a single lamp hanging from the ceiling to bounce off thick curtains, keeping the darkness at bay. Sitting opposite, a young man tilted his head forward, leaving much of his face obscured with jet-black hair draped around both sides. Dressed in a plain white t-shirt and black trousers bleached to beige in patches, he regarded his visitors through narrowed eyes.

Harris pushed on a plastic smile, her slender cheeks bunching as she spoke with a silken veneer to her husky tone. "Mr Chalmers, do you have any idea why we're here?"

The guy grunted as he shrugged. Harris notched up her smile. "Can I ask what your occupation is?"

The man grunted again, his hair moving sideways as he shook his head.

"Do you have any hobbies you can tell me about?" Harris said, watching his pencil-thin eyebrows rise. "Are you a hairdresser? Do you provide manicures? Nail art perhaps, or is it swimming pool maintenance? Do you clean concrete? Perhaps you're an entrepreneur and do a little of each?"

His thin eyebrows fell.

Fisher stood and looked around the room. "Laurence," he said. "I think you should show my colleague a bit more respect."

The man shrugged again as Fisher turned to Harris. "Do you mind?"

With a glance at her watch, she nodded and the guy's shiver was almost imperceptible, with only the swing of his black curved hairline giving any clue as Fisher stepped forward.

"You want to help us because underneath that harsh exterior you're a good guy and a useful citizen," Fisher said.

"Are you ready to help?" Harris asked as Fisher sat back down, and without a word the guy sat up straight, letting his long black hair fall back to uncover creased cheeks and lumpy matted flesh across his face.

"Next," Harris said as Clark picked up the call. "You'll need a half mile cordon and EOD. He's got about a kilo of two-year-old AP in his basement. He's too scared to move it since he gave himself acid burns. Your man will wait in his front garden."

As they walked to the car, they could already hear the sirens in the distance and, with the blues lighting the night's sky, she turned to Fisher.

"What you said to him," she said. "That was creepy. A bit new world order."

Fisher couldn't help but smile as he nodded.

Luana

Present

In the time it took her to prepare, many of the cars had left their spaces and she found a spot where the thick orange light didn't quite breach the fallen darkness. Strolling in through a marked staff entrance, she smelt the extract of flame grilled food as she breezed past the roar of kitchen fans. Her thoughts turned to her once beautiful nurse, reminding her to eat.

Shaking away the interruption, and walking through the almost empty restaurant, none of the couples in close huddles gave her a second look and a barman at the far end didn't halt the cleaning of a glass. Light footing her way through the long corridors, she soon spotted the night maid delivering fresh sheets and didn't pass up the opportunity, relieving her of a pass key which she wouldn't miss until she woke up with a splitting headache.

With her thoughts turning to which of the four hundred doors they waited behind, as the sound of pleasure caught in the air she grinned, hoping she found the pair fucking and she could destroy their world with him inside her.

Arriving at the corner of the wide reception lounge, she found papers spooling from the printer at the desk, beside which a blond guy tapped at a keyboard, double taking in her direction with warm blue eyes responding to her smile.

"Is Julian Rowse around? It's my first shift," she said, arriving at his side. "I'm Laura," she added, thrusting out her chest before offering her only hand.

"I'm Rodan," the young man said, reaching out with a gentle grip. "Mr Rowse is on holiday. He must have forgotten," the young man replied with a smile. "But it's fine," he added, leaning over the counter. "I'm sure I can show you the ropes."

Within five minutes, he lay back on a bed, his trousers around his ankles as she straddled him, but before he reached the point of no return, she shuffled up his chest. The last thing he saw was her grinding on his face, her pleasure turning to his pain when he couldn't breathe, unable to force her away and taking his last breath as pleasure surged up her centre.

Jerking with the sensitivity between her legs, she took a moment before she slumped to the side and pulled her knickers up. Then, with a glowing smile, retraced her steps to the stack of abandoned pages flowing onto the reception floor.

39

James

Looking away from admiring the shadowy candlelit dining room, Fisher smiled as he tipped his glass towards Harris sitting opposite. She returned the gesture.

"What's on your mind?" he asked as she looked away.

"The case," she said, glancing at the bar.

"Which one?" he asked, following her gaze.

"The rock, of course," she said, looking over after a moment.

He nodded. "If rocks have the habit of spewing out dangerous gases, you'd think we'd know about it. At least the university would have protected against it. Those places are health and safety mad these days," he said.

"Anyway, we're not getting anywhere fast. It's an early night for me, and I recommend for you too," Harris said. "I'll be knocking on your door before first light."

Fisher smiled as he stood, following her to the waiting lift, where she pushed the button for the top floor.

"Night cap?" he asked, then added. "Or should I scan for bugs?"

"Sleep," she said, her cheeks dimpling before her expression stiffened. "And stay in your room."

"If you're concerned I'll do something stupid, why don't you bunk down with me? I'll grab the sofa," he said, unable to stop himself from smiling.

"I'm only next door," she said as the lift chimed and opened to the soft lighting of the corridor, where he followed her down its length to the stairs before dropping a level to an identical corridor with so many doors. She unlocked a door a few paces down the hall, then handing him the key as she entered, she held out her palm for him to wait.

"All clear," she said, backing out. "Good night."

He couldn't help but linger as he watched her disappear into the corridor.

Luana

Present

Within ten minutes, she'd found ten occupied rooms booked without reservations. A minute more and she knew five of those checked in at around the right time but, as expected, none to a name she recognised.

One room, a riverside suite with a balcony, was on its own, whilst the other four, two sets of two side by side, were booked only two minutes apart.

Committing the room numbers to memory, the steel blade glinted as she pushed it under a stack of crisp white towels pressed under her arm as she left the floral-smelling laundry behind.

***

James

Wide-eyed, Fisher lay on his back, unable to think of anything but Harris on the other side of the wall, his mind wandering to a future where they could be together. Hoping to carry on the thought, he rolled to his side. Feeling the hard Glock under his pillow, he turned again in search of comfort, but could do nothing as the metal siding appeared, his focus fixed on her curves as she came around the glass.

Thankful when his eyes sprang wide with her touch, he drew a deep breath in the darkness.

After dragging the remote control from the bedside table, he stared through the TV, looking beyond a movie he had vague memories of.

Luana

Present

The middle-aged guy with teenage jet-black hair, supporting the pin-thin woman as they giggled and stumbled along the corridor, paid her no attention as they passed.

Stopping at the first of the numbers in her head, she waited until the slurred voices retreated around a corridor before her gaze found the dim flickers of light from under the door. Standing to the side, she knocked, before resting her hand between the towels as she gripped the cold steel between them.

***

James

His breath rushed as he woke, pushing his hands out against the metal arm before grabbing the Glock by reflex alone and pointing it into the emptiness.

With a deep breath, he slid himself up the bed and, feeling for the stem of the lamp, he clicked the switch. The room stood empty; the door undisturbed and he set the Glock on his lap.

Luana

Present

Her smile grew as she listened to movement on the other side. Her soft call had done the trick, and she tightened her grip on the buried handle. At the sound of padding feet, she pulled the steel to the surface and stepped to the side when, after the chain rattled against the frame, the door opened.

***

James

The rattle at the door shook him for a second time, his hand tightening around the grip as he pulled his head from the pillow.

Freezing, he listened in hope it was his imagination, but it didn't take long to realise the knock was insistent. Hearing the woman's voice, he sat up and stared at the door as his head journeyed from dreamland.

"It's Harris," she said.

Setting the gun aside, he jumped from the bed.

40

Fisher stumbled back as Harris bounded in, pushing the door closed behind her.

"You couldn't sleep either," she said, wrapped in the hotel's dressing gown, her face illuminated by schoolgirl excitement until, spotting him in just black boxer shorts, she looked away.

Feeling somewhere between reality and a dream, he sat back on the bed.

"The same nightmare?" she said, catching his eye. "I thought I heard you."

Fisher gave a shallow nod, watching her brow dip before she stepped forward and reached out for his shoulder. Her touch was enough to bring him into the moment.

"Look at this," she said, pulling her iComm from the robe's pocket. "There was an incident at Luana's hospital."

Fisher squinted at the screen, but she'd moved it before he'd focused.

"I made a few enquiries," Harris continued. "They found a nurse suffocated after Luana disappeared from the hospital. She's the prime suspect."

"Why…?" Fisher said, cutting himself off as he pressed his eyelids together.

"Remember, we don't know who she is. Everything she told us, everything we thought we knew about her, was a lie," Harris said, filling the space.

Fisher slowly nodded. "We already think she'll try to get back to one of *those* places. What else could she be up to?"

"I don't know," Harris replied, her lips pinching together. "But we need to be more careful. She might not know where they are, and maybe she has an axe to grind against you."

"Her hand?" Fisher asked, and Harris nodded.

"And if she's capable of killing someone that was looking after her…" she replied, nodding, knowing she didn't need to finish the sentence. "It's a good job you got different room numbers assigned to our stay tonight, or I might have been more concerned."

"Should we stay in the same room?" Fisher said, glancing at the ruffled covers beside him.

"I'll see you bright and early," she added and headed out of the door.

41

With the first rays of sun spilling over the horseshoe of bungalows in the quiet cul-de-sac, Harris knocked at the gloss-red door. At her side, Fisher glanced at the borders filled with rows of colour, ready to bloom. Looking up when a plump old lady in a floral dressing gown cracked the door open, he reminded himself that appearances meant nothing.

"Shall I?" Fisher asked with a broad smile.

"Next," Harris repeated as the call connected. "We've confirmed she sent the death threat to the MP, but, and I quote, 'they didn't build the bypass, so what's the trouble?' I think we can scrub her off the list."

Standing at the second door of the day, lit by the low morning sun, they were surprised to find it still on its hinges, let alone locked, unlike the communal entrances to the neighbouring three-storey concrete blocks of flats in the less than picturesque part of town. The brown tarnished intercom matched the paint as it flaked from the double doorframe. Fisher pushed at random numbers, missing out one, and within three tries they were inside and knocking at the aged inner-door. With smiles pinned to their faces, they watched the peephole as the spot of light disappeared and the door clicked open a moment later, sending a pungent stench outward.

"David Render?" Harris said to the slow-moving figure who'd appeared through the smoky haze, his frame thin and gangly. If it wasn't for his full height, with his stooped frame, they could have mistaken him for a child. He'd been an adult for three years, according to the comprehensive file they'd just read, but squinting and with dry, leathery wrinkles, he might have been twenty years older.

"Who's asking?" he said in a scratchy voice, as if not exercised in some time.

Harris smiled and stepped to the side, giving the man his first sight of Fisher.

The change was immediate, his demeanour going from a sloth to a cheetah in the blink of a bloodshot eye, his slight frame shooting past Harris like an animal on the plain, jumping down the first group of second floor stairs before the pair turned to give chase.

"Can't we just shoot him?" Fisher shouted, hoping the words would bring a quick end to what he could see unfolding, but as Harris glanced back with a glint in her eye, he knew they had no choice.

Bursting past the front doors, Fisher watched the wraithlike shadow disappear around the building's brickwork, but rounding the corner, all they found were the chain of flats, each a dishevelled carbon copy of where they had just left. A Victorian brick viaduct dissected the landscape two blocks ahead.

Pulling up to a walk, Fisher reached into his pocket, drawing out his iComm before Harris turned to ask. With the icon tapped and the familiar concentric circles radiating out, Fisher pointed to a double set of doors made from wooden slats where, at the base, a black liquor matted dirt to the concrete.

Greeted by the stench of rot, a strained wheeze welcomed them before turning to a coughing fit. They waited on either side of the door, neither ready to venture into the stink. It wasn't long before the door sprang open and the man, green-faced, bolted out.

Harris was ready this time, kicking out her leg and sending the young man sprawling across the ground before he realised what had happened, his understanding only just arriving as she pulled him up with his arms up his back and pressing his cheek against the warmth of the brick wall.

"Playtime's finished for the day," she said, forcing his thin wrist higher up his sweat-soaked t-shirt.

Leaning against the building, Fisher looked him in the eye before patting at the man's tracksuit bottoms and pulling out a tightly bound bag the size of a golf ball. With a shake of his head, he dropped the bag onto the floor.

"Did you set fire to the school in Chatteris?" Harris said, tightening her grip to stifle his struggle. His face contorted, but he kept quiet. "One more chance," she said. "Did you set fire to the school in Chatteris?"

When only distant bird song filled the silence, Fisher leaned close and pressed his thumb and forefinger at the guy's sweaty neck.

"You have nothing to worry about," he said, his voice calm before pulling his hand back and stepping away.

"Did you set fire to the school in Chatteris?" Harris repeated, watching as the guy closed his eyes and the tension fell away from his muscles. "It's not working," she said, looking over her shoulder.

"Let me try something," Fisher said.

"What?" she asked, her brow furrowed with the question.

"I don't know if it will work again," he replied, lifting his chin. "Turn him around."

Harris did as he asked and the man put up no fight, his eyes slits as she pressed against his chest, pushing him against the wall. He didn't flinch as Fisher pressed his palm against the man's shoulder.

Harris took a step to the side, poised to retake her hold as she glanced between Fisher and the man, watching as he pressed his lids together, then taking another step away as Fisher spoke.

"Tell me everything you know about the school fire," he said, his deep voice rumbling in his chest.

The man's eyes sprung wide and he shook his head, the motion slow at first, but building with every moment.

"It got out of control," he said, his expression contorting as if surprised at his own words. "I only meant to set fire to the office."

His head continued to shake from side to side. Fisher pulled back.

"He touched up my sister. Everyone knew he was a paedo, but nothing stuck," the guy said, spit gathering at the corners of his mouth.

"Who?" Harris asked, glancing between his confusion as he rocked his head and at Fisher's concern as he swallowed hard.

"Kilter. He taught at the school," the man replied, barely able to get the words out for the motion of his head. Raising his hands, he pressed his palms against his temples and the movement slowed, then came to a stop. The pair stood in silence, watching the man's eyes narrow as he appeared to look off into the distance.

"Were you alone?" Harris said after a pause.

"Yes," the man replied, his voice strained. "Can you stop the pain?"

The pair swapped looks just as a tone rang in Fisher's head.

Harris nodded and Fisher turned away.

"Hello?" Fisher said, answering the call.

"It's Doctor Finch. I'm sorry you've not been able to get hold of me, but I've been rather busy." The man's voice was loud and brash.

"Doctor Finch," Fisher said, repeating his name for Harris's benefit as he turned to look at her.

"Conference him," she said, raising her eyebrows.

"Hold on two seconds please," Fisher said, before taking the phone from his pocket and turned it to Harris with a shrug.

"Just use speaker phone," she replied, looking between the phone and the man whose face reddened.

With a few taps on the screen, Fisher held the phone out between them.

"Thanks for calling," Fisher said. "We're trying to find more information about the research one of your predecessors was carrying out."

"Ah yes. Prof Waffen. Chapman mentioned something. How can I help?" said the voice from the speaker.

"We need to know more about a rock," he said, looking Harris in the eye. "Well, rocks."

"Enrol," the voice replied with a laugh. "It's never too late to find a new calling."

Fisher forced a chuckle and watched as the kid looked over before his eyes pinched closed with his palms still at his temples.

"It's more to do with storage of gas in rocks. Is that possible?" he said.

"Of course." The answer was immediate. "Certain types of rocks can store large amounts of compressed gas, in the right conditions."

"So they could be a source of fuel?" Fisher asked.

"Yes. Yes," the doctor replied. Fisher nodded. "But it wouldn't last long in the atmosphere."

"How long?" Fisher asked.

Thoughtful noises came from the speaker. "A few months."

Fisher smiled and looked up at Harris.

"A few months. Thank you, Doctor Finch," he replied.

"You have my number. If I can be of any help, please give me a call, or if you want me to send a prospectus," the professor said, laughing as he hung up.

"He's full of shit," the man against the wall said, the pair finding him shaking his head.

"Are you an expert in geology?" Fisher asked, raising his brow.

"No. But I'm also not a gullible numskull. What have you done to me?"

As Harris pushed her hand back to the man's chest, Fisher stared over, then looked at his upturned palms.

"Clark," Harris said. "We need a meat wagon."

Luana

Present

"What happened?" the man said on the other end of the line.

"They're good," Luana replied.

"We know that already. One of them is the best, and the other is much more potent than we've ever imagined," he said.

"Than anyone?" Luana asked, her voice unsure.

"It doesn't matter now. We're calling it off. They're off the case and you should be too. Stand down."

"What the...? I can't just... What am I supposed to do?"

"I don't give a shit. You're dead. Do what dead people do," he snapped.

"You're leaving him out here. What about the plans?" she replied, glancing around.

"We've got an alternative. Your guy's time will come. We've got another."

"I'm not stopping. I'm bringing them in and I want payment."

"What payment?" he said.

"A new hand," Luana spat.

"Stand down. That's the last thing you need," he replied.

"Fuck you," she said, before chucking the phone.

42

James

Waiting in the silence, Fisher looked over the wide table and the bright engineering trade journals providing the only colour in the otherwise dull conference room. It took ten minutes for a procession of three to appear at the door, each dressed in a suit and shaking hands as they gave swift introductions.

The first was whom they'd come to see; a tall engineer in charge the day of the explosion. His hair was too dark for his age, not matching the progressing wrinkles circling his eyes as he sat opposite. Waiting for them to settle, Fisher put the face to the words in the report he'd consumed on the brief journey over.

To his left sat his supervisor, on which they had no information. She could have been older, but didn't try as hard to hide the peppered grey strands matching the two-tone of her sleek-edged designer glasses. Flanking the engineer on the other side sat a lawyer, a short guy with a bulbous nose holding up the bridge of a rounded pair of glasses curving with his features.

"Just to be clear," the lawyer said, his voice high and nasal as he adjusted his glasses. "The Health and Safety Executive's investigation found my client had no liability for the accident. The original police investigation found no evidence of any wrongdoing."

Harris smiled, having told Fisher to expect the lawyer on the way over. "The knack," she'd said, "when faced with such, is to let them get whatever they want to say out of their system."

"We're not here to find fault," Harris replied. "We're here to clarify details for a separate investigation," she added, waving her hand in the air. "It's a paperwork exercise to ensure there's no link to our current case."

Fisher watched the two engineers relax into their seats.

"I'll do what I can," the tall engineer said as he looked

between the two of them. The lawyer's stare fell back on Harris.

"Can you run through the events of the day, please?" Harris said, her voice soft.

The lawyer leaned further forward, his eyes narrowed and lip curled upward. "Those events are already documented in the Police report."

The engineer sat forward. "It's okay. I don't mind," he said, glancing sideways. "The day started like any other. I arrived at seven am and gave the morning toolbox talk."

"Was everyone you expected in attendance?" Harris said as the engineer paused for breath.

"Yes," he replied. "I gathered the ground supervisor and his team and we discussed an issue which I'd solved the evening before."

"What was the problem?" Fisher asked, and the engineer looked over.

"Whilst digging out the foundations, we found geology that wasn't meant to be there."

"What do you mean wasn't meant to be there?" Fisher asked with a tilt of his head.

"Sloppy prep work by the surveyors. It's been there for millions of years, of course, but the surveyor screwed up the searches and gave us a big headache."

"What was the solution?" Fisher replied.

"To use a controlled explosion to blast it out," he said, his words matter-of-fact. "I did the calculations the evening before and confirmed we only needed a small charge. We were fortunate the amount was below the threshold for national permits."

Fisher nodded, his eyes widening with a thought. "How much do you know about rocks?"

"I studied geology for two years at Oxford before I figured out civil engineering would pay the bills," he replied with an open-handed gesture.

Fisher looked at Harris, but she kept her attention on the engineer.

"Then what happened?" Harris asked.

"The team agreed with the solution and confirmed my calculations. My boss, at the time, signed off the permit and the demo specialist arrived within a couple of hours."

"Had you worked with the specialist before?" she said.

"The company. Not the guy," the engineer replied as Harris nodded. "I checked through his paperwork and it was all in order. We cleared the site, and the contractor laid the charges. We were in the middle of nowhere, so there was no one else to inform. As the contractor spooled out his line, the charges went off early. A fragment of rock hit him at the base of his skull and killed him instantly."

The engineer swallowed hard, and he looked down at the table. As Fisher felt a vibration in his pocket, the supervisor spoke.

"No one knows why he'd primed the charge. The correct procedure was to roll out the line to a safe distance, then connect up."

Harris looked at Fisher, then back to the engineer.

"I'm sorry for making you go over this again. I think it's clear there's no connection with our investigation, but we had to check," she said and the engineer looked up, pushing his glasses up his nose before everyone stood.

"Do you mind if we speak in private?" Fisher said, and the engineer looked to his left and right. "It's nothing to do with the case," he added. "But another sensitive matter you might advise on."

The supervisor shrugged, and the lawyer pinched his eyes together until the engineer nodded with a smile. As they left, Fisher drew in close and watched the engineer's eyes grow wider.

"It's nothing to worry about," he said, placing his hand on the man's shoulder.

"Okay," the engineer replied, not hiding his apprehension.

"Can a rock store gas?" Fisher blurted out, and the engineer raised his eyebrows, his mouth curling at the edges.

176

"Absolutely. Many types of rocks have tiny pockets, each storing whatever gas was around at the time they formed," he said, relaxing his stance.

Fisher nodded. "So it's feasible for a melon-sized rock to store enough gas to cause an explosion?" he asked.

"Oh no," the engineer replied, shaking his head. "I'm talking about massive underground ranges. The amount of gas in a square metre would be very small, plus you'd need to drill or otherwise fracture the material to drive out the gas."

Fisher turned to Harris, then back to the engineer, narrowing his eyes as he spoke. "So can rock make gas?"

The engineer shook his head.

43

Clark picked up the phone on the second ring as the smell of greasy food wafted across the car park. Fisher looked longingly as the busy lunch-timers disappeared under the golden arches, only to reappear moments later laden with grease-stained brown bags.

"I'll send another case over. This rate we'll be done by Christmas," Clark said, his voice devoid of any humour.

"We've got information on the university fire case," Harris said.

"Have you found a link?" Clark replied, unease in his tone.

"To the bombings? No," Harris said. "But we need a little help from Technical."

A long pause filled the space, but Fisher knew Clark wouldn't second guess her intuition and eventually his voice came back over the line.

"Ring them direct. I don't want to know anything," Clark replied right before he hung up.

***

Luana

Present

"Hey Susie," Luana said, smiling into the phone.

"Lara. Oh my God. I was hoping you'd call. I didn't think I'd given you my number," Susie replied, followed by a nervous laugh.

"You were in a state. How are you doing?"

"I'm, uh, really great," Susie said, her voice high and excited.

"Can we meet up?" Luana asked.

"Sure," Susie said without a pause.

"Great. I was thinking maybe dinner or something."

"That would be lovely," Susie replied.

"You could bring a friend along if you like," Luana said, her voice soft.

"I know just the person who'd love to meet you," Susie replied.

"Perfect," Luana added. "I'll call you soon."

***

James

"So what did he give us?" Fisher said, sipping from a paper cup as he scanned the trading estate's busy car park.

"This one's a current tip and came direct from the MET's Anti-Terror line," Harris replied, and he saw the interest in her eyes as she blew the steam from her cup, turning away only as a Police car caught his attention pulling up to the drive-through window. Before he knew it, the police officer in the passenger seat met his gaze.

Fisher turned away, still feeling unfounded guilt when he was around a police officer, despite his new line of work.

"The caller said he's a member of the Honourable Fugitives," Harris said and as he turned, he found her waiting as if she knew he'd need an explanation. "They're a group of cast outs from the Outlaws," she added and paused, watching his brows rise. "They're a one-percenter motorcycle gang?" Not seeing any kind of recognition in his face, she spoke again. "An organised crime group. They're sworn enemies of the Hells Angels."

"A one-percenter?" Fisher replied, scrunching his brow.

"A criminal motorcycle gang," Harris said. "They're a

179

law enforcement nightmare in the US."

"What about here?" Fisher asked.

"In 2007, the Outlaws gunned down a Hell's Angel and we're always getting reports of increased activity. It's the same across Europe."

"So are these Honourable Fugitives known to us?" he replied, relaxing his expression.

"They're low level, but yes."

"What was the tip?"

"They approached the wrong person, someone with a conscience, for help with a job," Harris said, scanning the iComm's screen as she ran her finger up the glass.

"What was the job?" Fisher asked. "I'm assuming we're talking a criminal enterprise, not shelf stacking?" he added with a raised brow.

"Crime," Harris replied, glancing up but with no hint of a smile. "They gave no details, but a couple of days after five of their regular guys disappeared off the face of the earth, only to reappear six days later with some story about booking a last-minute holiday and bragging about how they'd each ordered a custom-built ride from the US. One of them looked like he'd been shot in the hand, but he wouldn't say how it happened."

"When was this?" Fisher replied.

"They reappeared a week ago," Harris said, causing his eyebrows to raise.

"What else do we know?"

"A lot, for once. We have names and addresses."

"Can't we use FALCON to find out where they went?" he replied.

"Clark already did. They didn't leave the country, not using their own documents, at least. ANPR shows they didn't travel using their registered vehicles."

"I guess we need to find out where they were two nights ago," Fisher replied as she nodded.

"Let's have a chat with the guy with the lame hand. He should be the easiest to persuade."

Fisher returned her smile.

***

Luana

Present

Her gaze followed as the BMW pulled past the white and blue of the police car before they swung out into the evening traffic, then her view sprung back to the cop in the passenger seat of the panda car. Their eyes locked.

He smiled, but then his mouth fell slack, as she knew it would.

44

James

The squat house sat dark in the fading light, its bulk shouldered either side in the glowing terrace. With no answer to the rap of knuckles, the pair moved to the next only a few streets away where a limp chain hung shackled to a drainpipe, confirming it was the file-noted wife and perhaps the two children burning the night away.

They moved on, no point alerting them. At the next, dark windows of the first floor flat formed a simple conclusion. They were together, and the file told them where to find them.

It was a member's only meeting place. An unassuming door between two shops; a newsagent and a betting office covered in bright signs. Outside, upwards of twenty custom bikes stood angled against the curb. If not for bikes they would have missed it, as only a single brass plaque waited at the door, the letters HF barely visible to advertise what was behind the door.

Parking in a packed municipal car park thirty seconds down the road and on the other side of the street, they turned back to find a man standing at the anonymous entrance, his rotund gut hanging over his jeans and curtained by a tired black leather waistcoat. With a cigarette stabbed below his nose, a long grey beard covered all signs of his mouth.

"Wait there," Harris said as she jumped from the car.

Fisher watched as she went around to the boot, but turned his attention to the street and its pavement dusted with shoppers dragging children from one low-rent shop to another, each of them oblivious to their surroundings.

Squinting along the street, he could barely see the door in the distance and it wasn't long before Harris sat back and pushed a stubby tripod with legs made from a string of ball joints into the base of her iComm. She flexed the legs and sat the mount on the dashboard, manoeuvring the camera to point down the street in the vague direction of their target.

With a few deft clicks, a pristine image of the brass letters came into sharp focus. Pulling the screen's image out with a slide of her fingers, she had the closed door front and centre with the man with the significant heart attack risk nowhere to be seen.

Fisher flicked through the case file on his phone, reviewing the five images of who they sought, each a photo from a different time. Three from driver's licenses, the other two mug shots, but all repeated the same sun wrinkled skin and hair shades of black running to silver framing their faces. The smoker wasn't one of them, although it wasn't easy to tell them apart.

Holding his gaze on Harris's phone, he didn't dare look away, barely blinking in fear of missing something. As he stared, he caught Harris not looking, instead peering the other way.

"Relax," she said, as if reading his mind. "Let the tech do the work," she added just as a shrill bong sounded from the phone and the image bordered in red, freezing a woman with a pushchair on the screen. A moment later, the photo shrunk and moved to the bottom left.

Harris leaned forward, tapped the gorilla glass, selected *Activation Zone* from the menu and drew around the top portion of the door with her finger.

Fisher watched the phone stay silent as a couple walked in and out of the frame. Relaxing back into his seat, the pavement filled with shoppers as the streetlights blinked on as one.

Only then daring to look away, with Harris gazing out of her side window, thoughts formed of what he'd be doing if his life hadn't taken such a sudden change. If Susie hadn't disappeared that night in North Wales.

That life was gone. He no longer hid from who he was. Smiling, he turned to Harris, staring at the back of her flowing strawberry blonde.

He couldn't help but wonder what she was like at the

start of her career. Nothing like him, he knew. Not nervous he was always doing the wrong thing. She'd worked towards her career since she was very young, even though she hadn't known it.

Before he'd met her and started his adventures, he'd barely left the house for fear of his ability causing more suffering. Now he'd learned to relax, and with the backup of the agency, he'd grown in confidence, every day figuring out more of what he could do and how to limit its unintended consequences.

Focusing back out into the street, he watched the thinning flow of the people he was charged with protecting. With the recent attacks and the disruption to the world's air travel still felt around the globe, for once, people like him would be in the front of their minds before they were swallowed up in mundanity again. The way it was meant to be. People needed to be aware of threats, but the security services would be on the losing side if the citizens they protected were in constant fear of someone breaching the barrier.

Cracking a window with a touch at the control, he revelled in a sharp chill across his face.

"Not quite Mumbai weather," he said without turning, but when she didn't reply, he looked over. "Quiet music?" Fisher said and found her soft smile, then clicked on the radio playing eighties pop. "It's my first stakeout."

"Is it everything you expected?" Harris said, her tone neutral.

"And more, thanks to the company," he replied and watched her cheeks bunch as she failed to hide her smile.

"Don't relax too much," she said, nodding back to the street.

Fisher turned to a police car rolling along the road with two officers scouring across their view. As the white of the car disappeared around the end of the road, Fisher's phone vibrated.

"Hey you," Fisher said with the handset to his ear.

"Hey," Susie's voice came back, and he imagined her

bouncing on her heels with excitement.

"What's got into you?" Fisher asked.

"I've met someone," she replied.

"Ah," Fisher said, straightening up in his seat.

"Not like that," Susie said, then paused. "Well, maybe. Anyway, I want you to meet her."

Fisher didn't speak, instead looking over at Harris with a raise of his eyebrows.

"Oh great," Fisher said, hoping she'd not noticed his pause.

"Don't sound so shocked. Anyway, you'll understand when you meet her. Next time you're home, call me. Love you."

"Love you, too," he replied, clearing the call, then sitting in silence as he looked out of the window, unsure how he felt.

"What's up?" Harris asked, turning towards him with concern on her brow.

"Nothing," he replied, shaking his head and regretting the snap in his tone.

"That's not what it sounds like," she said as Fisher angled towards her.

"She was just calling to let me know she'd met someone," he replied, doing his best to consider his words.

"That's a good thing. Isn't it?" she said, raising her brow.

"Yeah, of course. I was just a little surprised it was a girl."

Harris beamed with a smile.

"We're not in the dark ages."

"No. It's not that. I'm not bothered. It was just a shock. She's never shown that sort of interest, apart from the odd drunken dare," he said.

"As long as she's happy," Harris replied as Fisher nodded, still unsure why the news bothered him so much.

Luana

Present

Luana sunk back in her seat as she dry-swallowed from the squat white plastic bottle. Then, drawing a deep breath, she closed her eyes.

As the first ebbs of sleep licked at her consciousness, she forced her eyes wide and sat up, staring through the window across the two rows of parked cars. When she settled on the two dark shapes in the furthest row, she let her breathing settle.

She'd parked nose to nose with a faded yellow VW camper obscuring her from the road. To her right, a low-slung sports car kept out of her view. Dogs and their walkers spotted the vast open grass to her left as adults strolled with kids of all ages, taking in the last fits of the summer despite the pending darkness. Behind her, a last row of cars bounded the park, rolling on into the distance and the escape route she hoped she wouldn't need.

Rolling her tongue around her dry mouth, she took in a sharp breath as pain spiked in her missing fingers, drawing a wave of nausea. Leaning against the steering wheel, she stared across the tarmac.

"What are you watching?" she said to herself. "You're so cold. A kid could have done better."

When her gaze caught on the blue clear plastic on the roof of the white car, she slunk back into her chair.

***

James

"What's with all the cops?" Fisher said as the yellow and blue Battenberg sides of the Range Rover passed across their view.

As if ignoring the question, Harris watched the unmoving door.

"It sounds like Susie's coping now," she said a moment later.

Fisher nodded. "Yeah. She's moved back to her flat with Kate and she still calls me two or three times a day," he replied.

"It's sweet," she said. Fisher heard the smile in her voice.

"Yeah," he said with a sigh.

"You're her hero, remember?"

"I know, but I don't want to be her crutch. I won't always be around."

"Are you going somewhere?" she asked, with no concern in her voice.

"You know what I mean," Fisher replied, turning to the opposite end of the street. "Maybe this new love interest will help."

As he spoke, he watched a young couple cross the road, both with long flowing hair and dressed in American Army cloth jackets from the seventies. The guy clasped his arm around the woman and she carried a beige woollen bag over her shoulder. He was unsurprised when they drove off in a battered yellow camper.

***

Luana

Present

With a high treble, black smoke plumed across her view as the air-cooled engine spluttered to life. A gust of wind cleared the thick air from the faded yellow camper disappearing along the run of shops, leaving behind what felt like a gaping space, exposing her to prying faces.

A wave of nausea closed her eyes, and she pulled a deep breath as she reached out blind for a water bottle in the footwell. Slowly, she opened her eyes, and finding no one peered her way, her breathing slowed. Fighting the urge to puke, she cursed the pharmacy codeine that dulled the pain well enough but inflicted her drowsiness and a sickly pressure that took the edge off her game. With a rush of panic, her gaze settled back on the shadowy forms.

With no idea how long had passed, a wisp of air through the thin gap above the window pinged her eyes wide until they settled on a blue BMW saloon. To the observant, the men dressed in black up front and the heaped black boxes on the dash were as good as fluorescent stripes. Its indicators flashed toward her as a blue Fiesta did the same.

Shuffling up in the seat, her gaze stayed fixed as she leaned down to her left and fingered the cold round of metal between the seat and the dusty console. Finding purchase, she pushed the reassuring weight under the jean of her skirt as the parking space in front filled with the Fiesta, its passenger a stout middle ager with a face thick with dark makeup. They were not a classic profile for a traffic violation.

The cops weren't watching her. Instead, they scoured the view with their momentary stare, catching on all faces except hers. So far, at least. The driver's stance was the same as he pulled the BMW into the car park and followed the lane, passing behind the pair she watched. The cops were out of sight, but soon they would snake around the car park to come behind her, boxing her in, perhaps forcing her to make a choice.

Too soon she saw the BMW in the distance, unimpeded and travelling at a crawl. Squinting, she could just about see the passenger talking, his head swinging from side to side. The driver's scowl fixed ahead, watching someone with a great intensity, and despite her wishful thoughts, she knew it was likely to be her.

With a turn of her head, she kept her gaze fixed. Lifting

her leg, she pulled the warming six-shooter onto her lap. She'd decided they'd be armed, at least with a Taser, and she couldn't give them a chance.

She'd shoot first. A single shot to each in the face. The best way to bypass their protection. She'd made the same shot with a perfect score on the static range, the same too when the target moved. All four shots remaining were for his companion, but she'd have to get in fast. That bitch would be armed and her skills were a match for her own, but without the edge of surprise.

There would be no bullets for Fisher. He'd be armed too, but slow. He had no battle edge. No field experience. A civilian, for all intents. She would have time to use their weapons against him, to run the voltage through his body and take their car.

No.

She'd have to keep the stolen one, unless they had an automatic, but she wouldn't be able to keep it long. They were already calling through the number and she readied for the alarms to ring.

The police car came level with her bumper at her back and then stopped, leaving her with no view inside.

Her grip tightened as she searched in the wing mirror.

45

James

Clearing the call, Harris turned to Fisher. Her gaze trained past him on the door mirror and the rear of the stationary BMW.

"I think someone's looking for us," she said.

Seeing nothing out of place after a quick glance around, Fisher caught her eye.

"Clark just told me a young man was found murdered at the hotel this morning," she said. "That's why there are so many cops around."

Fisher's eyes grew wide, surprised to find the gravity of her words not reflected on her expression. The same couldn't be said for him. "Murdered? By whom?"

"A young brunette with a streak of blonde," she said, looking away from the mirror. "She made no effort to hide from the CCTV and they also found a housekeeper, bound, gagged and locked in a cupboard. She'd been there all night."

"Could they see her hands?" he said, his eyes still wide.

"Yes," Harris replied. "A pharmacist also died in a robbery a few miles away," she added, looking back at the mirror.

"Painkillers and dressings?" he said, turning to his own door mirror as the police BMW drove out of view before leaving the car park.

"Yes."

Fisher watched the car disappear around the road's curve in the distance, but about to speak, a loud tone from the iComm pulled at his attention. As his gaze fell on the image of the door slamming closed, along the bottom edge of the screen were two bearded bikers fixed in time as they stepped through the opening. Reaching over, Harris tapped the screen and the biker's images grew.

"Dave Therman and Andy Leyland. Positive ID," she said, looking at Fisher.

As they turned back to the screen, Harris zoomed the

image out with her fingers before centering on the pair stepping out from the newsagent's door where they stood side by side, each unwrapping the cellophane of a silvered pack of cigarettes. Looking so similar at first glance, each had a portly frame, large coronary bellies and thick black leather waistcoats adorned with badges like overgrown boy scouts.

Their faces were much the same, with full salt and pepper beards combed to a point and long greying hair tied in a ponytail stretching their sun-aged skin tight on their foreheads. The only distinguishing features, apart from the bandaged hand, were Leyland's thick black eyebrows sculpted to points on either side of his face and the dark spots between Thurman's yellowed and missing teeth.

Leyland stood ripping at the rectangular package with his mouth and not the fingers hidden under the weave of the cream bandage. Thurman spoke as he lit his cigarette, then his friend's.

"If only we could hear what they're saying," Fisher said just as Harris reached out and angled the iComm so they filled the screen.

"I can lip read," Harris replied, her gaze intent on the image as they turned away from the camera, their protruding round stomachs replaced by a colourful emblem emblazoned on their backs. The full size embroidery depicted two rising skeletal bat-like wings, each covered in the flag of the George Cross, between which a plate-armoured arm held an ornate staff ending in a twist high.

"Disrespectful bastards," Harris muttered. About to question her outburst, he kept quiet when the camera zoomed out and the frame filled with another pair, both near mirror images of the first, with only the colour, twist and cut of their unkempt beards distinguishing them. He didn't need to check the file to know Stephen Buckley and Marcus Scott had joined the party, leaving only one not in the shot. The image zoomed out as Harris slid her slender finger along the screen, but he was nowhere on the street.

"What now?" Fisher asked, watching the group laugh

as smoke rose from the loose circle.

"We wait," she replied, her eyes slick with a glint. "It's just a shame there are so many witnesses."

***

Luana

Present

She pulled a deep breath as the police BMW slid out of view.

With her heart pounding, each powerful beat thumped at the stump, sparking pain through the absent palm and along the length of each missing digit. Letting go of her breath, she clenched her jaw as nausea lapped at her throat.

The tablet's effects were lessening, shortening the time she was pain free. Taking more helped at first, but the weakness, the nausea, and the unpleasantness in her stomach built over time. The long-term effects on her liver were of no concern. A fresh body waited, but anything that took the edge off her game could be fatal. To her, her prey, or his significant other.

It wasn't long before a new strategy emerged, distracting her from the phantom she couldn't itch. At first, a pinch. A sharp nip on her arm and the relief went on for minutes, but her brain caught on to her trick and it became her armpit, her inner thigh, her breast.

Her head flew back as the tip of the pen jabbed, reeling in the endorphin surge. Soaking in the calm, she looked down at the ink on her thigh mixed with her scarlet flow as a single tear splashed.

Dropping the pen, she covered her eyes as she wept.

Reappearing from her hand, her face clammy, she dry swallowed two more pills with her eyes closed, soon revelling in the rush and sinking into the bliss.

46

James

Concentrating on the screen, Harris bunched her cheeks, shaking her head as the full beards hampered her skills. Reading nothing of use from their lips, it wasn't long before Leyland exchanged a left-handed shake with Buckley and Scott and their expressions turned serious before they broke out of their group, turning their backs to walk in opposite directions.

Without looking away from the screen, Harris twisted to Fisher, the first of a smile budding in the corner of her mouth as she leaned forward to disconnect the tripod and push the iComm into her pocket before she pulled at the door handle.

They were out just as Leyland and Thurman's bulk came into focus along the street, then soon passing by and crossing the road. Harris led Fisher onto the opposite side where they followed a few paces back, listening to the bass of the men's laughter.

"Should we split up?" Fisher whispered.

"You're not ready. And you know that," she said, not looking over.

Pleased with her answer, although he wouldn't admit it if asked, Fisher glanced at the dark clouded sky, then back ahead to where short fence panels and low garden walls replaced the thinning line of shops.

"I think they're heading for Leyland's place," Fisher said, his voice still low.

"Let's leave a bigger gap," Harris replied, reaching out for his wrist to slow him as the footfall thinned and the traffic on the road increased.

Without warning, the pair in leather took a sharp left down another road, forcing Fisher to watch as the traffic between them zipped along. Just as their targets disappeared into a housing estate, a small gap opened and they rushed across to a chorus of horns.

Turning the corner where they were last seen, the pair eased around with hesitation until they spotted the bulk of two figures further along the lane.

"Where are they going?" he said and Harris shook her head before glancing behind.

"Leyland's place is the other way," she replied. "I don't like this."

"Shall we go back and pick up one of the others?"

"They'll be long gone by now. Let's stay with them a bit longer, but the last thing we want is a confrontation. Hang well back and if anything goes down, just do what I say," she said, looking over for the first time.

Fisher nodded and watched as a distant Leyland fished something from his pocket and pushed it to his ear before turning to their right and out of sight. Hurrying their stride, they arrived a moment later to find a long row of garages with tall streetlamps, their glass covers encased in wire mesh, lighting either side of a rough concrete road as their targets turned down a distant corner.

"Do we carry on?" Fisher whispered, leaning close, but when she didn't reply, he watched her looking over her shoulder to survey along the brick-terraced street.

After she nodded, they found themselves along a line of prefabricated garages either side of a wide concrete road. They were identical apart from the myriad of doors types, colours, and states of repair. Some had fallen and exposed rotten junk.

Walking with a quickened pace and with the echo of their footsteps the only sound, arriving halfway along, the grunting pop of engines reverberated from behind.

47

As the engine's growl continued to build behind them, the pair stared ahead at the two leather-clad bikers who'd reappeared from where they'd walked.

"Don't pull your gun unless you're prepared to kill," Harris said, surprising Fisher with her calm tone, before, without debate, she turned and put her back to his.

Fisher glanced behind to find what he'd expected; Buckley and Scott in open-faced helmets sitting astride their low-slung bikes. Turning to face forward, he watched the blank expressions of the bikers they'd followed to the bubble and pop of echoing engines.

Straining, he could make out Leyland to the left, his features drawn as he licked his lips and rolled his tongue around his mouth. Thurman walked to his right, his face red and dowsed in a heavy sweat. With each step, the curl of their lips tightened, their eyes narrowing with intent.

Feeling their aggression radiate, his fear spiked, bringing with it a desire to run, but with the brush of Harris's warmth against his back, the apprehension ebbed. Fisher narrowed his eyes and fought to slow his breath, then raised his right hand, outstretching his palm.

"That's far enough," he said, projecting his voice.

Thurman hesitated, his Doc Martens staying on the ground as his eyebrows twitched. Leyland's pace wavered, but too soon Fisher let out a smile and broke the spell as the sound of the motorbikes grew from behind.

Their bearded faces hardened and their feet pushed on, sending a chill down his spine.

"Not again," he said under his breath and forced his hand out further. "I'm going to kick your asses," he bellowed.

Thurman's shoulders let go of a shiver as Fisher's voice boomed, then a rider-less chopper skidded across the concrete from behind, sending sparks spraying as it smashed a garage door to splinters.

The pair in front glanced at each other before peering

around Fisher when a pained cry called out from a pair of middle-aged smoker's lungs losing their air.

A moment later, the growl of a motorbike flashed by at his right, with the other rider dressed in his emblazoned jacket wobbling past him on his American bike, narrowly missing the two others before he lurched to a stop, pressing hard into the suspension forks. Unsure what to do next, Fisher watched him climb from the bike, letting it fall to the ground before standing beside the other two.

"One down," Harris said, loud enough for them all as her warmth left his back.

With a flash of Thurman's yellowed teeth, the moment passed and, after a glimpse across their line, the trio charged. Scott held his head down, rushing like a bull and aiming the hard round of his helmet square at Fisher's chest whilst the other two sped with fists balled towards Harris. Knowing they'd figured out the bigger threat, Fisher felt a flash of empathy, but it soon passed as he stepped forward, pushing his hand out and calling.

"I'm going to fucking kill you."

When the charging man didn't pull up or lift his head, out of the corner of his eye he saw Harris lower herself into a shallow squat. Despite wanting to see her in action, doling out blows from whatever martial art she'd picked, he instead had no choice but to hope some instinct would surge and save him.

Still with no inspiration, and about to raise his fists, the helmet shoved the wind from his lungs, but stumbling back, Fisher didn't fight the backwards drive. Instead, he pushed down against the back of the helmet, forcing the attacker to slow against his weight. The man's fists flailed either side as Fisher pressed with all he was worth whilst somehow keeping upright. Scott soon stumbled and Fisher didn't relent, increasing the pressure on the back of the helmet until its brim cracked against the concrete.

Not wasting any time, Fisher bundled on the man's back, ignoring the muffled calls as he grabbed Scott's arms and raised them high.

"Stop," Fisher shouted, then with a shudder, the man beneath him went limp.

Glancing at Harris, Fisher caught his breath and the sight of her swiping away blow after blow from the pair pulled away all thoughts of what had just happened. Jumping up and about to turn the man over to check for signs of life, a high-pitched cry grabbed his attention.

Finding it wasn't Harris as he'd feared but the contorted face of Thurman spitting a wad of blood and teeth onto the ground, Fisher backed away, walking in a long curve around to Buckley's side and steering well clear of his partner's defence. When the guy saw him approach, he stepped away from the fight, squaring up to Fisher, who thought he saw resignation somewhere behind his eyes.

"Give up," Fisher called, cocking his head to the side.

"We can't," Buckley replied, the last word stifled as he launched a fist, narrowly missing Fisher's cheek. Sidestepping the blow, Fisher caught a draft of fresh, minty breath that gave him pause enough for a jab to glance against his right shoulder.

Having only ever thrown a single punch in anger when he was fifteen, it felt like he was back in the playground, awkwardly punching the air as he dodged tattooed knuckles.

Stepping to the side, he realised his agile advantage over the man's lumbering weight. Moving out of reach of another blow, he watched Buckley's frustration build as he failed to land another shot. Fisher mirrored his foe and waited, bouncing on his feet from side to side until the next jab came and Fisher pulled back just enough to feel the rush of air as the arm reached its full extent. He ducked back in, not realising the other fist followed and took a weak thump to the shoulder, but sprung his own fist with all he could muster. Connecting with the rough jaw, he let his weight carry through, the mat of wiry hair giving no cushion as the bones in Fisher's hand compressed and the biker's head shot back.

With wide eyes, Buckley shook his head, blinking and

glaring over as if seeing double.

Not waiting for his opponent to settle, Fisher stepped left as the biker's delayed gaze followed. With a step the other way, Fisher leapt forward, landing a second blow and sending him to the floor to join the last guy Harris had toppled.

Glancing over to her steeled expression, she looked down at the fallen men, their forms crumpled in various states, and, raising a brow, she nodded over as their eyes met.

A moment later and Harris had checked on each, placing two in the recovery position and raising Leyland's blood soaked hand in the air to stem the bleeding.

Massaging his aching right hand, Fisher looked down over the shattered nose and the sunken eyes of the last beaten man, his menace transformed to frailty, each of them looking more like grandfathers who'd been beaten and robbed, not hairy street thugs. But he didn't feel bad as he stepped to Buckley who tried to stand.

"Stay down and empty your pockets," Fisher demanded, unsurprised when he complied, pulling out a wallet, a handkerchief and what looked like a rolled up tube with a screw top.

"Gluebags," Harris said, stepping to his side before turning to a noise at the street entrance where they found another leather-clad figure riding slowly towards them, then without warning, he dropped to the ground with the echo of a huge gunshot before darkness sprayed over the garage wall.

***

Luana

Present

Her eyes shot open, filling her view with dull, orange light. Panic thrust her upright before her gaze settled on the deserted grey BMW. Pushing the start button, the compact engine jumped to life as her head twitched either side. Still in a daze, she squealed the tyres around the car park.

It wasn't until she was back on the main road that she saw their backs disappearing around a corner and into a housing estate.

Smiling to herself, she took a deep breath, her stump throbbing as her gaze turned to the digital clock in the middle of the dash. It wouldn't be long before she was due for more painkillers, but now wasn't the time to take off her edge. Since she'd been young, pain had always been an excellent motivator.

Watching the two low-slung bikes follow the pair, her smile grew at the chance to make the strawberry blonde disappear.

48

James

Whipping her Glock out from under her jacket, Harris sidestepped to the garage doors, glaring at the distant road before swinging around.

"Shoot them if they try anything," she called, her expression deadpan before spinning back around, then running along the wall with her aim out past the motionless body in the distance.

Fisher wanted to call her back. He wanted her to wait for the sirens in the distance to get close. Instead, he did as he was told. Grabbing his pistol, he looked at each of the men, scanning across them with the weapon. He found each face pale, their eyes wide in amazement as they lay about the concrete. Scott was the only one not moving.

Laying on his side, Thurman tried to sit up, and with blood dripping down his chin, it was his eyes Fisher caught first. Watching his attention move to the business end of the Glock, the man's head soon lowered before slumping to the blood splattered ground. His fight was over.

Moving to Buckley, the man's eyes watered as, with a bloodied finger, he dabbed at his jaw whilst rolling his tongue inside his mouth. Taking another step, the Glock lowered by Fisher's side, Buckley couldn't have looked more beaten.

"Why did you do it?" Fisher said, breaking the silence before glancing at Harris as she neared the entrance, still hugging the line of garage doors.

"I don't know," Buckley said, wincing through his pain.

"Those you hurt were innocents," Fisher said.

"Nobody died," the man replied, staring at the ground.

"You've seen the news. You were part of something much bigger," Fisher replied, bringing his aim up to the man's forehead.

"We were told to make some noise. That's all," Buckley said, his voice sombre.

"Noise? That's what you call it? Who's in charge?" Fisher said, taking a step forward.

"Someone from the club," the biker replied, looking away. "That's all I know. Honest."

"You're a family man," Fisher replied. "What if someone hurt your kids?"

Buckley's head sagged further. "I don't… I don't know why we went through with it," he said, fighting to be heard above the sirens.

With a glance at the entrance, Fisher drew a sharp breath when Harris was gone.

"Who's in charge?" Fisher bellowed, but when all the man did was shake his head, anger tightened his chest until the squeal of tyres somewhere close caused him to draw a deep breath. Holstering his gun, he knelt, clamping his hands against the sides of Buckley's head, holding him tight as the man squirmed.

"Tell me everything," Fisher demanded through gritted teeth, feeling him shiver, then his whole body shake.

"I don't know," Buckley replied, before howling as if in pain. Fisher pulled away, wiping the blood from his hands down the man's jacket. "I'm sorry," Buckley repeated as the intensity of his shivers increased.

Fisher stepped back to avoid the flick of blood and drool from the guy's mouth.

Catching movement out of the corner of his eyes, he turned to find Thurman getting to his knees. He halted as Fisher looked over.

"I'm sorry," Buckley said again, his voice wet and muffled.

"I'm sorry," came another voice, the words weak. Fisher turned to find Scott staring with dried, clotted blood from his flattened nose, matting his beard like a Halloween mask as tears washed lines down his cheeks. Sobbing, he told him everything.

Luana

Present

Studying the quiet line of brick terraces, she watched from the shadow between the streetlights as a car pulled into a tight space a few doors down.

The headlights soon died and Luana eyed the size ten brunette and her hands straightening the fitted skirt. Fighting the urge, after watching the long legs disappear behind a wooden door, she glanced across the street to the only gap between the terraces and the first of what she guessed were a line of many garage doors. After thumbing the numbers on the phone, a high-pitched male voice answered.

"BT. Can I have your requestor code?"

"Three. Eight. Seven. Six. Two," she said as the pop of a pair of bike engines spoilt the quiet. The voice repeated the numbers against the background of heavy key presses.

"I'm sorry, but that's coming up as an expired number," the voice replied.

Smashing her fist into the open wound on her inner thigh, she clamped her mouth to stifle her cry.

"I'll call back," she said with a tear rolling down her cheek before dialling another number, then watching the bikes disappear between the gap.

"Leicestershire Police. Tigers Lane front desk."

"Hi. This is Joan Peters from the British Telecom Law Enforcement Line. We've issued new requester codes following a breach of security earlier this week. Can you confirm your fax number, please?"

After a pause, the woman read back a series of digits.

"Thank you. We'll issue the new codes in the next twenty-four hours. For our security, can you confirm your current code is two, nine, five, three, eight, one?"

"No," the voice came back before pausing. "It's eight, nine, four, seven, seven, eight."

"Oh yes, sorry, I was reading from the wrong line. I've

authenticated your code. Please continue to use the existing code until you get the replacement."

Without pause, she was on another call and, with the phone pressed between her ear and right shoulder, she scribbled down a number.

"Hello," came Susie's voice.

Luana took a deep breath and pushed on a smile.

"Hello," Susie insisted.

"I can't stop thinking about you," Luana replied, her gaze resting on the bright red pills in the dashboard pocket.

"I was hoping it was you," Susie said, her smile obvious.

"I need to see you."

"I need to see *you*," Susie replied, coy and quiet.

Luana watched a second bike pull up to the garage entrance before the rider drew something long from a dark duffle bag.

"I've got to go. I can't wait to meet your friend too," she said, hanging up the call.

49

James

With Fisher's bumps and bruises checked, the blue light above their white Audi Q7 reflected against the dark streets of Cambridge as they caught up with the convoy, tucking in behind a Battenberg Mercedes Sprinter with darkened windows.

"A member of their club approached them a couple of weeks ago. They'd not met him before, but it wasn't unusual for travelling members to visit," Fisher said as he leaned towards Harris beside him. "One thing led to another and the group met the man at an outward-bound centre in the middle of Wales. The next thing they knew, they were being taught to make bombs."

Harris's brow raised. "One thing led to another?"

Fisher nodded. "His exact words. He didn't remember much about the time between meeting the man and finding themselves in Wales. It's how they all felt. At some point, they agreed to make and plant three devices. They were told where and when, but were given no reason."

"And no one said anything?" Harris asked. "Apart from a bit of petty crime when they were younger, none of these men had any history?"

"None of them thought what they were doing was unusual at the time. It's like they were brainwashed, but without the ideology," Fisher replied. "After more than just their devices went off, they realised they were part of something big, but by then it was too late and were in too deep to go to the police."

Neither of them spoke for a brief moment.

"That shotgun was loaded," Harris eventually said.

Fisher nodded. "Someone's done us a favour," he said as they came to a stop outside an address they'd been at a few hours earlier.

Each of the long convoy's doors flew open as they

ground to a halt, disgorging a sea of anonymous figures and overwhelming the three-bedroom house. With the building cleared of Thurman's startled wife and two kids, Fisher stepped out, soon passing the cordon radiating across the neighbourhood as police officers shed their heavy armour and knocked on doors to clear the street of bleary-eyed neighbours.

The remaining officers soon made way for a corporal and his lance, who carried a heavy tool bag. Both dressed in green, brown and black DPMs as they stood next to Fisher and Harris by the back door. With a simple nod, the pair followed the explosive ordnance disposal team across the short lawn and into the deserted house, glancing either side to confirm the normality they'd been told to expect and were soon out of the back door and under the ever-darkening sky, looking over the wooden workshop bathed in light with tripods set on the grass.

The weathered workshop seemed solid enough. Its long tongue-and-groove sides were almost as wide as both the garden and the house. Lacking windows, the only breaks in the structure were the double doors on the end face, which ran to ground level with a wooden ramp, its grain thick with a line of tyre tracks following the short gap to a gate in an eight-foot fence.

Fisher waited by Harris's side, watching as the two men in fatigues continued onward. After the lance corporal placed the heavy bag on the grass, they tracked the perimeter of the outbuilding, stopping at arm's reach to examine the edges and joins by Maglite. A moment later, the lance stepped to Fisher's side where the three watched as the corporal repeated the search until the spotlight lingered on the door.

"Did you bring the key?" the corporal said, turning to his junior.

Nodding, the lance corporal pulled the bulk of an orange-bodied circular saw from the bag, unclipping the plastic guard and setting it out of the way as the toothy blade glinted in the floodlights. Taking the power tool by the bulk of the battery, the corporal made eye contact with Fisher and he smiled, speaking in a hoarse northern voice.

"Afghan taught us many things. But the number one lesson is don't use the front door if you want to stay in one piece."

With a high-pitched whine, the saw revved to life.

Following the lance's lead, the pair stepped back against the house whilst watching the corporal along the middle of the wooden wall as he made light work to slice out a neat oval. With the shape's outline joined at the bottom, he moved to the side just as the panel fell onto the grass, wafting out the sweet smell of sawn wood. Still holding the smoking saw, the corporal pursed his lips around a cigarette, nodding through the darkened opening as Harris stepped up with Fisher.

Peering in, the lance corporal held out the torch like a relay baton, his cigarette flapping in his mouth as he spoke in a contrasting southern accent.

"Have a squiz if you want, but don't touch anything."

After a glance at Harris, Fisher stepped with light feet beside her as she took the torch and pointed it through the new opening, the beam chasing eerie shadows across the cluttered interior.

At first glance, they saw nothing unusual. Pots and paintbrushes, tools and tubs, tubes and all manner of trinkets lining densely-filled shelves. Then, with a glance over her shoulder, she looked back at the corporal, who nodded as he discarded the charred butt.

Stepping over the sawn edge, she moved into the darkness and Fisher followed, pulling out his iComm. After clearing the list of missed calls, he flicked a finger at the torch icon, then concentrated on the spacious interior.

It soon became clear it was a workshop, not your common garden shed, although the shelves were still crammed with old paint tins. A lawn mower sat upright in the corner and forgotten curiosities waited in unlabelled jars whilst the floor was lined with drums of oil, tubs of liquid in assorted colours and, to the left, a gloss-red tool chest filled the wall from floor to ceiling.

Across half of the opposite side wall, tools hung from hooks and nails, the other half crowded with wooden cabinets. In the centre of the space, a darkened metal platform waited with a hydraulic ram welded to each side and bright-yellow hoses ran under the floor. Gleaming mechanical parts lining an oil soaked bench confirmed it was a biker's haven.

Flicking the wide beam toward the bench, a low mechanical hum drew Fisher's attention. The drone belonged to a gleaming white freezer underneath the oily worktable, but his curiosity soon turned upward to a blowtorch welded to a metal frame with the nozzle pointed high, its rubber hose winding down the front of the unit to a bright-orange propane canister.

Long, thin fluorescent tube lamps hung just above their heads in front of polished metal reflectors focusing their light on the workspace. Following the row of lights, he traced cables to a metal-clad switch near the entrance they should have used. As he stepped towards the switch, a harsh southern voice cracked the air.

"Let me get outside of the exclusion zone before you push that button," the lance corporal said with a smile raised in the corner of his mouth.

"Nah. You're alright," the corporal said through the opening.

Fisher hesitated. "Are you sure?" he said, glancing at Harris for reassurance. The corporal shrugged, then stepped into the workshop and, taking the Maglite, he scanned over the protruding steel conduit.

"It should be fine," he said, grinning back.

Fisher glanced at Harris again and watched her brow raise.

Taking a gulp, he pressed the switch, unable to stopping himself from clamping his eyes shut.

50

Blinking as his pupils contracted from the bright light overhead, Fisher spotted rows of tubes like the one Buckley had pulled from his pocket. Gluebags, Harris had remarked.

Counting ten tubes, each identical, Fisher stepped up for closer inspection. Resting on the width of a thick twist cap, the unbranded tube looked naked without a wrap of colour. Not fearing any trap or menace from the object, he picked up the nearest, knocking its neighbour off balance and sending the entire group scattering across the bench. With a glance at Harris's narrow-eyed scorn, he untwisted the cap and moved the end up to his nose.

"Got you," Harris said, just as Fisher smelt the unmistakable hint of toothpaste. Joining at her side, he searched for what had raised her excitement.

Apart from the oil-soaked workbench, the place was cleaner than his kitchen, and, with more storage than his meagre bachelor pad, it was better equipped. It was only as Harris pointed out a length of steel scaffold tube, its ends cut at oblique angles, resting on the centre of the bench next to a tub of metal bolts that he realised what she'd spotted.

Peering inside what looked like Iron Man's pick and mix, random nuts and bolts, rusty nails, spiralling screws, ball bearings and sharp triangles of browned glass, lined up behind the pole stood a row of multi-coloured glass bottles ranging from dark brown to milky white and transparent. Each bottle, plastered with a brand he'd never seen, had only a little liquid remaining. The labels were white, with different bands of colour around the middle and three bright-red spheres circling a single italic word. *ChemicSLS*.

Turning back through the oval hole in the wall, he pointed at the bottles. "Can we?"

Stubbing out a cigarette on the underside of his boot, the corporal stepped forward and, after a cursory look, moved a hot glue gun to the side before pulling each of the bottles out. Eyebrows raised, he glanced over.

"TNT," Harris said before he could.

"Sulphuric acid and nitric acid," he said, nodding.

With a glance at Fisher, and wearing a faint smile, Harris's mouth straightened when she saw the tube Fisher held.

"That's a serious habit," she said, looking over its spilled companions on the bench.

"It's toothpaste," he said and, taking his hand, she brought it to her nose and frowned.

After calling the details into Clark, who handed the case off to the regional MI5 office whose job it would be to assist the police with sifting the site and following up each of the leads, it was dark by the time they arrived at Harris's car.

Excited and with a sense of hope that by using the same approach they'd find more foot soldiers and perhaps the mastermind for the plot, Clark refused to give them another case until the morning.

In no hurry, they drove from the carpark. It was early evening and soon the sun was nowhere in the sky, the air chilling with every passing moment. The roads were quiet, aside from the strung out line of police vans outside the gang's clubhouse, but with few cars around, they wound their way through the high street, meandering out of the city in silence. It was only as Harris pulled the car into a parking space on the side of the street, then killed the headlights, that Fisher watched her staring through the rear-view mirror.

"What's up?" he asked.

"Sorry?" she said, her tone absent minded.

"What's going on?" Fisher said, twisting toward her in his seat.

"Nothing," she said with a shake of her head before looking away from the mirror and meeting his gaze. "It won't be long before you're off to the Brecons for training."

Fisher nodded.

"And I want to sort this rock out before you go. I hate loose ends."

Fisher turned away, the dip and return of his head

slowing as he peered through the windscreen, reminded of how he'd felt being apart for weeks when undercover with Farid.

"I think the doctor has it," he said, hoping to push the thoughts away.

"Agreed," she said, her blank expression unchanged. "He had opportunity, and he's a fraud, or he lied to us." Not waiting for Fisher's response, she pulled out her phone and dialled a number, its ring soon echoing from the speaker.

"You're supposed to be resting," said a tired Welsh male voice.

"Hello to you too, Caplin," Harris replied in a flat tone to the nighttime cover operator. "I just need a favour."

"Give me a minute." The voice cut out, replaced by Clark's muffled tones.

"I said in the morning," Clark said.

"You know me too well," Harris replied.

"LanfordStamp PLC. Two Grandchester Meadows," Clark said, responding to the unasked question, reeling off a Cambridge postcode before hanging up.

As Harris tapped a note into her handset, Fisher looked back, open-mouthed.

"Huh?"

"The doctor's other employer and his home address," Harris said, still typing.

"And I'm the one with the superpower," Fisher replied with no idea how Clark knew what she'd ask for.

Harris shot him a look like a schoolteacher peering over non-existent glasses, then burst out laughing, her dimples deep in the cheeks. "A superpower," she said, still chuckling to herself. "He just wants the night off."

"So where now?" Fisher said.

Harris looked at her watch. "Let's see if he's home for the night," she replied, before firing up the engine and turning across the road.

Luana

Present

Without slowing, she watched the stationary BMW as she passed. With no junctions in the near distance, she had no choice but to disappear from view. Despite this, she remained calm, telling herself it was a coincidence they'd pulled over. Even if they realised someone followed, they wouldn't know who it was.

She'd made her moves by the book, staying at least three car lengths back and not panicking when she lost them around a corner. Still, they'd spotted their tail, or was it a well-timed precaution?

She knew herself to be an outstanding lone-operator, with no backup on the phone, and no second man behind her. She knew the drawbacks of her methods but also how it played to her strengths, only having to deal with her own ego.

As the road rolled out in front with blackness behind the trees and the rough hedgerows lining either side of the carriageway, spotting a turn she pulled left from the thin traffic, spinning the car in a half circle as the Tarmac became pitted and worn. With her lights off, she watched at the narrow entrance for the low riding grey flash of a BMW, unsure if she'd be able to see it through such a small gap.

Fidgeting for comfort, the pain wouldn't let her settle. She was overdue her next dose, but the moment wasn't right, despite the added ache in her head. She had her reasons for being wary of headaches, but without the pain keeping her alert, and with the dulling effect of the pills, if the sickness didn't overcome her, she'd be asleep in seconds.

After ten minutes, she admitted the night was lost, and with tears welling, she moved the tender stump, searching for any added comfort, then pulled the car onto the main road and passed by where she'd last seen them, screaming as she smashed her head against the door pillar.

51

James

The closed windows were dark with no movement beyond as the pair watched the Victorian three-storey house bathed in streetlight. With no steam escaping the boiler flue jutting out above the sash windows high on the top floor, or any other sign of life, it was the opposite to all its neighbours, where backlit shadows moved behind the curtains.

Harris's iComm soon agreed, showing none of the red dots in the centre screen, until, as she was about to turn off the screen, a faint red dot appeared in the space. Fisher looked up, but seeming unconcerned, Harris didn't pause before pushing the phone back inside her jacket and moving over to the driver's side of her car.

"I should have asked Clark if the doctor lived alone," Harris said, her voice quiet in the car.

"It's a big house," Fisher replied, and she shook her head, her eyebrows lowered.

"He would have said," she replied as if to herself, before moving the car into a space a little way down the street.

After tapping on her phone and flicking her fingers up and down the screen, she pushed it back in her pocket with a satisfied nod. Then taking something unseen from the boot, they strolled back in the house's direction.

As Fisher walked, he looked either side, glancing inside each parked car, then to every house window and door in search of anyone watching or out of place, almost jumping at each passing car before Harris jabbed him in the ribs with her elbow.

"Relax. You're making it look like we're doing something wrong," she said, whilst keeping her attention ahead.

Fighting against the desire to continue searching, when they arrived at the short gate, it felt like the walk had taken forever. Pleased to follow Harris up to the house and out of reach of prying eyes, he made a noise between his lips when he spotted the yellow ADT alarm box high on the side of the wall.

"Monitored alarm," he whispered, only for Harris to turn with a smile.

"It's a dummy box. There's no account for this house," she said, leaving Fisher gawking back and watching her pull on a pair of thin transparent gloves before she set about testing the door's resistance with her palm. With no change in her expression, she pulled what at first looked like a Swiss Army knife from her pocket, the streetlight glinting along the long metal prong as one end pulled free from the body.

As if using the key, she pushed the pick into the lock, aligning the pins in the barrel before the door soon opened, revealing the darkness behind.

Letting go of his breath when the alarm didn't sound, after a step, Fisher turned and pushed to let the latch click home.

***

Luana

Present

With the call placed, she'd set the wheels in motion.

More time would have been ideal, but sooner or later the pain would take her off her game, or she'd take those red tablets and her mind would be changed. She knew her feelings were genuine. She meant the brunette no harm, but her objective was everything, her reminder too constant to pay heed to wanton feelings.

Sitting back in the darkness, her breath slowed as she focused on the pin prick stars glistening through the windscreen, blissful and void of pain. Closing her eyes, she told herself it would be just for a second.

52

James

With the darkness almost total behind the heavy door, and
with dust drying his throat, the wooden floor creaked with
every cautious step in the wake of Harris's shadow. Twitching
his head to every vague shape, he caught the outline of a door
looming to his left.

A dull thud from about their heads sent his eyes wide.
Willing his pupils to adjust, he glanced up a long flight of rising
stairs as he fumbled for his phone. Before he could light the
screen, he felt her hand on his, pushing it away, then following
her glance to the head of the steps, he caught a dark shape
close to the ground, slinking low to the floor before letting
loose a low purr and sauntering away.

Paying it no heed, Harris opened the door. Following
close behind, he squinted at dark shapes in what he guessed
to be a living room. Frustrated at not being able to light the
place up, he paused when he heard the ruffle of her jacket then
screwed up his eyes at a soft metal click. But instead of a bright
light, a wide beam of red brought the corner of the room to
life.

"It preserves night vision, and it's harder to see from
outside," Harris said, her voice so low.

"Huh?" Fisher replied.

"It's something to do with cones and rods. Google the
rest." Hearing the smile in her whisper, he looked over the
soft furniture highlighted scarlet, but finding nothing out of
place, they crept further before the eerie light went out. As she
pushed another door wide, a faint orange glow drifted in
through the large kitchen windows.

Not searching the room, they soon arrived back at the
foot of the stairs and climbed as the snap of the wood under
their weight cracked like thunder filling the silence. Moving
their feet to the edge had little effect and, halfway to the top,
the pair stilled at the bass note of a car door echoing in the

darkness.

Guessing Harris would know the car's make and model from the tone, when she climbed again he was sure it didn't match the doctor's profile and arriving at the first floor, her red light bathed the landing.

Ahead, the stairs continued higher still whilst a short corridor with four doors waited to the right. One door was closed, whilst the others were open and inviting. Following in her wake, a wooden desk dominated the first room, a study glowing orange from the street.

Tracking her beam, his gaze ran over disorderly stacks of notepads beside rock fragments stuck to plastic backing boards. A rabble of books leaned at the side, but he couldn't quite read their worn spines.

Pulling on thin gloves, he squinted at the desk while Harris shone the light around the surrounding clutter. About to pick through the piled notepads, Fisher held still before turning to Harris, her face lit in demonic colours. As their eyes caught and he saw the smile twitch onto her face, he knew she'd heard the same rattle of a lock from below.

***

Luana

Present

The dash lit as she turned the key in the adapted ignition centred above the radio.

Straining, she leaned across herself, thumbing the plastic control until cool air licked at the edges of the misted glass. Staring at the red digits above the ignition, she ground her teeth together, annoyed at the extra hours' sleep, before relaxing back into the seat.

Closing her eyes, she drifted back to that night with

James Fisher, even though it felt like a dream. He'd had her all night long. So tender. So real, along with the delicious ache the morning after.

He'd woken something inside her, surprising herself at what she'd felt. An emotion so deep, never touched until then. Something she'd never got close to before, at least with a man.

Smiling, her thoughts drifted to a sexy blonde she'd shared only a few words with. Not knowing her name, the wave of joy was still crystal clear in her head. That stolen moment in a darkened room.

Her second had been a sultry brunette, and her last real time, a frenzied few minutes of wild abandon before she'd had to leave the place she'd called home. Then came the knot in her stomach and the realisation that what James had done wasn't real.

Her guts felt hollowed out. He'd cheated her. He'd preyed upon her needs. He hadn't asked her permission to push those thoughts inside her head. He'd fucked her all night long. He'd forced himself upon her, at least in her head.

None of it was real. He'd never been inside her. He'd barely touched her, but the memories remained. He'd raped her in the way it mattered.

Staring out as the windscreen cleared, she spotted a halo of light moving across her view, its source hidden behind the tangled hedge separating the loose gravel car park from the crumbling road. Anticipating the arrival, she hoped that if someone would disturb her calm, it would be him.

Sharpening her wits, she looked around. Already feeling the throb of her pulse in her stump, pain licked as she chided herself. She'd driven a mile or so from where she'd lost her prey. Finding a country road snaking its narrow route, she felt hidden out of the way. Dry swallowing a double dose as the engine ground to a stop, it was only then she checked her surroundings.

Dark fields of grass encompassed the car park on three sides beyond the chaotic knots of an unbroken hedge. She heard the babble of a river close by, but with only one way out, she was more concerned about her first mistake. Smashing her fist into her thigh, the welt grew a little larger.

Drawing back, she gritted her teeth, knowing she'd parked in clear view of whoever was coming, when she could have settled either to the left or the right to give a tight angle for any peering eyes glancing across the gravel. Writhing against the second wave, she nodded to no one. Having left her seat belt clipped in, she was prepared to smash her way out. The last option at least, and she'd have to ditch the car, leaving behind the one stroke of luck she'd had since the day she'd left.

The keys had been easy to get, almost given away. It was an automatic transmission and was fitted out with all the useful aids a person with only one hand would need. The disabled badge was the icing on the cake, but as with everything, there was a price to pay. Hers was the smell, and it wasn't strong enough for her to deal with yet.

The sight of the white car pulled her back, the stare of headlights blinding as they paused across her, then eventually moving to linger at her side. The inside of the car lit up with an eerie light, the screen of a mobile phone or other device. It was enough to get a glimpse, and she liked what she saw.

Leaning forward, she flashed her headlights twice.

53

James

Her smile was the least he'd expected. With his own expression wide with horror, he could do nothing but listen as feet pounded, cracking the dry steps. The sound echoed as if just beyond the door.

He watched her disappear into the darkness, leaving behind her faint orange aura before she reached out, gripping his jacket collar and pulling him close around the waist.

Tight against her warmth and in the door's shadow, he held his breath as the house fell silent.

***

Luana

Present

With its tyres crunching the gravel as they rolled, the fluorescent chevrons grew vivid with each flash of her main beam.

Its window hung low as it pulled alongside, and lifting her hand, the dark-clothed officer lit up the interior, raising a confident smile.

***

James

In the dim orange glow, her gentle breath glanced across

Fisher's cheek, not faltering with a sudden crack of dry wood from the corridor. A moment later, she pulled him closer still when the heavy weight against the steps rose above their heads. As a door slammed up high, the floorboards echoing in its wake, her touch fell away. Taking a step back, he stared into her eyes, unable to draw himself away.

About to speak, although saying what he wasn't sure, a thud of bass rattled through the house, soon joined by the scream of drums and a thrash of guitars, the racket enveloping them. Relaxing at the shroud to hide their movements, they both smiled before Fisher turned to the door, stopping only as her hand rested on his shoulder before he could leave.

"Where are you going?" she said as he turned to meet her, yet her words were barely heard despite knowing from her expression she'd shouted.

"But…" Fisher said, glancing high.

"We've still got a job to do," she replied before turning back to the desk.

Knowing the discussion was over, he glanced back to the open door, then shrugged as the red light came on then soon sharpened to a beam of blue sending motes of dust sparking as she lit up the cluttered desk.

After several glances back to the door, Fisher stepped to her side, and he picked through the desk's contents. Moving past piles of student papers scrawled with red ink, he leafed through a stack of books on so many subjects. Most were thin crib guides on geology or similar topics, together with thick hardbacks about far-off places, Antarctica and Australia among them.

Periodicals were at the bottom of the pile. *Oil & Gas. Energy Global* and *Offshore Magazine*. As he moved them to the side, his gloved finger brushed against a sticky note poking out from the glossy pages of the latter, its yellow still vivid in the blue glow. Opening the page, he glimpsed a sculpture of tall, silvered pipes against a bright blue sky, their lengths contorted, spiralling and intertwined. As he read with speed, the light shot away, his gaze following it along the side of the desk. Holding the magazine in his hands as he moved back, angling it against the window, he attempted to capture the orange glow.

"I need light," he said, shouting above the din sending dust from above.

"Hang on," she called back, her attention elsewhere until a beat later, her light came around to illuminate a pile of thin cardboard-jacketed files. Fisher flicked the first open, where his eyes went wide to find a glossy photograph of a beautiful rock. Out of a rounded, dark, inky grey base, long, deep purple crystal shards rose, their edges clean and vicious. At the foot, rounded bubbles of what looked like molten, milky grey rock appeared to float, their rough surface flecked with tiny pin pricks of white that seemed to flicker off the page.

Glancing at Harris, he found her staring too, and only as he turned around did he notice the wider photograph where the rock nestled on a bed of cotton wool resting in a transparent box, which nestled inside a Styrofoam rectangular plastic container.

Pulling out his iComm, he snapped a photo as he continued to stare, until out of the corner of his eye he caught a glint of light from the curve of a glass bottle.

The bottle was like the one he'd seen before, the familiar logo of three bright red balls and a band of deep purple wrapped around its middle. Moving to take a closer look, his foot knocked against something under the table where he found a Styrofoam container, like in the photo.

Wide-eyed, he peered down before grabbing Harris's arm to get her attention. Stooping forward, she reached for the white lid just as they felt the slam of the front door below them.

Luana

Present

A smile swept across her face as the policewoman's eyes sparkled the instant before the window shattered, the deafening echo sending black shadows from their high perches and into the night.

As the body settled, she knew she didn't need to check for a beat.

Resting the smoking cylinder on her lap, she replaced the spent cartridge for another full of lead as her gaze came to rest on the gap in the hedge line. She closed her eyes and listened as the constant trickle of water caught her attention.

A tiny screen flashed in the dark somewhere amongst the mess inside the white Volvo as she opened her eyes.

Feeling heavy as she pulled herself up and into the chill of the night, she found the driver's seat mercifully clear, the body almost clean with just a flap of jagged skin sagging down onto the black of her uniform as it leaned at an awkward angle towards the opposite door.

She remembered a trip they'd taken after a short break to regain her strength from the minor operation. They'd spend days on the desolate moors somewhere west, crammed together in discomfort where he resumed his morning routine, which soon turned to the night as well, or whenever the urge took him. By day they stalked beautiful animals, deer and sometimes livestock. By afternoon, if they were successful, he made her plunge her hands in and slice them apart with a knife. A week of sticky blood and a few perforated guts and she lost her childish unease of the gore, but disgust at the smell never left her.

With her hand through the window, she pulled at the door handle and the central locking released with a snap. Moving around to the boot, she looked over the crammed bags of kit and a tall stack of traffic cones. Soon her rifling hand found what she was looking for and, thumbing the plastic control, the light of millions of candles shot through the plastic lens, basking in a circle of trees in the distance.

Standing on the lettering of the bonnet and with the beacon lighting her path, she soon spotted what she looked for, a short distance across the grass. With her night vision in disarray, she chucked the unlit torch through her open window and squinted towards the light of the radio clipped to the headless torso.

The smell hit her as she leaned through the open door. The thick copper, distinct from any other. Human blood, she would always argue, had its own unique smell, sweeter, richer than any animal's.

He'd always said it was in her mind.

Don't linger on what you've just done. Don't think too deeply about what you are about to do, he would say, not hiding his disappointment. *Get the job done and move on. It smells different because you care.*

But they both knew it wasn't empathy or regret. The tests had confirmed that at an early age. It was more of a morbid fascination that kept each of the deaths in her mind and, after all, wasn't that the reason they singled her out?

Even as she took the earpiece, she thought nothing of the ridged, skin-covered cartilage she pulled it from. Opening the stab-proof vest was a little more gruesome, the blood already congealing, seeping between the zip's plastic teeth, committing her deep into the car before she could reveal the warmth beneath.

With the wire loosened and the Airwave radio retrieved, she was thankful the PIN was still the force default and it hadn't changed since she'd memorised the list. The warmth still radiated as she pushed in the earpiece and clipped the handset to her belt. The bright yellow Taser was next, then came gadget after gadget as she rifled through the rest of the Aladdin's cave. With a single shove, the body toppled to the side, slapping like a slab of meat against a chopping block.

The engine's power pulled them up through the hedge, and yanking the wheel to the right, she opened the door with the car still moving and left it to idle toward its wet resting place.

54

James

With Harris's warm chest pressed against Fisher's back and her breath hot in his ear as they waited back in the nook, they listened in the din to make out what they could of the new arrival. Not daring to peel from their space to seek reassurance from their electronics, Fisher tried to steer his concentration from her touch, and to what he knew he should pay attention to. It was only as a deep shout tore through the racket, sounding on the other side of the door, that his focus went to the voice he recognised.

The music quieted within a few beats, its thump leaving its mark as a door slammed overhead to an exasperated out-pour of breath and the sudden clatter on the desk as something sailed in through the door. Feeling her tense, he imagined her poised to move, her slight motion sending out a thrill.

Realising his lips had turned to a grin, Fisher wasn't sure if it was the danger or her body, but the thought fell away as renewed steps came from the corridor until a door closed and metal slid against metal.

He turned, forgetting for a moment how close they were, his nose only a hair's breadth from her forehead. Moving back as far as their space would allow, despite wanting to do anything but, he pulled himself together, knowing it wasn't the time for anything but getting out of there.

"Toilet," they mouthed together, each nodding as they stepped from their space, and Fisher's gaze followed hers to the Styrofoam box nestled under the desk.

Harris nodded at the white of the cube. He looked over, then took a step forward, treading as light as the dry wood allowed and lifted the featherweight lid, only to find it empty. No rock. No plastic box inside.

Turning to share his disappointment, she was already gone. Light footing it to the threshold, he found her at the top of the steps peering down, her expression reminding him of the ear-splitting creak of wood as they'd climbed. Still, she didn't ponder for long. Faint noise from behind the closed door and the footsteps above to the albeit lower background of metal pouring from the speakers edged them on.

He watched at the top of the steps as she leaned down, planting her hands on the handrails before swinging her body down six steps at a time. Her arms bulged in the thin of her jacket as her aerobics skills played to the full. Between each landing, she pushed her feet to the extremes on either side of the step and, as the muscles relaxed, the wood still gave the tiniest signature of protest. Repeating three times more, she was at the bottom, and holding the front door open to the orange glow, casting a shadow over the stairs. She glared up, expectant towards Fisher as he waited with his arms like jelly.

The toilet flush was his starting gun, and he swung forward, planting his feet to the boards. The protest was louder than he'd hoped, but still nothing compared to what he'd expected. A second leap and a large third and he was at the bottom, but hadn't mimicked Harris's gait as she'd landed and the wood beneath gave in, shouting with what sounded to Fisher like an ear-splitting creak.

Looking at Harris, she held her look only for a second before she turned down the corridor where Fisher's gaze shot to find a middle-aged woman with her eyes wide and holding two white saucers with dainty white cups. The cups slipped as she pushed her hands to her mouth, the scream filling the void.

Luana

Present

Rising steam, the odd ripple of water and the pop of bubbles were the only remains as her car's lights cut through the night and the engine turned over. Sniffing the air, she knew her stump was due for a dressing change, but that wasn't the source of the smell.

Winding down the window, the car crept across the gravel.

55

James

"That's got to be it?" Fisher said, unable to keep the excitement from his voice. Harris nodded, slowing the car to just above the speed limit. "We can check with Bissette in the morning, but I'm right, aren't I?"

"She didn't describe it in detail, but it fits."

"But why was the box empty?" Fisher said, shaking his head.

"Maybe it's for transporting? From where I don't know."

Fisher reached into his pocket and pulled out a pass strung with a black lanyard. Harris double took in his direction when she saw the photo of a man neither had met, but according to the details to the left, it was Doctor Finch, Chief Project Scientist for LanfordStamp PLC.

Harris smiled. "You're learning."

Fisher tried to suppress his smile as she raised her eyebrow. "But he'll realise it's missing in the morning."

***

Luana

Present

The radio chatter was sparse, a slow night for the police and it was clear the cute officer had broken protocol, not notifying anyone before investigating the car park.

Still, Luana had put five miles between them before parking amongst night worker's cars packed long against the metal of a warehouse.

With a glance at her phone, beside the time, she saw nothing. Only Susie and one other had the number, and it wasn't from him she wanted to hear.

At that moment, the radio handset rang loud until she thumbed down the noise. The direct call came and went unanswered. The second too. The third was to all handsets. A colleague reported last sighted two hours ago. A car despatched to wander in her last location, still a few miles from where she lay slumped and submerged.

Luana's head bobbed as a dispatch caught her ear, pulling her upright with a twinge down her right. Two burglars, in itself unsurprising, but the suspects were a man and a redheaded woman, and it happened only seconds before. Throwing the radio from the window, she pressed the throttle to the floor.

56

James

Standing transfixed, their thin reflections stared back from the glass-lined walls where in front of them bright lights washed over a vivid green map of the world. The land masses were unnatural, the coasts angular and pointed as if built from plastic building blocks. Their collective gaze darted to locations pinned with lurid logos, the three balls of ChemicSLS and a loud, fiery red encapsulating the word LanfordStamp.

Fisher's survey trailed from Norway down to South Korea, then over Australia before pausing on the rounded words blotting out Cameroon and over to the East Coast of America, then heading down to Peru where he caught his reflection lingering at the bottom of South America.

He saw his jacket. The badge he'd picked from the doctor's desk hung around his neck. The image of the head, even in the wraithlike reflection, looked nothing like him, but still the security guard had let him sign for a red visitor pass for Harris and he'd waved them in like he'd seen them many times before.

His pocket vibrated, but he let the call go unanswered. A second came in quick succession and he pulled it out to find Susie's face smiling back. Harris shook her head as he looked over.

"It's not a good time," he snapped, his voice hushed but still echoed along the empty corridor.

"Sorry," she said, timid.

"Look. You can't keep on calling me every five minutes. You need to stand on your own feet again, and soon." Silence replied, and he felt a pang of guilt as he waited for her response. He was about to apologise when she spoke.

"I was just calling to invite you to meet my new friend. I'm sorry," she said, and the line went dead.

He looked at Harris, his brow raised.

"You needed to be tough on her," she said, and he drew a deep breath. "But maybe not that tough," she added, watching his shoulders deflate.

A distant noise pulled his attention and, in unison, they turned down the corridor. Passing darkened windows to their left, behind which lights in far off buildings burned, to the right they walked by smoked glass doors, each sign written with a departmental function.

Estates. Fleet. Purchasing. Finance. HR. IT. They found the next opening barred by a plain glass door with words stencilled in the same formal dark writing. *Bunsen Block.* Behind it they found a long corridor, its considerable length well-lit as it guided them to another building.

Before noticing the card reader, Fisher pushed at the handle. It held fast, then the entire door haloed with red as he ran the stolen card through the digital reader. With a look at Harris, who shook her head, they soon found the door to *Aston Block* was the same. As were *Carver* and *Dana.*

Frustrated, they returned to the map.

"Head back to security?" he said, lifting his chin.

"Risky," she replied. "Finch could notice at any minute."

Turning away, she moved along the corridor and he followed, retracing their steps before passing the glass where she rested her hand on the door marked for Finance. As Harris pushed through, she turned with a sly smile. Her expression soon diminished when each door held firm against the downward pull of the handles. After heading back the way they'd come, as she stepped into the glass-lined hall where a bright light shone from the other side of the glass.

Standing still, they spotted a white pickup, its flaring headlights moving away as it turned, instead highlighting a dark clothed passenger with a long black torch sweeping its beam out of the window.

"Stay calm," Harris said, her voice stilted as she moved down the corridor and started towards the tall map, but soon stopped and held the HR door open.

Fisher counted five desks in the average-looking office, four with computers, phones and chairs, each of their surfaces clear of clutter. The last desk held a printer, a fax, and other office clutter. In the time it took to review the detail, Harris had found another locked door, freeing the mechanism before he looked over.

With the light on, he followed her into the windowless cupboard where stationery piled on shelves to the left and five tall metal filing cabinets lined up against the other two walls. Groups of letters labelled each drawer.

Not delaying, Harris pulled at the first cabinet and the draw marked A-C. The lock complained against the slide of her tool but popped open as he knew it would.

Finding a mass of faded green cardboard suspension files hanging either side, each tagged with see-through plastic clips, inside were smaller folders with printed name labels. With her finger as a guide, she scanned the list, slowing at the start of the Bs, then stopping on a name. Turning to Fisher, she raised her brow.

"Interesting." The word slipped from her lips as Fisher leaned in to read the tag.

Stephen Buckley.

Pulling open the file, she found it empty, then sliding her digit to the next, it was in the same state, before moving to the next. All were empty too, and she moved to the adjacent drawer. Those were empty and so were the next three below. The other two cabinets were also sparse apart from the last drawer, which was full of papers for employees from U-Z. She pinched open a file at random and pulled out the bundle of papers for a David Vines. The stack showed details of their progression in the company. A list of their projects, past and present. Their office and home addresses, along with emergency contact and bank details. One detailed a disciplinary.

With Fisher leaning close and scanning the rest of the folders, they found faded sleeves for each of the bikers. All were empty, as were many more.

"They must be digitising the files," Fisher said, his stare fixed on the empty file for Geoffrey Finch.

"Thanks, Sherlock," Harris said, turning away.

The office seemed darker as Fisher stepped past her.

"Where are you going?" she said, but he didn't reply. Instead, she watched him circle around the nearest desk, sitting in front of the computer, his face glowing blue as he turned on the monitor.

"It's locked," he said, staring at the username, *Bernadette Harper*, in the centre of the screen. As he stood, walking around the room, he squinted for detail at the various posters and printed A4 sheets of paper on the walls.

Pausing beside a page by the door, Fisher nodded to himself as he read down the name of emergency contact numbers for the department, drawing back when he couldn't find Bernadette on the short list. Instead, he found three names, each with a senior role, and he turned, walking back to the desk where he sat, his gaze lingering out of the window.

"What are you doing?" Harris said and as he looked over, he spotted a pile of pages in a tray. Wheeling the seat closer to get a better look, he picked up the wad from the plastic holder and found the top sheet was an induction form for an employee who'd started that day. He was in the Estates department. A porter, his details on the same format of form he'd seen Harris pull out of the filing cabinet, and on it was his home telephone number.

Pulling up the page, he found the same underneath. A science intern, then another. Thumbing the pages, they were all the same, and he started from the top again, paying attention to the department listed at the top of the page.

A name soon made his eyes go wide. It was Bernadette's. She'd started the day before and her first project was to digitise the forms, including her own.

Drawing the desk-phone close, he pushed the receiver up to his ear and tapped in the digits from the sheet as he glanced at the wall clock.

"Perfect," he said as he listened to the rings. It took ten

before a woman answered, her voice slow and groggy. With a glance at the form, he confirmed she was only nineteen.

"Hello?"

"Can I speak with Bernadette, please?" Fisher replied, his voice hard-edged.

"Speaking," she said with a question in her tone.

"It's Jake from IT at LS. I've been called from my bed to deal with a network emergency that's threatening to take out the entire system here."

"Oh," she said, her voice high.

"I'm in your office and we've traced the issue to a nasty little virus on your computer," he said, hearing a sharp intake of breath.

"I... Oh... I..." she said, unable to get the words out.

"Don't worry. We'll deal with it, but in order to clean up this mess by the time everyone turns up for work tomorrow, I need your password."

"Sure. No problem," she said, before hurrying out what he'd asked for whilst he tapped out the digits on the keyboard.

"Look," he said as the screen changed. "I know you're new, so I won't mention it to your manager. If you don't hear from us in the morning, no one will ever know."

"Oh thank you. Thank you," she said in a flourish.

Fisher hung up and Harris couldn't help but smile before he went to work with the mouse.

"What?" he said, clicking icons.

"I'm impressed."

Fisher's eyebrows narrowed. "Clark hacks all the time," he said, dismissing her words.

"He'd have me plug something into the machine and he'd remotely install software to smash down the digital walls with the power of one of our supercomputers. It's not the same."

Fisher shook his head. "I just went for the point of least resistance. She's a new employee and at a low level. She wants to be super helpful and doesn't want to cause a company-wide catastrophe. If she's got caller ID, she'll see I'm ringing from her phone, so most people would give over the details."

"Even so. I'm still impressed," she said, perching on the end of a desk. "Have you done this before?"

"A little. With a crowd of friends at uni," he replied, off hand.

"And it was nice what you did at the end," she said.

"There was no point in causing collateral d…" he replied before cutting himself off. "Bingo. Whose file do you want to look at first?"

Patting him on his shoulder, Harris came around the desk and bent closer to the screen and the window of a database application with Fisher scrolling a list of names. When she didn't reply, he clicked on a random name and an electronic copy of the employee's record loomed across the screen. With a click back, he was at the list again and let go of the mouse as Harris moved her hand toward it, watching as she scrolled from the top, before stopping on Stephen Buckley.

"He's a lab technician," she said as they read. Although he worked in B Block, the file showed he wasn't assigned to any project. It didn't take long to find each of the biker's files, confirming they all worked at the company in a low level position. After glancing at the last, she panned down the list and found there were over three thousand active employees.

"Can you grab the database?" she said, and without speaking, Fisher moved the mouse pointer to the bottom right of the screen, running it over a shield icon.

"The ports are secure. I can't override them," he said before scrolling back to the top of the page where, in the top right, he moved to a text box, tapping in a name.

The record for Doctor Geoffrey Finch appeared without delay. The picture was the same as the one on the ID Fisher wore around his neck. Reading on, he'd been at the company for over twenty years and his qualifications were numerous. They started with a university degree in chemistry from Cambridge, then added business qualifications before a second and third degree followed in very specific chemistry and chemical engineering disciplines. Soon after, he achieved a doctorate in chemistry. Then three years ago he got a geology degree from Baker College Online, with another doctorate following two years later.

Fisher glanced at Harris.

"How is this guy holding a head of department's seat in a Cambridge University with a doctorate obtained only two years before?"

Harris didn't reply, still taking in the information. "Scroll down," she said, and Fisher did as asked, surprising them both at the short history of projects. All were about fuel generation from alternative sources, then came a longer list showing where the projects were based. He had an office at each of the seven locations shown on the map in the corridor, plus an eighth. Rothera Research Station, Antarctica. His office in the complex they stood in was in the locked D Block.

"Why is a geologist working on fuel generation?" Fisher said, squinting as he turned around to catch her eye.

"Why did he train to be a geologist when he was doing so well in advanced chemistry?" she replied.

"And why go to all the trouble to get the chair at Cambridge?" Fisher asked as his mind raced for answers.

"The rock," they both said, nodding in unison.

"It all leads to the rock," Harris added.

Fisher nodded. "They must have figured it out, too. Despite everything we've heard so far, it can only mean that somehow this rock is generating hydrogen," Fisher said, rushing out the words.

"That fits with the fires and why they were so difficult to control. I guess they were still trying to understand it. I bet they paid a huge amount for the placement, but the university likely insisted on the doctorate. But do you understand what this all means? Water in. Hydrogen out."

"I think so," Fisher said, the words coming out slowly before he turned back to the computer and slid the mouse to the active project and clicking on the first where a list of staff and locations filled the screen. Scrolling down, the list stopped at twenty-one names. The two at the bottom were greyed out in italic font.

"Why is he familiar?" Fisher said, pointing at the last name.

"Johannas Hall. You were supposed to arrest him in Australia," Harris said.

"Shit," he replied and clicked the record before a near replica of the photo from the Interpol file jumped onto the screen. He stared into the sullen blue eyes of the dead man.

"Scroll up," Harris said without warning, her hand moving to the mouse. He let go, and she took control, the screen sliding up, the pointer circling the list of offices. "Bergen."

"That was the place he burnt down," Fisher said and Harris nodded.

"Maybe it was an accident if he had the rock?" she replied, looking over.

"But he ran," Fisher replied and Harris furrowed her brow.

"And they wanted him back," she said.

"Or something he had."

"The rock?" she said, tilting her head.

"The laptop?" they both added.

***

Luana

Present

"So they're off the case?" Luana said into the phone.

Her view, framed by the car door, was of a long street-lit road, rolling down to an illuminated security check point with red and white barriers crossing the tarmac. To its side, a sign announced *LanfordStamp PLC, Cambridge Unit* in blue and green letters with the backdrop of a mass of low-rise buildings. Behind that, a jumble of fat metal pipes twisted and turned into towering metal-sided warehouses, before rising to thin cooling towers pumping vast white vapour into the sky.

"Do you know what time it is?" Zio said, not hiding his frustration. Luana looked at the clock in the centre of her dashboard and her smile grew.

"Do you want to know where I am?" she replied without answering his question.

"Let's not play games."

"I followed them home. I'm outside Facility Four," she said, smiling.

The line went dead, then it rang and she didn't wait to answer. Rather than the bark of orders, a woman's sobs melted her heart.

***

James

"Who has the laptop?" Fisher said, looking up from the screen.

"Interpol, or the AFP. But perhaps ASIO kept it because of the murder?" Harris replied.

"Huh?"

"Australian Federal Police and Security Intelligence Organisation. Like Five here," she said, looking out of the window.

"So we can get it?" he replied. Harris nodded, but as the lights sprung on, she dropped to the floor, dragging Fisher off his chair by his arm.

Squinting in the bright light when Harris let go, he followed her crawl toward the window.

"What the fuck?" he said, but Harris didn't reply as she tentatively raised her head above the sill. After a few seconds of hovering, she dropped down, turning his way with the bark of a pack of dogs in the distance.

"The whole place is lit up like it's midday with fluorescent jackets running all over the place, and loads more trucks," she said, only catching his eye for a moment before glancing toward the door.

"For us?" Fisher asked, following her look.

"Do you know of anyone else who's broken in tonight?" she said as she turned back. Fisher shook his head even though she was already crawling toward the door. Following, they stood as they reached the bright hallway and walked toward the main corridor.

"Shit," she said under her breath, peering out through the door glass to the thoroughfare as a flash of bright yellow passed by.

Reaching inside his jacket, Harris touched his arm. "They won't be armed."

Holding still for a moment, he told himself to relax. "Why don't we just hand ourselves in? I'm sure I can convince them to let us go," he said.

"There are too many people involved. It won't work," she replied without looking back.

"What are they going to do if they find us? Call the police? You can get us out in minutes," Fisher said, and she looked back, her face pinched in a scowl.

"I don't get caught," she said, just as her expression relaxed. "Besides, who says they'll play fair?"

Fisher peered forward, ducking a little when another spray of colour passed along his quick view of the corridor. "We need another way."

Harris shook her head. "Apart from smashing a window, there's no other way. They've already checked the corridor, so it should be a while before they come again," Harris said, her hand already turning the handle as the unmistakable clap of a gunshot punctuated her words.

With her hand rushing inside her jacket, Harris pulled out her Glock, edging into the corridor.

"A revolver," she whispered. "And close too. They may not be here for us after all."

"Then who?" Fisher said, gripping his pistol as he stepped to follow.

"Her," Harris replied, not holding back her volume as she looked at the figure standing further down the corridor.

57

"Surprise," came Luana's voice, her tone as light as if she'd just spotted the pair on a Sunday afternoon stroll.

Fisher twisted to the greeting, his gaze falling on her curves and the long thin barrel of a six shooter raised above her head, her other arm held at her side.

"Put the gun down," Harris said, not lifting her gun despite the light tap of Luana's feet as she stepped toward them.

"Oh, this," Luana said, rolling her wrist as Fisher made out more of her detail with every step. Opening her mouth about to speak, she hesitated as heavy footsteps echoed in the distance. Lowering the gun, she pushed its bulk into the band of her skirt, beaming with a smile.

Fisher's breathing quickened.

"Hi James," she said, smiling over with an edge to her voice. Her eyes were a little red, but still their sparkle drew him in and he took little notice of her pale, gaunt complexion.

"How are you?" he replied, his voice soft, and he loosened the grip on his gun.

Her smile dropped, but flickered back. "As well as you'd expect. Thank you for asking," she replied, then turned to Harris. "Do you want to get out of here? I know a back door."

"How?" Harris said, the confusion in her tone unfamiliar to Fisher.

"A misspent youth," Luana replied.

"What are you doing here?" Harris said, stepping toward her with care as Fisher followed. "Were you following us?"

Luana sneered as she dipped her head. "I thought you'd seen me. I came to help. This place is better protected than you know. It's a good job you didn't get into one of those blocks," she said, raising her brow.

"Why are you helping us?" Harris said, glancing to make sure Fisher stayed with her.

"I'd save the questions for the car, I think," she replied, shifting her gaze though the window as a bright beam swept from outside.

"Give me the weapon," Harris said, reaching out whilst raising her own a few degrees.

"Don't you trust me?" Luana said, pressing her hand to her chest.

"We've seen your trail," Harris replied, and Luana couldn't help but smile.

"You're good. Anyway, I don't need it now. We're together," she said, pushing her hand to her back as both Harris and Fisher raised theirs towards her.

"Oh James. Don't hurt my feelings," Luana said, taking the gun by the long barrel and bending to place it by her feet. As she stepped back, the other two moved forward, Harris taking the lead. Pushing away her Glock, she picked up the weapon and slid the chamber out, the brass tinkling as they fell into her pocket.

"Turn around," Harris said, watching as Luana sighed, her shoulders sinking before she did a pirouette. Harris turned, locking eyes with Fisher for what felt like a long time. "Where now?" she eventually said, stowing the revolver inside her jacket as if they'd come to a silent agreement.

Without further word Luana turned around and headed back the way she came. Glancing at each other, they followed and after a few steps, Fisher pushed away his gun. Arriving at an unmarked grey door, Luana looked over her shoulder, motioning towards it.

"Can you do the honours? It's a little heavy," she said, stepping to the side.

Harris took the lead and turned the round handle, hefting it open with her shoulder before she checked across the view. The smell of propellent stuck in Fisher's nose as he followed the procession into the dull light of a short concrete hallway. Searching, he scoured every corner, despite being unsure what he was looking for.

He found that the landing soon turned down concrete

steps, the raw grey walls opening out into a brighter passageway, its floor clean and painted dark red. Turning back, he was surprised to find she hadn't forced the lock and the card reader continued to blink with a faint green light, rather than hanging off by its wires.

Hurrying to catch up, at each turn, he expected a trap, or an accomplice lurking with a raised weapon, but none appeared. No one pounced from a hidden nook. Instead, they soon arrived at a set of steps and a door, which Luana climbed up and moved her hand toward her pocket.

"Slowly," Harris said at her side.

Luana did as she was told, taking care as she pulled out a white card. The door opened after a single swipe where the floodlit glory of a car park bathed them in light. Rows of towering lorries parked side by side and, after rushing between their ranks, the light haloed against the bulk of the trucks. At the end of the long line of HGVs, Fisher counted ten identical white Ford Mondeos in a neat line. Luana led them to the first. As if knowing the door was unlocked, she pulled at the handle of the passenger side before grabbing at the sun visor for the keys to fall.

"Who does that?" Fisher said, lowering his brow as he turned to Harris.

"It's a pool car," Luana said. "Take it or leave it. But if you're coming, then one of you should drive," she added, waving her stump in the air, for the first time bringing it to their attention.

Swapping a glance with Harris before he climbed into the driver's seat, he was still surprised when the engine came to life with a turn of the key. Harris settled behind him as he meandered the car around the driveways with the campus lit from tall floodlights. It wasn't long before, turning a corner, they met a pickup waiting at a junction. Too busy staring at the big guys in the cab, it took him a moment to realise it was his right of way.

"Move it," said Harris from behind and pulling up the clutch, he nearly stalled as he moved away from the line whilst forcing his attention to a tall, closed gate blocking the road ahead.

With a glance in his mirror, he saw the pickup follow a short distance behind and, without moving his head, Fisher stared through the mirror. The men's expressions were blank as he pulled up to the white gates striped with red lines and a round stop sign in the middle.

Luana leaned over herself with the card and Fisher took it before examining a reader outside the door of the gatehouse. Yanking at the manual window winder, it lowered at a frustrating pace before he pushed his hand out and realised he was too far away.

The pickup stopped behind and Fisher's gaze lingered in the mirror where they looked straight at him. The guy on the right held a radio at this mouth.

With his heart pounding, he opened the door and leaned out, pushing the card up to the reader, but nothing happened.

"Slide it," Luana said, and Fisher looked back into the car. "Slide it," she repeated, motioning with her stump. "On the outer edge."

Pushing his arm out again, the card caught the edge of the reader and he slid it down the side. Still, nothing happened. The door of the pickup opened, and he moved the card again.

The guard strode over when the gate remained closed.

58

As the guard drew bigger in the side mirror with each step, sliding the card down the reader, it slipped from Fisher's fingers. With his heart in his mouth, he glanced from the reflection to the sound of a metal groan where he found the gates parting in the middle. Looking back, the guard was almost in reach and, with his hand moving under his jacket, Fisher stomped on the accelerator and sent the car surging through the widening gap. The wing mirror thumped against the gate as they headed into the night.

The campus detail soon faded into a distant dome of light, and as he listened to Harris's directions, he glanced over his shoulder to the passenger seat where Luana cradled the soiled bandages. After arriving in the quiet residential street where they'd left the BMW under the full bloom of a streetlamp, less than a minute later he was driving the German car with Harris beside Luana in the back and the child locks set.

"Take me to my car," Luana said, her voice cutting through the low hum of the engine. Looking in the mirror, Harris peered back before her hazel eyes turned to the other woman's raised stump. "It kicks ass if I don't dose up."

Reminded of her screams as Miller sawed, he watched Harris nod her instruction.

After driving by to confirm all was clear, Harris took the keys from Luana's pocket and threw them at Fisher.

"There's a white plastic bag in the boot," Luana said, looking at him with sunken brown eyes.

Unzipping his bomber jacket, he walked around the blue Ford Focus, his gaze landing on the disabled badge resting open on the dash. Peering in through the windows, he saw no obvious traps and no one lurking under the window line, ready to pounce. Standing to the side of the car's rear, he pressed the fob's lower button and the boot lid popped with a clunk.

When no one jumped out and no gun shots ruined the

still of the night, he pulled up the metal. Gasping, he staggered back.

Regaining his composure after a moment, he glanced at Harris, but he knew he couldn't look away forever.

The pungent stench and gaunt, frail skin told him the man couldn't be saved. Reassuring himself that there was no danger, Fisher stepped forward, taking the carrier back resting on the man's lone, liver-spotted hand, then shut the smell away as he pulled the boot lid closed and wiped his prints clean with his jacket.

"Sorry. He came with the car," Luana said with a smile, as if she'd used the last of the milk. Fisher looked at Harris and knew he didn't need to make it any clearer.

"Where now?" he asked just as he finished checking through the white carrier bag, finding a bottle of white pills, a single blister pack with two red tablets and a pen, its end clotted with scarlet.

"We're heading the same way," Luana said, taking the offered bag.

"Sorry?" Fisher said, squinting at her.

"No need to apologise. We're both after the same thing," she replied, delving through the bag.

"What are you talking about?" he said, after a deep breath.

"You're looking for her, aren't you?" Luana said, but neither of them replied. "I know you are, because that's what I'd do. She'll probably be where I'm going."

"Where's that?" Harris said.

"The farms," she replied.

"The farms?" Fisher asked, still squinting. Luana nodded as she opened her mouth and pushed two pills in.

"You must have worked out what they're doing?"

His expression dropped, unsure about any of what she was saying. Did she mean the place they'd destroyed in Chile? Had she just confirmed what he suspected? If she had, was it the liquid that saved Harris's life they were farming?

"What are *you* going there for?" Fisher said, staring at

Luana.

As she waved her stump in the air, he caught the sickly aroma of decay.

"Head to Cambridge town centre," Harris said. "There's somewhere we can use."

"What about me?" Luana said, like butter wouldn't melt.

"You're coming with us," Harris replied, her tone business like. Luana smiled as Fisher pulled the car out on to the main road.

"Am I under arrest?"

"We're not the police," Harris replied, deadpan. "But they'll want to talk to you soon."

"You don't treat a friend like that," she said, looking at the pair.

"You're a wanted criminal," Harris replied, watching the road. "For two counts of murder that we know of."

"Three if you include the guy in the back of her car," Fisher added.

Harris sighed and Luana leaned towards him.

"Four, if you count the biker with his brains up the wall."

"That was you?" Fisher said, his attention switching between the dark road and the mirror.

"Remember, she's a liar," Harris said, taking a deep breath. "She's not what you think."

"Who did you shoot at back at the facility?" Fisher added.

"No one. It was just a warning," she replied, looking away as Fisher and Harris swapped glances.

"I may not be your sister," she said, rubbing her temple. "But we go way back." As she finished talking, she fished inside the white bag.

"Tell me everything," Fisher said in the mirror. "Please," he added, his tone softening.

"Now, where would that get us? You'd get all emotional and that wouldn't do." She dry swallowed two more white pills and slunk back into the leather, closing her eyes. A few moments passed before she spoke. "Anyway, why should I? If you're turning me in when I've helped you twice already." Luana looked down at the bottle of pills before turning to Harris. "Do you want some?"

Fisher watched as Harris turned away, then he looked back at Luana, unable to stop staring as she forced her breathing to slow.

"Remember, we have mutual goals," Luana said after a moment.

"What's your goal?" Fisher said, his tone low. She waved her stump in the air.

"To do what *you* should have done."

Fisher looked back at the road. "What's that got to do with LanfordStamp?"

Harris watched, her brow furrowing. "Don't talk to her until we get her secure," she said with a shake of her head.

A smile grew on Luana's face. Fisher already knew that wouldn't happen.

"Look, I'll jump first. I'm talking about finding those facilities, popping one open and juicing one of our friends so I can get my hand back. I guess you two are trying to find mummy. Am I right?"

"No," Harris shot back.

"No," Fisher agreed. "But we are looking for the same places."

"Fisher," Harris snapped.

After her sharp word, they drove in silence through the quiet streets before a red set of traffic lights bathed the inside of the car. Luana took a deep breath, exhaling before speaking.

"Did I tell you about my new friend?"

Fisher's eyes met hers in the rectangle of the mirror before he turned back to the road.

"She's an actress. Low rent at the moment, but there's promise," she said with a thin smile.

Feeling his heart pick up pace, he concentrated on the empty road.

"Only the other day she was telling me she's been through some tough stuff," Luana added.

Fisher looked at the mirror as a car moved up behind them. Biting his lip, he searched through their conversations, trying to recall if he'd mentioned Susie to this woman.

"I told her I'd help her out with a trip to clear her head. It seems like her friends have deserted her."

When the traffic light shone green, an image of Luana's topless body sprung into his mind. Back in Farid's flat, they'd talked for hours. He remembered opening up, telling her about Susie. The image shattered with a horn bellowing from behind. The engine revved as its tyres screeched, billowing smoke as it pulled past. The light went back to red as it raced off into the distant darkness.

Paying no regard, Fisher pulled out his iComm and his heart sank when he found the screen was blank.

No messages. No voicemails. No missed calls.

He tapped in her number from memory, her picture appearing as he completed the string. Her voice came back at his ear. She hadn't changed her voicemail since she'd returned from captivity in Barbados. He knew the message off by heart. He'd listened to it every few hours for comfort as he raced around the world to get her back. Which he did, but could she be gone again, this time because of him?

He pulled open his door just as Harris did the same with hers, her slight frame already blocking his path to their passenger.

"She's messing with you," Harris said, her voice raised as she held onto the arms of his coat. "We'd know already if she'd gone missing."

Not hearing her words, his anger built as their last conversation filled his head. He'd shouted at her. He'd told her not to call. She'd hung up without her usual sign off.

"Don't think about it," Harris said, shaking his arms. "Get in the car and we'll get her processed. Do it the right way this time."

Stopping his struggle, Harris released his arms, and he

turned to head back to his door, but as she moved away, he walked around the car, his breathing strained. The image of Harris shaking her head hardly registered and all he saw were his hands pulling open the passenger door and Luana's wince as he drew her down to the tarmac.

"She's fine," Luana said, straining against his hands wrapped around her neck. Feeling pain sear at his left temple, he staggered backward to find Harris looming over Luana, her hand curled in a fist.

Incredulous at her blow, he rose ready for a battle, but as he reached full height, the rage had drained, shock filling the space.

Instead, he peered down at Luana. Her skirt had ridden up to her white knickers, but his gaze didn't get that far, instead lingering on the weeping wounds near the space between her legs, a hole matching a blood clogged pen he'd found in the plastic bag he'd retrieved.

Catching her eye, he remembered the same look of vulnerability she'd worn at Farid's apartment, the face that made him choose her over all of those other beautiful people. The expression that had almost made him lose control.

As the tension receded with the pain, he walked to the driver's door and collapsed onto the seat. Without speaking, Harris helped Luana back into the car. Slamming her door, Fisher pulled through the red light.

"What do you want?" he said, his breathing hard as he threw the car around the streets of Cambridge, slamming to stop at the barrier arm of an anonymous concrete building.

"Just to be part of the team until I get this sorted out," she replied, sincerity dripping from her features, the pain obvious as she lifted her stump from her lap. Fisher let a deep sigh escape. "Look, I'm not a monster," she paused, peering down at the bag. "With the right medication, at least."

Through the barrier, he pulled the car into the only space by a set of metal double doors and he turned in his seat, his glance landing first on Harris, then on Luana's expression full of wanting and strain. To him, at least she seemed incapable of anything bad, even though she'd admit this was far from reality. Feeling as if he felt her truth, he looked at Harris, realising she hadn't got out and was looking right back. He turned to Luana. Harris did the same.

"Where are these farms?" Harris said before he could.

"I don't know," Luana replied, her brow knotting for a moment.

"What *do* you know?" Harris replied as she twisted towards her.

"A little. Are we staying in here?" Luana replied.

"Everything changes when we step onto the tarmac. We need to know how we're dealing with this first," Harris said, staring at Luana.

"And you want to know if I'm worth the risk."

They both nodded.

"Why do you know your way around LS?" Fisher asked.

"I was brought up there," Luana replied.

"It's a chemical factory," Harris replied.

Luana shook her head. "It's not just a factory. It's a research lab and a huge office complex. There are houses for the staff. It's more like a small town than anything else."

"So your parents were scientists?" Harris asked.

"I'm an orphan."

"I'm sorry," Harris said.

"Don't be. I'm not. I had a great upbringing and when I grew up, they gave me a job," Luana said, lifting her chin.

"What did you do?" Fisher asked.

Luana's face twisted, as if struggling to form the right words.

"I was a sort of security guard," she eventually replied.

Fisher's eyes narrowed. "So why were you in Farid's apartment? Why Chile?"

"For you. I thought you knew," Luana said, moving her head to the side. Fisher's eyes narrowed further still. "They trained me in procurement."

"They sent you to procure me?" Fisher asked, and

Luana nodded. "For whom?"

"I never knew," she replied.

Fisher glanced at Harris, who looked at Luana.

"Is that still your job?" he said, and she shook her head before Harris spoke.

"Why won't they give you back your hand?" she said, glancing at the stump.

"They think I'm dead," Luana replied.

"In Chile," Fisher stated, and she nodded.

"Why don't you tell them you're not dead," Harris added.

"I tried, but my mentor doesn't want to know. He said I've failed."

Harris looked at Fisher as he raised his eyebrows. "Failed?" she said.

"You're still here, and of course there's the thermobaric missile. It counted against me, apparently," Luana replied, raising her eyebrows.

"Tell someone else," Harris said.

"I don't know anyone else," Luana replied with a shake of her head.

The three sat in silence, exchanging glances, and it was Luana who broke the silence.

"See. We're all on the same side."

Fisher turned and stared through the windscreen at the car park packed with vehicles, but his mind soon filled with thoughts of that place and the photo of the family wedding, then drifted to Harris's wound healing as he poured the liquid.

"How do we find what we want?" he said, turning in his seat and looking at Harris, but still seeing Luana's blooming smile as she spoke.

"You were close," she said.

"Where?"

"Moments ago," Luana replied.

"LS?" he asked, still looking at Harris, but registering Luana's nod.

"I think we've burnt our bridges," he replied.

"I can get you back in," Luana said, her brow raised.

"Why would you?" Fisher asked, looking at each of them.

"We're a team now. Right?"

59

"This better be good," said the projected image of Franklin's bark-rough face as they opened the door of the conference room deep in the bowels of the Cambridge building. His features sagged with fatigue as his gaze bored through the lens. Gone was the grandfatherly persona that had sat opposite Fisher while he'd told his life story only a few short weeks before. Now before them was a calculating powerhouse of strategy, but with red ringed eyes and pale skin, he looked so tired, and not in the best of moods.

It was only as he sat, Fisher noticed the second image. The screen split down the middle with Clark to the left, his eyes shadowed.

"It is, sir," Harris replied as she settled herself into one of the two leather swivel chairs behind the conference table. Fisher watched as Franklin didn't react.

"I'll let *you* know," he replied, looking off screen.

"It's…" Fisher said, but Harris cut him off.

"Infinite energy, sir," she said as Franklin's eyebrows twitched. "We've identified a material that splits water into its components." Fisher stared at Franklin, but the smallest movement of his brow gave nothing away.

"LanfordStamp has this?" Franklin said. "You're sure?"

"Yes sir," Harris replied, shooting a look at Clark. Fisher watched in the silence as Franklin contemplated what he'd just been told. Fisher wanted to explain the discovery's significance. He wanted to call out how it would change the world, but knew not to interrupt the man's thought process. Instead, he watched in silence.

"Where is it now?" Franklin said, startling Fisher as his deep voice reverberated.

"We don't know, yet," Harris replied.

"Find it," he said, and his image disappeared as Clark took over the entire screen.

"You didn't explain what it means," Fisher said, looking over at Harris.

"It's on the list," Clark said before Harris could reply.

"Huh?" Fisher mumbled. "What list?" he said, looking between the pair.

"We have a list of human advancements we watch out for," Clark said, staring at Harris.

"I don't understand," Fisher replied, glancing at each of them.

"It's a list of advancements that could change the fundamental way we all live our lives," Clark said, and Fisher narrowed his eyes at what this could mean.

"What else is on the list?" he soon said, settling on Clark, who smiled, but it was Harris that spoke.

"The cure for old age. The technological singularity. Self-replicating nano bots."

Fisher smiled.

"Yeah. I've read those books too. But why infinite energy? I understand the implications. The petro-chems go out of business. So what?" he said, holding his hands out at his side. "The world heals from the greenhouse death. Things get cheaper and we're no longer tied to the price of oil. Nations no longer go to war over what's buried in the ground."

Clark wore a tenuous smile. "Without oil, what limits the price of goods?"

Fisher looked back across the table. "How much they cost to produce," he replied.

Clark nodded. "Raw materials. Energy. Shipping. Fuel. Infinite energy means free energy. The cost of goods falls through the floor. What's stopping us from making everything? The raw materials become the new boundary. Imagine 3D printing coupled with a free energy source. You can make anything you want. Capitalism collapses. Governments go out of business. The world runs out of raw materials. What do you think the next war will be over?"

Fisher took a deep breath as he considered the words. Eventually he looked over at Harris. "All because of the rock?"

"Imagine if there's more of it buried somewhere, or we can unlock its secrets and synthesise it," she said, nodding.

"What are your leads?" Clark said, his voice returning to the matter-of-fact tone Fisher was used to.

"Johannas Hall. A scientist on the project. They killed him for a reason and we need to find out why. The contractor attempted to take his laptop."

"Where is it now?" Clark said as he tapped at his keyboard.

"The AFP seized it with the rest of the evidence from the job in Australia," she replied.

"On it," Clark said as his gaze diverted to the left of the camera and his typing became more energetic. "What else?" he said, still tapping.

"We go back in to LanfordStamp. It's the key," Fisher replied when Harris didn't.

"Do you need backup?" Clark said.

"No," Harris replied.

"Do you think it's there?" he said, looking at the camera.

"It's likely," she said.

"When are you going?" he replied.

"Now," Fisher said.

"With no preparation?" Clark asked as he looked at Harris.

"Oh. We've been preparing," she replied.

60

"I know you can't talk," Clark said over the open link. "But I've got news."

Fisher glanced at the back of Harris's head in the row in front, her strawberry blonde only just visible at the edge of the black baseball cap as it slid beneath the collar of her blue overalls, which matched his and everyone else's on the bus. The same blue overalls that had stopped them carrying their Glocks.

Staring out past the condensation covering the cramped minibus windows, the sun was still a few hours from reappearing over the horizon.

"The Aussies haven't got the laptop," Clark continued. "Interpol took the case along with the evidence, and they can't find it."

Fisher watched the almost imperceptible tensing of her shoulders.

"It was in transport to Lyon, but it didn't make it. We'll have to hope there's a backup. Find out what you can about Johannas."

Fisher caught himself nodding, then shot a look to his side, but the Asian woman next to him had her head tilted down, her wrinkled skin still covering her eyes.

As the minibus stopped, each worker stepped off without saying goodbye or thanking the driver. Fisher pulled his dark blue overall straight as he followed the old lady doddering down the steps, his breath misting in the cold of the pre-dawn as he followed the line and slipped in front of Harris in the queue for the security hut.

Even though they knew their faces were likely plastered under the counter, it was easy to get photo cards issued with a level high enough to get them onsite and both soon slipped through the cold metal turnstile into the sprawl of low-rise buildings standing vague in the distance.

With the floodlights which had blanketed the campus a few hours ago now dim, the stars hung bright in the clear sky, leaving their view filled with shadows sprawling on the horizon and spotted with the odd triangle of light and the flash of anti-collision beacons on tall towers.

Attaching themselves to the stream of workers, they came to a halt in a long line of slumped forms, queueing alongside a low rise utilitarian building, most of its windows dark. Peering at the head of the queue, a fierce middle aged woman filled the wide double doorway, her tall, bulky form illuminated by a powerful light above. With a defined, angular jawline, and although a waterproof coat hid much of her body, he pictured the bulge of muscles and broad masculine shoulders tensing her clothes.

With the occasional forward step, Fisher watched as the stern woman ticked at her clipboard and exchanged short stone-faced words, handing each at the front of a queue a sheet of paper from the board. Even though she moved to the side, they had to make themselves small to squeeze past before disappearing beyond.

He turned away, urging his eyes to adjust as he thought about where they would start their search.

Luana had given them a few pointers, but still, unsure what exactly they were looking for, they knew it wouldn't be easy. The rumble of an engine interrupted his thoughts, and he spotted a pickup with *Security* stencilled across its white side. It swung around from behind a building and pulled up at the head of the line before rocking with two beefy security guards in fluorescent jackets lumbering from the cab's rear doors.

To the purr of the idling engine, the shadowed faces of the guards sauntered along the line with their attention swinging to each of the workers. Fisher looked ahead to Harris, but finding her staring straight ahead, he realised the mistake he'd made.

His blood ran cold as the driver in the pickup stared straight back. Silently screaming for self-control, Fisher held his gaze whilst doing his best to look downcast, tired, and bored. The stamp of boots slowly lifted his head, and he watched a torch beam linger on each face.

As one after the other the workers drew away from the bright light, Fisher steeled himself to react, forming the words in his head, then reforming again as he calculated the consequences and the mass of witnesses who'd watch him force his suggestion.

Too soon, the light spun around to his face, seeming to skip Harris altogether. Blinded, he pulled his hand up to his eyes, exaggerating a reflex to shield from the light.

"Hands down," came a bass command.

Fisher filled his lungs, tensed and readied himself.

61

Softening his scowl, Fisher dropped his hands to his side and found the sharp brightness gone with the guards turned away. Instead, they looked over at an adjacent square of concrete half the size of a football field, which he'd not noticed until daylight flooded from the top of tall posts.

He followed the turn of their heads to the roar of engines and a convoy of four pristine Land Rover Defenders in polished black and chrome, their thick alloy wheels and checker plate edges gleaming in the artificial day.

A volley of swears snarled between the two guards as they glared at the sixteen opening doors and dark clothed figures climbing out, their steps almost in time. To collective groans from the two in fluorescent yellow, each figure collected heavy duffle bags from the vehicles before marching out of the light.

As the last stepped into darkness, Fisher steeled himself, but the stereo squark of voices from the guard's radios pricked his interest. The voice wanted them back at the control room, and without a backwards glance, the pair mounted the pickup.

Recovering his nerve, the line grew shorter while he watched flashes of fluorescence swarm across his view, in pickups and on foot, in pairs and alone, each heading in the same direction.

Facing forward, he realised there were only two others in front of him and his thoughts turned to Luana and her excited expression as she told them about her tried and tested trick for getting back on site after she'd played out. Her smile had widened as she described waiting in the queue before the supervisor assigned a role. Then, once they left them alone for their task, the security patrol would have no cause to question them. After that, they could slip away to explore, not to be found missing until the end of their eight-hour shift.

Not knowing where in the vast place held the answers, they planned to access the computer network for Clark to join in the fun and guide them, perhaps finding a finger pointing to an unmarked location on a satellite image.

They hadn't planned on the bolstered security.

As an ex-military base, an airfield during the second world war, a garrison shortly after, the front portion of the campus spread out with one and two-storey buildings whose facades were devoid of flair or imagination. Built somewhere in the fifties or sixties, the frequent whitewash didn't hide their age. Sat alongside were buildings added over the years, a short tower and row of five low rise circular metal containers, with no windows and just a square of glass on top, their use looking vaguely chemical. Behind the sprawl of squat buildings, the scene turned to a modern twisting metropolis of pipework and stainless steel towers rising into the sky, all different heights and each visible only as shadow.

In front, Harris stopped at the outstretched arm of the female sentinel as she took a long look, running her gaze from the cap on Harris's head, down to her Doc Marten boots. Finally she spoke, confronting her with a harsh Slavic accent, demanding to know if it was her first time.

As Harris nodded, subdued, the scary woman's head came to the side, looking past her strawberry hair to Fisher.

"You too?" she barked as Fisher stared at her hooked nose.

He nodded, and she sneered in return, baring a set of crooked, off white teeth. He struggled to stifle a smile, thinking back to bad Halloween parties from his childhood and followed in Harris's wake, squeezing past the woman's bulk, his nose flooding with a perfume of chemical cleaner and vinegar.

Behind the entrance was a corridor lined with six cleaning carts arranged in a row, each filled with sprays and potions, cloths and tools. At the front a galvanised steel bucket hung, the mop lying flat across the cart. A cowering worker stood at each except two, their stares fixed on the floor. Taking their places at the last remaining carts, the supervisor stood with her back blocking an open door and her hand moving along the line, snarling the first four letters of the alphabet.

Damn it, Fisher thought as he heard Block D reeled off. Dismissing the thought of intervening, he instead focused out in front as the trolleys clattered around the corridor.

With the person in front of him disappearing out of sight, the woman muttered over her shoulder before snapping her head around, her stare sending a shiver down Fisher's spine as she motioned him forward.

Her hook nose bore down on him, but before he could speak, she pushed the pen underneath the clip at the top of the board and grabbed Fisher's left hand, pulling it in front of her face, squinting.

"New," she said, shaking her head. "You," she said, pointing a finger at his face, "with me." Then she looked around his side to Harris behind, her expression still downtrodden, and barked, "restaurant."

Turning towards the door, she shouted something sounding Slavic and laughed. Seconds later, an overweight man in an ill-fitting blue shirt, the cleaning contractor's logo stretched across his breast pocket, ovals of dampness hanging from the armpits, came out of the doorway, yellow teeth bared as he laid eyes on Harris.

Hearing Harris's unintelligible mutter under her breath, Fisher wasn't surprised she knew what they'd said. Before her reaction unfolded any further, he replied to the supervisor's sharp call, pushing the trolley as he followed with its contents clattering as she marched at pace deeper into the building. Their path twisted and turned through stark corridors and he tried to make mental notes of the route, but with only numbers on the doors, he soon gave up, instead concentrating on other details. The make of a digi-lock. The brand of a white klaxon. Storing each fact away for Clark when he could talk.

"You've got to be joking," Harris said in his head, the first time he'd heard her since walking away. When no other words came after, his attention turned to a door opened by the supervisor with the pass around her neck. Fisher followed, using the trolley to catch the door before it slammed shut, and found himself in a long corridor, the floor bright red, the ceiling and walls white and fresh as if it was only just painted. Along the corridor bins overflowed outside closed doors, but Fisher's interest was more on the solid-looking doors themselves. A quick look along the corridor revealed a name plate he understood. A toilet, and he stopped outside.

"Sorry. I need to go," he said. Without waiting for a reply, he abandoned the trolley and rushed through the door before standing at the urinal. "It's crawling with security contractors. They look specialised, good military." A single cough replied from Harris.

"Harris agrees. How many?" Clark's crystal clear voice came back in his head.

The door squeaked on his hinges and Fisher held his reply.

"Put that dirty thing away. You're not playing with it on my time, unless you've been really good."

After motioning to zip up his flies, he turned to find the supervisor standing at the door, sneering at his crotch. Trying not to look at her face, he stepped through the gap she'd left, which was only just big enough, her perfume of polish engulfing him as he passed.

"Where now?" he said, standing in the corridor, then watched her point to the door opposite and the name plate for the Security Operations Centre where low radio chatter echoed.

62

As the Wicked Witch of the East, Fisher's new name for the supervisor, disappeared behind the Security Centre's door, he glanced around for somewhere to hide in case anyone came out whilst she got the keys, or whatever she was there for.

Turning away, he peered along the empty corridor, pausing on each door spreading out in front of him. Each were the same as the next, as far as he could tell, and bulleted with numbers which meant nothing to him. Still with no one in sight, he turned back and as he did, he spotted the next name plate along. After glancing at where the witch had stepped, he moved closer to the small, silvered letters, reading again.

Investigations.

Twisting around with a start, he found her stood in the doorway, her nose wrinkling as she beckoned for him to follow inside.

As Fisher moved, Clark's voice came on the line.

"When it's safe, let me know where you are."

Only just able to manage to cough a response, Fisher used all his will not to turn and run or do anything but enter the nest of guards who would know his face off by heart.

Stepping over the threshold, with relief, he found the place wasn't teeming with men as he stood with the bulk of the door hiding him from the main room. To his left stood a wooden worktop with row upon row of empty radio charging units. Below, shelves held LS branded folders with bold lettering describing security manuals and operating procedures, above which whiteboards filled the rest of the wall, leaving little space between the scrawl of multi-coloured handwriting listing radio channels, names and dates of maintenance work.

Leaning forward, Fisher's gaze ran tentatively across a crude schedule of security equipment faults before halting on two blurry photos, moving only as the witch's voice snapped.

"Here," she said, pointing to the floor further in the

room and her pinched expression told him to do anything but follow her instructions, knowing it would bring unwanted attention.

Stepping past the door with a tentative step, he focused to his left, but catching Harris's blurred image, he realised his nervous demeanour would draw questions.

With a silent breath, he pushed his shoulders back and glided the trolley forward. Then, with a glance to his right, he saw a dark counter ran along the width of the room and a section to her right folded over on itself.

Two plump guards in pale blue uniform sat beyond the wooden boundary, both with hair shaven to nothing. One manned the front desk but stared down at something behind the counter. The other sat to the right, facing a wall of colour CCTV monitors, three flat screens high and four wide. Only the bottom right corner monitor showed anything other than a rotating view of the campus. Instead there were green lines of text, fresh additions adding at the top to push old entries off. As he watched, a red added, then a second, but soon followed with a green.

Not able to see the detail of the text, a label on the thin edge of the monitor read *Sentinel Access System*.

As he turned his head, keen not to get caught lingering, he couldn't help his eyes widen where he saw Harris on the top left-hand screen. She was one of two people in the shot as she stacked chairs beside the fat man in overalls watching.

Forcing himself to look away, he pushed the cart to the witch's side where she plucked a tall can of polish and a yellow cloth, then motioned the can in circles.

"Spray this, then polish round and round," she said without a hint of sarcasm in her accented voice. "Then the same on the desks."

Placing the items on the counter, she took a long multi-coloured duster from the cart and ran it over a few blades of the venetian blinds. "Like this."

As she twirled the long pole, dust caught in the light, but before he could point out the flaw in her system, she gestured to the mop and bucket.

Looking back up, she raised an eyebrow, and he replied to the unvoiced question with a nod, catching a rag as she chucked it from the cart. "Then get on your knees and dry. We can't have any of our most important people falling over."

Fisher nodded as one of the men snorted, then grabbing a roll of black bags from the cart, the witch headed to the door, slapping him on the ass as she passed.

Dumbfounded at the sting of her touch, he decided to get the job done so he could get the hell out of the room as quickly as possible. Turning the cart, he pulled on pink rubber gloves, and despite every fibre of his body calling to keep his face from view, he sprayed the counter furthest away from the guard and settled in to polish the wood.

With the coffee rings and grime lifting as he polished in circles, his hearing attuned to the low volume of the radio chatter. He listened to the various call signs, each two letters spoken phonetically along with two numbers, before passing confirmation of a completed task. New orders always followed, often to unlock a door somewhere or relieve another patrol.

After skimming the entire surface, he turned to get a dustpan and knelt in front of the cart, his head angled up as he swept invisible debris from the floor. Looking at the whiteboard again, he saw himself and Harris fixed in time, both of their faces looking at the camera. Miming emptying the pan into a black bag held open with a hoop, he took the duster and can of polish and moved behind the counter. When the guard glanced over, Fisher looked away.

There were four desks behind the counter, three with empty chairs, their surfaces clear aside from neat stacks of paper piled in a corner. A round guard sat at the fourth desk and he held a cable from the radio in his left hand, where it snaked down to the receiver on the desk. By the other, his palm rested on the pad of a CCTV controller and a custom keyboard as his fingers nudged a thin joystick rising where the number pad should be.

Watching from the corner of his eye, every so often the man would bring the receiver to his mouth and talk, his fingers tapping at the controls, forcing images in the wide bank in front of him to change, zoom or pan at his command. When the guard turned to Fisher, all he could do was smile and bury his head back in the swirl of polish as he sprayed the adjacent desk.

It was a few long moments before he felt safe enough to look up. When he did, he recognised some of the places from the night before, others from what he'd seen on the way over. There were many he didn't recognise.

He stopped swirling the cloth as his gaze caught a pair of the guards dressed in all black walking along a corridor. Each time they moved out of view, the image switched, replaced with the nearest camera tracking their progress. Their manner was so much different from the guards he'd seen hours ago, their stance controlled. Their stride had purpose that oozed with every movement.

He knew the walk well. Military, but more refined. Disciplined to the nth degree. There was thought behind their expressions, a battle-hardened edge in their look. A force of last resort for hire. Ex-Special Forces.

Despite the rising dread, he turned from the screen and his gaze settled on another. The tunnels Luana had led them down where he found another pair of men, their walk a carbon copy. With movement in his peripheral vision, Fisher turned away just as the guard at the desk looked over, forcing him to push his weight into the cloth circling the table.

When no one raised their voice and no alarm went up, he slowed his breath just as his hand slipped, sending papers scattering across the floor.

"Shit. I'm really sorry," Fisher said, dropping to his knees to corral the pages.

"Fuck's sake," the guard blanched and Fisher kept his head low, knowing they'd both be looking right at him.

"Sorry," Fisher repeated as he gathered the loose pages, but when he saw a map of the campus amongst them, it took all of his effort not to pause, instead he placed it on the top of his gathered pile as he focused on its detail.

The map itself wasn't unusual. He'd seen satellite images of the site, but his interest hung on the labelling, the word *Server Room* jumping out at the edge of the building he was already in. As he gathered the last page, he knew he'd have to stand, but as his gaze fell on a red broken line pointing to a square underneath the large circle of grass at the centre of this site. A label called it the Archive.

Knowing he'd already paused for too long, after glancing up to make sure neither of them were looking, he folded the top page, choosing to ignore the detail on the other side, instead, sliding it into his pocket before standing and returning the pile back onto the table, butting the edges of the sheets together.

Rushing through the rest of his tasks, with desks clean enough to pass a casual inspection, and with a spray of polish in the air for effect, he walked back to the cart, scanning the white board for as much information with voices in the corridor getting louder.

Gripping the handle, he turned the cart through half a circle and watched as four guards dressed in blue overalls bounded into the room, pushing and jostling with laughter as they blocked his route.

63

An all too familiar dread gripped at Fisher's chest as he kept his head low, shuffling forward as the new arrivals blocked the corridor with ridicule and laughter pinging between them. Glancing at the bottom edge of the door, his heart sank when he realised he had no choice other than to advance in the hope they would move, too engrossed in their banter to care.

Resigned to the manoeuvre, his eyes widened as a voice he recognised came from the corridor, its pitch grating against his every being. The voice filled the room with jeers and a tide of wolf whistles aimed at Fisher. He was thankful that at least they'd noticed him enough to clear a path.

Guided into an adjacent room where she stood outside chatting with the guards, it was little more than two desks and chairs. Repeating the same process, he spent the entire time thinking over more and more imaginative ways he could ditch the witch and get to the server room. It was only with the shock of her hand against his butt a second time that a plan formed, cemented with each contact after he cleared the third, fourth and fifth rooms.

With the sixth room clean, he listened to the squeak of boots closing in from the corridor and as he stepped out, he spotted a pair of blacked-out guards whose steps were in perfect time, their heads swinging from side to side in search of their prize.

His thoughts flashed to Harris. But she could take care of herself. Pulling the bags from the bins into the corridor, the witch appeared from another room.

"I'm done," he said.

Her smile was immediate. "Great. Now I've got something to show you," she said and took his cart's handle, dragging it behind her.

Lowering his brow, Fisher followed along the corridor, stopping when they reached an unmarked door where the lock chimed as she pushed it inwards.

"In here," she demanded, before standing to the side

with the door at her back.

Fisher peered in as a pungent mix of chemicals and stale air told him it was a cleaner's cupboard. At the rear of the small room, silver-foiled pipes ran along the wall from the floor to the ceiling.

"Get in," she said, her brow raised as she waved him in. Doing as he was told, she pulled the cart in behind him before the door levered into its gap. Feeling the warmth radiating from the pipework, he turned to find her face so close, then guessing what was coming next, he didn't move as she pushed her mouth to his.

Their lips glided and contorted with her energetic motion, and he couldn't help feel the power of the moment as she ground her crotch against his leg, her hands coming around to where their bodies met.

With their mouths still interlocked, Fisher grabbed around her waist before turning her with a swift motion. Her breathing deepened as he pushed her against the warm insulation. Groping for the zipper of his overall, she didn't hide her frustration when it wouldn't move.

Pulling away from the kiss, she greedily sucked air as he pushed his body against hers. Pressing into her, he yanked her pass from her neck, discarding it before his fingers nibbled at her blouse buttons.

Dropping her hands to her sides, she let the cotton fall from her shoulders to reveal the lace of her bra hugging her E cup breasts. As she thrust out her chest, he grabbed the blouse in both hands before pushing her against the pipes and blindly tying her hands together at her back with her top. Rather than pull away, she relaxed, letting a deep moan slip from her lips as he tied the last knot.

Backing off, he dropped and fumbled with her trouser button, her chest heaving as she let an excited groan slip. Shuffling the trousers to the floor to reveal knickers matching her bra, he caught a waft of her excitement as she stepped out. Knocking her bare legs on either side with a firm but gentle touch of his knees, he bent back down, securing each ankle to the tangle of pipes with her trousers. Even as he pulled back, she writhed in pleasure, the bonds tightening as she tugged.

"Now fuck me," she said, her voice low and breathy. Fisher put his finger to her mouth at the sound of voices in the corridor.

Not frantic or hurried, the conversational tone soon disappeared, and she smiled, her eyes begging for him to come close. He did, slipping two fingers to the side of the thin lace just below her waist and, with one sharp pull, she gasped as her damp knickers came away. Slowing her breathing, her eyes half closed as she pushed her hips out for his touch.

Motioning for her to open her mouth, he pushed the knickers inside as she did.

Even with her void crammed, he saw her smile. It only dropped as he pulled a rag from the cart, tying it around her mouth to stop the thin lace gag from falling out. Stepping back, her eyes went wide as he watched to make sure she could breathe. Leaning close to her ear and held by the bounds, he saw her sudden doubt.

"I'll be back to finish the job. Just wait," he whispered.

Zipping up his overalls, he swept up her ID from the floor and turned off the light. Listening over her muffled protests, he pushed the trolley out into the corridor.

"Cleaners cupboard. Room P0045," he whispered.

"Roger," came Harris's reply.

"I've got the server room's location. Can you join me?" Fisher said, not expecting a response.

"Ten minutes," she replied.

"Great," Fisher said, guiding the trolley, his head down despite the empty corridor.

"Be careful," she replied, her voice strained.

Retracing his steps to the security office, his head bobbed upright for a look before shrinking back at the first distant sound. To his relief, turning the corner he found the corridor still clear, the control room's door still ajar, with distant radio chatter the only sound. Not pausing, and without a glance inward, he passed the control room, resting his iComm on top of the trolley.

With concentric circles radiating off the screen, he saw the room next to the control centre was empty with just two red dots pinging from where he'd first cleaned. Still, as he stood outside the Investigations Office door, he stopped and listened, forcing his breathing to pause as he tried to hear past his pounding heart and push the handle towards the ground.

Finding the door unlocked, and not waiting to thank his luck, he pulled the trolley inside and pushed the door home, delving himself into darkness. Standing just inside, he reached out, squinting as the lights burst on.

The room was only big enough to fit two desks, their front edges butted together, their contents standard and dominated by a flatscreen monitor with cables snaking from a mouse and keyboard. Plastic trays lined the edge of the desks, each overfilled with paper crammed with text. Battered metal filing cabinets lined the walls and, not pausing, he pulled at the top drawer of each but was unsurprised when none gave.

One day he'd know how to have them open in a second, instead he had to make do with the piles of pages on the desk nearest the door. Flicking through the sheets, he skipped lists of numbers and names, discarding them to the side.

About to move to the next desk, he held his breath at laughter in the corridor. Turning his attention to the bottom of the door, he regretted turning on the light when he realised the gap at the floor could let a cat in, let alone the light spraying out into the dim corridor.

With excuses building in his head, the sounds died to a muffled rhythm of chat falling off into the distance, but still he picked up the wad of pages and shoved them into the waste bin before moving around to the second desk.

Even before he came around, his gaze fell on a colour picture of Harris's grey BMW in the bottom corner of a sheet of paper square in front of the keyboard. Surging around the desk's side, his leg clattered with a thin metal bin the witch must have discarded in the middle of the walkway.

Swearing under his breath, his attention shot back to the entrance, but the silence was the opposite of comfort.

Before the clatter of the metal, he was sure he'd heard distant voices. Letting his breathing fall back, he stared at the car, transfixed on the image of himself and Harris inside, the photo taken from a high angle that could only have been from a bridge or a traffic camera.

About to grab the sheet, which bared no logo or originator's markings, his head snapped up as he caught a smell where he focused on a paper cup of brown liquid he'd not noticed before, and a wisp of rising steam.

64

Fisher's eyes sprung wide as he fumbled with his iComm, but before he could do anything, a voice boomed from the other side of the door. With the flurry of orders still echoing, Fisher watched the handle move. Sliding the phone into his pocket, he dropped to his knees as the door clattered into the cleaner's cart.

"What the fuck?" a deep voice called out as the wood sent the trolley thumping into the wall of cabinets.

"I'm sorry," Fisher said, standing with a forced smile. "I'm almost done."

In front of him stood a middle-aged man in a pair of baggy grey trousers and a white shirt. A plain grey tie hung under an ID pass. The collar was loose around his neck, and Fisher's stare fell to a dark bushy eyebrow running the width of a deep red face.

"It's been cleaned," the guy replied with no attempt to hide his contempt. His features hung low and tired, but Fisher thought perhaps he saw a growing glint as he waited for a response. Fisher didn't reply, instead holding his gaze, mesmerised by the single eyebrow as the guy's head turned at an angle, his eyes pinching as if he were trying to remember something.

"You've never seen me before," Fisher said, feeling he had no other choice, before glancing out to find the corridor empty at the man's back. Returning to look the guy in the eye, he found his brow wrinkled and his mouth opening but with no words coming out as he let go of the door and walked around the desk.

Feeling himself relax, Fisher moved in the opposite direction whilst watching the guy scour the surfaces as if searching for anything out of place, or an excuse to disbelieve Fisher's words. Hoping he would sit so he could leave, Fisher stepped towards the door with his thoughts heading to where he'd meet Harris and how they'd get into the server room. Only half noting what the man was doing, he hurried a look over his shoulder then moved for the door, but about to leave, he glanced back, finding the guy staring at Fisher's face on a sheet of paper in front of him.

Before the guy's lips could part, Fisher held the fingers of his right hand in the shape of a gun, wrapping the other around the bottom half. He held his breath as the old guy's mouth fell open and he staggered back, falling into the chair.

Realising he hadn't spoken the suggestion, Fisher's eyes went wide because, by the fear in the man's wrinkled eyes, he believed there was a gun pointed at him.

"It was going so well," Fisher said, forcing himself to relax. "Why couldn't you just listen to me?"

The guy looked back, raising his arms.

"Talk to me," Clark said, not hiding his alarm.

"Some guy stumbled into an office I was searching," Fisher replied, trying to stop his breath from racing as the pair stared at each other.

"Where is he now?" Clark replied, his tone unchanged.

"Sitting in front of me."

"What's he doing?" Clark asked, his voice rising.

"Just sitting there," Fisher said, his words slow.

"Why?" Clark hurried out.

"Because I'm pointing a gun at him."

"But…" Clark replied, but Harris cut him off.

"Shit."

"Thanks for the support, guys. Now, what am I going to do with him?" Fisher asked.

Only silence followed for what felt like a long time.

"Can you lead him out of there?" Clark said.

"I'm next to the security command station," Fisher replied.

"Shit," Clark said, echoing Harris, but Fisher barely heard it when a knock rattled the door at his back.

"It's me," Harris whispered, sending Fisher's heart racing as he twisted the handle. Looking up from her iComm, she looked between the man in the seat and Fisher's clasped hands.

"What the…?" she said before shaking her head.

Fisher shrugged, and she drew a deep breath before stepping toward the guy, whose eyes seemed wider than Fisher thought possible.

"Hello, Mr…?" Harris said.

"Dack. James Dack," he said, hurrying the response.

Harris smiled, baring her teeth as the guy glanced at the photo on his desk without moving his head.

"Yes, it's me," she said, and James Dack nodded. "And yes, it was us who broke in last night." Her tone had lightened. "So you can see we've got some pretty big balls, metaphorically speaking, coming back in here."

James Dack nodded.

"And along with the lump of nylon pointed at you, I hope you realise you shouldn't fuck with us."

James Dack continued to move his head up and down.

"I need to hear you say it," Harris said, bunching her cheeks. "Please."

James Dack stopped nodding before glancing at Fisher where he lingered on his outstretched fingers.

"I won't fuck with you," he said, turning back to her.

"Great," Harris replied with a bounce in her voice. "Now follow me," she said, beckoning him towards the door.

With the guy out into the corridor, she motioned for Fisher to put his hand down.

"I know just the place," Fisher whispered.

65

"It's crowded, I'm afraid," Fisher said as he used the stolen pass to unlock the cupboard, then watched Harris's lips bloom with a smile at the sight of the half-naked witch. Within a few minutes, they left the investigator in a similar state of undress, his trousers gripping his legs to the pipework, his shirt binding his hands and his tie stuffed in his mouth as he faced his colleague.

"I leave you alone for less than an hour," she said with a raised brow.

"We might have done them a favour. They could be the perfect match," Fisher said with a muffled laugh. "How did you ditch yours?"

"That fat pervert?" she said, her eyes narrowing. "Let's just say he has a newfound respect for women, or at least it will take a few months before he can touch anything else he shouldn't."

A shudder ran down Fisher's spine at the thought of what she'd done, but as he pushed his hand into his pocket, he remembered the map.

"Take a look at this," he said, drawing out the page. Harris unfolded the sheet with her eyes widening as she scanned the drawing, then turned it over to the detailed layout of the building they were in. Side by side, they rattled the cart down the dim twisting walkway, slowing for each echo in the corridor. It wasn't long before they were outside a door with a long number stencilled in matt grey letters, its purpose only indicated by the map.

Pausing, Fisher pressed Dack's fob against a black rectangular reader and a bass tone replied, the sound echoing as the reader pulsed red. Harris shook her head at the unasked question and he slid the pass into his overalls, watching as she lifted her iComm against the reader.

"Is there anything you can do?" Harris said to Clark, but before he could respond, Fisher pulled the witch's fob from his pocket and pressed it up to the side of the plastic. A quiet chirp pinged from the glowing green rectangle and he turned to Harris.

"Someone's gotta keep it clean," he said, raising his eyebrows.

Air sucked in around the door as he pushed it open before dragging the cart over the threshold. They were in a wide room with a wall of triple glazing separating the thin lobby from racks of dark boxes blinking with a galaxy of lights. Multicoloured cables sprayed from their fronts, each ordered in bunches and snaking to cable trays, winding their way across the floor and ceiling.

Standing side by side, Fisher spotted a thick glass door with a second card reader mounted to the right. As the first door slurped back into place, he turned to Harris before pressing the witch's pass against the reader. With a loud buzz, the reader haloed in scarlet.

"Follow me," Fisher said as he manoeuvred the trolley back to the corridor, but glancing back, he found she hadn't moved. "I'll explain," he said, beckoning her out.

Not waiting to see her follow, he grabbed the metal bucket, pushing his fob against another door only a few steps away. This time, he expected the smell of the cleaner's room.

With the bucket full and foaming with suds, he pushed a knee-high, yellow *Wet Floor* sign into the centre of the corridor just outside the room before resting the wet mop against the wall. Harris didn't hide her confusion.

"Make yourself busy," Fisher said as he motioned toward the cart. "The CCTV in the server room isn't working, so security is swinging by every hour to check it manually. I don't know when they were last here."

"How do you…?" Harris said, but Fisher cut her off.

"On the whiteboard in the security centre."

Nodding, she glanced at her iComm, then plucked a rag from the trolley before dropping it on the floor.

They waited ten minutes before they heard the echo of heavy boots and keys jangling in time with a faint whistle. Both turned from the noise, their motions starting up. His mop swung from side to side whilst she slid the cloth back and forth along the skirting. When the footsteps arrived, Fisher glanced up to find the oldest permanent guard he'd seen so far. With short, but not cropped hair, the fifty-something guy paid them little attention as he peered through the outer server room door. As he turned around, their eyes met and Fisher froze, still pushing the mop. Seeming to hold each other's gaze for seconds, it was only as his radio chirped that he turned and spoke into the handset as he walked away.

The moment his fluorescence was out of sight, Fisher pushed the mop along the side of the cart, rolling the trolley into the cupboard and hurling the sign after. With the fob back at the reader, within seconds the door sealed into its hole and Harris moved past him, standing at the glass door, reaching out towards Fisher.

As he handed over the cleaner's pass, she pushed it against the back of her iComm, her fingers darting across the screen as the outline of a progress bar appeared. Its bare contents tracked bright green from the left.

With whatever process had taken place completed, she tapped at the screen then pushed the iComm against the reader, watching as a series of numbers cycled.

"It's trying to mimic the proximity pass. Even if this works, we still need to figure out who might have access."

With Fisher nodding, she turned away and spoke into the air. "Clark, find a list of IT employees and their payroll numbers, please."

"Got it," Clark's voice said in Fisher's head, then in the following silence, Fisher pivoted on his feet, taking in the room. Apart from a round bin, the bag not yet emptied, and a metal table to the right of the door, the lobby was bare. A black phone handset rested on the tabletop, and underneath was a single drawer.

"The IT department has fifty employees," Clark said, cutting into Fisher's thoughts. "Can you narrow it down?"

"Try the highest paid ones first," Harris said, hovering her fingers over the screen of the iComm as it pushed back against the pad.

"Chris Holms.10292."

Harris typed the number on the on-screen keypad, then Fisher watched the green progress bar empty before filling from the left. A moment later, the reader flashed red.

"Next," Harris said.

"Tia Cousin. 11210."

Just as Harris tapped the last number on the screen, Fisher remembered the security centre monitor with the lines of text.

"Stop," he blurted.

Harris kept the iComm to the pad, turning with a furrowed brow. "They can see when a pass doesn't work. If we keep getting failures, the guys in the control room will know what we're up to."

Harris paused. "We'll have to take the risk."

Fisher scowled, shaking his head.

"Have you got another plan?" Harris replied as she turned and tapped in the new number.

He didn't, so kept quiet and moved to examine the table where he pulled open the drawer. Inside, he found a thick pad of lined paper, the cover folded back. A pen and a pencil lined up at its side. Cringing as the reader barked another denial, he picked up the pad and flicked through the pages. Despite finding each sheet blank, he ran his fingers over the first, pulling it close to his face, then turning and twisting it in the air to angle it against the light.

Seeing feint indentations, he traced their lines with his finger before placing it back down and with the edge of the pencil, rubbed a light covering of lead, marvelling when he saw *@lanfordstamp.com* appear.

With the rest of the string unreadable, the bark of the reader pulled him up straight and he screwed the page in his fist, tossing it into the bin. Watching the ball of paper sail into the metal, it brushed at the side before falling. Standing, he walked over and took the bin in his hands, then pulled out the bag and emptied the contents onto the table.

Sifting through the dry rubbish, he used the pen to clear the used chewing gum and tissues to the side, isolating three crumpled sheets of paper. Unfolding them, he found one was his, and flattened the other two against the table.

On the centre of the first page was a sketch of a technical drawing, with the symbols perhaps something to do with the CCTV. The second page was a nonsense doodle. The scribble of someone on the phone, alongside the digits of an external phone number. It was out of the area, the noughts shaded with blue biro. He glanced at the phone and the grid of numbers, then at the two-line screen showing the early hour and the name *CMB-Server Anti-Room*.

It was a standard Avaya office phone with a large keypad of numbers and function buttons that ran across the top. The first was programmed to fast dial for reception, then security and the facility's helpdesk in turn. The fourth was for the porter's office. To the right, he saw redial.

Picking up the handset, he listened to the tone, and the display showed a question mark. He pressed the redial button and the number from the crumpled page showed on the screen. He pushed the button again, and it changed to a four-digit extension. After another press, it flashed with Security. A final tap, and it was back to the first number.

Fisher glanced back to Harris as she stared at the red pulsing reader, its bark dying back, and he cycled the button to the four-digit extension and pressed the large green button to dial. Listening out for an answerphone to take the call, when a deep male voice greeted him with a short phrase Fisher didn't catch, he was lost for words.

With Harris's fingers at her iComm, he pushed his hand out, waving her over.

"Sorry," was all Fisher could come up with.

"Blake's phone," the voice repeated.

"Oh. Hi," Fisher stumbled, his stare fixed on the bin at his feet. "I hadn't expected anyone to pick up the line. I was going to leave a message. Whilst cleaning the server room lobby, we found a twenty-pound note on the floor. I figured it might have been dropped by whoever used the phone last." Fisher paused, but when the voice didn't reply, he stumbled out the first thing that came into his head. "Anyway. Can you tell him I'll drop it over to reception on my way out?"

"Oh my God," the voice came back. Fisher's eyes couldn't help but widen. "That's so honest of you. Tony was in the server room last. So it could be his. I'll come and get it to save you the hassle of taking it over. Thanks, man, I'll be there in five." Fisher was about to protest, but the line was already dead.

"We've got about two minutes before we have company," Fisher blurted out.

"Clark, is there a Tony on the list?" Harris said, leaving Fisher fumbling in his pockets.

"Shit. Have you got a twenty?"

66

Tapping the only Tony's employee number into the phone, Harris handed over a twenty from a pocket deep beneath her overalls and Fisher ran down the hall to the cleaner's cupboard, opening the door moments before he heard soft footsteps. Turning, he found a man in tatty jeans and a faded black Guns N' Roses t-shirt with blond hair hanging past his shoulders, walking over and holding up his palm.

"I can't get over this. Most people would keep their mouth shut," he said, taking the note and pushing out his other hand.

"Thanks," Fisher replied, shaking the hand just as he heard Harris's voice in his head.

"It didn't work. Maybe because he's off shift?"

"Hey," Fisher said, and the guy's eyes flickered as if startled. "I've not seen you around here before. Do you work nights much?"

The guy's eyes widened, and he showed off a yellow-tooth smile. "Yeah, I seem to get more than my fair share, but at least it's quiet."

Fisher glanced down at the badge hanging from his lanyard, but his ID faced the wrong way. "Anyway, I've got to get on. It was nice to meet you…" Fisher said, leaning forward and raising his brow with a question.

"Adam. Nice to meet you too," the guy said, winking then walking away just as two security guards came through the door at the end of the corridor.

"Thanks, Adam," Fisher said, raising his voice.

Without turning, Adam lifted his hand, then nodded to the guards as they passed each other.

Looking at his watch, Fisher turned back to the cleaner's cupboard. "They're doing their checks early."

It was Clark's voice he heard first. "There are two Adams," he said, before reciting their corresponding numbers.

Fisher pulled the trolley from the cupboard, shutting

283

the door before drifting along the corridor and wiping invisible dirt from the wall.

"Shit, I'm in," Harris said. "The lights… they're connected to the reader and now I can't turn them…"

"What's happening?" Fisher said when the line went dead. "Clark?"

"I'm getting no signal from her handset," he replied.

Picking up the pace, Fisher slowed as he approached the corner, then after taking a deep breath, peered around the bend. Finding the corridor empty, and passing no guards coming his way, he stared at the door, unsure what could have happened.

Pausing for only a few moments more, with his cloth in one hand he used the pass in the other and pulled the door open. The blood drained from his face when he found the anteroom empty and his mind raced as he tried to figure out where they'd dragged her off to.

"What's up?" Harris said, accompanied by the drone of fans. Letting out a breath, Fisher turned to find her holding the glass door wide. "You look pale."

With a grin blooming, the colour flushed back to his cheeks. "What happened?" he said as he followed her through the door, where she held a thin metal box.

"I found the light switch," she said, nodding to a grey metal clad switch on the wall. "They didn't check in. They must have been another patrol."

Following as she stepped back amongst the computers, he watched her pull a network cable from a loop of spares hanging from a hook on the wall, before plugging one end into the box then stepping to a stack of network switches, their edges flashing with a glorious green and yellow dance. With a satisfying snap, she pushed the connector into an empty port, then grabbed a longer cable and plugged it into a second, before hiding the box in a thick bundle of cables.

"Let's go," she said, walking toward the opening in the glass.

Fisher hesitated as he pulled open the door, but Harris

nudged him forward, urging him into the stream of foot traffic that had built in the corridor. Clark's voice was back in their heads.

"I'm in," he said, and for the first time Fisher realised he hadn't heard him speak since he'd entered the main area of the Server Room. He continued to talk as they walked along the corridor towards the admin building they'd been in last night.

"I've got door control and CCTV." His laughter burst across the line. "And I've found the problem with the camera," he said, relaxing his tone. "There's a lot of activity around the block. Do you want a diversion? How about I set an alarm off on the other side of the site?"

The pair looked at each other before Harris nodded. "I'll give you a cue."

Stepping from the building's relative comfort, the beginnings of a cloudless day haloed the twists and contortions of metal rising on the horizon. Steam rose from tall towers with the columns of white climbing ever higher in the windless morning. Like the corridor, the paths and roads had filled with activity, forming ant-like processions with cars and people snaking from the entrance, splitting this way and that.

Their attention soon found three black clad guards gathered, sentry like, around the entrance to the Admin Block. Everywhere they looked were a new stream of people, each lining up to pass a black Land Rover by each entrance. Despite the vast lines of people queuing to be checked, a guard glanced over, but Fisher was sure they were too far away, too lost in the crowd to see their detail.

"I think now would be a good time," Harris said, and hearing Clark's acknowledgment, they joined the flow, swapping lines several times and changing routes back and forth as they made their gradual way closer to the Admin Block. They didn't have to wait long before the squeal of sirens came from all directions and Clark was back on the line as faces in the crowds turned to each other with slumped shoulders.

People's directions changed and lines dissolved, moving instead in some other way as crowds formed at assembly points dotted away from each building.

"What have you done?" Harris asked and Fisher followed her focus on the entrance, where now only one guard stood, stiff with his finger at his ear as the Land Rover eased its way off the grass and through the crowds, increasing pace.

"Not good," Clark said.

"What?" Harris replied.

"The alarms are linked, I guess," he said.

"That's affirmative, but it's done the job," Harris said, moving with assurance towards their goal as Fisher sped to stay at her side. At first, the remaining crowds hid their direction, but it wasn't long before the masses were away from the buildings and they found themselves isolated with a single guard standing between them and the building's entrance. With a little more than a few car lengths between them, he looked over.

Fisher followed as Harris continued on her course, even as the ex-solider raised his left wrist to his mouth. Getting closer, Fisher lifted his hand which curved as if cupping a bowl.

"You don't recognise us," he whispered, watching the guard's hand still travelling to his mouth. Before it could reach, Fisher bounded forward and called out.

"You don't recognise us."

"X-Ray, this is…" the guard mouthed, then stopped as Fisher shouted the words with his hand almost close enough to touch.

"You don't recognise us," he said, quieter this time, relieved when he saw the guard's shiver, the discomfort running along his spine. Their stare's locked as the man drew back, his eyes narrowing before he turned away.

"This is Foxtrot Five," the man said as Fisher held his breath.

67

"Cancel that last message," the guard added, still facing away as the pair stepped past.

They found the corridor empty, but Clark had already told them as much. With the three-toned siren still ringing in their ears, they strolled towards the doctor's office, guided by Clark. Harris defeated the swipe lock with a tap as if it didn't exist because the doctor's payroll number was on his tax records. The physical lock was no slower than if Harris had used the actual key and not her wear-smoothed picks. The moment the door opened, the shrill din stopped. Coincident timing, both agreed with only a sideways look.

Clark confirmed the crowds were already spreading thin as Harris rolled the lock back into place with her thumb after closing the door behind them.

The doctor's office turned out to be a lab. Split into eight sections, each had two tall desks butted at right angles. One with a monitor, the other with a sink and tall swan neck tap Fisher recognised from his school science labs. Along the far wall were a long run of windows with closed venetian blinds sealing out the emerging daylight. The rest of the walls were whitewashed and alternated between rows of shelving and tall fume cabinets with coils of silvered ducting rising to the ceiling.

With the desks clear of clutter, there was no work in progress. No personal effects scattered the space and the shelves along each wall lay empty, the cabinets devoid of any contents. Instead, the floor was spotted with a stack of black plastic packing crates, the intertwined lids sealed shut and ringed with bright orange, tamper evident tags.

Turning in unison with Harris, Fisher spotted a wall of glass in the far right corner with a door at its side. Moving as one, Harris grabbed the handle first, easing the door open with a push. The office they found was as bare as the lab, apart from two stacks of boxes in the corner. One, a pile of three black crates, the other two high and bright orange with writing stencilled on the side. CMB S2 and CMB S3 in bold black letters. Instead of tamper evident plastics tags, these were ringed with thick padlocks either end.

Stepping inside, they turned to the right where they found the giant door of a strongroom. In the centre was a large, silvered wheel with spokes running outward from the edge. And it stood ajar.

Glancing at each other, they moved to the side before peering in through the thick gap and a small room the size of a bathroom with silvered walls and rows of empty shelves.

"They're moving out," Harris said.

Fisher nodded and turned back to the boxes. "Can you get in those crates?" he said, but Harris had already reached for her picks.

As she set to work, Fisher moved to the window, peeking through the gap in the blind and the daylight where crowds had reformed neat lines. When the locks clattered to the floor, he turned back.

"They've been reassigned," she said, shaking her head. "This stuff's going into storage."

"Storage?" he replied, wide-eyed when she held up a single sheet of paper she'd taken from a stack of loose pages.

"It's an instruction from their board. They shelved the project and everything is going into storage. It's dated a week before Bergen went up in flames."

"The rock?" Fisher said, but Harris nodded as she rifled through the rest of the contents.

"They must need the rock for something else," Fisher said.

"Unless it's in storage," she said, looking around the room.

"There's a box missing?" Fisher said, after inspecting each container.

"CMB S1," Harris said.

Fisher nodded.

"Guys," Clark said, startling Fisher before he remembered the open line.

"Did you get that?" Harris said, looking over at the door.

"Yes, but you have company. Two porters with trolleys about ten seconds from your position."

68

"Are you sure they're coming here?" Fisher asked, his voice urgent.

"They're outside the door," Clark replied, sending Fisher's gaze darting to the entrance before flashing back to Harris, who was about to slip the page into the box.

"Wait," he whispered, holding his palm out. She held still, watching him pull out his iComm then take a picture. After nodding for her to let the page go, she handed over the locks before she moved past the steel door.

With locks pressed back in place, and with just enough time for Fisher to follow, the gentle beep of the lab's electronic lock and the swift roll of the barrel signalled for them to be quiet as together they tucked down either side of the opening, staring at each other across the gap as they listened to a pair of male voices.

By the slow pace and depth of their voices, Fisher guessed one was much older, and a local. The other spoke with a London twang as they bickered about who would take which box. The discussion didn't last long. The deeper voice dominating, and with his gaze still focused on hers, Fisher's shoulders relaxed, despite the chatter growing louder.

Soothed by the unwavering grin he'd grown used to in the tight places they often found themselves in, he assumed she still experienced the same rush of hormones as situations escalated, but it was how they empowered her that was so different.

Fisher marvelled at how Harris always tuned in and was ready for any scenario, any fear and adrenaline pushing her on; not holding her back like it would for most people.

It was Harris who broke their trance, slipping out through the gap when he realised the voices fell silent, having lost himself in the oasis of her eyes for how long he didn't know.

Following behind, he found the boxes were gone, and Clark's voice came back on the line, the link having quietened as they'd entered the strong room. He confirmed he was tracking the porters along the corridor.

"Show us the way," Harris said.

"They've just split up. One with the orange crates and the other with the black…" Clark said, cutting himself off. "Why am I showing Fisher with them?"

Neither filled the silence, and it was Clark's huff of breath that told them when the penny dropped.

"Don't let Miss White find out you've let your iComm out of your sight," he said as Harris smirked.

Fisher's smile dropped as he pictured himself explaining to the woman in her lab coat with the wiry cranial interface in her hand.

"Stay with the orange crates," Harris said, then turned to Fisher. "You won't need me soon. You're nearly all grown up," she added, smiling as she double pushed her home button.

"I can't tell if you're serious or not," Fisher whispered as he listened at the outer door.

"I'm not sure either," she said through her smile. "What's it looking like out there?" she asked, her expression straightening.

Hunched over her screen, the pair watched the green dot representing Fisher's phone as it followed a circular route whilst Clark described the journey along the corridors of the admin building then through a door into a corridor which, from his description, sounded like where Luana had taken them the night before.

"It's clear," Clark said and Fisher didn't hesitate, rolling the tumbler between his fingers and pushing the door release at its side before peering out. Finding it vacant, he stepped out. Soon rounding a corner, Clark's breathing changed, halting altogether, as if muting his microphone.

Glancing at each other, he came back. "Pick up the pace."

"What is it?" Fisher said, striding at her side. "Shit. I left the cart."

"Don't worry," Clark soon said. "The semi-naked guy and his undressed friend were more than a giveaway."

It was all they needed to break into a run as Clark urged them to a door on the right, where they rushed down steps and into the concrete corridor with the dark red floor. With the propellent smell from the following evening long gone, it had replaced instead with stale dust on their lips as Clark continued to guide them further. "I lost your iComm a few hundred metres ahead."

"What's there?" Harris asked before Fisher could.

"I think it's the building not shown on the plan," Fisher said as they hurried, stopping only as Harris raised her hand, then pressed the back of her palm against his chest. Leaning forward, Fisher heard it too. A faint, tuneless whistling. "Where's that coming from?" he whispered.

"I don't know," Clark replied, his words elongated, and Fisher pictured him concentrating on his bank of screens. "Got him," he eventually said, and Fisher turned to Harris, hoping she'd know what to do next. "The porter is coming back your way. I didn't see where he came from. It must be a black spot."

"We need to hide," Harris said before Clark had finished, but glancing around, there was nothing to slip behind. "We'll have to back track."

"No. There's two guards patrolling the corridor where you entered," Clark said, rushing out the words.

Fisher expected her to swear when he cursed under his breath before repeating the fruitless search, but as he turned back, he found her peering towards the ceiling, her expression fixed with concentration.

Following her gaze with the whistle rising in clarity, he looked along the wide steel cable tray slotted with elongated holes as it hung down just below the ceiling laden with cables. With a nod, she looked over and he closed his mouth when he realised it had fallen open at the multitude of questions filling his head.

Giving him no time to protest, she crouched to one

knee and cupped her hands like he'd done for her in Snowdonia a lifetime ago. The insistent whistle stifled his complaint, and he knew he needed her help, but it likely wasn't true the other way round. Stepping onto her hands, she barely moved as she held his weight and stretched up to grip the thick pillar of steel fixing the perforated sheet metal.

Puffing and panting as he strained his arms, he couldn't help but grunt as he pulled himself up, despite the burn in his biceps. Eventually he left only footprints in her hands. With his legs tucked up and stretched out, his body parallel with the tray, he felt the metal sway as he shuffled in the small gap left between the ceiling and the bright cables bedded on top.

Despite feeling like he could topple at any moment as the screws gave away their grip to the concrete without care for him, he settled in. With the high pitch of the whistle so close, panic caused him to look over the lip of where he hung, but she'd vanished and had already tucked up on the length just ahead, giving no sign of any strain she'd spent in her ascent.

Together they watched from above as the whistling porter walked, oblivious, leaving only footprints in the dust and the decaying echo of a sneeze as he rounded the far corner.

Looking back to Harris, he watched her angle herself down, the tray barely reacting as she lowered with such control and grace, which was nothing like his descent. Dust rained down, the air rushing from his lungs as his boots clomped as he landed, then with a glance up he found his hiding place marked with a curve, bowing where he'd waited.

He didn't hold the thought for too long, instead running at Harris's side as a klaxon wailed from somewhere unseen.

"Have you got a visual on where he dropped off the crates?" Harris shouted above the noise, her breath barely stretched, despite still running.

"No, and I've just lost you on CCTV," Clark replied to the sound of tapping keys in the background.

"Bad timing," Harris said and slowed at the sight of a heavy red door barring their way, the steel criss-crossed with metal banding running around the edges and circling the lock.

Searching for a card reader, Fisher found none, only hinges as thick as his balled fist, the gaps thick with dark grease. Relieved to find the corridor empty, his gaze landed on the cable tray that had saved them once already. Following its length towards them., hope raised his heart rate even higher, but finding a metal plate welded across the gap as it went through the wall, he deflated.

"I don't suppose you kept any of those E-bullets back?" Fisher said, and her glance told him all he needed to know.

"I can't find the door anywhere on their system," Clark said. "And the guards are closing in."

Fisher looked back, but spotted no movement.

"We're looking right at it," Harris said, staring at the door. She glanced over at Fisher and he knew she'd felt the vibration, too. Leaning forward, he placed his hands on the metal just as it complained and crept towards them.

Instinct caused him to look up at the cable tray, but he already knew there was no time to lumber back up before whoever came from behind the door. With another glance back the way they came, he knew they only had one chance, and he followed Harris, stepping to the corner, hoping the opening door would keep them obscured.

Voices soon cut through the high-pitched call of the alarm, but he could only pick out a few curt words, and no matter how hard he concentrated, he couldn't distinguish how many there could be. He needn't have tried so hard when with the door barely a third open, two men in black jackets strode through, their hair cut tight at the back and sides as neither of them looked behind and soon the door's swing blocked all view when Harris dragged him further into the crease.

Breathing a sigh of relief, he prepared for the door to stop, readying himself to rush around the side and slip in through the opening. As the space they waited in continued to shrink, he pressed his hands at the warm steel to slow its motion. Feeling the vibration of cogs somewhere deep inside, it pushed back, his pressure having no effect, and he realised they had no choice but to make their move or be crushed to death.

As a warm hand pressed against his arm, he knew Harris had come to the same conclusion. With only enough space to slip to the side, he grabbed her hand and pulled, side-stepping as quickly as he could. Emerging from the metal's shadow, he drew a deep breath, despite the soldiers sauntering away still filling much of the view.

Looking back, he realised she wasn't out, and the gap behind the door was getting so tight. Still holding her hand, he yanked hard, pulling her out, but not far enough before the heavy metal pressed her shoulder against the concrete and he heard the pop of a joint.

69

Harris's face contorted as Fisher pulled, but somehow she made no sound. Gripping with both his hands, he heaved at her with all his might, and she stumbled out, grabbing her arm which hung slack at her side as the door banged against the concrete before reversing its direction.

Recovering his breath, and unsure what to do, he glanced to the oblivious walk of the two black figures someway off in the distance. Turning around, he found Harris already staggering past the door, its steel as thick as his forearm, and in through the opening. Paying only enough attention to see the corridor beyond empty, the walls filled with only a few doors on either side, he followed her, stumbling in before she leaned against the wall. As the door sealed closed, it left the klaxon's high call behind.

With her eyes closed, Harris remained standing and cradling her arm before she took considered breaths then moved into the centre of the room where, much to Fisher's distress, she fell to her knees, and clutching her shoulder, lowered her back to the floor.

"It's dislocated," she said, panting. "I need your help," she added through halting breaths.

Relieved at her diagnosis, rather than suffering from crushed bone, he knelt and nodded, eager to do what he could to stop her agony.

"Don't touch," she snapped and he pulled away.

"What should I do?" he said, hurrying out the words.

"Stand up," she said, and he followed her instructions. He watched as, with her good arm, she rummaged through her trouser pocket before coming away empty-handed. "When I..." she said, halting for a pained breath. "When I say," she repeated a little louder. "Pull my arm at forty-five degrees and as hard as you can."

Fisher shuffled on his knees and swallowed hard

"Move my arm out at a right angle to my body," she said, looking over, then squeezing her eyes tight.

Fisher tried to relax, then readied his arms out without touching her, watching as she stuffed her mouth with the cuff of her sleeve. As he took the weight of the bad arm, she pressed her mouth closed, her cheeks bunching as she tensed before nodding.

Without delay, and in one gentle move, he guided her arm through ninety degrees from her body, then rested it on the floor. With a deep breath through her nose, she removed her other hand.

"Whatever I say, or however much I fight, you need to pull slowly, but as hard as you can until it's back in place," she said, her mouth dry.

"How will I know it worked?" Fisher said, his voice breathy.

"You'll know," she replied and pushed her hand back over her mouth. Just as he reached out, the air erupted with a new klaxon.

"Do it," she said, her voice quiet behind the scrunched material.

He took her hand and wrist, then squeezed his eyes closed, then pulled, her scream chilling his bones.

70

Almost before the echo of her shoulder clunking back into place had died, Harris stood. With her face a picture of relief, she tested the joint with tentative movement.

"Thank you," she mouthed over the air thick with the siren and Fisher pulled himself from the floor as she interrogated her phone's screen and rounded on the door to the left of the corridor. "It's in there," she said, glancing between the phone and the door.

"Can you get us in?" he said, finding the round of a traditional barrel lock. Replying with a nod and not her trademarked wry smile, she'd already unfolded her picks.

"But first this one," she said, turning and stepping up to the identical door opposite which wouldn't have been out of place in an office with over-painted lines and round handle.

Fisher didn't question her choice when he spotted the label plate in the top half.

Armoury.

Neither of them tried to speak with Clark, already realising his silence when the door sealed. Instead, Fisher's mind filled the seconds it took with a nauseating reminder of her shoulder popping back into place.

"Maybe it's just batons," he said as the lock clicked, but seeing her brow raised as the thick door opened, and the smell of light oil, he knew he'd misplaced his optimism.

Following her in, the lights went out, but after a brief pause, the place glowed with light from her phone. Two long rows of metal shelves were stacked with M4 Carbines, the assault version of the classic American rifle, each sitting on their butts with the business end pointing to the ceiling.

Between the two shelves, black pistols rested, each similar but smaller than the Glock, beside empty magazines. And four guns were missing. Their absence was more concerning than what they looked at.

With Fisher following her turn, she played the torch beam over a large wooden box against the wall, with no top and deep with sand, he'd seen something similar before. A safe place to load and unload their weapons.

A tall metal cabinet stood by its side with a deep-set circular lock. At its side, a row of nightsticks with a handle at a right angle hung. On a shelf below were two bright red boxes lined up side by side. Someone had ripped open one bearing the head of an eagle.

"Eight clips. Ten rounds each. Two boxes of fifty," she said as she backhanded the phone to Fisher. Keeping the beam forward, he watched as she slid an empty plastic tray from the box.

"Shit," Fisher blurted, still watching as she pulled open the second, this time half filled with brass shining in the light. "Why are you smiling?" he said as her grin flashed in the light. Harris had already moved to the rack on the wall, pulling the empty magazines and slipping rounds into each.

"It's a game changer," she said, already done with the first. Fisher's brow twitched. "It changes our rules of engagement," she added, pushing a full magazine into the butt of the pistol.

Leaving the room, they were each heavier to the weight of a loaded SIG Sauer P226 pushed into their overall's pocket, Harris unable to let the moment pass without listing in a low voice the name of their new weapons, along with her disdain for the slow double action on the first shot and the unacceptable ten round capacity of the magazine. As she spoke, she pulled the armoury door closed, its self-locking latch engaging.

With the thin of her set of metal picks back out, the metal twanged in the lock as she snapped the blade. Turning in unison, Harris switched the phone to active IR, and they followed the green glow to the door opposite, where Fisher took the phone and watched her hands blur at the lock.

With the gun drawn, and letting the second heavy door seal at their backs, the klaxon retreated to a whisper again. Moving the phone out of sight, the pitch black heightening the aged, stale air. With a delicate touch on his arm, Harris took the phone, the screen lighting the contours of her face green as she turned on the spot to take in the room's eerie rendering.

Sidestepping him with the camera, she leaned up to the wall, and with a metallic click, long fluorescent tubes popped and flashed bright as they came to life over their heads. As the light's crackle faded to a low hum, Harris turned and flicked the door latch before they took in the room.

Just as she turned, a waft of air brushed his face with the rising harsh hum of faraway turbines complaining for lubrication. With a glance up, he spotted two large stainless steel louvres recessed into the far wall, then took his first look at the towering shelves stretching out in the wide room the size of a high school gym.

Together they strode the perimeter of the rectangular room, their entire view filling with containers, cartons and boxes of all sizes, each sitting on thick metal shelves. Many boxes were of dense, aged cardboard, each tied with nylon rope and bound in the middle with a padlock.

To the right, the containers looked untouched by age, orange plastic boxes stacked three high in some places. Passing row upon row, their footsteps echoed while the boxes aged, their size shrinking and the space between them lessening. Passing the last, they came to a raw concrete wall, its rough industrial finish just visible between the wooden shelves crammed with cardboard folders arranged in all colours of the rainbow.

Some were more worn than others. Their colours faded and corners rubbed light, whilst others were crisp with the pigment still vivid. Oversized cardboard dividers stuck out from various points in each row, jutting out with a bold letter in the top corner.

Drawn to the folders, Fisher stepped closer and out of the corner of his eye, Harris pushed her gun into her pocket before staring at her phone as she disappeared between the shelves.

The first file he pulled came just after the section

marked with a C, and was somewhere between beige and light orange, its apparent age neither new nor old. On the front was a name written with care, *Adam Castleton*, besides which stood a number five marked and the words, *Type 4*, underneath in the same fountain pen ink. A date Fisher presumed was the guy's date of birth, *2nd June 1978*, came next. It described him as a male before it showed his address. He wasn't a local, instead from London. Before that, it showed 2011, a year Fisher guessed was of some significance. The rest of the front was blank.

Although feeling empty, inside he found two loose sheets of paper. A form, some sort of medical document covered with barely legible scrawl and two cartoon style drawings of a male body, each with an oversized head. On the left, it depicted a featureless person staring out from the page with their hands stretched out to the side. The other was of the same drawing but side on in the same pose.

An inked cross marked the centre of the head on both cartoons. Fisher attempted to read the scrawl again, but it contained too many acronyms.

The second page was a high-quality printout of an x-ray film. Even without a day studying medicine, Fisher knew the mass wasn't meant to be inside the guy's head.

Hearing Harris, he looked up and spotted her moving between the piles of boxes. Pushing the file back in a random place, he plucked the next, this time a darker orange.

Skipping the name and the age, his gaze went straight to the bold seven in the corner and *Type 3* underneath. With a similar form at the front, it ran to three pages and the biro marks were in different places on the cartoon. To the left and close to the front of the head. As before, an x-ray followed. This time it was the original film, and showed another mass, smaller than the last and matching the location on the cartoon. The third document was a form from an accident and emergency department, dated ten years ago. The details described that he'd presented to the A&E at Addenbrooke's with a head injury, which concluded with a referral to a specialist for further investigation into the unrelated mass inside his head.

Remembering waking in the hospital, he pushed the file back.

So much had gone on since then, he'd not given it a second thought.

Scanning along the sea of cardboard sleeves, his gaze caught on a deep red file, in the corner a ten and a Type 4. He glanced at the name on the file, *David Simon*, born 31st August 1984. Unsure why he thought the name would stick in his mind, he scanned the wall of files, still not understanding the significance of the colours. Looking higher at the next row, he counted only a few dark red files amongst the sea of beige and orange.

Cameron Roberson. A7, Type 1 in a faded dark orange file, its thickness singling it out from the crowd. He read through the pack, skipping to the last page of the report dated two years ago. He read through the clipped English on a sheet titled *Profile*.

Observations showed the subject's abilities appeared to have reached their plateau, making tracking and further investigation difficult. A recent operation to detain the subject for study failed when he used his abilities to evade, and he disabled three operatives. Studies of the affected concluded the damage irreversible.

Fisher read the line again, unable to stop himself from imagining what the damage could have been.

Moving on, he found the last two lines inked bold and underlined twice.

All future type ones with a potency greater than five are to be detained at an early stage before abilities reach full bloom.

Consider JFM10T1 extremely dangerous, should he advance to his potential.

Fisher looked up from the words, searching for meaning as he stared into the distance, but as he rolled the thoughts over, his vision came from a blur, his gaze running along the continuous parallel line of folders packed against each other, only stopping on the large handwritten F separating it from its neighbours.

His feet seemed fixed to the spot and his legs felt heavy as he tried to step. With the first file just out of reach, moving in time with the pounding in his chest, he traced across the anonymous spines, then pulled out a wedge of folders.

Toby Fearn came into view, but he pushed it back into place. Feasel, then Finch, came after a beige file. The name was next to a large four. The words *Type One* beneath.

The next stole his breath. With his surname written across the orange file, he searched his memory for the name. Annabel Fisher. With no recollection, he heard a heavy noise from the corridor, followed by the sound of snapping plastic a few rows over.

Pushing forward to the last of the files, he opened a gap in the row on the shelf with the tips of his fingers, leafing to the faded pink of a dog-eared jacket, its contents substantial, but the name on the cover showed no more Fishers. The bold black mark confirmed the guy had died over ten years ago.

As he slipped his fingers into the next, and the one after, he pulled apart file after file as disappointment tugged at him when he hadn't found his name, sure the code mentioned in the last one was him. But if it was, then what did the M stand for?

71

With his breath thick in his throat, Fisher's gaze darted the short distance between the markers for O and N, before finding M in the row above. Although the row stood out of his reach, he soon spotted the faded pink edge of a scarlet folder.

On tiptoes, he pulled himself high, just about able to tug at the corner. With not enough purchase, the card fell from his grip, sending pages fluttering across the floor. Peering down and scanning the fallen sheets, his attention drew to the red cover.

Type 1. Solid in dark marker, his name jumped from the scarlet, giving him his first understanding of the initial. *Montez*. The surname in brackets after Fisher.

Shaking his head, he forced himself from lingering on the name, instead scooping up the closest sheet to find medical notes from his brief stay in hospital. After a flash of the van hitting for a second time, he read the summary.

No apparent injury, but he requires an appointment with the representative from the U of Cambridge to review scans of a mass in the brain.

Appointment missed, ran in red across the sheet pinned behind, the words scrawled in a hurried hand.

Looking back to the floor, he found the page he'd dreaded. A cartoon of his oversized head with the cross of ink buried deep inside, the notes pointing it out as the anterior insular cortex. Choosing a perfect print of a life size x-ray next, its date matched the report and was only a couple of months old. Had it been such a short time since this all began?

Seeing the mass the size of a pea, the thought fell away.

Closing his eyes, he concentrated as if trying to feel it inside, but shook his head when everything felt like it always had.

Glancing at each of the gathered pages, he recognised the handwriting from many of the other files.

Continued observation confirms the subject is still in first stages, with the next milestone expected in a couple of years. However, the timeline is affected by environmental conditions. It is clear the subject will reach stage three a few years after, and we're very hopeful the subject will continue to stage N, the stage of which has never been observed in a Type One before.

A loud clunk at the door pulled Fisher from the words. Despite a desperate need to look at each file, interrogating every page for answers to his growing list of questions, he stuffed the sheets back into the cardboard.

Feeling the need to look for Luana next, the girl raised in this place, he scanned the files for her name. But Montez was her lie, and his, but differently. Pausing at the sound of Harris fumbling somewhere a few rows over amidst the muffled klaxon, his gaze fell on a black jacket amongst the Ps.

As he pulled the wide cardboard free, taking more care than he had before, he realised there was more than one black file in his hand. Two bulged with pages, the other thin and limp, but reading a word in red across a white sticker on the front, he realised why.

Deceased. He pushed it under his arm and opened the next. Hunter Penfield. Female. Born 3rd December 1985.

Its pages were filled with multiple films. The earliest was of a baby with a mass in the same place as his. A dot on the image. As the heads grew on each film, so did the mass, but with age, growing bigger in proportion and not round like Fisher's or the others he'd seen. With each film, the spikes grew further outward like the protective capsule of a conker. Spikes twined out like tendrils from a wild creeper. In the last film he saw the mass much larger, its alien-like suffocation of the brain near indistinguishable from the native matter.

Glancing back at the cover, he found a white sticker in the corner he'd missed. She was a Type 1, like himself, but above it was the number four. Scouring through the notes, he searched for an address, when a square of thick paper fell. A photograph of a little girl stared back from the floor. With her head shaved, the red of a fresh scar along her hairline made him wince.

Fisher slipped the glossy polaroid back between the pages and continued leafing through the sheets. A heavy sound caught him from the door, but when he glanced over and the noise had stopped, he turned back, sending the files spilling from his grip. Cursing as the pages fluttered to the floor, he dropped to his knees and scraped the papers into a pile. The word *Profile* at the top of a page made him pause, and he read the scribble beneath.

The subject exhibits a captivating likability by those in her proximity. Previous extensive reviews have determined we should limit human contact, and we have taken several steps in order to remove all possible contamination, including isolating siblings and her mother. The only measured change, however, is the deterioration in the subject's mental state. We have yet to determine if this is an environmental factor or a result of the primary condition.

It has been a year since the subject has been restricted to one main contact and there had been reports of a physical relationship between the two which resulted in a pregnancy. This could not be allowed to go full term. Examination of the early stage embryo determined the offspring was viable.

Fisher's heart sank as he read the reports. Only once did an author ask that, even in the surroundings of the questionable ethical framework, and the subject being over the age of consent, if what they subjected her to was justifiable. Isolated and insular, she was in no position to give consent.

The ink changed and so did the hand that wrote it, the words more scientific and recording a tendency for mood swings along with an ever-diminishing empathy. He re-read a phrase buried in the middle of the text.

Both are likely due to the seeding location. Had the effects been stronger than a level five, the risk to wider society would mean the project would be terminated. A large dose of prednisone has found to be the only way of holding back the symptoms. Although opioids had a similar result, the side effects were significant and dosing difficult to judge.

Fisher looked up, squinting as he turned back to the words. The last entry was six months ago and ended with a stark outlook. The mass was still growing, and they didn't know how long she could cope.

Pulling his stare from the page, he looked around the room. Feeling a deep sorrow and desperate for perspective, he drew a breath.

As he turned the last page, the files dropped from his grip again as Luana's pale, smiling face stared back at him from the floor.

72

Shaking from his stare, he reassembled the pages into the sleeve, pulling out the thin file from under his arm.

Joshua Penfield, deceased. From the date of birth, perhaps she was a twin.

With a glance at the last file in his hand, he corrected himself. A triplet.

They'd died five years ago, almost to the day. Fisher watched the tumour grow in the macabre flick book of x-ray films at his fingertips. The shadow of a dot growing. The feelers of the anemone feeding out, encircling the brain at a rate that made the black writing at the head of the file inevitable. The last page reported the obvious. His brain crushed from the inside, the vice like pressure incompatible with life.

A photo pinned at the top made Fisher gag as he looked at Joshua's brain sat on stainless steel scales with blood drooling from its surface and long pink tendrils encasing the grey matter.

With one black folder left, he drew a deep breath, taking heart in the file's thickness. It's weight similar to Hunter's. The name read Lucy Penfield. Looking back at the row, he was relieved to find no other black folders.

The first page could have been a carbon copy of her sister's, but as a thump of steel against the door echoed the warehouse, that was as far as he got.

Harris rounded the shelving, pausing for a moment when she saw the files. She carried an orange plastic container, the black words CMB1 stencilled on the side and with two iComms resting on the lid.

When steel rammed hard against the door for a second time, they glanced over but saw no movement.

Fisher stepped over and took his iComm.

"Thanks," he said, his voice low and head still lost in the words.

"They've shelved the project," Harris said, pulling open

the leaves of the container, her iComm in her hand. Fisher didn't need to voice his question. "I don't know where it is, or why they shelved a discovery of such monumental importance."

"Maybe they don't understand the significance?" he replied, not raising his voice.

"They do," she said, her eyes pinching as she read the single sheet of paper, leaving the container empty.

"Maybe they're going to bury it?" Fisher said. "The project, not the rock."

Harris spoke again, shaking her head.

"A corporation with a conscience turns down trillions to save the status quo?" she said. "I don't think so. It's more likely they've found where it came from."

"Or another use?" he replied, staring at Harris.

"Something more significant than infinite energy?" she asked.

He nodded, turning towards the shelves of files towering over him.

"What are these?" she said, stepping forward, but before he could answer, the thump of the metal at the door was replaced with the high-pitched squeal of a cutting wheel. "Time to go," she said. "Are you okay?" she added when Fisher didn't reply.

"The answer's here."

"The answer to what?"

"Everything," he said, then paused as he looked back at the rows of cardboard sleeves. "To what I am. To where I came from. They've been cataloguing for years. This is bigger than the rock."

"You're not making sense," Harris replied, her brow furrowed as she stared at the files. "We've got to go."

Fisher pushed the three black files under his arm and grabbed the pages spread at his feet, the bundle pinched in his armpit as he peeled away from the shelves. He paused for a moment, staring back at the towering folders.

"Come on," she said. Only her tug at his arm broke his

gaze and he followed her along the rows until she stopped, eyeing the door and the gaps between the shelves.

"How do we get out?" Fisher said, his eyes flitting around the vast room.

"I don't know," she replied. Fighting the urge to run at her heel, he followed her calm walk, despite the shrill call of the attack at the door.

As if finding purpose, her pace soon increased, as did his, rushing as he clutched the folders tight.

Arriving at the far wall, Harris pulled crates from the stack, their lids snapping open as she rummaged through the contents, stopping only when silence fell around them. With caustic fumes filling the air, they both peered at the door just as a thump of metal called out like a dulled bell.

Fisher spun on his heels, leaving Harris to continue her search and rush around the room's perimeter only to confirm there was only the one door. His despair cut short when a deep groan came from up high and he looked up to the air vents in time to see both stainless louvres seal closed. Still staring at the louvres, Harris soon joined at his side.

Halfway back to the wall, he'd spotted the ceiling broken up by a hatch in the room's far right corner. Swapping glances, Fisher's eyebrows raised before he turned back to the hatch's over-painted edges in between the wall and the first shelf, and then his gaze found a rust-pitted ladder sticking out from the wood to hang below, set back from the wall but it ended with sharp edges where a long time ago it had been cut, leaving only four rungs behind.

"Fuck," Fisher shouted, his anger echoing around the chamber.

With a deep breath as the pounding on the door continued, he took comfort in Harris's blank expression until the hum of the lights and the brightness vanished, plunging them into darkness. The hectic grind of the power tool lit up again, its screech growing louder with each moment.

Fight or flight, that was normally the choice, but all they could do was hope there weren't too many people for their bullets.

Light sprung out from Harris's hands, illuminating her face before she turned her phone around, sending shadows dancing across the shelves and wall.

In the new light, he sized up the shelf he stood beside, then leaned against the unit's thick pillar. When it didn't give, he pushed harder, adding more pressure. When it still didn't deflect or complain, he relaxed.

"Not going to happen," Harris said, pointing the beam to the thick bolts holding the shelf against the floor. Grabbing the uprights as best she could whilst holding the phone, she raised her foot and climbed.

Fisher pushed his hand out, trying to gauge the distance they would have to cover before they could reach the bottom rung, even if they could climb the shelves in the darkness. With one arm still pinning the folders, he reached out, watching the walls shimmer as her torch cast a meagre dash of light, until the full beam shined in his direction. She was at the top, but even with her arms outstretched, she was only halfway to the wall, which even for her was too great a distance to make.

As the constant scrape of the grinding wheel paused, replaced with the thump of weight banging shoulders against the door, the whine of the grinder was soon back to work. With Harris's light shining from above, Fisher shoved the folded cardboard under his belt, tightening the buckle by two notches, then gripped the metal struts and climbed.

With each step the metal swayed but he was soon by her side staring at the painted edges of the escape hatch and the rust covered uprights of the short ladder.

"What now?" he said, turning towards her as she shone the beam across the gulf. Shaking his head, he looked at her again, this time taking no comfort in her unflinching expression. "We can't make that," he said, still shaking his head.

"You know the other option," she replied.

"Your shoulder?" Fisher replied, but she dismissed him

without looking over. "If you miss, that's it."

"Don't miss then," she said. "Use your light," she added, pointing to the ladder before pushing her phone into her pocket just as Fisher's light came on to reveal the hatch again and the metal that looked paper thin.

With his eyes widening, he felt the shelf swing as she shuffled forward to teeter on the edge, then moving back and forth, she built a rhythm. About to leap, the white noise of the grinder ceased, replaced by another heavy clank against the door.

On the second bang, the note changed, and he felt the door was ready to give. Harris turned and Fisher stared along the path she was about to take, his heart beating for their future together as he fought the urge to hold her back.

On the third bang, she pounced, the arc of light shaking as Fisher steadied himself with the metal beneath him reacting like Newton's Third Law said it would. He held his breath as she sailed through the air, but she was too low, Fisher guessed as his shoulders slumped, enveloped by a cloud of depression as her shadow traced the wall.

On the fourth bang, the note was much higher, the volume loud. The door was about to give, but Fisher's attention held as Harris's fingers brushed the metal post and, finding no friction, she fell into thin air.

On the fifth bang he saw her suspended, the fingers on her other hand curled white around the bottom rung where it held. His heart leapt as the metal remained strong and she stifled a pained scream as she pulled herself up enough to grab with both hands and curl her legs around the last rung.

On the sixth bang, the door seemed paper thin. Shouts from the corridor echoed and by the seventh she was safe, climbing two rungs up, her eyes catching the light, cat like, as she beckoned him through the air.

On the eighth bang, Fisher stood transfixed at the gap. She shined her torch to the ceiling and he pushed away. Urging himself forward, he knew this was no time to prove himself a failure.

With the ninth bang, the door was done and with it came a mass of long torch beams piercing the cloud of dust scattered by the fall.

No tenth bang came, but on the missing beat he hunkered down and with all his might sprung across the gulf, pushing his hands out as he willed himself onward in the hope he had done enough to cover the impossible distance.

He had done enough; in fact, too much. He'd jumped higher than he thought possible and had paid for it with too much distance which he only realised when his shin smashed into the short cutoff at the bottom of the ladder. Doing his best to ignore the searing pain as the raw edge sliced through his overalls and skin, he focused on grabbing a rung.

With both hands, he circled the metal, then dropped, tensing, ready for the pull of his weight. As his mass caught, the momentum was too much and his grip wasn't enough for the sudden effort, the cold metal tearing from his hands. With all but the occasional spray of light from below, he could no longer see where he was trying to grab as he fell.

After what seemed too long to be of any use, his finger caught something, but even though his hand reacted in an instant, it was too late and his fingernails scraped against the metal. Somehow, he knew there was one more rung left before certain death and, hooking his hands, pushed them forward just as the tips smacked the rung, but gave no purchase.

73

Time slowed for Fisher like people say it does. In the darkness, he heard a barrage of noise from below. Muffled, deep screams merged with his thoughts of the concrete floor racing towards him, but just as the panic bit, he felt a calmness descend as a sudden pressure entangled his wrists and an agonising pull yanked him to a stop midair, his shoulders straining at the sockets and the pages slipped from under his belt.

For a moment he toyed with pulling free from the grip, letting himself fall so he could scoop up all the words that could have so much meaning, but as light dashed across his view and he saw Harris, upside down, hair hanging towards the floor and her features contorted with effort, he realised the stupidity.

A shout of realisation went up from below and Fisher felt himself rise, the grip on his wrists tight. As he rose, his fingertips reached the steel and, helped with an upward pull, he took his own weight and forced himself higher, past her legs curled around the bottom rung of steel.

Holding tight and with his feet on the metal, he climbed with her hands against his back, pushing him higher and guiding him around the side of the ladder. Hanging, he blinked as she righted herself and scurried up on the opposite side of the metal with the bright light blinding them from below.

A calm voice echoed up as they both regained their breath. The words from the unseen man were low and tinged with a German inflection.

"That's not your way out. You'll be sure to die, if that's your choice."

Fisher flinched as a shot echoed around the room and Harris touched his hand to steady him. The light below wavered as shouts caught the air, the brightness easing as torches turned away. Glancing at Harris, another shot rang off but quieter this time, as if not even in the room.

Within an instant of the second shot, Fisher felt a hand

pull him tall as a third rang off in the distance. The reply was much closer. An order barked for a ceasefire.

Standing hunched over with their feet on the lowest rung and their fingers gripping the highest, their backs arched against the flat of the panel in the ceiling, where together they pushed between the two sections of the hatch.

Grunting with the effort, the painted seams gave with a tear and a crack and they didn't delay in rising into the darkness, then climbing as the steps continued into a brick chamber, which ended in another hatch, extinguishing their excitement. What greeted them wasn't another thin wooden panel painted shut, but solid steel banded with thick rivets at each edge, its surface rusted over where the life-saving control wheel should have been.

A single urgent shout rang up from below. The lights had sprung on and, looking down, Fisher saw the spread pages covered the floor, dotted with black spots with new marks appearing as the blood dripped in a steady stream from his ankle.

The shout repeated, the word louder despite the two leaves of the hatch dropping closed to force out all light.

"Fire."

The violent reply came in an instant. Multiple fingers itching to play tightened against curled metal and sent hot lead ringing out at a deadly rate. Both pulled their legs high to their chest, arms straining as they clutched at the top rung with their feet balanced on the one below. Squeezed as high as they could, rounds tore at the wood beneath them before embedding in the brick and pinging around the tiny space. All they needed was an off balance ricochet, and they were done for.

Having pushed his eyes tight, he opened them to find Harris clinging on with one hand and holding the pistol out towards the remains of the hatch with the other, as if waiting for the first face to appear through the mess. Fisher shook as her first round released, then again with her second. Her rounds did for the panel, as well as for a man in their limited view below, but he knew it would only delay the inevitable.

Without warning, something jarred against the hatch at their heads, followed by the grind of metal as if someone turned the control on the other side. Looking up, he found the cut spindle turning, and for the first time, he saw uncertainty in Harris's expression. Not knowing which way to point the gun, she aimed upward, then back down, firing when someone appeared to drag the body away.

Light shone from above, but despite the renewed shots from below, when they hadn't both fallen at the new arrival's hands, Harris bounded up the ladder and disappeared, leaving behind only a fresh breeze.

A hand reached down, and it wasn't hers, but still Fisher scrabbled higher, although with much less finesse. Taking the offered grip, he was soon out, left squinting at black boots, black combats and a bomber jacket before settling on a wide smile of a stranger, surprised to find no malice or gun pointed in their direction.

Pulling himself over the edge, he watched Harris with fascination, glaring at her smile as she rolled her injured shoulder.

"Your faces are a picture," the guy said between deep belly laughs, his own a smiling mass of white teeth too big for his mouth.

Staring at the man who Fisher guessed was in his late thirties, his gaze caught on a side arm holstered at his waist, but before he could question what was going on, the man stopped laughing enough to speak.

"I'd get the fuck out of here if I were you," he said.

"Who the hell are you?" Fisher said, looking between the pair.

"Tommy," Harris replied, lurching forward to hug the man.

"Tell Biggy it looks like there's a few of us back on the market," Tommy said before handing Harris a pass on a lanyard.

Not waiting to be told twice, Harris grabbed Fisher's

arm and they ran towards a pedestrian turnstile and the car waiting on the other side.

74

Climbing into the rear of the car, they found a first aid kit on the back seat. After giving the driver a questioning look, Harris barked out a road name. Fisher watched the roads as they headed through a maze of residential streets, not looking at Harris as she poked and prodded his leg wound, tearing at the overalls before she wound the first turn of a bandage.

"You'll have to do the other one," Fisher said, with the pain subsiding as he looked at the rags hanging from his right knee. The corner of her mouth turned up.

"Here's fine," Harris said toward the front before opening the door with the car barely at a stop.

Slamming the door after Fisher hobbled from the seat, the car vanished around a corner moments later.

"I take it you've worked with Tommy before," Fisher said as he sucked through his teeth with each painful step.

"A long time ago," she said, her brow narrow as she nodded. Again, he thought better of delving deeper.

Back at their car after ten minutes, they hardly spoke, the conversation only starting as they pulled into the service station car park and they spotted the blue and white police tape cordoning off the shattered glass scattered around the wide opening that had been the window of Luana's room. The room they'd left her at before meeting with the LanfordStamp minibus.

"Stay here," Harris said as she pulled her slender frame from the driving seat.

Watching her walk across the car park, he'd already forgotten about the aching wound as the all too familiar hormones coursed through his veins to focus his concentration and prime him for another round of action.

With no need for fight or flight, the surge of adrenaline left tiredness in its wake, along with the feeling there would be many more hours before they'd process what they'd found. He watched Harris as she glided across the car park with no signs of strain in her gentle sway.

"The police have her, if you hadn't guessed," Harris said as she pulled on the seatbelt and stared out at the missing window just as an employee swept up glass.

"What happened?" he asked.

"There's been a shift change since the arrest, but it sounds like someone tipped off the police after seeing the TV news report. They arrived with armed units, but she put up a fight. Three officers were killed, and she tried to commit suicide." Fisher stared back, wide-eyed. "But they're just rumours," she added.

"What now? We need her," Fisher said and Harris nodded.

"I can't see any other way. It's going to be hard to get hold of her, if it's true," she said, her words tailing off.

"We have to tell Clark," Fisher replied.

It was her turn to nod, and he answered within two rings.

"I know," Clark said before either of them spoke.

"Where is she?" Harris replied.

"Cambridge nick. They won't let her go without very good reason," he said.

"What happened?" Fisher cut in.

"The preliminary report says after an initial foot chase, she came of her own accord."

"Is she injured?" Fisher hurried out the question.

"No," Clark replied. "No shots fired." The pair looked at each other, shaking their heads.

"The window?" Harris asked.

"She smashed it through with a chair when they knocked at her door, but they had the place surrounded. She didn't have a chance."

"How do you know all this?" Fisher asked.

"She says you're her lawyer, and she's asking for you," Clark replied.

They sat in silence until Harris spoke.

"Have they interviewed her?"

"No."

"We better get there before they do," Harris said, starting the engine.

"Can you get her released to our custody?" Fisher said, looking across at the driver's side.

"She's suspected of murder. It will take a while. I'll call ahead, for all the good it'll do," Clark said before silence followed.

"Thanks for saving our bacon back there," Harris said.

"I just made a call," he replied and hung up, only to call back ten minutes later.

His first call got them a prescription. The second got them into the station and in front of the custody sergeant. As he denied their first request to see her, Fisher stared at the white board at their backs. Cell FM1. Murder times five, written under her initials and followed by a large question mark.

The desk sergeant called the inspector who sent it further up the line, leaving them standing in the austere room behind the custody desk, their view fixed on a grainy image of Luana in the cell, her body twisting and turning against the restraints as she slipped and slid over the blue plastic mattress. Beside them, an officer kept a constant vigil on the screen.

Fisher turned back to the sergeant, handing over the white box they'd picked up on the way over.

"She needs four tablets," he said, and the sergeant stared back. "It'll calm her down, but she may not want to take them."

He took the pills without a word and they watched on the screen as the officer spoke. Then she offered her open mouth, where he placed a pill one after the other.

Fisher's gaze fell away from the screen as the sergeant left the image and another officer in uniform arrived at the desk with a thick grey moustache, dark hair close cropped around the edges. The crown on his lapels made him the most senior in the district. Fisher watched as the man moved alongside Harris first, offering his hand out. The officer cocked his head towards a sergeant who sat a few desks down, then nodded at the door. The door closed as the sergeant left.

"Chief Superintendent Stewart," he said, shaking Harris's hand.

"Have you had time to confirm our identities?" she asked as he repeated the greeting to Fisher.

"Yes, but it changes nothing. Without a warrant, the prisoner is staying here."

"You understand this is a national security issue, don't you, sir?" Harris replied, raising her eyebrows.

Stewart nodded, but his stern expression didn't move.

"I have an officer missing and she's the chief suspect, let alone the other hits her prints flagged on PNC. What have you got?"

"I'd be breaking the law if I told you, sir," Harris replied with her head to the left.

Stewart nodded in the reply, the thick grey hair twitching on his lip as if hiding a smile.

"You can have five minutes with her. That's the best I can do."

Harris shook her head. "She's coming with us to London."

"Then we have an impasse, but you're welcome to stay here until she's charged. But I assure you she won't get bail."

Harris took the bulk of her phone from her pocket and pushed it to her ear. Stewart watched with surprising patience, looking at Fisher as Harris's mouth moved into a smile, her gaze never leaving the officer's. After a few seconds without speaking, she closed the call. "You're just wasting my time now. She's coming with us."

The chief superintendent puffed up his chest as his cheeks pinked.

"Nothing's changed. I have a station full of officers that will keep her here. I'm afraid you're going to have to…" he said, his words halting with a knock at the door.

"Not now," Stewart barked.

The knock repeated and without waiting, the sergeant's head appeared around the wood. Stewart snapped his head in the direction, his face red and puffed.

"There's a phone call for you," the sergeant said, his voice meek.

"Take a God damn message," he barked and turned back to Harris.

"Sir," the sergeant insisted.

"What?" Steward shouted.

"It's the Home Secretary."

75

The chief superintendent didn't return from taking the call. His replacement, a pale-faced inspector, hurried them through the process of de-arrest, surprised at the former captive's calm demeanour as he removed the restraints and ushered them out of the station. As they drove, Fisher thought he saw the red faced Stewart scowling from a top-floor window.

Both Harris and Luana slept until they reached the city. Each time Fisher glanced at Luana through the rear-view mirror he winced at the sight of her deathly pale face, his concern compounding when she barely roused as they arrived in the underground car park where two nurses, flanked by a pair of men in suits, took her off in a wheelchair. Fisher followed Harris to a conference room where Clark's image filled the wall, looking up from his desk as they walked in, his eyes bleary.

"What did you find?" Clark said without the usual pleasantries.

Fisher rubbed his eyes as he took a seat. "Everything and nothing," he said. "And they've found another use for the rock."

Clark's expression mirrored Harris when she read aloud the page from the archive.

"What new use?" Clark asked, looking over.

"We don't know if that's true," Harris replied.

"Where is it?" Clark said, his eyebrows raised. Harris shook her head and rifled inside her bomber jacket, pulling out a crumpled page.

"It left for Bergen two months ago," she said and Clark nodded, blowing from between his lips.

"Anything else?" he asked, looking around his desk.

Fisher glanced over to Harris and she nodded.

"They're conducting a research project," Fisher said. "It appears there are lots of people that have certain abilities. Some like me." Clark nodded, his expression unchanged. "They have a wall full of records. Over a thousand, I reckon, but I didn't understand most of what I read." He bit his lip. "They have a file on me," he said, shaking his head. "I should have been more careful," he added, looking down at the desk.

"What was in the files?" Clark said, his brow narrowed.

"There were lots of x-rays of people's heads," Fisher said, looking up.

"Do you know why?" Clark replied.

"Each showed a mass," Fisher replied. "A tumour I guess."

"Did you see your X-ray?" Harris asked, her voice quiet.

Fisher nodded. "Mine's smaller, compared to some I saw." He watched her take a deep breath, her shoulders relaxing as Clark continued to look at him.

"What else did you find?" he asked.

"Three files stuck out. They had records from an early age," he said, looking away from the camera above the projected image as his thoughts turned to the chestnut shaped mass.

"Fisher?" Clark said, and Fisher blinked, the image disappearing as he looked back at Clark.

"Their masses were large, horrible and contorted. They showed their growth through the years and I saw nothing about trying to get rid of them, or make them smaller," Fisher said.

"But it's not linked to the rock?" Clark asked after a long silence.

"There was no reference to the rock anywhere," Fisher replied.

"Okay," Clark replied, seeming to notice Fisher hesitate. "What is it?"

"I want to go back," Fisher said, looking at each of them in turn. Harris closed her eyes and raised her chin.

"It'll be cleaner than an operating theatre by now. And we'd need a warrant and a small army to enforce it," she said, not looking over.

"What about your friends on the inside?" Fisher asked.

"They'll be long gone by now," she replied.

He drew a deep breath. "I have to know."

Harris opened her eyes and looked over at Clark.

"There will be other ways," she said, before the room sunk into silence.

"I'm sorry about this," Clark said after a long moment. "But we have to get back on track. I have to give the board an update in…" he said, his eyes widening as he glanced at his watch. "Three hours. So far, I've got nothing to tell them, and all progress on the original cases has stalled."

"The rock went to Bergen and according to what we found, Johannas Hall went too," Harris said.

"And the place burnt down," Fisher added.

Clark nodded.

"We don't know if it was an accident or deliberate, but they knew how dangerous the rock was," he said.

"Anything on the laptop?" Fisher asked as he turned back to the projected image.

Clark raised his chin. "Like I said before, I don't think we'll ever find it, but I've analysed the ISP traffic from Johannas' rental for the week before they killed him, and I've tracked down his online backup service."

Fisher sat forward, but Harris didn't move, already reading Clark's flat tone.

"But it's encrypted to 256 bit," Clark continued.

Fisher's shoulders slumped, and he pushed himself back into the chair. He didn't need Clark to explain they would die of old age before they would crack the password, even with all the world's super computers on the job.

"Did you find anything to help narrow down the search?"

"Like a Post-it note with his password on?" Fisher said, watching as Clark's eyes lit up, then droop as Harris shook her head.

"Send over the link, just in case something comes to me," Fisher said.

Clark nodded just as they heard the trill of new mail.

Sitting in silence for what seemed like an age, Clark perked up, igniting their pair's enthusiasm. "They found the plane."

Not knowing what it could mean, their shoulders slumped, but Clark continued anyway. "Remember, I said we were missing a couple of planes? They've just found the last one on a remote strip in India."

Fisher nodded, but only half listened. Instead, he tried to remember what he'd seen in the file.

"It looks like the pilot went nuts," Clark said, causing Fisher to take notice. "He killed the co-pilot and disappeared."

"What happened to the passengers?" Harris asked.

"A little hungry, but otherwise okay," Clark, looking over at another screen.

"Any motive?" Harris said, narrowing her eyes.

Clark shook his head. "This is hot off the press," he said, looking at another part of the screen. "They only found the plane an hour ago and information is still coming in. Whilst they organise replacement transport, they've impounded it until they can give it a thorough going over. I imagine they'll interview everyone involved when they get them to the city. The Indian authorities have asked the MET to investigate as most of the passengers are British."

Fisher's mouth opened in an involuntary yawn. "Sorry," he said.

The infectious reaction broke out on Clark's mouth and he raised his eyebrows.

"Did the tests come back from the toothpaste?" Fisher asked, about to stand.

"Yes," Clark replied. Leaning out of shot, they heard the rustle of paper before he reappeared with a printed sheet of A4. "Traces of Fentanyl and a substance yet to be identified, but it appears to be biological."

Fisher glanced over to Harris, his brow low before turning back to the projection. "How are the bikers?"

"They're all experiencing mild side effects associated with withdrawal. Well, the three of them we could test, at least," Clark said.

"What about the fourth?" Harris asked.

"Oh shit, sorry. There's so much going on at the moment I'm not sure what I've told you and what I haven't," Clark replied.

"So?" Fisher said, not hiding his impatience.

"Sorry. The guy," Clark replied before pausing as he clicked at his mouse. "Scott. Marcus Scott. They admitted him to a secure unit."

"What…? Fisher started, his mouth dry. "What's wrong with him?"

Clark glanced at Harris, then back to Fisher.

"He had a psychotic episode. I've seen the video interview, and that's the only way I can describe what happened."

Despite staring at Clark, Fisher didn't see him, unable to stop thinking about Cameron Robertson's file.

"What's wrong?" Harris said, leaning over.

Fisher swallowed. "Nothing. I hope," he replied after a moment.

"Let's take a break," Clark said in the background, and with a nod from Harris, his image disappeared.

"I think we should ask Luana what she knows," Harris said as she stood. "Then get some rest."

Fisher nodded as he trawled the fading pages in his memory.

76

Side by side at the door, they watched Luana's pale face, the globes of her closed eyes sunken into their sockets. She lay near-unrecognisable with her arms at her sides in the hospital bed and a clear tube disappearing into her stump. A white coat floated past, breaking their stare, its owner pulling up the chart at the end of the bed and running a thumb and forefinger through a white moustache before pulling off delicate round glasses as he turned.

"Doctor Sutton," Harris said, stepping across the threshold.

"Agent Harris," he replied, wrinkles tight in the corner of his eyes.

"How's she looking?" Harris said, staring at the bed.

"The wound's infected. She's severely dehydrated with a racing tachycardia and severe headaches. We've given her something to help her rest. By all accounts, she's had the worst recovery regime imaginable," he replied, raising a brow.

"She needs to keep up with the prednisone," Fisher said over Harris's shoulder.

The doctor looked back at the chart. "For?" he said, shaking his head.

"We've seen her without it," Fisher replied, stepping back behind Harris as she nodded toward the doctor.

"It won't do her wound any good, or the infection," he said, but to Fisher's surprise, his voice filled with more interest than concern.

"Call it an operational requirement," Harris replied, and he didn't hear more than the scratch of a pen as Harris followed the doctor out of the room.

Fisher stood at the doorway, his gaze settling on the rise and fall of her chest, but when he looked up, he was surprised to find her eyes open. Despite killing so many who by no measure deserved it, he couldn't forget the sickening contents of her file.

"How are you doing?" he said in a quiet voice.

Glancing down at her limb that ended too early, Luana's voice croaked as she looked at Fisher with big eyes, her bright blue pupils sparkling in the fluorescent light.

"I keep telling myself it's only temporary."

Not knowing what to say, he nodded as a soft smile warmed her face.

"Can I ask you a question?" Fisher said.

She nodded, holding eye contact.

"Susie's okay, isn't she?" Fisher said. Since they'd picked Luana up at the police station, he'd called Susie five times. When Clark didn't know where she was, Fisher was about to stop the car and pull Luana awake to drag the information out of her when he got a text.

I'm okay, but you're right. I need to fix myself. Sorry.

"She needed some time away," Luana said. "I helped her out, that's all."

Feeling tension leave his shoulders and with the guilt filled lump in his throat almost gone, another question came to mind.

"Did you ever meet a guy called Johannas when you lived at LS?" he asked and watched as Luana's eyes brightened.

"Johan Hall?" she replied, her tone rising.

Fisher nodded and her smile widened as her eyes glazed. Fisher pulled up a seat from against the wall and sat down.

"I think he had a crush on me," she said with a childish giggle. "He used to bring me flowers every day for six months. Then he just stopped visiting. I guess someone had a word." Her smile shrank away. "Why do you want to know?"

Fisher looked into her eyes, but feeling Harris's presence at the door, the answer fell away.

"It's nothing, I'm sure. Get some rest and I'll visit again soon."

Fisher stood, and she sat up in the bed, the pain clear on her drawn features, her eyes wide as she spoke.

"Don't leave me here. When you find out where they

329

are, come and get me. You owe me. Remember?" she said, then turned to Harris. "Both of you."

***

The hotel lobby was much as Fisher remembered it. Light grey uniforms. Efficient smiles. He couldn't recall if it had been a week, two, or maybe a year since he'd sat in the dark corner nursing a drink. However, since then they'd remodelled the reception with a new tall, dark wooden desk on the adjacent wall. The old wood where he'd watched their colleague slaughtered was nowhere to be seen. Instead, there was only space, and it was as if it was all in his head.

Harris gripped his forearm as they walked through the door held open by a doorman, another new fixture, and he guessed perhaps he was more than just to welcome, perhaps with a firearm within easy reach under the long woollen coat.

"Are you okay?" Harris said as Fisher felt the warmth of her touch through his jacket.

Fisher nodded his only reply, keeping his voice to himself and locking the door at his back after she spoke.

She would wake him at two.

Stripped to his boxers, he lay in the plush bed, and after setting the alarm on his iComm for a few moments before she would arrive, he stared at the webpage on his screen.

The stark plain white showed no corporate logo or instructions, with just two text boxes waiting for his fingers. Tapping in Johannas's name in the topmost, then checking the Interpol file to make sure of the spelling, he stared at the wall as he counted his breaths, then tapped in *LanfordStamp*.

Tall red characters blinked at the top of the screen. *Ingen Tilgang*. The googled translation provided no surprise. He tapped out the guy's date of birth to the same result. The Interpol file was a mine of information but with the fifth entry, his town of birth, the whole screen went red, the boxes disappearing.

Five minutes counted down in their place and his eyes drifted to the dark TV screen.

Frustration pulled at his insides as he unlocked his phone with his touch just as Clark's name loomed large in the list of contacts.

"You're supposed to be resting," Clark said as he answered, his voice stiff.

"I need to get my mind clear," Fisher replied.

"What are thinking?" Clark said, his tone softening.

"Have you had any feedback on those other cases?" Fisher asked.

"Not much," Clark replied, surprised by the question. "The MET are handling them now."

"So you've heard nothing about that lad? The one who burnt down the school?"

"Like what?" Clark asked.

"Like is he okay?"

"I haven't heard," Clark replied, speaking again after a pause. "But I can find out for you?"

"No," Fisher replied. "It's fine," and he hung up the call.

Resting the iComm on the bedsheet, he'd said too much and closed his eyes, despite knowing sleep was unlikely.

77

The familiar drum of rain echoed in the warehouse and Fisher stood transfixed to his suit as it reflected from the familiar glass box sitting just proud of the gloss white floor. His eyes refocused, staring through the glass to the stainless steel plinth and the naked body laying on top with his hands clamped on either side.

As if on rails, his gaze followed the same route they'd taken so many times. Unable to move from the course, it passed over white scars, the shaven head and through the second pane to her smooth naked curves.

But it was different to every other time he'd been at this place. His body didn't react in the same way.

Desensitised, perhaps. He watched as she operated the controls and, feeling a twitch in his eye, he noticed writing etched into the corner of the glass. Despite being unable to turn or squint, he tried to concentrate on the word at the edge of his vision. The characters were familiar. *JFM10T1*. His eyes ached, and he tried to blink, surprised when his sleep filled mind obeyed, his eyelids fluttering away the pain.

Taking in the view, he watched Harris move toward him, but he soon spotted something else in the distance. He couldn't move his head or look elsewhere no matter how hard he tried, but his concentration took no notice of the familiar play, instead he poured his effort into watching a tall figure engulfed in shadow. After a moment, his mind spasmed and the view reset, forcing him to watch her move to his side. He could see the figure still watching, but when a faint voice spoke for the first time, he could no longer pick them out.

Detached from the view, he watched as the body, his body, twitched behind the glass, and instead of the emptiness he felt every other time, he caught a reflection on the left side of the glass. Another case rose into his thoughts and panic electrified his soul with a question.

Had he seen this all before?

His body twitched and somehow he turned his head to

the side. Shocked at first with the ease of the movement, despite that, it was like someone controlled him, but only allowing him to move within allowed bounds. Somehow, he took in the new image.

A woman, not Harris. Her two hands were a surprise. Across her shoulder was the curve of a crossbow. He didn't fear, even as the woman smiled.

His gaze followed her as she moved, his body in tow, fixed on its path as he turned to the left and walked backwards to the second glass case. His brain fought for control of his eyes as they ran across the naked body of a woman, her skin firm but wrinkled. Looking up, he found another etched code. *AJM10T2.*

Through the glass, he found a third case with a wrinkled man bound inside. As Harris curled around his body, he focused on glass cases vanishing into the distance. When his head snapped around, she'd gone, leaving him staring at his face inside the glass cell.

"It won't be long," Harris said as she always did. "I love you," he heard her say as she pulled a lever and arms rushed down inside the procession of glass cases, colouring his view with scarlet.

With sweat beading on his chest, Fisher pulled himself up from the bed, panting for breath. Scouring the hotel room, he searched for the insistent knocking.

"It's two o'clock," Harris called through the door and Fisher stared over, then leaned to his side, grabbing his phone as it chimed. With the last of the nightmare falling away, she called again. "Are you okay?"

"Give me ten minutes," he said, repeating the words with volume before her footsteps replied.

Climbing from the bed, he grabbed a thin square of note paper and pen from the desk, scribbling the fading memories.

Hunter Penfield.
Man in the shadows.
JFM10T1.

Shaking his head, he remembered no more details.

"There's something else. I'm sure," he whispered to himself, then scrawled again, but couldn't read the incoherent scribble.

Letting out a sigh, his alarm chimed for the second time, and he scrabbled back to the bed and slid the icon across to silence the alarm and, by habit alone, he tapped in his pin, revealing the login page for the backup service.

Without thinking, he removed Johannas's name and typed. *Hunter Penfield*. Not pausing, he switched to the other field, tapping again. *JFM10T1*. The screen flashed green, and a folder appeared with a single document.

Tidsskrift.

Journal.

He clicked the link and took up the iComm's offer to translate.

78

Journal

This is my truth.

My name is John Hall, and I'm a neuroscientist, a certified physician working for Lanford Chemicals Ltd. I am fifteen years in research that will soon reveal the secrets of the human brain and unlock the potential for its development. History will compare the steps we will take to the transistor's invention, or the printing press, or antibiotics multiplied a thousand times.

I write this journal not for anyone in particular, but for all those who have worked tirelessly to achieve this greatness. This project is my proud legacy and the legacy of the hundreds of people who work beside or before me.

To some, the details of this project will be unpalatable, but to those who can look past the glancing cost and consider the words of great philosophers, there are other techniques and breakthroughs with high human costs, but they have still brought society to where it is today.

Yes, we look back at the Nazis and shake our heads, disgusted by their ways, but still we use the methods and tools born from the fruits of their labour. Humankind built modern medicine and surgery on the backs of forced human trials and bodies stolen from the ground, but with them we save lives.

This is not an expose. It is a reminder that human history is littered with decisions made for the masses and not for the few, much akin to war. I want the facts to be clear. This work is undertaken in the same vein; it is a considered scientific endeavour made by great men that has been ongoing for over half a century, and all for the greater advancement of humanity. It should not be considered the cruel work of a few.

My only concern is when I die, I want people to see the facts before they make their judgement. If you're reading this, then I am dead and it is my last wish to make it public.

My work started on the backs of many great scientists who have come before me. In the nineteen seventies, Eldridge and Gould theorised we were in the midst of Cladogenesis, a new species rapidly splitting from Homosapien, the species that had been the human race for the last half a million years. The theory was based on burgeoning research into genetics and allowed them to formulate their theory of Punctuated Equilibria.

Their published work was based on the lowly land snail, but behind closed doors their ideas had come from the top of the food chain, the Homosapien. They named their theoretical new species Homopotius. It wasn't until a few years later empirical measurements cemented the Eldridge Gould theory firmly in science and they became the forefathers of research into the first tentative steps into the unknown.

For millennia a wide section of civilisation across all religions and faiths have harboured a belief, or a will to believe, at least, that humanity is not just the sum of all of its flesh and bone, and there were secrets to discover about our true capabilities. Anecdotal evidence ripples through history about humans being more. Scientists and pseudo-scientists have been reaching out since the birth of the species, searching for that something.

It was while supervising such an investigation at a University in Norway that Gould's research group discovered a documentable and repeatable case of what we now call the Type Three. The subject was able to read the minds of other people and stand up to robust scientific scrutiny.

The reader may ask why, if they knew this, why was this information kept secret? It wasn't greed as you may suspect and it wasn't a need to keep the special information to themselves for their own end, but an understanding that the information was so powerful and would change the world, they had better understand it before they set it out.

Those were the motives back then, anyway.

Once it was decided to keep the project secret, a like-minded corporate backer was found and under a promise not to release the information until the work was deemed complete and the world was considered ready, they set about a worldwide project to test and catalogue as many people as possible, honing methods and increasing their understanding of the biological mechanisms as time went on.

As the months passed, new examples of Type Threes were found at a rate of around two a month, then by chance they discovered the first Type Four, a young man who was able to regenerate flesh at an enhanced rate. Realising the scope of what they were looking for was much wider, they tested subjects again, subjected them to more and more, at this time, non-invasive tests and scrutinising medical records, all in the name of a *drug trial.*

The project was costly for the commercial backer and despite the injection of cash from a number of wealthy donors, they couldn't save the firm from being taken over. The project continued and with the fresh influx of cash, its pace increased, but they saw the first cracks in the motive of those putting forward the capital.

By now the project had categorised four distinct types, adding the Type One, which with the ability to influence his fellow man, and still the rarest form, and the most difficult to test. Then Type Two, the ability to locate other Homopotius on a geographical axis.

It was found that the potency of the abilities would vary from subject to subject, originally a scale of one to four was used, but they were forced to increase the upper boundary many times over, the last moving from a top number of seven after the Montez Line, a family rich with new subjects, was discovered nearly twenty-five years ago.

The scale started with one, which was considered being your average Homosapien, all the way up to ten, where the abilities, or potential later abilities, defied all previous understanding of both the laws of physics and biology. A subject with a potency level of three would be borderline Homopotius. An example of a Type One with a potency of three, or 3T1 in shorthand, would be a charismatic world leader. To put this in context, we have so far only found three subjects with a potency of ten, all of which were traced by their DNA to the Montez Line.

The second part of the project was focused on the causes, or physiological triggers, behind this great cladogenesis, but with the lack of suitable imaging and only occasional dead subjects to study in detail, it was a testament to the team's skills and insights that not only did they establish the leap was associated with a mass in the subject's brain, but were also able to identify that the location and size of mass is directly indicative of the type and potency of behaviour observed.

The team identified the mass would cause the generation of a new type of hormone secreted into the blood during an episode and formed an offshoot project.

Part of the team investigated if it was possible to graft the abilities into a Homosapien brain. The research yielded positive initial results and human trials began. It was found possible to 'seed' a mass in the brain at the embryonic stages. Infant and adult trials were completely unsuccessful, but embryonic manipulation had a statistically significant viability rate of nought point one percent.

Despite the death of each of the four live subjects before they grew, they were mature enough to be tested. The four days of their lives had given them enough time to gather experience and the process was refined, boosting the resulting success rate by a further point one of a percent.

We debated for some time over the statistical significance of this round, as all four surviving subjects for the second round were from a single host and had split from a single cell. Despite the outstanding results, the project was suspended when the company merged with Stamp Pharma, but at least we were able to keep the three offspring, one dying shortly after birth, the cause never made available. Over the coming years, we confirmed we'd successfully seeded Homopotius traits in a Homosapien host and had two 4T1 females and a single 4T3 male to work with.

I spent the next few years analysing the huge catalogue of subject data, looking forward to the days when I would actually sit in front of one, either alive or dead, or hurriedly analysing a subject's blood with speed because after only a few minutes out of the body, the exciting parts decayed to nothing.

Over years of direct observation of our spawn and passive interaction with other subjects, we identified a few key areas, including how the abilities of the subject would themselves evolve over time. We'd seen abilities normal by the standard of a T5, that would over time make leaps, to T7 level, and we were soon able to estimate the potency of the individual subject by their blood line, along with the location and size of their mass.

I would also take time out to join the team, studying the three children as they grew up and their abilities manifested. The two twin girls were a pleasure to be around. Separated at birth and with no further contact between them, it was a necessary control measure, we later found. I would kid myself it wasn't due to their masses, but as they grew into young adults and bloomed as women, they were the spectacle of the campus. Capable of great affection, they were banned from all contact because of the trouble their magnetism was getting everyone into. Instead, they were deprived of all but one contact and put to useful work.

We were all itching to take what we had learned and conduct a third round, to improve on the potency and to iron out the one imperfection. As the continuous examinations throughout their early life discovered, the seeded masses in their brain were unlike a 'naturally' occurring mass in two ways.

The first was that the mass continued to grow. We hoped one day the size would plateau.

The second was the shape. Whereas the true Homopotius had a near spheric mass, those of the seeded types grew spiky tendrils reaching out into the head, causing interaction with normal brain function which manifested in the three subjects in different ways.

A postmortem confirmed the male's death was caused by the mass crushing his brain from the inside. The only cure sure to work would be to irradiate the mass like a cancer, killing it, but the owners decided there was too much to learn and not enough time, so they were left to live out their predetermined course.

Drugs treated some symptoms and allowed us to exert control.

The project took another turn late this last year when my path crossed with another researcher who was looking into a fascinating project yielding amazing results, promising itself as a near infinite energy source. Despondent and with the lack of scientific skill on the team, with a security clearance as high as mine, I joined the research on a part time basis. The scope of which was to identify the mechanisms whereby the material, in the form of a beautiful, but coarse rock, would split molecules of water into its constituent forms.

After a few days, I hypothesised the material may be able to split other compounds into their constituents. It would later turn out this thought was the start of the end for my work at LanfordStamp. This was also a time when I had taken delivery of a fresh batch of 7T1 blood, corked in a protective atmosphere. I was excited and tested it in the same lab whilst in parallel running several compounds through the rock material. Overworked and tired, I accidentally mixed the two experiments. The results astounded even my wildest imaginations.

The blood foamed from the rock like one of those failed volcano demonstrations that bad schoolteachers do with baking soda and vinegar. Already I knew the compound had changed, but when I saw it under the microscope, I observed it wasn't decaying, and the structure was different in a surprising way.

After further tests we found it had indeed stabilised. We already *knew the application of the blood of a T4 would endow healing properties upon the imbiber, with the stronger the potency, the more powerful the effect and that changed little with distillation through the rock. However, we had enough of a rare sample of 10T1 blood and found once run through the rock, even a drop had a stark effect, making the Homosapien subject so suggestible to command he could be made to do anything. Even to take their own life.*

The shock stayed with me for days and I battled with my conscience, but before I could make a decision about what to do with the information, I found they already knew. Their action was quick. They halted the energy project and pushed all the resources on to gathering more samples and testing them through the rock.

I was soon approached by a man from outside the team. He introduced himself as from top level management of the group's parent company. I never found out his name, but he was American and with skin like the colour of fake cheese, he came with a British female companion.

She was a different thing altogether, with floating strawberry hair and an air about her I wasn't alien to, and more importantly to me, she would have made an interesting subject, maybe a five or six. Certainly no less than a four.

***

Startled by a bang at the door, Fisher sat up in shocked silence with a film of sweat covering his body, the image of his partner's striking hair bright in his thoughts.

As the knocking came again, he looked at the clock, realising it was twenty minutes since she'd last been at the door, but rather than rushing to answer, his thoughts turned back to his recurring nightmare as Harris let the mechanical arm swing down inside the glass cage.

"Fisher," she called through the door.

He stood, shaking off the thoughts as he turned off his phone and pulled the door wide to find Harris standing on the other side with a question on her lips.

"Are you okay?" she said, looking him up and down before peering into the room.

"Sorry. I lost track of time. I'll get dressed and meet you at breakfast," he replied.

"I'll wait. Just in case you forget," Harris said as Fisher closed the door.

Sitting at the table, he barely noticed the empty dining room as he continued to devour the journal with the plate of cooked breakfast cooling and her seat empty.

***

My mood changed when they instructed me to get rid of all but a handful of my research team, with the rest to abandon all lines of investigation except for methods of mass producing the distilled super blood, as they called it. It was at this time I had stumbled on an interesting line of enquiry, a compound when put through the rock which had an interesting effect on the growth of the seeded subject's masses.

Told to concentrate on how to package the transformed blood for delivery in something innocuous like moisturiser, or one of their many other product lines, my protests went unhindered, informed in no uncertain terms I would be the next to go if I chose that path, along with a promise that I would never work in research again.

When I reported the objective was impossible without a continuous supply of 10T1 blood, without hesitation, the woman informed me the supply would soon not be a problem.

The project moved to Bergen, but even being back in my home country brought little comfort. The next few weeks were a blur, working most hours on testing. After using up the last few drops of the 10T1, I moved on to a 7T1, which was equally in short supply.

They sent infrastructure and manufacturing engineers to discuss the processes required, all without letting on what they were designing. Running out of super blood, I asked for more and the American came alone. They told me the flow of 10T1 had stalled; my heart was glad, even though I had never met James Fisher, having studied his files, the sparse observation videos gave me a sense that I knew him and I was happy they weren't harvesting his natural resource.

The process would require a constant stimulation of his abilities, and I could think of only one way that would be possible. I also heard on the grapevine that our Chilean research facility had been destroyed. Unsure if the two were linked, I kept quiet. Even the thought of asking gave me a chill.

The American did, however, promise me they would get hold of a 7T in return for an estimate of how long the effects of what I would produce would last.

Pausing when he asked, I wasn't wrestling with the question. I'd already carried out extensive tests. It was my conscience I battled with.

As he pushed for an answer, I meant to lie, instead I told him it would be hours and not days. The guy laughed because they already had a solution to that problem. I also confirmed that although the effect would be less, it would produce the results they were asking for.

I couldn't help but laugh to myself because I had equally intimate knowledge of the only 7T1 we had on file. Although he had less potential potency, he was older than James, the 10T1, and his skills were at full maturity.

I knew from experience, pinning this guy down was going to take something major.

That's when I first realised this was something more than to get people to buy more wrinkle cream and I took the first opportunity to get away, leaving the rock under running water to cover my tracks. The force of the explosion gave me a head start, and a hope they'd consider my body vaporised at the epicentre.

Still, with access to the databases, it looks like it worked.

Every day I check and there's no new information on James Fisher or Cameron Robertson.

When I first started this journal, I was arrogant and young, ready to make the world a better place, but now I hate that it took me so long to realise the part I pla...

***

Finding no more words as he scrolled, Fisher thought back to

Johannas turning in his chair just before the bullet took his thoughts away forever.

Looking up, Harris had returned, and for the second time he'd not noticed her movements. He'd not noticed her stare, and he looked back, wide eyed, with his thoughts only partly in the restaurant.

She spoke, but he didn't hear the words and blinked, forcing himself to listen.

"I said, what are you reading that's so engrossing?" she said, leaning into the table. The husk of her voice sent a chill down his spine, the effect so alien compared to when he'd hung on everything she'd said.

"Oh, nothing," he replied, knowing his tone was less than convincing, but he held his gaze. "Have you ever worked with the Americans?" he said, watching the confusion rise on her expression.

"You know I have," she replied, tilting her head to the side. "You've met some of them. Don't you remember?"

"Yeah, sure," he said, annoyed at his stupid question.

"Spill the beans. What's going on?" she said, leaning across the table.

"It's nothing and we should get back," he said, watching her look down at his full plate as they stood, then followed her out onto the overcast street.

79

"What does Fentanyl do?" Fisher said to Clark's image on the screen, unable to miss the deep red shadows around his eyes.

Looking beside the camera, the brightness of Clark's screen reflected from his round glasses. "It's a synthetic opioid painkiller," he said, not turning as he spoke.

"And it's highly addictive," Harris added.

"There are easier ways to get a fix," Fisher said. "And why in toothpaste tubes?"

Harris shrugged, and Clark didn't acknowledge the question.

"Nothing surprises me these days," Clark said and Harris nodded before turning to Fisher.

"Did you crack Johannas's password yet?" she said.

Fisher shook his head. "Not yet," he said, looking at the blank page of a notepad.

"Someone has," Clark said. Both Fisher and Harris looked up. "I got a call from the provider."

"Did they trace it?" Fisher asked.

"Yes," Clark replied without a change in his tone.

"And it came back to me?" Fisher replied and Clark nodded.

"So what's the password?"

Fisher stared in silence at the image on the wall. "I don't want you to see it?" he said after a pause.

"Why?" Harris said, raising a brow.

"It makes for uncomfortable reading," Fisher replied.

"We're all adults," Clark said in his usual tone.

"I can tell you what it said," Fisher replied. The other two exchanged looks before turning to Fisher as he stood from the table. "But give me a minute. I need to speak with Luana."

Harris rose, stopping midway as he raised his palm.

"Alone."

***

Fisher watched Luana sit up in the bed, still dressed in a thin white gown and sipping from a large plastic cup. She looked pale and gaunt, as if her beauty had all drained away.

"I wondered when you'd be back," she said, resting the cup on her leg.

"I know everything," Fisher said, perching on the edge of her bed. "I'm sorry, Hunter," he said, standing, and she nodded as he left.

***

The pair sat in silence as Fisher recounted the main body of the journal, leaving out the description that matched Harris and omitting the American's accent. It was only as Fisher mentioned Cameron Robertson that he saw any reaction, and it was Clark's momentary dip of a brow.

"Luana is a twin?" he said after Fisher finished.

"Her real name is Hunter Penfield," he said, nodding.

"And somehow I know that name," Clark replied, looking out of camera shot.

"Penfield?" Fisher asked, uncertain.

"No. Robertson. Cameron Robertson. At least I think I do. I've read so much these past few days. Let me see," he said as he worked unseen at the keyboard. "Bingo," he said, making Fisher jump as his eyes lit up. "He was on the plane."

"What plane?" Fisher replied, as Harris's brow mirrored the same question.

Clark nodded. "The lost plane," he replied, his eyes widening as if it were a silly question. "And they should land in half an hour."

"Are you sure?" Fisher said.

Clark nodded as if barely able to keep his excitement in

345

check. "He's on the passenger list for the plane that landed at the Hyderabad strip when the UN grounded all aircraft."

Fisher looked wide-eyed at Harris as he tried to gauge her lack of reaction.

"I think he means are you sure he's on the passenger list for the return jet?" Harris said, glancing at Fisher.

Clark's eyes widened further still, as if asking himself the question. It wasn't long before he was tapping at the keys again, then banged his fist on the desk. "Shit. No. He's not."

Fisher ran his hand through his hair as Clark continued to type, his gaze rising from the bottom of the screen as if searching a list. "He was on the flight when it landed," he said, his eyes flicking either side. "But no. He's not on the replacement."

"He's not the captain you mentioned? One of those that were injured?" Harris asked, the question clear on her brow. "You said everyone was still on the plane apart from the pilot."

"What was that last name?" Clark said. Fisher looked at Harris and she replied with a nod.

"Robertson?" Fisher asked.

"No. Not that one," Clark said, hurrying out the reply.

"Hunter?" Fisher replied.

"The last name," Clark said.

"Penfield," Harris added.

"Holy shit," Clark replied, pausing for a breath as he stared right back at them. "She was the pilot."

"Who was?" Fisher said, almost squinting as he tried to keep up.

"The sister."

80

"This can't have all been about getting one man?" Fisher said, looking at them both, open-mouthed. "Could it?"

"There must have been an easier way?" Harris said with a shake of her head.

"I think the bombs were a test. Perhaps what happened on the plane was as well," Clark replied.

"A test of what?" Fisher said.

"Controlling people. The unidentified compound in the toothpaste," Clark replied, raising his brow.

"You think they put my synthesised blood in there?" Fisher asked, rubbing his forehead.

Clark nodded and Harris raised an eyebrow.

"Johannas knew how difficult it would be to get to Cameron," Harris said. "The chaos gave them a great opportunity to get his plane down."

"But they couldn't have known where they would land," Clark said. "Could they?"

"I don't think it mattered. The world was in turmoil for hours and if the sister is half as accomplished as Luana, then she'd have taken care of the rest," Harris replied, sitting forward in her seat.

"Okay," Fisher said, leaning back. "It looks like they accomplished all they wanted. What happens next?"

They both looked back as if they were about to speak, but neither did.

"We all know there's only one reason they need a continual supply of our blood," Fisher said.

"Mass production," Clark replied as Harris nodded.

"How long has Cameron been missing?" Harris asked, looking at Clark.

"Two days," he replied.

"So he could be anywhere by now," Fisher blurted out. "And we're sitting here!"

"Let's think about this. Johannas said they were building a new factory," Harris said, as Fisher looked over, his

347

brow low.

"Russia. The Congo. Australia?" Fisher replied. "But those are only the places we know."

"And they're the hidden sites," Clark said. "They've got facilities all over the world," he added as he tapped at the keyboard. "They've got factories and bases of operation in Norway, the East Coast of America, the bottom of South America, Peru, Cameroon, Australia and South Korea. The subsidiary firms would double that list."

"Where do we start?" Fisher said.

"Let's just look at new factories," Harris said.

Clark tapped at the keyboard.

"According to their website, they've just built two more plants," he said, reading from the screen. "One in the Mumbai suburbs, and the other in East China."

"What's the official line on what they're producing?" Fisher said, and the pair waited whilst Clark's eyes flitted around as he read.

"China is coming online in a month and produces cosmetics," he said, then paused before his eyes went wide. "Mumbai…" he said, his eyes moving again, "… is a toothpaste factory. Billed to produce over eighty percent of the entire world's consumption."

"Shit," Fisher said as Harris mouthed the same.

"LS owns the top five brands across the world and produces ninety percent of the supermarket own brands too. That gives them a seventy-five percent share of the world market. Shit, indeed."

"If they add the same stuff to all that toothpaste then…" Harris replied, cutting herself off. "We have to shut it down. How long have we got until it opens?"

"It opened last month," Clark replied, the pair watching as his brow raised. "The new factory received funding from the US government." The projected image changed to a picture of the American ambassador for India, the woman they'd met earlier, shaking hands with a group of men outside the front of a concrete building as smiling children crowded

348

at her feet. "It was opened by the ambassador a couple of days ago."

Silence followed as they stared at the photo.

"What's with the kids?" Fisher eventually said. Clark read more before he spoke.

"They also built an orphanage for street children. It's probably something to do with planning permission."

Fisher nodded. "So, how do we shut the place down?"

"I'll present what we found and I'm sure we can have the locals close it by the end of today," Clark said, tapping at his keyboard, but before he could continue, Harris stood.

"No," she blurted out. "We go there and close it down ourselves."

Fisher looked at Clark, then back to her. "Why us?"

"We'll do it right," Harris said, her voice quietening as she continued. "India is rife with corruption. The bureaucracy alone could take forever. And the journal says there's an American involved. That could complicate things," she said, and Fisher's thoughts went back to Johannas's description of the American's companion.

Regretting not letting them see the full text, he wanted her to deny it all. He hoped she'd say it matched so many people's description, but instead, she wanted them to go to the last place on earth he should be. The place where his dream might come true.

"Okay," Clark said. "I'll make the arrangements."

Clark's words startled Fisher from his thoughts and as he looked up to the projection as the Welshman continued.

"Before you go. How did you know the arson kid had a screw loose?" Clark said, and Fisher's eyes went wide.

"What?" Fisher said, his heart racing.

"I checked him out after you asked," Clark replied. "They've admitted him to a secure facility. He went nuts."

"That's not the language we use," Harris said, her brow raised, but she wore a thin smile.

With his heart beating hard in his ears, Fisher took little notice. Pushing back his chair, he stood, almost running to the door.

"Wait up," Harris said as she followed, her voice grating against his nerves.

Stopping as he reached the door, he didn't turn around. "I've changed my mind."

"About what?" she replied.

"Joining the agency," Fisher said, feeling her hand on his shoulder. Her touch felt like such a weight, and he turned in the hope she'd let go.

"I'll call you back," she said as she moved her hand. Without a word, Clark's image disappeared. "What's happened?" she asked and although the words were soft and seemed to come easily, he couldn't tell if they were sincere.

"Is it true what some philosopher said?" Fisher replied, unable to meet her gaze. "The needs of the many outweigh the needs of the few."

Harris smiled, and Fisher's brow lowered, unsure if she was mocking him.

"Unless you're one of the few, them maybe, I guess," she said. "Who are the few you're talking about?"

"Andrew. Susie. Everyone I touch. Me, perhaps," he said, lifting his chin.

"Is it because of what you saw in those archives?"

"Partly," he replied.

"James. Talk to me," she said. "Let's work it through," she added and as she looked into his eyes, he felt himself relax, but then words from the journal leapt into thoughts. If she was a type one, what was to say she wasn't manipulating him like he'd done to her when they'd first met?

Desperate to scream his frustration, somehow he kept quiet. He wanted to tell her what he feared. He wanted to ask who she really was. He wanted to tell her about how his abilities were changing again and how it was affecting those he touched. He wanted to tell her the truth about the recurring nightmare. He wanted her reassurance, but most of all, he wanted to trust her.

"Is it me?" she said, squinting. "Have I upset you? I

know I can be so focused at times."

"No. It's not you," he finally said and Harris smiled, but he told himself to stay strong.

"What is it then?"

"I'm putting everyone in danger," he replied, knowing that also was true.

"But Susie's alright," she said.

"It's not just her," he replied as his thoughts raced. "There are other things I need to do. My priorities have changed."

"Like finding your mother? We can still do that together," Harris said, her voice becoming urgent with an uncharacteristic edge of emotion slipping in.

He didn't know if it was from a belief she would fail some hidden mission, or perhaps she was concerned about him.

"I was afraid of this," Harris said as she turned away to stare at the blank wall. "I've seen you change since Andrew, and each time you found something new about your past."

"The lies they built my life on, you mean," he replied and Harris nodded as she looked back.

"I've only known you for such a short time but…" she said before stopping for a breath. "I think you're changing."

Those weren't the words he wanted to hear. He wanted her to confess it all. He wanted to know what she was doing, or how she felt about him.

"Will they let me leave?" Fisher said.

Harris looked at him for a long moment before nodding.

"If you're not a threat."

"I won't be," he replied.

"Are you going back into hiding?"

"No. I don't think I could," Fisher said.

"They'll want to know," Harris replied. Fisher turned and opened the door, but stopped as Harris spoke, her voice soft.

"James."

He turned around, unable to do anything else when she used his first name.

"Is it what's inside your head?" she asked, reaching out for this arm.

Fisher shook his head and pulled his Glock from the holster, then placed it in her hand, butt first.

"Keep it," Harris said, offering the gun back, but Fisher turned and pushed open the door.

81

Walking through the steel-arched gate, Fisher expected the guard he knew stood out of sight of the road to draw a hidden side arm and block his path. When they didn't, he thought perhaps the door at his back would open for a discrete voice to call out. They'd put forward a deal and barter for his service. When after a few steps nothing happened, he set aside preparing his reaction. His legs instead carried him unhindered along the busy main road, the sky darkening as he stepped onto the bridge with his gaze falling to the turbulent water below.

Maybe she hadn't told anyone. Perhaps it suited her to have him out of the way, unarmed and with no iComm.

His thoughts drifted down the river and he let them carry away with the steady stream of boats, his mind reassuring him there was no great plot for his capture. No plan to squeeze out his juices.

Life would go on. Harris and Clark would still save the day.

He'd had his chance, and it was clear the life was not for him. Doubts over his abilities had taken him back to those not too distant times, secluded and alone, being a version of happy.

He couldn't help but question if he could be like that again. With Andrew dead, his relationship with Susie on the rocks, it was a new life, not an old one he needed. That and to get very drunk to forget how Harris made him weak at the knees.

It wasn't even dark as he hit the third bar, a drink in each to make himself a moving target while he considered his next step. To get away was his first and only decision. He would need to go far, not wanting a reminder of what he could have been to others. They'd had a taste and Franklin hadn't liked it one bit.

The vodka woke him from his stare, fumes evaporating at the back of his throat. He pushed himself to his heavy legs and strolled back along the street.

A car horn howled as he was about to step into traffic, his mind rolling over the same information. His gaze fell on the road as a black cab jostled for space in the beginnings of the rush hour. He looked to his left and saw the cafe across the bridge, the place he'd sat in for half a day watching Vauxhall Cross, a building he'd known nothing about. He'd not got far after three drinks down. Turning on the spot, choosing not to step across, instead he followed the bustle of pedestrian traffic.

He wasn't going home. He couldn't go back to that place. Itself a symbol of his old life.

Someone would pick him up in minutes and it held nothing over him. He fumbled inside his bomber jacket pocket and pulled out the passport, thumbing to the back. Blank and useless without the iComm. A fake was in order, easy to get if your name was Carrie Harris, or Trinity.

He smiled to himself.

His new life would be outside of the country, his decision cementing with each step. The silent toast with a shot of clear liquid sealed the deal, despite beginning to lose its taste.

He thought back to his bank balance of over a million pounds. It had slipped his mind over the last few days in the whirl of activity signposting these recent weeks. He'd had every intention of handing the money Farid had paid him over. By now, the insurance companies would have settled. If he'd have given it to his ex-employer, the money would have added to their vast coffers; a drop in the ocean. Operating costs for half a second, maybe. In the morning, he would make a withdrawal, despite his unease that they probably knew all about it.

His thoughts turned to Andrew. He wanted to call him and arrange an urgent meet, and he'd be there in an instant. They'd talk into the night. Their heads would be sore in the morning and they'd arrive at a plan. But he was dead, of course, which was no one's fault but his.

Another vodka passed between his lips. Susie should have been there too, but he'd fucked her up as well. He had given her that time and now he had to leave her be.

Then, of course there was the job. He would miss it like crazy, even though his time had been so short. He wouldn't miss the inevitable battle with Harris, the ultimate reason he'd left. She'd betrayed him. At least there was a good chance, and the ending could only go two ways. Him locked in a cage, doomed to live terrified and in agony, or to destroy the one he loved. He pressed another shot of clear liquid against his lips.

As he strolled, cool air brushed across his face and he noticed night had finally descended. Perhaps it had been there for a while. He had no idea of the time. Traffic was light, headlights blinding him as they crossed his path, and he didn't know where he was, nor did he care. Smiling, at least he couldn't betray himself, and turned into a bar on the corner of the street.

Well past midnight, he settled with a tall bottle of beer, half emptied into a glass as he sat in the corner booth of the dingy place with the chatter of after work drinkers in suits long gone, leaving his thoughts turning to sleep. He was sure he had enough in his pocket to find somewhere, no matter how late.

With his glass almost empty and his surroundings too, he watched a scattering of couples huddled around tables and stuffed into the dark booths. His vision hazing, he looked up from his near last sip. Revelling in the cool taste, his gaze caught on the doorway where a leggy brunette stood balanced on killer heels, a thin red dress clinging to each of her curves, sending shockwaves to rattle his soul.

She scanned the room and their eyes met, lingering for a second too long.

Fisher took a gulp of air.

"Oh shit. Not again."

82

Beer lapped at the inside of the glass as Fisher pushed the last sip away. His gaze rested on the slender woman's long bare legs as she stood and took her drink, sharing a laugh with the barman, who didn't take his eyes from her face. He watched as she scanned the room, the rows of empty tables on either side, but he knew her gaze would settle back on him. And it did, with a soft smile, but he was determined that her innocent look wouldn't melt his guard.

She soon glided towards him, her expression not a surprise as he tried to guess her opening line.

"Is there anyone sitting here?" she said, her voice dripping with musk.

Fisher didn't hesitate and opened his mouth as he smiled. "Help yourself," he said and stood.

Not waiting to see her reaction, he headed towards the door, stopping just moments before he walked into a mountainous black guy, barring the way. It was only when the guy didn't move that he realised perhaps it wasn't the woman who was there for him.

"You're kidding me?" he said to himself, but the words were loud enough for all to hear. "Are you looking for me?" Fisher snapped at the unmoving barrier.

"Eh, yes," he said, the words redefining Fisher's understanding of how deep a voice could go.

"Oh. Okay," Fisher replied, taking a step back as the guy somehow stood taller. Fisher took another step back, watching in hope of understanding the guy's thoughts. All he saw was confusion.

Taking the upper hand, Fisher brushed his palm across his chest, but found only a space where his Glock had been for the last few weeks. With his eyes flaring wide at the realisation, he watched the guy do the same as if they were both scrambling for their next option.

Knowing a delay would be his undoing, and not trusting what he could do after how much he'd drunk, Fisher looked across the bar, locking eyes with the guy behind who watched their unusual dance. The man then flicked his head to the doorway at the side with a sign in the centre. *Staff Only*.

Backing up, Fisher turned on his heels, and a little unsteady, he bounded toward the door. Without taking notice of whether the man followed, he ran in hope the door wasn't locked. With a light twist of the handle as he arrived, he pushed through, his momentum carrying him to the sound of smashing glass. Not looking back to wonder at the noise, he dashed past the kitchen and was out a door open to a yard facing a fence between him and his escape. Rushing up crates stacked to the side, he vaulted high and landed with a sharp pain as his bandaged ankle jarred on the concrete path below.

Giving no heed to the pain, he rose, then scanned both ways along the alley. Not lingering, he hobbled left, the pain easing with each step and he was soon out onto the street, its pavement filled with revellers heading home or searching for one last drink as the street sweeper's orange lights blinked.

His heart sank when two well-built guys jogged around the corner, their eyes locking straight to his. Fisher glanced over his shoulder to find another pair, almost a mirror image at his rear.

Without thinking to look across the road, he leapt from the path, only just able to dodge a cab, then a bus just as a motorbike sped across his path. He stopped only when his chest hit against something hard, sending him stumbling away. Hands caught him before he could land. Fisher looked up into Biggy's beaming smile.

Fisher matched the wide grin of the wearer and offered out his open palm, accepting Biggy's powerful handshake.

"You're fucking kidding me," Fisher said with relief as he looked at his new friend's bulk in the leather jacket. "I should have known they'd send your ugly mug to get me. Can't they leave me alone for five minutes?" he added, righting himself.

Too busy laughing, Biggy didn't reply.

"I'll come quietly," Fisher said, still smiling as he raised his hands. "Where are you taking me?"

"I've got a message," he said, as his smile dropped and Fisher glanced across the road to find his pursuers had vanished.

"Were they with you?" Fisher said. Biggy smiled and nodded. "Since when did they let women into your unit?"

Biggy raised his brow. "They haven't."

"You gotta be kidding me," Fisher replied with a shake of his head, then looked over his shoulder in the pub's direction.

"We need to talk," Biggy said, the smile gone as he guided Fisher down a dimly-lit alley with his arm around his shoulder. Turning his nose up at the stench of piss and rotten vegetables, he looked at Biggy when he stopped a few steps in.

"Go on," Fisher said, unsure if he'd slurred.

"They sent the locals to close the factory down. They even took a US embassy aid with them," Biggy said. Fisher nodded. "But they've disappeared."

About to speak, Fisher thought back to what Biggy had said, in case he'd missed something.

"So send someone else," he replied, shaking his head at the ease of the solution.

"They did, along with four of my guys." Biggy said, pausing as if to ensure Fisher understood.

"And?" he replied. squinting.

"And we've lost contact."

"Who did you send?" Fisher asked, standing straight as he ran through the names of the team he knew, hoping it wasn't Lucky or Boots, or even Hotwire.

"They needed someone with your skill set," Biggy replied.

"Harris?" Fisher said, drawing a long, deep breath as Biggy nodded.

83

Fisher didn't hesitate. He didn't need to hear any more before he was in the car with the city's lights a blur at the windows as Biggy explained that the first shipments of the doctored toothpaste had already left India. His words were enough to keep the other thoughts at bay.

Harris was in trouble, and that was enough to quiet his whispers of a plot. It was his turn to save her. She was the victim, one way or another. And if she wasn't, then at least the doubt would be gone.

With the alcohol fog clearing with every word, the car rushed through RAF Northolt's parted gates where soldiers standing either side pointed their SA80 rifles at the ground.

The chilly night air ran fresh in his lungs as they pulled up to a compact jet beside which men in fatigues carried a steady stream of long olive green containers through the narrow door. About to get out, Biggy motioned to the glove box where Fisher pulled out his iComm and holstered Glock.

He followed Biggy up the steps where a waiting airman handed them both a steaming cup of coffee as Fisher looked over the polished leather seats, disturbed by the lethal luggage strung across them.

"Sorry about the mess," Biggy said, turning with a wide grin. Fisher closed his eyes at the beginnings of a headache.

"We're going alone?" Fisher asked, opening his eyes to find Biggy inspecting the crates. With a glance up, the big man nodded to the door, his smile widening at the heavy footsteps clattering against the metal.

"She'll be okay," Hotwire boomed as he led the way down the aisle, stopping only to grab Fisher by the shoulders and pull him into a tight embrace. "The fucking A Team is here."

Behind him Bayne, Boots and Lucky followed, each dressed in light coloured civvies as they fist bumped each other with their expressions fixed in that all too familiar way he'd seen before they headed into danger. Soon settled into their seats, a pair of RAF uniforms with bars on their lapels joined them before heading to the left.

With the guys seated and Fisher ready to sleep, he felt the first vibrations of the engines spinning up. About to close his eyes, Biggy stepped into the aisle.

"Full briefing at four hundred hours and touch down at five hundred hours," he said.

Fisher glanced at his iComm.

"That's only five hours. How the hell will we get there so fast?" he blurted out.

"The same way Harris did," Biggy said, slapping his hand against the fuselage. "In the fastest passenger bird in the world."

"At least for the next few months anyway," Hotwire chipped in. "The Gulfstream G650, and she's a sexy bitch."

A roar of dissent filled the cabin as empty cups and other soft clatter rained down on Hotwire, only stopping as Biggy put his hand out.

"Get some rest, guys. Save your energy for the bad guys," he said, then touched a discrete switch at his side, the lights dimming as he sat down.

With a quick look around, Fisher found most already had their eyes closed. He followed suit, in hope he'd be able to sleep.

***

Feeling pressure on his shoulder as he rested his hand on Harris's naked buttocks, Fisher's eyes shot open at the sounds of Biggy's voice. Forcing himself to wake, he twisted around to find Hotwire pulling back from between the seats. It took another few minutes of barely catching Biggy's words before he'd left the nightmare behind, and he paid the briefing his full attention.

With the sun streaming through the windows, the punchy presentation finished, setting out the obvious primary objectives of penetrating the facility, then locating and securing Harris before halting production in whatever way they could.

Much to Fisher's surprise, rescuing the men that had gone with her and recovering the rock were secondary.

"We have a lock on her communication device, but it hasn't moved since it arrived. That's our starting point. Questions?"

Hotwire stood and Fisher half turned toward him.

"What about the other woman?" he said, and Fisher's brow lowered.

"What other…?" Fisher said before Biggy interrupted.

"Consider Hunter Penfield hostile until we know otherwise."

"Luana?" Fisher blurted out. "She's there too?"

Biggy nodded. "Sorry. I assumed you realised. Hunter travelled with Harris, but we believe she's turned against her."

Blinking hard, Fisher shook his head at the thought of Harris trusting that woman, but in the pit of his stomach it made sense, knowing it would take someone with Luana's skills to beat Harris.

Sitting back in his seat, Fisher tried his best to calm and forced himself to go over the briefing again, reminding himself of three extraction sites.

"Don't worry," Biggy said, crouching in the aisle beside him, and as if he could read Fisher's mind, he spoke in a quiet voice. "It'll be okay. Just stick with the team. If it goes tits up and we get separated, go with whoever runs first. Rendezvous at Tulsi Lake at the eastern extreme."

Fisher gulped, then Biggy caught Hotwire's eye. "Stick together you two."

With a slap on his shoulder, Fisher turned to Hotwire's wide grin.

"Out of all of us," Hotwire said, glancing around. "I think you're the best equipped."

"Right," Biggy said, his voice sharpening. "Get kitted up. We need to be ready as soon as we touch the ground."

To the rattle of seat belts being unclasped, Fisher watched the team break from their seats, then edge around each other searching the crates and cracking them open to pull out weapons and kit, before stripping down to bare chests and pulling on thin skin coloured vests and holsters, planting knives, small pistols and all manner of deadly paraphernalia about their bodies.

Fisher stared with intrigue, watching Boots hand over rectangular blocks of deadly plastic. Black stencilled writing marked out the explosive PE-4 as Bayne secured it into the webbing over his vest. Catching Fisher's eye, as he pushed long white cords into his own covering, he called over.

"Don't worry. It's a lot stabler than Bayne," he said, tapping a block against his head as he wore a toothy grin.

It wasn't long before their civilian clothes covered everything up and they strapped on handguns holstered at their side, throwing water skins across their shoulders, then securing stockless MP5s in the small of their backs and hoisting great flowing smocks to cover the aggressive kit-out. With the Star Wars look not lost on Fisher, Hotwire's move towards him drew his attention.

"I thought we weren't expecting much resistance?" Fisher said, not hiding his frown.

"We're not, but planning for the worst keeps us alive," Hotwire replied. "What do you need?" he asked, but before he could reply, they glanced at Biggy.

"Not today," he snapped, motioning for Lucky to put the metre long General Purpose Machine Gun and a bandolier of finger thick bullets back in its case.

"Nothing. I think," Fisher replied, turning back to Hotwire and watching as he unclipped an olive drab trunk before plunging his hands in to draw out an aluminium case.

"Clark thought you might need this," Hotwire said, watching Fisher's eyes light up.

Getting to his knees, Fisher flipped open the catches where everything looked brand new inside the Aladdin's cave of the portfolio case he'd hoped he'd eventually call his own after Harris had shown her his.

Wide eyed, he spotted a second Glock in a foam insert beside which was a space for the gun sat in his holster. Spare clips stuffed to each side, along with rectangular boxes of rounds huddled around the outside. Lifting the top layer, he found a new ultra-thin protective vest which he pulled out and lay to the side.

Underneath it were a series of knives of all shapes and sizes along with a skin coloured carrier for the largest. Stripping off his black jacket, he unclipped his holster and Glock before peeling off his shirt, then unfolding the vest, he slid it over his head. It felt like home. On top of the vest, he pulled the knife carrier over his head and secured it with the blade under his right armpit, before pulling his shirt back on, followed by the jacket and holster.

Standing in the aisle, he felt unstoppable.

Kneeling, he revealed the next layer and found a camouflaged gun striped with olive and fluorescent yellow. Hotwire leaned down at its side.

"Let me," he said and pulled the weapon out.

"Is it a Taser?" Fisher asked, watching Hotwire's fingers wrap around the grip.

"Not quite. It's a Stazer," Hotwire replied to Fisher's frown. "Whereas a Taser incapacitates a target for a few seconds, this will keep the target down for ten to thirty minutes."

Fisher nodded. "And it's safe to use?"

Hotwire laughed. "Safer than the Glock, my friend, that's for sure. Flip the switch on the side, and either press the front against the target's skin and push this button," he said, tapping a red square on the side. "Or pull the trigger to fire electrodes up to ten metres."

Examining the gun, Biggy called for them to sit as they descended. After Fisher slipped the Stazer into a holster he'd strapped at his side, Hotwire leaned forward in his seat and handed over a folded smock.

"Do you need anything else?" he said between the

seats. "It's already mighty hot out there, so keep it to a minimum." Fisher shook his head. "But bring plenty of ammo. It's better to be safe," Hotwire added, his voice quiet but intense.

Fisher bent down and filled four empty clips with brass before stuffing them in his pockets. Sitting back, he tried to relax into the well-fitting seat, slowing his breathing to counter the effect of the steep descent, the pilots more used to defensive landings into hostile territory than guiding a luxury jet into a friendly commercial airport.

Outside, the blue sky soon turned to white cloud, the puff of cotton wool thickening as rain striped the windows with Hotwire mumbling under his breath, some curse about Mumbai in the rainy season.

Fisher watched at the window as the dry ground rose, the wheels kissing the tarmac with the barest of touches before he recognised the airport they'd flown out of only a few days before. Seat belts released as they taxied, but Fisher kept his buckled, watching the rest continue their preparation. Within minutes, they drew up to a remote area next to a road on the other side of the tall perimeter fence.

Turning back into the cabin, he found each of the team staring out of the windows, whilst Biggy held a phone to his ear.

"Where is he?" he said in a raised voice as he scowled. "You're fucking joking. We'll wait ten and that's it." As he hung up the call, he turned back to the group. "The yank's delayed," he said to the collective drone from the men. "We give them ten minutes and then we'll source our own transport."

Each of the men pulled out phones, and either pushed them to their ears or tapped at the screens. To Fisher's surprise, Hotwire made a call in what, by his ear, was a fluent Indian dialect. Within the ten minutes, each reported that numerous alternative arrangements were in place. Biggy just needed to give the command.

"You have five minutes," he said, not waiting for a

reply before hanging up.

Within two, Boots spotted two desert-brown Humvees on the horizon, then waiting as the trucks came to a stop just outside the door, Biggy stood as it lowered to form the steps. Fisher pictured hands around the cabin under smocks, patting their weapons, undoing catches. Each was ready for the unknown, despite their deadpan expressions. The rain had stopped as he stepped into the day, the sun already hot on his skin and the ground drying at his feet as he repeated Harris's reaction from earlier in the week.

"Connor Fucking Tucson."

***

The pain was gone.

Feeling almost completely at ease in a pain-free haze, she lay with her eyes closed in the dim light of the hospital bed. Still, she wasn't quite able to shake the sense that something wasn't right. She knew about her limited life expectancy, the remembrance coming back as a slow drift and with it came the reminder that she'd had a plan, although its details were out of her grasp.

As the lights brightened, she saw a face that filled her with delight.

"He's gone, hasn't he?" she said to the familiar strawberry blonde stood by the bed, dressed for action in black combat trousers and same colour jacket.

Harris nodded.

"For good?" A shrug was all that replied. Her plan came into her mind like a bolt of lightning through her chest and she sat upright, ignoring the pain flashing up from her wrist.

"I'm coming too," she said.

"I was banking on it," Harris replied and helped her lift the covers.

84

Rain hammered without noise against the thick armoured windows as Fisher listened to Connor, his body twisted in the front passenger seat as the American reeled off excuses.

After sharing a knowing glance at Hotwire at his side, Fisher stared out of the window, surprised at the luscious green landscape as they left the confines of the airport. He'd expected a desert rather than the abundance of trees and verdant hills rolling to the horizon as they followed dense traffic along the Eastern Express Highway. With the Humvee slowing, his heart raced before Hotwire repeated part of the briefing he must have missed, the part where they'd greet a truck, its once vibrant multicoloured paintwork faded from decades of blasting from the sun.

A dark, wiry man in baggy jeans and a t-shirt two sizes larger than needed struggled to pull the canvas back, his long black hair stranded with grey whilst thick hairs sprouted from his top lip. As Fisher's boots hit the ground, dust flew from the cover as it retreated enough to see the inside stacked with cardboard boxes but with a space supported with a sheet of wood to stop the stack from collapsing on what he guessed was where they'd hold up for the next leg of their journey.

Fisher watched Connor and Biggy in quiet discussion, the American's arms more animated than his voice. To Fisher's surprise, Connor climbed up the rusted metal siding, pushing himself between the boxes. Hotwire and Lucky followed, the gap barely wide enough for their shoulders. Fisher guided Biggy back to the Humvee before leaning to his ear.

"What the fuck?" Fisher said, watching Biggy's surprise melt and his expression harden. "I don't trust him."

Biggy raised his brow before glancing back to Lucky's bulk disappearing into the darkness.

"And neither did Harris," Fisher added, feeling the heat of Biggy's glare as they stared at each other.

"He'll get us in," Biggy said, his expression softening as

he rested his heavy hand on Fisher's shoulder.

"He'll get us killed, or worse."

"Leave him to me, and relax," Biggy replied.

"I think he's involved," Fisher said, before glancing back to the suspension creaking as Boots climbed up.

"How?" Biggy asked.

"I don't know," Fisher said, leaning closer as he lowered his voice.

"Tell me everything," Biggy said.

Fisher waited for Boot's backside to disappear, then for Bayne to take his place on the metal rungs.

"If you know something that could get us killed, now's the time to spill," Biggy said, removing his hand.

Fisher glanced at the truck as Bayne peered out from the shadow.

"I think Harris might be involved," Fisher replied, his voice a near whisper. He'd expected Biggy to protest or pepper him with questions, or at least be outraged. Instead, he nodded.

"She's more than capable," Biggy replied. "And perhaps it's not of her own free will."

"So what do we do?" Fisher said, recovering.

"Don't let the fucker out of our sight."

***

Nothing about the air journey surprised her, but she was pleased the pain killers kept her mind from the stump.

The other medication kept her mood level, but did nothing to temper her surprise when *he* met them at the airport and rode at their side in the sand-coloured Humvee. Still shocked by his appearance, she barely noticed his disinterest in her apology, waving away her concerns as she pleaded for forgiveness.

85

With Fisher's body wedged in between the cargo, rain battered the canvas. Humid air clung to his face, and despite drawing thick air with each breath, he knew, being the last in, he had the most comfort. They'd reserved his space that he might affect a change more subtle than a bullet.

With his cheek against the rough bed of the truck, he watched through the gap between the canvas and the rickety metal, his view a thin slit his left eye could barely register between each thump of the carriage against the potholes.

Pushing away memories of the last time he was cargo, Fisher was thankful they weren't on the water.

Giving thanks as the truck carried them onto fresh, smooth tarmac, the bitter bite of bitumen still in the air, he watched a procession of trees zip pass in touching distance of the clean-cut edges of the dark road. With the occasional mumbling at his back, Hotwire's voice rose over the engine noise.

"What do you see?"

"Trees," Fisher replied, but when the engine shifted in note and the brakes squealed, Hotwire remained silent.

Concentrating as the truck rolled to a stop, he realised the rain had eased. A chain link fence towered twice the truck's height but only ran for a few seconds before joining to a two storey building whose bricks were fresh, the mortar dark. The chain link carried around the building, disappearing into dense trees as they passed inside the perimeter.

"What was the building we passed?" Fisher said, listening as the message whispered down the line.

"The orphanage," Hotwire replied moments later.

A smile pulled at Fisher's lips as he imagined a large donation given by Harris, his expression dropping when Hotwire spoke again.

"We're almost there."

Taking more note of the curt tone than the words themselves, he tensed as the truck slowed again, listening to the fractured idle of the engine. Pushing his head back to the truck bed, the vibrations matched the grumble of the truck. Peering out of the slit, he found a clear plot of grass had replaced the trees, and a tall, spiked fence pushed out either side, undulating with the contours of the land.

A shadow passed across his view and he clamped his mouth shut before reaching backwards to signal to Hotwire. As he touched some unknown body part, the truck rocked before the cab door slammed with the engine still spluttering.

From somewhere close, he listened to a jumble of words, foreign to his ear, which, by the pace of the conversation and its building volume, sounded like the driver was arguing. Still, Fisher took heart that whoever they were, they could open the canvas at any place except where he lay and would see only what was written on the manifest.

As long as they expected the delivery. As long as Connor hadn't half-arsed the preparation.

Perhaps what he heard was nothing to be afraid of. Maybe it was just the way they went about their security checks, or negotiating the size of the bribe.

Still, the rise and speed of the voices didn't seem right, and as the driver stepped in to view, a thin guard in a khaki shirt with a Kalashnikov slung over his shoulder, followed, waving a sheet of paper.

On his last encounter in the country less than a week ago, he knew the police carried weapons, the airport patrolled with uniforms and guns at their side. He'd seen the military ordering the flow of tired and stranded passengers, but he wasn't sure if it was normal for a factory guard to tote an automatic rifle.

Not convinced, along with their continual rising pitch, he reached back a second time in the hope they would prepare for whatever would come next.

Unable to feel any reply, and with his hands stuck tight by his sides, he knew that any moment the guard could turn his way and would spot a lone eye peering through the small gap before he'd swing his rifle around to where the canvas and the cardboard offered no protection.

86

With a fat drop of rain darkening his uniform, the guard's voice tailed off as he turned skyward. Wiping a second drop from his forehead, he pushed the papers against the driver's chest before disappearing from the narrow view.

A moment later, the truck rocked, a door slammed and the engine roared. A stout building soon took up all he saw, then passing by a raised barrier, Fisher locked eyes with a man staring out of a window. When they both blinked, he was gone, replaced by trees as they swept around a corner.

Despite knowing the man wouldn't have known what he stared at, Fisher couldn't help but fret with each lift of the accelerator as the huge wheels splashed great swathes of water away from the road.

With the sun blooming as if by the flick of switch, it wasn't long before the Tarmac lightened in their wake and the truck slowed, coming to a stop. Only halting for a moment, they turned in reverse, the brakes squealing when they rocked for the last time. With Fisher staring at a raw concrete wall, the engine died, leaving the silence broken only by his pulse pounding in his ears.

Seeming to share Fisher's uncertainty, no one moved and only as a dazzling light forced his eyes shut, did he feel a pressure from behind. Forcing his eyes open, he found the canvas swept to the side and the driver beckoning him out. Shuffling from between the boxes, he ignored the offered hand.

Instead, he nodded in reply to the wide, yellow-toothed smile.

Hotwire burst out at his heels as the humid air weighed heavy on Fisher's shoulders. Biggy soon appeared from the dark, and Fisher followed him at the driver's side, walking the length of the truck, only halting as the native moved into the wide space of the open-sided building. A tall concrete canopy hung high above their heads with bright white lights in place of the sunlight. Beyond the cover, Fisher marvelled past the high fence at a vast forest and the last remains of water flowing at the edge of the road.

With a turn, he saw Hotwire motioning him closer, and Fisher moved past Connor, who'd just emerged, his face dripping with sweat. As he passed, he heard him snap in the driver's native tongue before the American arrived at Fisher's rear.

Forming a line with the others, they moved, hands rifling under their smocks. Fisher touched at the Staser's slim body as he placed one foot in front of the other with care. Boots took the lead around the truck's edge, emerging into the vast cavern, a behemoth of a loading dock and a berth for commerce, the place destined to be a hub for huge articulated lorries to unload between the stark white lines still bright against the black Tarmac.

Keeping tight to the left-hand wall, they walked its raw gentle curve running parallel to the opening. With no windows, tall hatches rested at even spaces where they hovered above the floor level and sealed with crisp, bright red shutters. A double set of doors came into view as they rounded the corner, their gleaming red finish seeming barely set.

Fisher caught up with Hotwire as the Indian driver led the procession.

"Where's he taking us?" he said in a whisper.

"He'll get us inside, then we're on our own," Hotwire replied with equal volume.

The slow march halted at the doors and Biggy stepped out of line just as a tone rang in Fisher's head. Sliding his finger across the iComm's screen before pushing it back under the billowing smock, he heard Biggy's voice. "Take point. You know what to do."

He did and repeated the instructions in his head as he jogged up the line with Hotwire following close behind.

Whilst together, he was the soft head of the spear and ready to neutralise any confrontation. Those that didn't involve guns, at least. The guys at his back would take care of any force, whilst he plunged back into their ranks for cover.

Walking past the digital keypad flashing green at his side, he took up his position, taking the strain of the open door from the driver and handing it off to Biggy.

Once they'd got their bearings, they'd split into pairs. Fisher and Hotwire would search for Harris and Luana, if she was near. Boots and Bayne were to stop production by making things go bang, whilst Biggy and Lucky sought their men and the rock, if not needed elsewhere.

Inside the tall room, cold air rolled over as the last of the crew piled into a corridor, its rough painted black floor sloping down to drainage grills at the base of whitewashed walls. There were two sets of identical doors, one to their left and the other dead ahead. Hung on the left, green signs pictured a crossed knife and fork, with male and female toilet signs over side doors. At their front, the gleaming double red gloss door showed nothing but a large yellow and black sign with an exclamation point at its centre. Both had digital locks at their sides. Above the doors in front was a whole second storey with two thin slits of windows that showed nothing but darkness.

The driver stopped at Connor's side, garbling something as he pointed at the digilock, then hurrying the way they'd come.

"That's as far as he goes. I have the code," Connor said, turning to Biggy, still pointing at the door to their left. "In the canteen, there's another security door like this, but we'll need a pass to get through."

Fisher peeled from the conversation, opening a call to the Brecons.

"Loud and clear," Clark answered. As Fisher turned back, he saw Bayne at the lock, peering at the simple brushed steel box for insight.

"It's a kill box," Hotwire said, breaking the silence. Fisher watched heads turn around the room, along the walls, then across the roof and back to the door behind them.

"Bollocks," Lucky whispered to Hotwire's back.

"Those windows up there," Hotwire replied, pointing to the window slits above their heads. "The roof is at least three storeys above. Pop those windows open and mow us down."

"Or it could be ventilation," Biggy replied with a raised brow and a smile.

"Three locked doors. It's a good job this place isn't fully operational, or someone would be picking our guts out of the drains," Hotwire said, turning to face the metal grates at the edge of the walls.

"Fisher. You're up. Hotwire, stand down. Let's not wait to find out if he's right," Biggy said, tapping in Connor's dictated code.

Biggy held the door open and Fisher moved into the wide space, spotting a long hatch running the length of the room. Steel roller shutters sealed all but two of the sections. Fisher estimated there were twenty clustered tables, but several were folded and only one populated. The men looked out of place, wearing flowing traditional dress with unkempt beards hanging down to their food as they nursed plastic cups and watched Fisher.

Ignoring them, he strode alone with purpose, his gaze flowing from side to side as he tried to keep his stance natural. Spotting the toilets first, he focused on a second double set of doors further along with a porthole window, a card reader and keypad at its side, then his gaze drew back to the open servery hatch as a lone Asian woman with a square of plastic hanging from a yellow lanyard, poured a sloppy white liquid into the bain-marie before resting her elbows on the counter. Staring into space, she only noticed Fisher as he arrived at the hatch.

Getting the pass was easy, convinced, despite his broken English, that he was collecting a bad batch of access cards to return them for repair.

Back in Hotwire's killbox, he sent a picture of the card home, then held it to the iComm. Once a soft tone informed him it had all it needed, Fisher returned the pass, brushing off her surprise at the speed of his work.

As the keypad glowed green and the lock clicked, they smelt fresh paint from the coarse carpeted stairwell. Fisher took the lead as they climbed the steps, soon arriving at another set of doors with only a green button to press. About to look through the porthole, he felt a hand on his shoulder drawing him back.

Fisher turned to find each of the crew, except Boots, examining a huge plan on the wall Fisher had missed.

As tall as the wall and with a luminous green background, the map of the site couldn't have been more obvious. A red cross hovered over the left of the circular building where they stood, its jutting teeth resembling a cog. The top three quarters, at least because there was a tooth missing from the bottom section.

Reading the labels written in at least three languages, the space between the top teeth was the main entrance, with a car park sprawling out to the trees. A canopy hovered between the teeth to the left and heavy stencilled words designated it as Loading A. It was where they'd entered. The space opposite had a similar canopy marked as Despatch A.

At the base of the space left by the missing tooth, a separate building stuck out from the cog wheel like a piece of pie removed from the whole. *The Energy Centre.*

At the centre of the incomplete wheel was a solid circle, linked to the main structure by thin walkways at each point of the compass. The southernmost walkway seemed to be the only connection between the lower building and the rest.

Each of the teeth carried labels. At the southeast, the letters described Hall A and a label noted it as Manufacturing. The tooth to the right pointing out to the north west was Hall B. A white sticker with the words, *Coming Soon,* was the extent of the detail. The centre building was much better described with a breakout diagram showing five different levels, listing labs, offices, and function rooms.

Despite finding nothing of use in the list, no server room or control centre in bright shining letters, Biggy tapped at the sticker.

"A prime location for some plastic," he said, turning to find Boots.

Grunts of agreement came from the huddle and Fisher pulled out his iComm, letting the green lines radiate off the screen before he pushed the phone up to the plan and the brilliance of Harris's iComm glowed in the centre of the core building.

"That's where we start," he said, turning to Hotwire at his shoulder. "Then we search for some sort of holding facility."

"How do you know she's here against her will?" Connor said from somewhere in the group.

Fisher scowled, turning to find him. "Anything to add Clark?" he said.

"Not without access to their network," he replied. "I've had no luck from outside. The security is robust and there's not enough time. I've picked up the Wi-Fi, but it's encrypted. I'll either need the passkey or a physical connection somewhere."

Fisher shook his head.

"Okay," Biggy replied. "We'll head this way," he added as he jabbed at the piece of removed pie. "I want this nice and easy. A quiet in and out."

Nods followed around the huddle and Fisher turned to Biggy who pressed the green button.

87

Finding the corridor's curve, only Hotwire remained at Fisher's side as the door swung closed behind them. They'd taken less than ten paces before their first test approached, a young oriental guy in faded jeans and a t-shirt too big for his slight frame. Thick glasses hugged his face as he strolled from a branch corridor ahead with his attention buried in a thick folder open in his palms.

It was then Fisher realised the absurdity of what they were wearing. Dressed like Mexican cowboys, they only lacked sombreros.

As an involuntary deep breath sucked into his lungs, he closed his eyes and spoke under his breath.

"We're meant to be here," he whispered, repeating the words as he focused on the man's jet black hair.

After glancing up to avoid a collision, the guy didn't look twice at the two amigos with no passes around their necks. Despite this, Fisher fought the urge to turn, holding himself back from charging along the corridor and banging open each door in search of her. Somehow, he kept his breathing steady before he saw their next challenge. A short brunette in a white lab coat, her wide eyes framed with thick glasses, her skin pale despite the pounding heat outside.

Giving him no time to speak, she looked up, her mouth falling open before her eyes turned to slits.

"Ariba." Blurting out the first thing that came into his head, he hoped in vain she'd think them in fancy dress. A smile took over her lips as she passed.

Buoyed with confidence, Fisher led Hotwire past the increasing amount of foot traffic whilst conscious of their surroundings as he searched for clues. Unsure if it was his demeanour, or another aspect of what he could do, no one raised the alarm, or questions before they arrived at a sign pointing along a corridor to his right where dark writing announced the IT department behind the double doors. With a glance over his shoulder, he followed the sign.

A second set of doors stood beyond as they pushed through, and another stood to their left, this time with a contact pad and a second sign shimmering with a film of protective plastic loose at the edges. With no window in the door, Fisher moved closer and listened. Hearing nothing, he glanced back at Hotwire staring along the corridor, then pushed his iComm against the pad.

After an abrupt request made to Clark, and drawn out seconds with only his pounding heart, a click reverberated through the door when it gave way as he pushed.

Inside, he found a room full of desks piled around the centre with technician's workbenches gleaming against the walls, each surface piled high with large crisp boxes emblazoned with the logos of global tech firms.

Only the two desks in the centre of the room had computers set up, their tiny LEDs flickering. As Fisher stepped forward, a young man's head appeared from behind a monitor, but disappeared, only to reappear a moment later.

Giving him no chance to voice the question his raised brow already asked, Fisher rushed forward, pushing the Staser's electrodes into the skin of the man's lower arm. Hotwire caught the guy's head as he slouched onto the floor.

"Biggy, we're in," Fisher said across the link then listened to Clark's instructions before following as he paused, his fingers a blur on the keyboard where the guy had sat, all to the background of Hotwire zip-tying the man's wrists behind his back.

Error message after error message poured from the screen and the instructions from Wales altered with each line of feedback. From the high pitch in Clark's voice, Fisher knew he had control before the avalanche of lines tumbled down the screen.

"Give me ten minutes and I'll see what I can find," Clark said, the excitement keeping his voice high.

"We need to move," Hotwire said, fumbling the slumbering body into a cupboard he'd dragged empty of its once-neat contents.

"Biggy, Clark should have eyes soon," Fisher said as he pulled at the door handle.

With the coast clear as he swept his head to either side, he strode from the room, holding the door for Hotwire. Back in the corridor, he urged a deep breath, reminding himself a goal early in the match didn't mean they would win the game.

Holding his iComm out, he watched the green of his dot as they moved past huddles of reds crowding in packs, the dots of other people spread out like noise. Soon spotting two groups of blue signifying the rest of the team who'd split to their own tasks, at a brisk pace, he pushed the phone under his smock as they passed the occasional red dot before pulling it out for the third time, his legs quickening when he saw Harris's green marker at the top of the screen.

With Hotwire's hand at his shoulder, Fisher slowed, and he drew a deep breath, knowing he'd let go of the confidence that had so far let them pass unchallenged. Realising the advice had been timely as the corridor's traffic soon built, still, few paid any attention, focusing instead on their little worlds. With the facility so new, no one understood what was normal for this place.

After a snatched glance at the screen, Fisher spotted the door to his right and their next divergence to lead to her iComm, or to Harris herself, if he still held hope.

The doors swung open before they arrived, held wide by a pair of youthful faces at the back of a pack that passed, taking no notice. Fisher paid them little attention in return, instead focusing on a door a few paces to the left.

With each footstep, someone new entered at the far end, but ignoring the traffic, Fisher plunged down the brushed-steel handle, then held himself back as he felt the lock's resistance. Feeling a pressure at his arm, Fisher looked up to find Hotwire beaming a smile.

"Did you forget the key again?" he said.

Fisher exaggerated a nod, and together they turned back, settling into the traffic before Hotwire bent to tie his shoelace and let the flow pass. Waiting until the swing of the far door told them they were alone, Fisher spoke.

"Clark, we need to get into G-128?" he said, reading the brass label as he returned to the door which he confirmed was still locked. "Sorry," Fisher mouthed, watching Hotwire flash his brow.

"You need a J-Suite key from…" Clark replied, but Fisher didn't hear the last of his words when, looking up, he locked eyes with Luana walking from the opposite end of the corridor in white jeans and a white leather jacket.

It was only when he noticed the tray of stacked beakers she carried did he realise what was wrong.

"She's got her hand back."

***

The building was new, the smell of paint a giveaway.

The drugs kept her from crying, talking, or fighting, but she could walk far enough to reach the chair with wheels. Despite her blurred vision, she knew there was someone in front of her. Lifting her stump, the words came out slurred as she pleaded for the only thing she wanted.

She couldn't do anything as they strapped her to the bed. She didn't resist as they pulled her tight, then tugged at the bandages. She didn't gag as the smell hit the back of her throat and held her mouth wide as they brought the glass up, the pink liquor frothing in the beaker.

She couldn't help but sob when she realised they were making her wish come true.

88

As recognition flashed across the woman's face, her eyes narrowing and cheeks bunching, Fisher saw the hatred pouring toward him. With no time to linger, he spotted the black of a handgun silhouetted against her white clothes as the tray fell from her fingers.

Clark spoke in his ear, but he heard the voice, not the words. He was too busy scrambling under his smock as a scream rang out from behind them. Before he could bring his gun to bear, her shot sent the screams higher. Hotwire fired next, the rounds spitting from just behind Fisher to embed in the plaster where she'd stood, a brisk leap across the corridor saving her life as she left their view.

With the screams muffled, it was Biggy's voice next over the comm, but before either of them could answer, Fisher felt himself pushed flat against the wall, pinned by Hotwire as he pointed to where he'd last seen her.

"Contact. Lone female. Lost visual," Hotwire said, his voice hurried but calmed as he released the pressure.

Fisher withdrew his Glock and stared at where Hotwire aimed. "Cover the rear. I don't know where that comes out."

Doing what Hotwire asked, he turned to face the other end of the corridor as the doors burst open and two men in grey fatigues rushed through, their expressions intense and pointing handguns.

Letting his aim drop just enough, Fisher fired three rounds, sending both guards collapsing to the floor, writhing in agony as they grabbed at their legs.

"Contact," he said. "Two guards incapacitated," he added with a shout cutting through their screams as he rushed over and kicked away their weapons. His heart racing, Fisher turned to watch Hotwire creep along the corridor to where the woman had run. Then, turning from Hotwire's progress, he picked a handgun from the floor and fired it point blank at the locked door.

As the echo stopped ringing in his ears, two more

reports exploded from guns at his side and before he could complete his reflexive turn, thrusting the borrowed weapon as he did, he spotted the wall scored with a trail of two bullets where he'd stood. Two more rang off with a different tone and he stared at Luana, sinking to her knees, her hand outstretched until a third ball of lead pushed her backwards and she fell face first on to the floor.

Fisher stood open-mouthed as Hotwire rushed over, disarming her with a swipe of his foot. As Fisher arrived at his back, he stared at the blood running down the white of her leather from a tight pair of oozing red holes and a third bubbling with scarlet.

Unsure if sorrow or guilt tugged at his gut, his thoughts flashed back to Farid's flat and the first time they'd met. The overwhelming need to protect her came back, but he knew she'd stopped being the person he'd spoken to for most of the night after she'd lost her hand. Instead, she was the bundle of trauma who'd they'd experimented on, abused and fed with lies. That was the woman that lay dead. Hunter. A merciful ending to a wretched life.

Hotwire glanced around, and as if spotting Fisher's pause, he grabbed him by the arm.

"Come on," he said, arriving at the door, which he gave a swift kick and sent it flying open. "All clear," Hotwire said, peering in.

"I have the CCTV feed," Clark said, his voice a welcome distraction. "You've got about thirty seconds before you're joined by a group of heavies carrying AK47s."

By the light from the hallway, Fisher found the space stacked with boxes, and he didn't need long to confirm they had the right place when in an open box lying on the floor on its side were black trousers and a bomber jacket he'd seen her wear before. Beside the pile was a thin white vest that had saved Harris's life at what felt like the beginning of time.

With a quick rummage in the box, he drew in her scent and found her iComm in her trouser pocket. Its main battery was missing, and the fake sim card removed.

A hand on his shoulder made him stand.

"Time to move," Hotwire said before letting go.

"Go the same way you came in," Clark added, his voice urgent as he described the multiple groups assembling. At least one group was already on their way. Breaking off the narrative, Clark's voice rose as he addressed Biggy, his impending need greater than theirs according to the gunfire beyond the walls.

Together they jogged, following Clark's direction, and before long Hotwire leaned with his arm outstretched and palm resting on the right-hand door as he peered between the crack. Just as his face brightened with a slither of natural light, he backed away and turned before ushering Fisher to follow the way they'd come. Overtaking him, Hotwire led them into the dark cupboard they'd broken into, pulling the door punctuated with bullet holes closed.

In the darkness broken only by the shattered wood, Fisher tried to slow his breathing as he held his Glock out. When garbled voices gained volume, he let Hotwire pull him further in.

89

Despite what he'd seen earlier in the dim light, turning and stepping over Harris's clothes, Fisher followed Hotwire deeper into the room. Travelling further than he thought possible, much to his surprise, the space opened out. Peering around to orientate himself, his gaze chasing dark shapes, he pulled back as a wide cone of light came from Hotwire's torch beneath the barrel of his assault rifle.

Seeing benches free of the trappings of experimentation lining the walls in the bright cone, he realised they were out of the cupboard and into another dark room.

Still hearing the rushed voices, Fisher followed Hotwire, who turned off his torch when Boot's delighted voice rushed into their ears, declaring he'd found their brothers in arms. His voice didn't remain high for long when he described finding them in an unlocked, empty room. Dressed in civilian clothes, they seemed to be only missing their weapons, and none of them responded to their rescuer's arrival. Their faces were blank and haggard.

"Keep them safe," Fisher whispered, shutting his mouth when he caught the shake of Hotwire's head as they crossed the dark room.

Following Hotwire's dark outline, he waited at a door. When voices had faded on the other side, he heard the handle twist.

With the door unmoving, unsure if it was Hotwire testing, or someone on the other side, about to speak, Fisher held his breath when the air filled with a hurried gabble of incomprehensible voices growing close, moments before a triangle of light opened from the cupboard where they'd entered. There was enough light for Fisher to see it was Hotwire's fingers groping and twisting the metal before light poured in to reveal the corridor.

Squinting, he watched Hotwire step out with his eye trained down the rifle's sight and the extended stock pushed into his shoulder. Turning to the left, but soon whipping around, he didn't hesitate, sending three rounds bursting from the barrel.

"Move," Hotwire shouted.

With a glance back toward the bustle of boxes skittering across the floor, Fisher didn't wait to see who emerged. Instead, gripping tight at his Glock, he rushed from the room as another trio of shots fired.

Jogging at Hotwire's shoulder, Fisher did his best to avoid looking at the writhing figures on the floor, or up at the sprayed blood tracing its slow journey down the walls. Concentrating instead on a set of double doors ahead, he spotted figures in grey overalls moving beyond the rectangles of glass running the length of the door.

Fisher turned, and in the corner of his eye he saw Hotwire had stayed put, but the thought fell away as he locked eyes with another who'd appeared behind them holding an AK47 in what looked like an awkward, untrained stance; the kind a boy would make after unwrapping a much wanted gift at Christmas.

Fisher hesitated longer than he knew he should; longer than Hotwire had moments before. The gulf felt like a lifetime, but when he saw the man's eyes narrow, Fisher pulled his trigger twice, sending the guy falling back, spraying bullets into the ceiling as he did.

"Contact," someone said in his ear, the word too frantic to know who it belonged to.

Edging toward the man he'd felled, Fisher glanced over his shoulder to find Hotwire still trained on the double doors they both knew were the only option unless they retreated.

"We need to keep moving. They're trying to pin us down," Hotwire said, his voice barely raised as he held his rifle single handed with the other fumbling under his smock. "Wait for the bang," he said, before pulling the pin from a round canister with his teeth and spitting the metal to the ground, then launching the container through the double doors.

Fisher pressed his eyes shut, turning away moments before the grenade exploded, but still he saw a blinding bright flash through his tight lids and the air felt sucked from his lungs.

They didn't linger, Hotwire tugged at Fisher's arm and he followed through the double set of doors, retracing their steps back to the staircase.

"Clark. Where now?" Fisher near shouted, his ears as if full of cotton wool before he glanced to a burst of three rounds from Hotwire, the bullets peppering the wall.

"Follow the building's curve and find the stairwell. Go up two levels and follow its shape again. Hall B is on a separate CCTV system and I'm not in there yet," Clark replied.

With gunfire echoing from all around, and not exchanging looks, the pair sped up past sprawled men writhing with their hands against their ears. When the background of screams receded, they arrived at the next door to find it opened out to the stairwell.

Fisher tried to mimic Hotwire's silent steps as he led them higher, peering through his sight, slowing as they neared the next level and a long empty corridor. Gripping his Glock double handed, he pointed it at the ground as he soon examined a double set of smoked glass double doors with *Hall B* stencilled in wide black letters.

Waiting at Hotwire's shoulder, together they stared at the glass, looking for movement that hadn't yet come.

Fisher was the first to move, his iComm in his hand as he presented it to the card reader at the door's side. Whispering for Clark to open it, a thunderclap of gunfire overtook the silence.

He repeated the call as the sound lulled.

"It's a different system. I can't even see it. If you can find someone's ID, then I can try again," Clark replied, harried.

His voice cut off sooner than expected and Hotwire stepped to Fisher's side, pulling a line of cord from under his smock.

"Use this ID," he said, drawing the cord along the height of the door and pressing it against the glass. "Back

386

away," he added, already turning and running down the concrete steps, not worrying about the sound his boots made.

The pressure of the explosion felt less than expected. Perhaps the gunfire and grenades already softened Fisher's hearing. Coughing through the dust, they ran back up the steps to find both panels gone, their remains scattered across the floor and embedded in the walls, leaving dust shimmering in the daylight from above.

Beyond the missing doors was a wide reception bounded by a series of opaque outer glass walls, cracked and shattered in places. On either side, white-washed walls rose at least three storeys where they met a glass roof. Doors waited on opposite sides.

Fat rounds of water hit the glass roof, falling from the greying sky, and it was Biggy's voice across the comm that pulled him back into the moment.

"We can't wait to blow the Energy Centre. Bayne's hit," he said, gunfire resounding in the distance and they crossed the floor to the right-hand side door, the ground beneath them shaking as the wall lights blinked out and a collective metallic click rang out as if every lock in the building relaxed its grip. Realising the opportunity, Fisher plunged the door open, but the darkness beyond only held for a second before a dull light glowed, the locks tensing again as auxiliary power took over.

Thanking his luck and with Hotwire pushing past, he followed his flowing movements, pointing his gun through the steep angles up and down a metal stairwell.

Following Hotwire down the stairs, Fisher kept light on his feet as he tuned into the silence. The steps were short and twisted to the left at a sharp angle. At the bottom, they found a single gloss-red door with no lock. Its only feature was a brushed metal hand plate.

Hotwire leaned up to the door with his shoulder before shaking his head and motioning with two fingers for Fisher to push it open.

As Hotwire stepped back with his MP5 pointed at the

door, he nodded. Fisher lifted his Glock and pushed through with the other hand.

A familiar antiseptic sting bit at his eyes and raked inside his nostrils with every breath. It was the same noxious cocktail he'd experienced in Chile which had dulled in his nightmare.

Attempting to blink away the caustic vapour, his gaze followed a long white wall to his left, its three-storey rise broken up by a metal walkway hovering two levels above and wrapping around the wall with lamps hanging below. The lamps were dull, only just highlighting the corrugated sheets playing with an orchestra of beats from the pounding rain.

With a wave of déjà vu, he peered across the room with his breath held and weighed down by his body. The thunder of the water above, the sting at his eyes, and the cavernous room filled with long lines of transparent glass boxes. It wasn't déjà vu. It was the dream he knew would come true the moment the wheels of the Gulfstream left the ground.

Dropping his arm to his side, the Glock so heavy in his hand, his mouth gaped at the grid of transparent cages, line after line disappearing to a vanishing point so far away.

Focusing closer, he stared at the glass boxes sat on metal plinths, the details of which he could have described with his eyes closed. But at least they were empty.

Letting his gaze drop, he took a sudden intake of breath. The floor was the last piece, a metal grid inlaid with the initials he recognised from Chile, and below which he saw raw concrete inlaid with drainage channels running off to the side.

He didn't know how long he'd been standing still, but with a nudge from behind, it was long enough.

About to move, he stopped after a single pace, his foot clattering the steel section against its neighbour, and he held his palm up at his shoulder. But he hadn't waited because of the noise. He'd paused because he'd noticed a difference. It wasn't so striking at first, but as he'd moved, he caught sight of each of the countless cases, a bound group of black corrugated pipes strapped together, running up from their sides to a metal tray hanging high in the ceiling before joining other bundles from their neighbours, each fattening the pile.

Squinting into the distance, the dull light clouded his vision, and although he saw the bundle getting wider, it disappeared into darkness before he saw where it ended.

"This is it," he said under his breath. Here he was, and he took a step forward. Somehow he'd arrived, just missing a gift box and perhaps a bright bow around his middle.

His thoughts turned to how easy it had been to breach their security. How after their initial discovery, they'd left them alone to wander about, turning this way and that until they stumbled upon the exact place they needed. There had been a fierce firefight, but their colleagues had taken the brunt. They'd left them alone.

"What is this place?" Hotwire said in a low voice. Fisher had almost forgotten he was with him.

"It's a farm," Fisher replied, the words doing nothing to change Hotwire's confused expression.

"What are…?" Hotwire said but stopped himself, still taking in the vast space, when a sound came from somewhere in the hall like the clash of floor grid against floor grid.

Footsteps.

90

Listening, they kept their movements slow and precise, but still they couldn't make out where the footfall came from, the noise baffled by the glass prisons. Its echo sounded as if an army were taking up position.

Plotting a straight course between the line of boxes in front of them, and with his Glock taking the lead, Fisher took a tentative step, but somehow the metal still clattered under his feet. When an echo replied, he missed a step before continuing.

Making slow progress, his senses fought for his attention as the long line of boxes seemed to go on, disappearing into the darkness as his own echo, and that of Hotwire's followed, replied by someone else's. How close they were, they didn't know.

Fisher glanced at Hotwire over his shoulder. The nod confirmed he'd seen the shadow through the boxes too and with a few hand signals, they agreed he would go back and circle around to trap the footstep's owner between them.

Soon alone, Fisher picked up his speed, the clank of the grid replying with no grace. He turned to his right, diving between cases as he chased fleeting glances of the shadow. He dived left, then right, matching the moves. When another clatter of steel turned him around to where they'd first started, he looked up to the long run of pipe joined by others before it travelled off into the darkness.

Seeing movement, at least he thought he did, he tucked himself up against a glass box.

The glass sent a shudder through his hand. Although colder than he'd expected, it wasn't the temperature but knowing there was only the single pane between him and being trapped inside.

The footsteps grew louder at his back and a sudden thought filled him with a question. Could it be Harris?

If they were the sounds of her motion, could they be carrying her towards him to complete the betrayal?

Spinning around, he tightened his grip on the Glock and straightened his arm to point at the metal grid clattering from behind.

As he turned, he saw her, but somehow he knew the ghostly figure was a figment of his imagination. Still, he couldn't point the weapon at what he saw.

He was screwed. He knew it. If she came for him, he'd do what she asked. He'd plead for her reason, of course, but having only met such a short time ago, he really didn't know her.

Had she ever opened up to him? Had she ever let him inside her life? It could all have been an elaborate plot. The last gasp when all of their past efforts had failed, and now they had used their best weapon and he was standing here, alone, waiting for the inevitable.

Trying to blink away her image, instead it changed and there was someone standing in front of him, at the edge of the darkness, but it wasn't Harris.

His arm tensed and he lifted the Glock toward Connor, who pointed a pistol in Fisher's direction as he chewed gum.

"Put the gun down," Connor called, but Fisher wouldn't do such a thing, despite the man lowering his own. Fisher's head twitched to the side as Hotwire noiselessly appeared between them, somehow managing not to rattle the grid with every step.

Hotwire turned to Fisher.

"It's just Tucson," Hotwire said, turning toward the man. "The rest of the floor is clear."

Fisher saw the question in Hotwire's eyes, asking why he hadn't lowered his weapon.

"What are you doing here?" Fisher shouted with an echo as he watched Connor look between the pair of them.

"Calm it," Hotwire said, his voice steady as he stared Fisher down.

"You don't know everything that's going on here," Fisher replied.

"Roger that," Hotwire replied with a slow nod.

"Answer my question," Fisher shouted again.

"The same thing you're here for," Connor replied. "Now put the weapon down."

"Not until you tell me how Harris and Luana got here," Fisher said.

Connor raised his brow, as if surprised by the question.

"We brought them here," Connor replied, the uncertainty clear in his tone as Fisher scowled back. "Brandon and I did it ourselves."

Fisher lifted his chin in defiance. "Where the fuck is Brandon now?" Fisher said, almost spitting the words.

Connor stopped chewing. "I haven't seen him since," he said, his words tailing off.

"Fuck me. Someone else we've got to rescue," Hotwire blurted out, turning towards Fisher.

Fisher and Connor shared a look.

"Bullshit," Fisher replied, and without warning, Connor darted between the glass boxes and out of sight. Fisher ran, leaping past Hotwire as his feet clattered against the steel grills. Hotwire joined the chase. Arriving where Connor had stood, Fisher looked about, peering between the glass cases and found the man's distorted blur a few rows away.

Running again, he charged to the side, moving to the left then right and back again as he rushed across the grid, zig-zagging with a great clatter at his feet as he followed the shadow with his gaze darting for clues.

Hotwire called out that he was splitting off. Two were better than one.

Fisher nodded without slowing, his senses overwhelmed with the cacophony of metal hammering around him, but satisfied he'd proven Connor's guilt.

The dancing shadow was out of sight and Fisher slowed, peering around in hope he'd pick him up again as he listened to the distance clank, uncertain if it came from Hotwire or the American.

Standing in the middle of the vast room and

surrounded on all sides by glass plinths, he turned to where the bundle of pipes were the biggest, but he still couldn't see where they ran to. Instead, he found a metal gantry running across the width of the vast hall, its weight held by lengths of steel from the ceiling.

Turning with care on the spot, Fisher moved with a sudden impulse at what might have been a shadow, but when his gaze settled, there was nothing there. Twisting back a quarter of a turn, he moved at something in the corner of his eye. Not a shadow, but an imperfection in the sea of glass.

The moment he stopped, he knew it was flesh, despite the distortions of the thick layer upon layer of glass.

Drawing a deep breath, the Glock trembled in his hand as he took cautious steps around the glass prisons in between. Travelling in silence and considering each move, he found the clamps gripping the grid to the steel frame, then the pale naked body inside.

The set up was the same as his dreams. A textbook match to the foul sight he'd seen inside the apex of that mountain, right down to the contour of muscles defining the man's tight lines and the clamps stopping any movement, even though his sallow expression showed no sign of resistance. The man's closed eyes and lustre of the hair gathered around his head, the cannula and wide tube snaking from his forearm and the decomposing mess under the clamped wrist that made bile boil in the pit of Fisher's stomach were the same.

Despite all his attempts, Fisher didn't wake from what he hoped was a dream.

Instead, he turned away, stopping halfway through a deep breath and coughing on the thick stinging air his lungs hadn't quite got used to. As he did, he saw another person to his right, trapped and held down. With a hint of brown on her skin, she paid no attention to Fisher, even though his feet clattered against the grating.

They'd brought her here, left her unshackled, and she'd tanned. But that wasn't it. He'd known all along the woman they'd shot wasn't right either. She was too pale, her features off.

But there she was in the box. Her long perfect body laid on her back, the shoulder-length brunette hair. That streak of blonde.

His gaze followed the curve of her shoulder, down her arm, across her pert breasts, her nipples hard, down to her flat stomach and across the wisp of light brown pubic hair, to the only part of her he'd not seen before. The full pink flower between her legs.

Embarrassed for her, his gaze wandered back up and to her other hand. They'd healed her, after all. It was Luana. This time, there was no question.

The dead girl was her sister, or the fourth sibling that may not have died soon after birth. He looked over his shoulder at the pale guy, his gaze catching on the tubes and shackles that were missing from inside her prison.

Staring at Luana, he held himself still. She looked amazing, vital, just like Harris had after he'd administered the serum, but he couldn't see a single rise or fall of her chest.

"Beautiful, aren't they?" came a deep American voice reverberating around the hall.

Fisher span on the spot and zeroed in on a figure standing on the gantry that crossed the room's width. He was closer than he'd expected.

Fisher squinted, but still the figure hung in the darkness with only the silver of his handgun on show. It wasn't pointed in his direction. Its focus lay somewhere over Fisher's head. Somewhere he couldn't bring himself to turn and look.

"Connor?" Fisher said, his voice sounding wild in the echo against the constant rattling of the rain.

The voice laughed in reply.

A second joined in from behind Fisher, but it wasn't an echo, or from Hotwire.

Without thought, Fisher turned to find what could have been a mirror image on the metal grid, an equal standing two lengths of the cases behind him. His body and face were in shadow, his gun pushed out and pointed high at his double on the gantry.

"Put the gun down," came the same voice, but with the rain and echo, Fisher couldn't tell who it was from. One of the weapons clicked. A safety releasing, the thought filling him with dread. Still, neither moved as he looked between them.

"What's going on?" Fisher said, forcing his voice above the rattle over his head. No answer came, and he swung his aim up to the gantry before letting it hang limp to his side.

"Two on one. Now wait. I have something to do before I get to you, Mr Fisher," came a voice that could have been either of the shadows.

"Whenever I worked with her, she's always given me a semi," the same voice came again. At first Fisher thought it came from the guy on his level, then the pound of the rain lessened for a moment and the direction seemed to shift high up into the hall. "Come out. Look who I've found."

It came from up the top. Fisher was certain when a figure walked from the wall.

He knew her form, although the walk was unfamiliar. The swagger of her hips less controlled, but as soon as he'd seen the silhouette and a glint of strawberry blonde as she passed to the side of a dull lamp, he felt a gulf of sorrow expand in his gut.

His worst dreams had come true.

91

Turning on the spot, Fisher searched out the man behind him, but midway, his gaze caught on the woman's lifeless body in the cage. Lingering for only a moment, he turned back, the Glock feeling heavy as he raised it toward the walkway.

"What have you done to Luana?" Fisher shouted over the hammer of the rain, unable to keep the pity from his tone.

Deep, guttural laughter replied.

"You mean Hunter? You must have figured that out?" the American called out.

Fisher drew in a deep breath as he tried his best to relax his trigger finger, still not able to endanger that woman, despite everything.

"We granted her wish," he replied, and a second wave of despair caught in Fisher's throat. They'd fixed her up, then put her in the box.

"How much more can you put her through?" Fisher called out, not caring that water welled in his eyes.

"She's like a daughter to me and she's happy. Thrilled, in fact," the American said. Fisher wasn't sure if he heard his voice soften.

The gun wavered in Fisher's hand as he shook his head, motioning behind him as the rain's beat eased.

"I'm afraid I had no choice," the American replied, and the rhythm of the rain hitting the roof stopped, filling the space with silence. "She screwed up. Once I decide, I have to stick to it. What would the board say otherwise? It's out of my hands," he said, his voice loud. "This way she'll make a contribution in her remaining time."

"The thing inside her head?" Fisher said, raising his chin and watched, just able to see the figure nod. "What now?" he asked, letting his arm down to his side.

"You know how this ends," the man up high replied. "I thought you would have put up more of a fight. After such a long time, I'm a little disappointed. When you didn't arrive with her, I thought that was it. But we're grateful you changed your mind."

"I was stupid," Fisher said, no longer looking up.

"That's not true, I'm sure. I hear you have a certain aptitude," he said, dismissing the reply. "But when she came alone, it made my life a little easier. She's almost nicer to look at than Hunter, but don't let her hear me saying that."

Still not looking up, he held his breath as he rushed to repeat the man's words to himself. Sure he'd heard right, he blinked the water from his eyes and turned to each case, despite knowing most of them were empty.

"Oh dear," the man said with a wide smile, followed by a bellow of laughter. Turning on the spot, he paused with his mouth dropping open. The laughter grew as he stared at what looked like someone else in a see-through prison a few rows away.

Stepping forward, he rounded a glass case, the figure clarifying with each move until he stood at her side. It was Harris, her unmistakable strawberry blonde hair flowing over a white pillow in the same pose as Luana, her body punctuated with faded scars, but more perfect than in his dreams.

"Oh my," the American called out as his laughter subsided. "You didn't think…" he said, but stopped himself with his hand at his mouth. He beckoned the figure at his side to come into the light whilst Fisher did his best to focus beyond the excitement filling the sorrow's void. If someone described Harris, the woman on the gantry would match it to a tee. But it wasn't Harris, he was certain.

Guilt soon replaced the other emotions. He'd been wrong all along. She hadn't betrayed him. He'd left her to come alone and let this man capture her.

"I would have loved to have Harris in on this, and perhaps I'm guilty of finding an assistant who resembles her somewhat. Does that mean I'm a bad person?" the American said. "Don't answer that," he added with a burst of laughter. "I don't think she'd be up for the paperwork. Do you know how much admin there is in running a multi-national company?"

Unsure how he should feel that his purpose was back, and barely listening to him speak, it felt like someone had turned on a thousand watt lamp inside his head. He knew what he had to do and raised the Glock up to the man laughing on the gantry.

"Be a man, Connor," Fisher bellowed, but neither of them moved. The man's gun remained pointed over his head as the woman reached inside her jacket.

"Enough," said the deep voice. A gun fired. Fisher ducked, pushing himself to the side and between the glass cases. As shots rang off from all around, unsure where to turn, he waited. The noise halted, replaced with the clatter of the metal floor at his back and up high.

Peering up at the gantry, the woman fell backward, bending at the middle before slipping past the rail. Caught by the side of a glass cage with a dull thud, she went out of sight as the floor clattered. The American was gone and when Fisher turned, he couldn't see the other man either.

He stood, glancing at Harris laying on her back, then he turned to Luana a few rows away. She'd moved.

Pushing away his Glock, he turned back to Harris, feeling around the base of her prison and much like those they'd destroyed in Chile, he had it open with a hard press. Finding different red wheels, one marked Fluothane, and beside which was a thin needle on a small dial, he twisted the valve to the left, and it fell just as a loud bang reverberated in the distance, followed by a muffled shot.

As the needle showed zero flow, he heard the metal floor sing with activity and he went for his gun, but pulled back when he saw Biggy with Hotwire at his side, then Bayne strung by his arms over the necks of Lucky and Boots, followed by a procession of morbid-faced men whom he recognised from the Brecons and on board HMS Daring.

Walking between the two groups was Brandon Sword.

With a glance at Fisher, he ran to Luana's cage, and he had her valve closed and the needle falling in quick time. Then he flinched at an American voice at his side.

"Come with me," Brandon said, his voice solemn.

"Where's Connor?" Fisher said, glancing around, his head twitching from place to place.

"He ran. I expect he's rallying his people. We need to be gone," Brandon replied, placing a hand on Fisher's shoulder.

"What about these three?" Fisher said, looking up at Luana's motionless naked form before turning to the spy chief.

"We'll come back for them. I've got something I need you to see."

About to move, out of the corner of his eye Fisher saw Luana stir. He turned toward her.

"We've got to go," Brandon said, but Fisher hardly noticed the touch at his arm as he stared at Luana blinking, then raising her hands. Her smile seemed to stretch right across her face, her perfect white teeth beaming as she wiggled her fingers. Fisher put his hand to the glass and she turned, but looked past him. Her eyes widened and she tensed. Her smile relaxed, and the glass dulled her voice.

"Zio?" she called out.

Not recognising the name, he was about to turn when he caught Brandon's reflection looming in the glass, then a shot rang off and pain bit at his leg before everything faded to black.

92

Vague images rolled around Fisher's head.

The metal grid racing up. His arm wrapped around a shoulder as Biggy fought hand to hand with his brother. Hotwire the same, but with a knife.

Too soon, the forest of glass ended, his head rolling down as his feet hit an obstruction.

Connor's three eyes looked up. One in the centre marked with a line of blood and wished he had the energy to be sorry he'd got it so wrong.

In the bright light and thick air, he was grateful when his breath eased as sweat soaked his body.

His view turned to the sky, clear and blue, and his head rolled to the side. He was laying flat as the ground below him rushed by. The bumps rolled his head from side to side. Then the motion stopped.

A tightness gripped at his leg, and he remembered the sharp pain. It was Brandon's muffled voice he could hear. It was his complaints in the background.

His head rolled to the side and trees filled his view as he blinked away the sting of sweat, clearing his vision, but not for long as the moments started to hang together. If only the pain in his head and a throb below his knee would let him think.

The two-storey orphanage came in to view as it merged with the treeline. They were soon inside and the heat turned to a chill, freezing his slick skin. His head tipped toward his feet and Brandon moved to the side, holding Fisher's free arm in a wave as a chorus of children's voices echoed a teacher's welcome.

He turned up from the streak of blood left behind by his foot and looked at the huddle of uniformed children. There were maybe twenty, each sat in a half-moon around a smiling woman. Their heads turned his way, each smiling as if without a care in the world.

As the fairy tale continued at the centre, after Brandon

pushed something at the side of the door, they headed through. The teacher's voice muffled as the light dimmed. They were in a carpeted corridor, the trail of blood no longer so clear. Fisher looked up as Brandon rebalanced his weight over his shoulder and he spotted a thick bundle of black corrugated pipes as if they'd arrived just as he had.

Falling to the floor, he felt a sudden pressure at his leg and pain leapt up before it dashed away as his head banged on the sound of a curse. His, or Brandon's, he wasn't sure.

Waking, he found himself slumped in a chair. Sweat ran into his eyes. He tried to pull his hand up, but found he had no control. It wasn't until, with the slow turn of his head, he saw his wrists bound to metal arms with thick black cord, weaved through steel rings welded to the bare metal chair.

With his head clearing, he tried his best to take in his surroundings.

Brandon bent over in front of him but facing the other way, his hands grappling with the corrugated pipes running high through a hole in the wall. As the man stepped to the side, Fisher saw a wide metal tundish. Out from the base there was another pipe, this time smaller, its surface smooth and snaking through clips on the wall and thin plastic valves before running to the top of a glass case and stopping at what looked like a steel shower head ready to spray its contents on the beautiful object below.

He'd seen the object before. An image, at least. He'd listened to its description, but the rock was so much more than the array of pixels or collection of words.

Absorbed in its contours, Brandon broke Fisher's stare as he moved towards him holding a thin clear tube he'd pulled from the bundled pipes.

"Hullo again, Mr Fisher. You're back in time for the best bit," he said, his voice falling to a lazy drawl.

"Why?" Fisher said, his throat so dry.

Brandon paused, lifting his head and looking him in the eye.

"Why?" he said, his smile widening. "Are you kidding

me, Mr Fisher?"

Fisher's eyes narrowed, his head throbbing.

"Are you seriously asking why I want to turn your blood, and those like you, into something I can feed us humans? Are you really asking me why I'd want it under my control? You of all people shouldn't need much imagination to understand what we could use it for. I'd have Russia on her knees in days. Even if we only use it to heal the wounded, I'd be unstoppable. But imagine if we could use your blood on their people. I wouldn't need any American boots on the ground to take control." His eyes widened as he spoke. "Imagine if I got this into the food at the Kremlin. The place would be mine to do with as I wanted."

"You keep saying I," Fisher said. "What about the board?"

Brandon laughed. "It sounds much better if I say they're in charge."

"It wouldn't stop when you've defeated the east, would it?" Fisher said, and the corner of Brandon's mouth turned up. "You've already shown the suffering you can inflict."

The man's smile faulted and he raised a brow, but Fisher didn't need him to answer to know what he had to do. Taking a deep breath, he tried to summon all his energy, ready to spit forward a command and send this guy crazy.

"Oh no you don't, Mr Fisher," Brandon said, fist flying in from the side, sending a stifling pain to his temple.

With his energy gone and barely conscious, he closed his eyes and tried to mutter commands. Unsurprised when nothing happened, he felt his sleeves rolled up his arms and he opened his eyes, wincing as a cannula jabbed into his wrist. Then, as Brandon moved away to an array of controls where he flicked a switch, a round pump like that in a dialysis machine turned, drawing his blood into the tube.

It was all he could do to look around the room, glancing anywhere but his blood disappearing as he waited for Brandon's remaining crew to arrive and cart him off to his home in a see-through cage.

When the door flew open, it was Brandon who turned with a start, staring at the two women in grey overalls, their hair flowing behind them, long and lustrous. Harris led the way, with Luana behind. Both looked so vital and alert, the opposite of how he felt, and with handguns poised and aimed at Brandon's chest.

Brandon's face was a picture of surprise, but it didn't take long for his eyes to narrow and his brow to fall.

"Okay, ladies. I'm glad you're here to help," he said, with no measure of insincerity in his voice.

They both laughed as they took in the room, their eyes widening as they saw the state of Fisher strapped to the chair.

"Hunter. Come on. Let's get him packaged," Brandon said when their laughter vanished into nothing. Neither of them moved their aims. "Come on Trinity. Let's not make this a thing. And Hunter, you know your place in this. Look, I gave you your hand back, and all is forgiven. Now, let's get on with the job and stop messing around before I change my mind."

Luana stood her ground, her expression impassive with Harris the first to move, edging around the room towards Fisher. She soon unpicked the knots and he pulled a hand free, ripping out the cannula through gritted teeth and letting his blood spill from the needle.

"No!" the American called out, but Luana raised the gun a little higher and he seemed to think better of moving.

Harris freed Fisher's other hand in short order, then pressed his palm on the pin prick dot to stop it from weeping. The elation of being able to stand soon fell away, replaced with a throbbing in his head and the stab of pain in his wet and sticky leg. Still, he watched Luana's expression as she snarled, the veins on the side of her forehead pulsing as he remembered what he'd read in her file. The abuse she'd gone through at the hands of this man.

With a gentle touch at his cheek, Harris moved his focus to her, standing at his side.

"Can you walk?" she said, but he didn't answer. Instead, she turned to find Brandon recovering upright, his cheek bright red as Luana withdrew her hand.

"Really?" Brandon said, touching at his face. "After everything I've done for you?"

Luana stepped toward him. "You told me to stay dead. Now it's your turn," she said and pulled the trigger, sending the American staggering back. Harris stepped forward, looking away from the black hole in his neat white shirt as crimson spread out.

"No," Harris shouted. "We do this properly," she added, pushing Luana's aim from the man laying on the floor.

"There is no justice for him," Luana replied, taking a step back and turning the gun toward Harris. "This goes up further than all the way. There is only one way to deal with him."

"No, it doesn't," Fisher said, despite the pain in his head and Harris moved her hand out to the gun and stepped forward, turning it away for the second time, but Luana moved her aim back toward the floor and shot twice more.

Paying Luana no more attention, Harris stepped back to Fisher. "Can you walk?"

Before he had a chance to reply, he saw Brandon moving, his hand reaching for a black box from his pocket where a red light glowed and a moment later a shrill tone announced itself from speakers.

Harris looked at the man, then at the box with the fabric covering in the corner of the room. The sound wasn't painful, but nonetheless seemed to penetrate their skulls.

"Don't kill him," Fisher said with his hands at his ears, but Luana shot twice more, the second round shattering the box and ending the piercing call. Brandon lay still.

"Search him," Harris said as she pulled Fisher's arm and draped it over her shoulder before taking his weight and guiding him toward the door.

"Look what he had," Luana said after they'd only taken a step, and together the pair turned around and saw her holding a small bottle of pink liquid they recognised.

"Give it here," Harris said and turned to Fisher as she

took the bottle. "Drink it."

Fisher shook his head through the pain. "Give it to him. There are so many unanswered questions," he said, forcing the words out.

Harris shook her head. "I think it's too late," she replied, not meeting his eyes.

"He was a bully. A manager. That's all," Luana said, spitting the words towards the body. "He wouldn't know the answers. You want to find your mother. For that, you need the head of the corporation."

"He was the head," Fisher replied. "He ran the whole thing."

Luana looked over, swapping her glance between Fisher and the dead man. "No. He was following orders. That's what he always said."

Fisher shook his head, until after pocketing the bottle, Harris turned him around. "That's because he was a coward."

Taking painful steps toward the door, Fisher stopped them both, sucking air through his teeth at the stab of pain from his leg. "The rock?" Fisher said, but Harris shook her head again.

"Fuck the rock. Fuck Brandon. Fuck everything. It's all a lie. Burn the place down to the ground and put a stop to this now," Luana screamed, before sobbing through heaving breath.

"She's right," Harris said at his side. "Boots has enough PE-4 to end this today," she added as Luana joined at his side and slipped his other arm over her shoulder as they walked with care through the doorway and along the corridor.

"Are the boys alright?" Fisher asked.

"They'll have more scars to make up stories for, but yes," Harris said. "They're just wrapping things up. You should see their faces when we woke and got out of the cases. Both of us naked with everything jangling around."

They laughed as Luana pressed the door release then pushed through into the nursery, surprised to find a sea of over fifty children standing and filling the room. But their shock soon turned to something else when they noticed each held some sort of blade raised towards them.

93

With a fresh scent in the air Fisher couldn't quite place, the door to the nursery stood open as more glassy-eyed kids arrived, each brandishing a different sharp weapon and staring at him supported between the two women. The front of the group stopped a couple of arm's lengths away. Realising the source of the mint tang in the air, and with the children's far away expressions matching those of the bikers and Biggy's missing men, Fisher knew what was behind it.

The high-pitched tone from Brandon's box of tricks must have triggered their stupor and utter compliance.

"There's no one here to give orders," Fisher said, shaking his head and as he did, the entire group took a step forward.

"He must have told them what to do if they heard the sound," Harris said. Fisher raised his brow, glancing over wide-eyed before turning back where his gaze landed on the striking blue eyes of a boy he recognised from the Mumbai streets, now standing at the front of the crowd. He was the one he'd helped behind Harris's back.

"Are you still sure shelter's what they needed?" Fisher said, stifling a weak laugh whilst watching her out of the corner of his eye. She glanced back as if over imaginary glasses until the children took another step, arriving an arm's length away.

"They're kids, for fuck's sake," Luana said, dropping low and slipping Fisher's arm off her shoulder.

"Luana, no. They're drugged. You haven't seen what it does to people," Harris said, leading the pair back a step. Luana glanced over her shoulder and smiled, raising an eyebrow before she turned and walked up to a girl whose head came lower than Luana's hips. After pushing the gun behind her back, she motioned the girl out of the way with the other hand. When she didn't move and Luana reached out to push at her shoulder, the entire short group swept their blades through the air. Sucking through her teeth, Luana jumped

407

back, grasping her hand.

"Shit," she called out, raising her pistol to the little girl's forehead.

"Really?" Harris said with a scowl. "Don't you dare. Leave it to Fisher," she added, catching his eye. "Do what you do."

Fisher swallowed hard as he stared at the short crowd before dipping his head.

"Hello there," he said, his words soft as he leaned forward as much as Harris's hold would allow, but he bolted up straight when, as one, the kids stepped forward, raising their blades as high as they could.

"What are you doing?" Harris said, eyeing him from the side as she pulled him closer to the door they'd arrived through.

Shaking his head, he looked back at the group, staring into the glassy eyes of the boy he'd given money to. He knew he could use his new ability to command them to put their weapons down, but if the same happened to them as those he'd first used it on, wasn't destroying their minds worse than shooting their way out?

"You're safe. Put the knives down," he said, his voice soft. Unable to bring himself to do anything else, Harris pulled him back as the kids took another unified step.

"Just do it. I know you can," Harris said, the kids not reacting to her voice. "Command them!"

Before he could speak, the door at their backs rattled, and he glanced over his shoulder to find Luana pushing at the hand plate, but finding it wouldn't budge.

"I can't," he replied, his voice trembling as the kids stepped closer and swiped their blades through the air, forcing the pair back further.

"Why?" Harris replied, raising her gun and shaking her head. "Don't force me to shoot."

"What I can do… It's changing," he blurted out. "I'll destroy their minds if I command them."

"It's a transition," Luana called from behind as the

children forced them back another step. "It happens sometimes when your abilities grow, but it's only temporary. You might be through it already," she added, her voice high with optimism.

"Might?" Fisher shouted, his call sending the children's eyes wide as they took another step whilst drawing down their knives, leaving Harris little time to pull them back.

"Trust in yourself," she said. "You've got this."

Fisher couldn't help but stare at the kid they'd met on the streets and his striking glassy look as he stared right back. Seeing Fisher's inaction, Harris pulled herself from under his shoulder and lifted her gun before settling her aim on the same boy.

"Make a choice," Harris said, her gun almost point blank. Fisher knew she'd do what she had to in order to protect him. To his left, with her cut hand held against her side, Luana pointed her gun out at the girl who'd caused it.

With tears welling in the corner of his eyes, he shook his head, unable to choose between their own deaths in a flurry of blades and bullets, or decimating the minds of the innocents.

"Focus. That's all it takes," Luana said, her calm sending a chill along his spine.

"Fisher," Harris shouted as the blades whipped through the air. All it would take would be one more half step and they'd touch steel; then the choice would be out of his hands.

"I can't," he shouted and as he did, they stepped again, but with nowhere the three could go, steel dove into his thigh and he couldn't help himself from calling out. "Stop!"

94

Shaking with the effort, Fisher stared as the air punctuated with the clatter of fifty or more lengths of steel hitting the floor. His attention didn't waver when each small face remained blank as he searched for signs of the damage he'd done.

His heart sank as tears fell from the corners of their eyes, and turning to Harris, his mouth fell open at the water rolling down her cheeks. Fearing she'd fallen to the same fate, unable to linger on the sight, he stared back at the kids, watching for pain or hands reaching for their temples as their brains fired off misleading signals.

The kid he'd helped on the street was the first to move, glancing at the girl beside him. She turned to face him, her mouth opening with a question. Although not understanding the language, the words told Fisher he hadn't broken her. Other words came from the rest, their chatter building to a hum until the main door opened and they all turned to find Biggy and Hotwire sweeping their MP5s across the view. Lucky followed with a wide dark mark surrounding an eye.

"What the hell?" Hotwire said, taking in the view.

"Shit man," Lucky said, gawking at Fisher. "You look awful."

Fisher's vision blurred as he peered at the blood rolling from the small hole in the crook of his arm and pooling on the floor from the wound at his ankle. His head swam at the sight and his knees gave way, his vision falling to darkness.

Outside when he awoke, he was in the back of a truck, a Humvee, he guessed. The lights were on inside and hovering over him were Harris's face and someone else he couldn't quite place, recognising only their long, lustrous hair.

"It's okay," he said, his voice like silk as he pushed a cup up to his lips.

Lifting his hand, Fisher pushed the man's arm away as he remembered the last time he'd seen him lying naked on his back, both in his dream and in the warehouse.

"But…" Fisher said, unable to get the rest of the words out.

Harris held her finger to her lips.

"You're concussed and suffered severe blood loss from three major wounds. You could die," she said as she went from his view. "But it's your choice. He wants to help."

Fisher closed his eyes and when he opened them again, he saw the beautiful, blemish-free expression of the man from the glass cage as he offered the cup to his lips.

95

Staring at the Hummer's roof lining, Fisher woke. With his head clear and the pain gone, despite a deep sense of hunger, he felt so strong.

Nothing ached as he sat up and confirmed he was alone. Peering down, they'd cut the legs of his trousers open, the cloth dark red and cardboard stiff. Bandages lay discarded on either side and dried blood covered his legs, but he couldn't see the source.

Staring out at the bright day, he felt a chill as the engine vibrated underneath him. Spotting a huddle of people to the right of his view, the deep throb of rotor blades pulled his attention away as a pair of Black Hawks sent dust swirling as they touched down in the distance.

The two women broke from the group and he saw it was Biggy and Hotwire and others he didn't know they'd been speaking to. The sailors soon formed a line to load large olive crates into the aircraft.

Heat rushed in as Harris dropped the tailgate.

"How are you feeling?" she said, looking him over.

"Perfect," Fisher replied without thinking. "The children?" he added with a spark of panic.

"Under observation, but they're fine so far," she said before throwing a folded flight suit on his lap. "You've got two minutes," she said, turning.

As she walked away, Luana stepped into view, not looking away as Fisher peeled off his stiff clothes.

"I'm dying," she said, looking at the ground.

"I'm sorry," he replied.

"You knew?" she asked, glancing up.

Fisher nodded. "I am sorry."

"It's not your fault, and it's time to say goodbye," she said and Fisher raised a brow. "I don't know how long I've got, but I don't want to spend it in some lab. I've had enough needles in my arm for a lifetime."

"I understand," Fisher said, nodding. "But maybe

there's a cure."

"There isn't," she replied, her voice still soft. "I just wanted to thank you."

"I thought you wanted to kill me?" he replied, pulling on the flight suit.

"I did, but now I really know you were just doing the right thing," she replied, then turned away before walking to a waiting car where the guy whose blood had saved his life stood.

Shuffling out, he watched the car disappear down the road.

"Let's go," Harris said, arriving just as he pressed the last of the poppers together. "She offered to go on trial, but she'll be dead within weeks."

"Where are we going?" Fisher asked.

"We're needed back in Coventry, if you're still interested. They're raiding LS headquarters. Perhaps we'll find your answers," she replied, tilting her head to the side.

Fisher's eyes brightened. "So that's it? Do you think because we've cut off the head, the rest will unravel?"

"I guess we'll find out. We have teams already on their way to every factory, those they advertise and those they don't. They're finished and there's no coming back," Harris said.

"But what about the rest of the people like me?"

"That's not a question I can answer on my own. Governments and the people will have to figure out what happens next," she added. "But for now, there's a long flight ahead of us," she said, raising her brow. "And you need a shower."

Fisher stood for a moment, watching her walk towards the Black Hawk, then he jogged to catch up.

"I'd want the same end as her," Harris said. It took Fisher a moment to realise what she was talking about.

"Most people would," Fisher replied, just as a tone announced a call. Her glance over told him she'd heard the same.

"Franklin passes on his congratulations on a job well

done," Clark said, his voice brighter than they'd heard for some time. "He'd have liked more discretion, but he's pleased we have enough for the raid. You're both invited to a dinner reception at the embassy."

"You've got to be kidding," Harris said. "What about Coventry?"

"You can pick over the details when you get back. Don't tell anyone I told you, but it's in your honour. Most guests won't know who you are, but they want to celebrate your success."

Harris screwed up her face, then smiled as she hung up the call and they climbed inside the aircraft before pulling on the offered flight helmets.

"Take us to Mumbai international, and have our bird on standby for London please. Make sure they know we'll be the only passengers," she said, and the pilot replied in the affirmative. Fisher looked over, his brow high with a question.

"Sometimes," Harris said, laughing, "the needs of the few outweigh the needs of the many," she said, pulling on her belt and closing her eyes.

Fisher couldn't help but smile.

"Oh," Harris said as she looked over. "Do you know which great philosopher said those immortal words?"

Fisher shook his head.

"Spock," she replied, grinning as she closed her eyes again.

Want more of Agent Carrie Harris?

Then you're in luck. I loved writing her so much I wrote her own series which takes her back to the very start of her career!

If you like high-stakes thrills, strong female heroes, and action-packed adventures, then you won't be able to put down these intriguing novels.

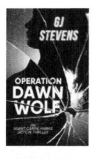

Visit my website for more details and a free copy of
CAPITAL ACTION!

www.gjstevens.com

All my books are available from Amazon on Kindle,
paperback & audio.
Search 'GJ Stevens'

Printed in Great Britain
by Amazon